DARCY'S
PASSIONS

DARCY'S PASSIONS

PRIDE AND PREJUDICE RETOLD THROUGH *HIS* EYES

REGINA JEFFERS

Ulysses Press

Published in the United States by
ULYSSES PRESS
P.O. Box 3440
Berkeley, CA 94703
www.ulyssespress.com

ISBN: 978-1-56975-699-7
Library of Congress Catalog Number 2008906996

Cover design: DiAnna Van Eycke
Cover illustration: George Goodwin Kilburne/Fine Art Photographic/Getty Images
Editor: Jennifer Privateer
Editorial Associate: Lauren Harrison
Production: Judith Metzener

Printed in Canada by Transcontinental Printing

10 9 8 7 6 5 4 3 2 1

Distributed by Publishers Group West

To my mother Peggie Jeffers
who taught me any book
is too valuable not to read
and
to my son Josh who
learned the same lesson
from me

PREFACE

I walk around the classroom explaining the nuances of dating and relationships in Regency England. My students know by now I am a self-described Jane Austen "freak" for most were in my World Literature class last year and know when I speak of Jane Austen's works my eyes sparkle with excitement. They listen as I describe Austen's six novels and the many sequels and retellings of her works I have enjoyed and have sometimes loathed. "Why don't you write your own book if you know all these things?" comes Will's suggestion, and the others chime in their agreement.

I laugh it off, but I have thought about it for some time. When I read any novel it plays in my head like a movie; I see the characters—their facial expressions; I hear the inflection in their voices. The characters live and breathe in my mind's eye, but no character has fascinated me, or for that matter any woman who ever read *Pride and Prejudice*, more so than Fitzwilliam Darcy. Who is Fitzwilliam Darcy? What brought him to be the man he is when he first meets Elizabeth Bennet in Hertfordshire? Why can he not allow her into his life as soon as the attraction starts?

When one reads *Pride and Prejudice,* he sees Fitzwilliam Darcy filtered through Elizabeth's eyes. In reality, he is a "minor" character who becomes a major part of Elizabeth Bennet's life. If one takes how long the journey from their meeting at the Meryton Assembly to Elizabeth's acceptance of Darcy's second proposal, the span of time is approximately one year. During this year, Darcy is with Elizabeth for a little over three months—from Michaelmas at the end of September to the Netherfield Ball at the end of November; for approximately two weeks at Easter time at Rosings Park; for less than a week at Pemberley, and another week upon his return to Netherfield/Longbourn. We know what he says and does during those three turbulent months, but what is he thinking each time he meets the woman with whom he is consumed? What does Darcy do to try to rid himself of thoughts of Elizabeth Bennet? How does he reconcile abandoning all he knows about fine society to love an amazing woman? What is he doing the nine months they are apart?

Most believe George Wickham to be the villain in this classic tale, but I am of the persuasion Darcy is both villain and hero— disdainful pride to benevolent rescue. Yet, I also do not believe anyone changes completely; Darcy's transformation must be based in all his previous experiences. The disagreeable social façade and the potential lover lie within the same man. That is the tale one finds in *Darcy's Passions*.

In writing this retelling, I meticulously read and reread *Pride and Prejudice* to keep the chronology of the events accurate to the original. Those details I combined with my own estimation of the character of Fitzwilliam Darcy. Because Jane Austen tells us little of what Darcy thinks or does, I employed dramatic license. Darcy's "passions" are threefold: his sister Georgiana, his ancestral estate, and his love for Elizabeth Bennet. Often these passions conflict and fight for dominance in his life. How he manages to find a balance between each facet is Fitzwilliam Darcy's journey from dutiful son to the master of Pemberley.

Having taught media literacy, I enjoy the video interpretations of Austen's works, and one will hear some of those characteristics in my writing. In reading *Darcy's Passions,* one will often hear Colin Firth's, the ultimate Darcy, voice in Darcy's lines, especially when Darcy meets Elizabeth at Pemberley, but I will also admit to being a Matthew Macfadyen fan. I enjoy Macfadyen's previous portrayals in *The Way We Live Now, Wuthering Heights,* and as Tom Quinn in *MI5* (aka *Spooks*). So, I mix Firth's haughty reserve with Macfadyen's vulnerability. In analyzing both actors, I am more inclined to look at the acting rather than the choices made by the director in his portrayal of the work. I use the Macfadyen version in my classroom—two hours versus six hours being easier to justify to administrators who are concerned only with test scores and want no "wasted" instructional time. Plus, Keira Knightley helps to keep the boys interested in what they first term to be a "chick flick." My Fitzwilliam Darcy combines the best of both actors as I play the scenes in my head.

The chapter titles are lines from *Pride and Prejudice* or other Austen writings. Several lines come from Shakespeare's *Much Ado About Nothing.* They are actual quotes I did not change and chose to use as originally written. One quote I chose to adapt within the text comes from the 2001 film *Serendipity.* I took the idea from an article written by Bev Graves, my son's eleventh grade English teacher at Worthington Kilbourne High School in Worthington, Ohio. In an online article, Mrs. Graves uses the quote as part of a writing lesson on obituaries. Later, I realized it came from the 2001 movie, but it speaks of "passion," and I chose to paraphrase it in the book.

The new characters' names come from my other interests. I love pro football, especially New York Jets' quarterback Chad Pennington, so one will meet Lord and Lady Pennington, as well as Chadwick Harrison. I voted repeatedly for Clay Aiken in Season 2 of *American Idol* and spent one summer going to five of his concerts in nine days. Therefore, I created Clayton Ashford. Austen gives Colonel Fitzwilliam no first name; Edward, my father's name, is used here.

I spent time researching social customs, fashions, terminology, and traditional celebrations. Resources for those are listed in the back of this book. *Persuasion* is my second favorite Austen work. I often say Anne Elliott and Captain Wentworth are Darcy and Elizabeth if he did not find her at Pemberley. Austen readers will recognize in Darcy's words Wentworth's declarations to rid himself of his love for Anne. Austen fans will easily note similarities.

My friends who have read the earlier drafts of this book tell me they hear my voice in Darcy's words. I am not sure whether that is a compliment or an insult. What happens to Fitzwilliam Darcy I tried to keep "real," but not didactic. Even if one has never read *Pride and Prejudice,* understanding *Darcy's Passions* will not be an issue. For regular readers of Austen sequels and retellings, I hope this interpretation will appease their interest in these two characters.

Regina Jeffers
Indian Trail, North Carolina

CHAPTER 1

" . . . your conjecture is totally wrong."

Fitzwilliam Darcy lounged lazily in the high-backed chair of the library at Netherfield Park, sipping his morning coffee and savoring the news found in his sister's letter. The rest of his party had not come down from their chambers as of yet, and Darcy so enjoyed these moments of solitude. A self-assured man, confident and independent, Darcy took care of himself and others because he saw it as a virtue. In fact, this was why he now found himself at Netherfield Park sitting with his back to the sun and smiling at his sister's opening words. When Darcy made a transaction with the Bingley family's firm and discovered Charles Bingley to be affable, but greatly in need of direction, he found himself thrust into the position of helping his friend transition into society. From the beginning the men cast a solid relationship although their temperaments differed immensely. Bingley's easygoing nature accepted without censure the stolid disposition Darcy possessed. Yet, their affection for each other seemed genuine, and both men counted the other to be his closest friend.

Taking another sip of the tepid brew, Darcy reread the first couple of lines of Georgiana Darcy's meticulously written missive.

2 October

My dear Fitzwilliam,

I pray your sojourn to Netherfield Park was without incident, and you found it to be pleasantly suited. Unexpectedly, Mr. Bingley took possession of this estate, but, clearly, he must establish himself in fine society. Hopefully, Netherfield will allow Mr. Bingley to find the happiness he deserves. As your friend, I find him to be dear to me also, and I give him all my devotion as I would you my brother.

Darcy smiled at the tact Georgiana displayed. She realized, obviously, Charles Bingley took Netherfield at Caroline Bingley's insistence and because of her need to present herself as a woman whose family held enough wealth to merit an estate, while also establishing Charles's position in society. Charles Bingley desired his sister's happiness so he let Netherfield Park in that purpose.

I assume you will enjoy Miss Bingley's company, as well as the society found in Hertfordshire. Your happiness plays uppermost in my mind. You have, Fitzwilliam, been my support in my worst of times. I can never repay you; truthfully, Brother, I fear you place your own life on hold to placate me.

His sister Georgiana experienced love of the basest form, having briefly given her heart to a familiar cad. Thank goodness Fitzwilliam Darcy arrived in time to save her innocence and her heart. For several months, Georgiana pined for this braggart, and as he gently guided his ward back, Darcy stewed at the audacity of the man. Thankfully, he found Mrs. Annesley, a companion, who turned his impressionistic, innocent sister into a culturally refined, although still very shy, young lady.

Darcy marveled at Georgiana's reference to Caroline Bingley. Although they never discussed Miss Bingley, Darcy knew his sister found Miss Bingley's advances too forward at times. Yet, Georgiana would welcome Caroline into her home and her family if Caroline pleased Darcy. In reality, Caroline Bingley pleased Darcy as much as any other woman. She possessed refined tastes; yet, Darcy felt nothing for her. He knew he must marry soon, but he always wanted more; he wanted the passion he witnessed in his parents' marriage. Unfortunately, he never encountered such feelings even though he met women of fine society regularly, all of whom would welcome his advances and his wealth. As far as finding Hertfordshire's society pleasing, the prospects of that possibility lay as thin in Darcy's mind as did his developing affection for Caroline Bingley.

Mrs. Annesley and I enjoyed a concert sponsored by the Prince Regent. Oh, dear, Brother, you never heard such music. It could pick one up and transport him to realms of emotional fantasies. Mrs. Annesley says we shall look for the sheet music, and Mr. Steventon will help me practice until I achieve at least a semblance of the concert's greatness. Then I shall give you a private performance, which I pray you will enjoy.

Although a slow process, Georgiana showed signs of recovering from her brush with romantic disaster. Since the age of two and ten when his beloved mother died shortly after his sister's birth, Fitzwilliam Darcy protected Georgiana. He became her legal guardian when their own esteemed father passed away several years back. Yet, Darcy really assumed the position when his father became ill. Only with Georgiana and a select few others would Darcy let his guard down. Her gentleness complemented his staunch manner; he adored Georgiana in a way few could understand. For the last five years, Georgiana's world revolved around her brother. With the age difference, Darcy and Georgiana each possessed the characteristics of being the *only* child, needing solo time each day to focus, to listen to soothing music, to meditate, or to read a book. Over the past few years, he became not only her brother but her parental figure as well; it was a great responsibility, but Darcy was groomed for responsibility.

Maybe I should see about getting a new pianoforte for my sister; it would give her such pleasure. "A birthday present, perhaps," he said aloud. He returned to the letter; he wanted to finish it before the Bingley household descended upon him.

Fitzwilliam, it has been a long time since I felt contentment, but I owe it to you, my dearest. Your love and kindness gave me the ability to go on. I will be once again your younger, sometimes precocious, sister. Give Mr. Bingley and his family my fondest regards.

Georgiana

Darcy closed his eyes and pictured Georgiana in his mind. For a fleeting moment, he vividly saw the sweetness of her smile on the purity of her face. Then he slowly folded the letter, savoring the moment, and placed it in the inside pocket of his morning jacket. The sound of Caroline Bingley and Louisa Hurst in the morning room interrupted his reflections. Darcy unfolded his frame, stood, adjusted his clothing, and strode purposely from the library to join his hosts.

"Ah, Mr. Darcy, I see you rise before the rest of our party," Caroline said as he entered the room.

Darcy made a quick bow to both Caroline and her sister. Crossing to the breakfast repast to refill his coffee cup one last time, he politely replied, "It is true, Miss Bingley, I prefer to rise early. It is a habit my late father instilled in me many years ago. This morning, besides your family's hospitality, I read a letter from my sister."

"How is dear Georgiana?" she replied without any true concern evident in her voice. *Typically Caroline Bingley,* thought Darcy; *she knew the right words to say in each situation, but Miss Bingley possessed no real emotion—no real thought of her own.*

"My sister enjoys her time in London with her favorite pastime—music," Darcy added quickly, hoping this would end Caroline's inquiries.

Unfortunately, Caroline rose and strolled over to Darcy, supposedly to refill the chocolate in her cup, but they both knew she wanted closer proximity to him. As a man of wealth and often targeted by women in pursuit of a husband, Darcy recognized her game. He learned to gracefully avoid the claims of these many potential mates with a haughty, prideful manner; with his fortune,

Darcy could offer indifference to such ambitions. As Caroline sashayed across the room playing up her feminine qualities, Darcy took on a familiar somber face. "I do wish Georgiana could have joined us at Netherfield," she said, refilling the cup and taking a step closer to him.

"She has her studies to which to attend," Darcy responded as he walked away, placing distance between them, and taking up a position by the window. Turning to observe the grounds, he continued, "Will your brother be down soon? I hoped to survey the estate with him today."

As if on cue, Charles Bingley sauntered into the room. "Come, Darcy, I am not that late, am I? We shall have plenty of time to look at my lands. Of course, they will never live up to your Pemberley, but it will be a fit beginning, do you not think?"

Making a slight nodding bow to his friend, Darcy could not help but get caught up in Charles's enthusiasm. "We should survey the fields, the fence line, and observe the homesteads on the estate. Then we may assess what to address immediately and what to delay until the new growing season. We should do so before the obligatory calls from your neighbors begin and before you decide to stay in Hertfordshire."

"I am most looking forward to meeting my new neighbors," Bingley replied as he fixed himself a plate of eggs and some fresh fruit.

"I fear," said Darcy assuming his superior attitude once again, "you will find little true society here in Hertfordshire. It is a country society, lacking in manners and refinement."

"Darcy, you should open yourself more to new adventures," Bingley teased.

Coming quickly to Mr. Darcy's protection, Caroline told her brother she agreed about the probable lack of society in the area. Louisa Hurst agreed by tutting her tongue in a clucking sound. Bingley's countenance brightened as he turned to his sister and said, "If that be so, Caroline, you will be credited with changing their lives forever. Every woman will want to copy your style, and men will be eating out of your hand."

Caroline dropped her eyes in a coy-like manner after darting a glance at Mr. Darcy's profile and hoping he found her "style" to his liking. Louisa agreed with their brother, and then they excused themselves to dress for the day.

Darcy changed to his riding attire and rushed toward the stables; he loved being in the saddle and being out in the open. Cerberus waited for him at the mounting block. Normally, a man of property rode such an inspection of his land in the springtime, but Charles Bingley made an impetuous decision. He only lately decided he should take possession of Netherfield Park, without the usual inquiries of the soundness of the structure or the condition of the land. Then Bingley "begged" Darcy to lend his expertise in what to address in the matter. Darcy's father spent time teaching his son the responsibility Darcy eventually assumed as the master of Pemberley. He began as a child to accompany his father on the spring inspection of the farms and holdings of their estate; therefore, Bingley's learning from Darcy fit the need. Ownership of land determined wealth. Darcy inherited Pemberley through a system of primogeniture. As Bingley's father made his wealth in trade, he held neither ancestral ties to the land nor any real knowledge of the accountability involved in owning an estate.

As the two men rode out that morning, Darcy, in his element, showed his friend the delights of and the responsibilities of being a man of property. Netherfield Park held areas where drainage needed to be addressed, but it also possessed immediate grounds offering paths and parkways for the pleasure of its owner. As both men mounted a hill to take a better view of the prospect leading to Netherfield, Bingley queried, "Well, Darcy, do I have your blessing in this matter?"

"Let us wait a bit longer, my friend," Darcy began, "until you spend a winter at Netherfield. A fine home in the late summer or early autumn may be a drafty pit in the winter."

"Darcy, you are the voice of gloom," Bingley laughed.

Darcy flushed with his friend's taunt. "Gloom seems like sound reason from my perspective."

Bingley turned his mount toward his home; as Darcy circled Cerberus to follow, he espied a glint of color moving along the road below them and to the right. Upon closer inspection, he realized a young lady walked along at a robust pace, nearly running. *How unladylike* he thought briefly. Yet, her obvious joy at ignoring propriety momentarily intrigued him, and he found himself smiling at the sight of such unbridled freedom. *She is delightfully happy.* He secured the memory of the girl before moving on.

Upon their return, both men washed the dust of their ride away and retired to the study to recapture their thoughts on Bingley's investment. "The lodge is stately and will serve you well, especially for shooting parties."

"The stream is adequately stocked, although the wooded area was a bit overgrown," Bingley observed.

"Being able to harvest some of the wooded area for heating purposes will serve the estate, Bingley, and you may choose to sell off some of it for profit. Yet, be sure seedlings are available to replenish the area."

"I never considered that, Darcy. Your counsel is invaluable to me."

"As for the house itself, the lighting in the dining room, morning room, and study is pleasantly suited, picking up the early light. Of course, for my taste, I hope, Bingley, you will address the library's need for comfortable furniture and adequate evening lighting."

"Darcy, I forget how much you pride yourself on the reputation of Pemberley's library. Although I am not the reader you are, I will certainly address your concerns," Bingley mocked.

Their conversations continued along this vein until dinnertime when the gentlemen dressed for the meal and escorted the ladies into the formal dining room. Congenial conversation followed the meal of several courses. "We received," confided Miss Bingley, "several cards and invitations from our neighbors. We expect some of them to call tomorrow to pay respects."

"I am anticipating becoming acquainted with the locals," Bingley beamed.

"Do not anticipate the local gentry to offer much toward polite society," Darcy returned to his earlier qualms. "Country manners, I find, are greatly lacking in a sense of decorum and can often be viewed as vulgar. No doubt many of your neighbors will be intolerable."

The conversation on what to expect continued over dinner and a game of whist. Bingley's usual gracious nature hoped for pleasant hospitality; the rest of the party felt the intrusions upon their privacy to be a necessary evil. Either way, those considered to be from "society" in Hertfordshire soon introduced themselves to the Bingley party.

Sir William Lucas and Mr. Bennet numbered among the first to call on Mr. Bingley. Sir William made his fortune in trade, according to Caroline, and the King honored Sir William with a knighthood after an address made at St. James during Sir William's mayoralty. Evidently, Meryton offered Sir William as the only titled gentleman in the village. Mr. Bennet, a member of the landed gentry, on the other hand, possessed a small estate in comparison to Netherfield. Darcy's smugness crept out when his suspicions of country society received confirmation.

"Mr. Bennet has five daughters, Darcy," Bingley applied to his friend as they played billiards after dinner. "Maybe we can find you a fitting mate among them; I have it on good authority they are reputed beauties."

"Please excuse me if I tell you how I find those prospects to be very distasteful; I plan to marry a woman of wealth and standing, one who will reflect well upon my family. Beauty alone could not be my requisite. I need a woman who is healthy enough to secure future generations for Pemberley. Of course, a woman with superior intellect and strength of character would be desired."

"What do you say to love, Darcy?" his friend asked incredulously.

"Love would be an asset, but my first concern must be what I owe to my family." Darcy studied his friend. "Duty comes before affection."

Bingley stopped and looked up from his shot, "Then I do not understand why you avoided marriage for so long. Surely by now you could find a woman who meets your standards. My own are not so stringent; I still hold with hopes of marrying the woman I love, no matter what her financial standing may be."

Arching his eyebrow, Darcy said, "Maybe Mr. Bennet has a daughter you will prefer."

"Maybe so," Bingley mused. "I think I will return Mr. Bennet's visit in a few days. It is possible I will be able to assess the truth regarding his beautiful daughters." He laughed as he played the next ball into the side pocket.

Mr. Bingley's foray to Mr. Bennet's manor of Longbourn offered no new realities. Unfortunately, he did not meet the young ladies in question. Their reputed beauty remained unconfirmed. The Bennets extended an invitation to dinner, but Bingley deferred; he had obligations in town and could not accept the honor extended to him.

Rumors swirled about Meryton; the Bingley party would attend the upcoming assembly. The rumors included exaggerations of the size of the intended party, thinking it to be eight to ten in number. In reality, after completing his business, Bingley returned to Netherfield with only his brother Mr. Hurst as company.

Dressing for the evening, Darcy did not anticipate a pleasing experience. Normally, he detested large gatherings, being animated and congenial only among his close acquaintances; in fact, in large gatherings he took on a different persona. Even among those of refined tastes, Darcy often withdrew within himself. Those who encountered him found a daunting scowl plastered upon his face. His attitude toward a gathering involving anyone who could afford a ticket bordered on pure disdain. He despised, according to all reports, dancing.

Of a like disposition, Caroline and the Hursts suffered an appearance at the assembly as a social duty to support their brother. A full moon shone brightly as the party descended from their carriage outside the Meryton Assembly Hall. Sir William Lucas welcomed them first, coming forward after the party disposed of their evening wraps. Ironically, as Bingley and his sisters stepped into the crowded assembly hall, the music stopped, and the dancers made their turn and came face-to-face with city fashion. After Sir William's amiable greeting, he ushered the group to a place of prominence in the room, stopping only to introduce his wife Lady Lucas and his eldest daughter Charlotte.

Crossing the room at the back of the Bingley party, Darcy became astutely aware of the impression they made on those assembled. He realized within five minutes both his and Bingley's financial wealth would be rumored among all those in attendance. This type of monetary evaluation played common among the upper class. Often he heard it said a single man in possession of a good fortune, must be in want of a wife. Darcy assumed the premise permeated the thoughts of those of a lower level too.

Shortly upon their arrival, the party met Mrs. Bennet and the elder daughter. Miss Jane Bennet, he found, had golden hair, eloquent Greek features, and deep blue eyes. Darcy thought Miss Bennet attractive; in fact, she proved the only one of any note in the room, but he possessed no real desire to make her acquaintance. Immediately taken with Jane Bennet, Bingley, on the other hand, requested a turn on the dance floor with her.

Darcy walked about the room, giving offense to all who viewed him. Although handsomer than Mr. Bingley and now rumored to have ten thousand pounds per year, most of the assembly found him haughty and formal and possessing a superior bearing. Soon, most shunned his disagreeable attitude; not accustomed to attending public assemblies, Darcy's disdain showed. He stood, being inhospitable, along the wall when Bingley came from the dance floor to press his friend into joining him. "Come, Darcy, I must have you dance. I hate to see you standing about by yourself in this stupid manner. You had much better dance."

"I certainly shall not. You know how I detest it, unless I am particularly acquainted with my partner. At such an assembly as this, it would be insupportable. Your sisters are engaged, and there is not another woman in the room whom it would not be a punishment to me to stand up with."

"I would not be so fastidious as you are for a kingdom!" cried Mr. Bingley. "Upon my honor, I never met with so many pleasant girls in my life as I have this evening; and there are several of them, you see, uncommonly pretty."

Darcy looked at the eldest Miss Bennet. "You are dancing with the only handsome girl in the room."

"Oh! She is the most beautiful creature I ever beheld! But there is one of her sisters sitting down just behind you, who is very pretty, and I dare say very agreeable. Do let me ask my partner to introduce you."

Darcy looked around, and his gaze fell on Elizabeth Bennet; he caught her eye and unconsciously quickly withdrew his. A momentary feeling of regret shot through his body, but he shook off his unfound interest in the woman while saying coldly, "She is tolerable, but not handsome enough to tempt *me*; and I am in no humor at present to give consequence to young ladies who are slighted by other men. You had better return to your partner and enjoy her smiles, for you waste your time with me."

Shaking his head in disbelief, Bingley moved back to the dance floor to enjoy his first celebration with his new neighbors; Darcy moved in the opposite direction. He took up his post along an adjoining wall. Standing there, his eyes rested again on Elizabeth Bennet; her enigmatic smile forced him to replay his response to Bingley's entreaty in his head, making him sorry for the way he acted. Then he noticed she meant her smile for him. She smiled, evidently, because she heard what he said and found it amusing. *How dare she ridicule his behavior with her smile! To whom did this woman think she directed her disdain?* His duty did not lie to those in this room; his duty rested with the people on Pemberley's estate; too many lives depended on him. Although he did not enjoy giving offense to the lady, maintaining his position seemed uppermost in his mind. He found her smile insulting. Insufferable!

Yet, as the evening progressed Darcy unwillingly noted although Elizabeth Bennet was not the remarkable beauty she was reported to be, she did possess a quality he could not define. Miss Elizabeth, Darcy conceded, proved herself in the dance forms, and he discovered to his dismay his eyes often fell upon her. Men and women alike sought her company, and he unconsciously became aware of her presence. She owned an unbridled freedom he saw some place else recently; Elizabeth Bennet approached the dance and ensuing conversations with an exuberance from which he had difficulty withdrawing.

CHAPTER 2

" . . . It is often only carelessness of opinion."

As usual, Darcy rose before the rest of the Bingley household. Sitting alone in the breakfast room at Netherfield seemed to be becoming a habit. Holding the coffee cup to his lips momentarily, he allowed his distaste for the previous evening's entertainment to play through his mind. He never saw such gaucheness gathered in one place and at one time—from the supercilious Sir William to the many women he observed of little intelligence, few true manners, and disagreeable temperaments. A shudder of disgust briefly racked his body when an enigmatic smile and an arched eyebrow played fleetingly across his memory. Darcy purposely shook his head trying to rid himself of the image. Disturbed by the vision but not knowing why, he rose quickly and strode through the hallways of Netherfield heading toward the stables. He should wait on Bingley to go riding, but it might be a long while before his friend came down. At the moment, Darcy needed to be free of the form and free of his feeling of uncertainty. Cerberus, thankfully, stood ready at the mounting block; and without realizing what he did, he turned the horse toward the same hill from which he saw the flash of color along the road several days before.

Darcy's energies depleted, upon his return to Netherfield, he found the Bingleys still sitting around leisurely in the morning room. Their respite into Hertfordshire society exhausted them in so many ways. Assuming an air of false hauteur, Bingley playfully turned to Darcy, "I see our friendship did not impact your decision to ride out without me. I hoped we could continue our survey of the estate. You wounded me, Sir."

"If you are honest with your reproofs, I beg your pardon most profusely, Bingley. Your hospitality is an honor I cherish." Darcy looked steadfastly at his friend.

Bingley realized Darcy did not comprehend he made the disparagement in jest. He gauged having Fitzwilliam Darcy as an intimate more than favorable, his good opinion a wealth upon which value could not be taken. Bingley knew if Darcy told him to quit Netherfield, his chaise and four would leave immediately; his friend would not lead Bingley astray. "Really, Darcy," flustered Bingley, not used to such self-reproach, "I value your opinions *and* your company." They gave each other a quick bow indicating mutual respect; then Bingley emitted a soft laugh to relieve the unanticipated tension while both men moved to the serving tray to partake of the items there.

Darcy turned to Miss Bingley before she lambasted her brother's tarriance among Hertfordshire's finest. He knew she wanted to gain his approval by defying her brother's successes last evening. "Miss Bingley, your refinement and charity were never so appreciated as they were yesterday evening."

Bingley joined in, "Yes, my Dear, you and Louisa were much admired. I received so many compliments on your behalf last night. I am indebted to you two in helping to establish our family's standing in the community. Your successes are our success."

Darcy knew Miss Bingley despised last evening; she confided as much to him several times during the assembly; yet, she said, "Your attention honors me. I pray my contribution to the evening solidified your presence in the community, Charles."

Leaving the ladies behind, the gentlemen retired to the study to continue their review of the Netherfield books and accounts. Darcy thoroughly enjoyed these hours of withdrawal from the niceties society placed on gentlemen; what transpired behind the study door remained within his control. It held no double-edged expressions to dance around—no prejudices—and no enigmatic smile hauntingly resurfacing in his memory.

However, those hours passed too quickly; returning to the company of the ladies, Darcy and Bingley suffered when Caroline Bingley could control her opinions no longer, and they now listened to the Bingley sisters decrying their neighbors' manners; the tirade started at dinner and increased in its vehemence. Miserable, Bingley suffered greatly, but Darcy felt far from being agreeable himself; he sat with a pronounced grimace. Bingley insisted. "I never met with more pleasant people. Everyone offered their attentions and their kind regards; there was no one putting on airs or offering false countenances; I was pleased to make the acquaintance of many of my new neighbors."

"Charles, you lack judiciousness," Miss Bingley intoned her contempt. "The women may be pretty by your judgment; yet, they lacked conversation and fashion. Were you not aware of their conceit?"

Bingley, at least, allowed censure could not be addressed to Miss Bennet. In frustration, he turned to his friend for sympathy. Darcy's honest nature allowed him only to concede Miss Jane Bennet as attractive, but "she smiles too much."

"Smiles too much!" Bingley nearly came out of his chair in disbelief. "I can think of no one of my acquaintance more beautiful."

Darcy, however, finally admitted, he saw a collection of people with no manners and little beauty. "I take no interest or pleasure at the prospect of renewing their attentions." Yet, as soon as he said it, he felt a twinge of betrayal.

Taking pity on their brother, Mrs. Hurst and her sister finally allowed Jane Bennet to be a *sweet* girl and declared their desire to know her better. They, therefore, established Miss Bennet as someone they admired and liked; Bingley accepted their praise of Miss Bennet and allowed himself the pleasure of thinking of her as someone he too *would like to know better.*

Over a fortnight Bingley continued to prefer the company of Jane Bennet to all others in Hertfordshire. Darcy observed his young friend fall in and out of romantic relationships before, but he never recalled Bingley to be more besotted. Bingley danced with Miss Bennet four times at Meryton, saw her one morning at his house, and dined in company with her four times. Unfortunately, as Bingley seemed about to give his heart to a woman clearly below him, Darcy discovered to his horror his own tendencies in that vein becoming more distinct. Every time Bingley found Miss Bennet's company, he placed Darcy, as Bingley's companion, in Elizabeth Bennet's presence. Each time as he swore to himself he would ignore Elizabeth, he found himself more enticed by her. Unconsciously, he placed himself where he could observe her, where he could listen to her conversation, and where he could interact with her. Although he rarely spoke to strangers, Darcy began to *plan* ways to afford verbal exchanges with Elizabeth. When they did converse, however briefly, a verbal swordplay occurred between them; he knew she desired an apology for his behavior at the assembly; Darcy also *assumed* Elizabeth Bennet knew he had a *right* to such behavior. His distinct station in life afforded him an air of superiority. Darcy determined she flirted with him through the verbal assaults, and they worked remarkably. He could not offer any culpability to Bingley; he felt in nearly as bad of a position himself.

As Bingley and Darcy discovered themselves distracted by the Bennet ladies, Miss Bingley's acute awareness of the changes in her brother and of his esteemed friend increased her fervent rebukes, especially those directed toward the second Bennet daughter. Miss Bingley congratulated herself when Darcy openly expurgated Elizabeth Bennet's failings. He made observations about Elizabeth's not having an appealing countenance; he said with a critical eye her figure lacked any point of symmetry; and he asserted Elizabeth's manners showed no knowledge of fashionable acceptance. Yet, as he publicly castigated Elizabeth's virtues, privately, the fact he found her face possessing a soul of its own as her dark green eyes danced with life tormented him; he recognized her figure to be light and pleasing; and he found her manners to have a relaxed playfulness. As Darcy's estimation of Elizabeth Bennet made a transition so did his appraisal of Miss Bingley. Uncharacteristically, he said so to his sister in a letter dispatched shortly after the assembly.

20 October

Dearest Georgiana,

Your letter of the 2nd brought me such delight; I would confess to having reread it daily of late as a way of keeping you lovingly in my heart. Bingley's estate possesses plausible attributes, and although it keeps me from your company, being in his service in this matter satisfies me. Miss Bingley and Mr. and Mrs. Hurst number among our party at Netherfield, and we suffer from varying degrees of country society. Duties of this nature, as you know, pain me, but I consent on Bingley's behalf.

We first undertook a local assembly. I found very little pleasing among those at the assembly, having experienced such behavior on prior occasions when duty called me to Lambton and other local villages. Detesting dancing with strangers only added to my discomfort. However, not wanting to discredit Bingley, I maintained my station with abridgement. I wish I could recall as much for Miss Bingley and her sister. I would never consider criticizing one of Miss Bingley's standing; yet, I found her behavior, in reality, not complimentary to her brother's desire. He does these things to advance Miss Bingley's status; yet, she repays him most unceremoniously. True, many at the assembly found them to be pleasant. However, I was not convinced; Bingley's sisters did not try to please anyone but themselves. The neighborhood, which lacks any sophistication, should not have been disposed to approve of their behavior. The Bingley sisters are fine ladies when they choose to be, but they allow their opinions of themselves to border on pride and conceit. Both Caroline and Louisa are rather handsome and each received private seminary educations. Miss Bingley possesses a fortune of twenty thousand pounds, although both women are, I fear, in the habit of spending more than they ought. They associate with fine society and have a right to consider themselves privileged, but they should consider how meanly they treat others.

Their pride is a common failing and is, unfortunately, found in all circles. We all, I believe, display pride in some real or imaginary quality with some people cherishing these feelings of self-complacency. Maybe what the Bingley sisters display is vanity, but I argue vanity and pride differ. A person may be proud without being vain. Opinions of ourselves define our pride; what we have others think of us is our vanity.

Thankfully, our family has the benefit of generations of knowing what society expects. With Mrs. Annesley to guide you, my Dearest, I fear no such behavior from you. Georgiana, I must regretfully close. Please do not concern yourself, my girl, with thoughts of my happiness; when it is time for my taking a wife, I will find someone who will give us both affection as the mistress of Pemberley and as a devoted sister. I am anticipating your concert for my benefit. I am sure it will be one I will cherish forever as I do all of our times together. Praying that you too find all the happiness you so rightly deserve, I am your affectionate brother . . .

Fitzwilliam

The evening's engagement took place at Lucas Lodge; again, Darcy found his thoughts taking on a contradictory form. Over the past few weeks, he developed an interest in learning more about Elizabeth Bennet. He desperately wanted to see more of her although he knew an alliance with such a family insupportable. Darcy *convinced* himself of late he held no real interest in Elizabeth Bennet; so little entertainment came to a man of the world in Hertfordshire society, and Miss Elizabeth became only a diversion for his hours of boredom; that was all she was to him; that was all she could ever be to a man of his quality, a man of property as vast as Pemberley. Darcy would never take advantage of Elizabeth Bennet as a former friend tried to do with Georgiana; he was a man of honor, a man of scruples; yet, he found his *diversion* with Elizabeth

Bennet to be an unanticipated pleasure.

As much as Darcy took pleasure in Elizabeth Bennet's vitality, her family appeared less than to be desired. Mrs. Bennet's connections proved poor, having brothers, one a country attorney in Meryton and another who resided in Cheapside in London. Mrs. Bennet, whose manners, openly profusive at best, had one goal: Find her five daughters suitable matches in life; Mr. Bennet, well read and a gentleman with an income of two thousand pounds per year, took very little interest in the activities of his wife and daughters. Jane and Elizabeth Bennet he *accepted,* but the three youngest were left to their own frivolities; one devoted herself to her studies to the point of being rude, while the other two openly flirted with every available man, especially with those officers of the local militia. Having observed the Bennets over a fortnight, Darcy convinced himself an alliance to such a family intolerable; and he feared Bingley might be choosing poorly if he continued to favor Miss Bennet. Of course, Darcy's interest in Elizabeth Bennet could never advance to that level: He just found someone in the area with an active mind, a person not of a dole character, whom he could observe from afar.

As the evening at Lucas Lodge progressed, Darcy took pleasure in espying on Elizabeth Bennet's interactions with Charlotte Lucas, various militia officers in attendance, Bingley, *and* her elder sister. He noted of late little escaped Elizabeth's attention. He watched as she complimented Maria Lucas on her needlework, causing the girl to blush excessively but out of reinforcing its worth rather than out of shame. He observed Elizabeth trying to reign in her mother's exuberance. Elizabeth, evidently, took delight in Bingley's attentions to her sister, but she did not suspect Darcy's growing interest in her. Darcy's desire to know more of her advanced throughout the evening; and as a way to converse with her, he eavesdropped on her conversations with others. His doing so drew Elizabeth's notice and, eventually, she told Charlotte she would confront him. Therefore, when Darcy came near her, although he showed no intention of speaking, Elizabeth playfully confronted him. "Did you not think, Mr. Darcy, that I expressed myself uncommonly well just now, when I was teasing Colonel Forster to give us a ball at Meryton?"

Flustered momentarily that Elizabeth Bennet took note of his attention, Darcy recovered his composure and said, "With great energy; but it is always a subject which makes a lady energetic." He knew he should walk on, but the need to remain a few moments more in her court overwhelmed him.

"You are severe on us," she replied. Darcy quickly assimilated the double meaning to her words. More than likely, Elizabeth still waited for the apology he owed her for his conduct at the assembly.

Charlotte Lucas, not wishing her friend to offend a man of such high standing in her father's house, tried to divert Elizabeth. "It will be *her* turn soon to be teased. I am going to open the instrument, Eliza, and you know what follows."

Elizabeth good-naturedly lamented, "You are a very strange creature by way of a friend!—always wanting me to play and sing before anybody and everybody! If my vanity had taken a musical turn, you would be invaluable; but as it is, I would really rather not sit down before those who must be in the habit of hearing the very best performers." The insult, coated in sweetness in order not to directly offend Darcy, found no such offense; instead, he searched the depths of her eyes.

Yet, Miss Lucas persevered, and Elizabeth added, "If you insist, dear Charlotte, it must be so." And gravely glancing at Darcy, she said, "There is a fine old saying, which everybody here is, of course, familiar with: 'Keep your breath to cool your porridge'; and I shall keep mine to swell my song."

She curtsied and walked toward the instrument. The mocked sincerity with which Elizabeth spoke was not lost on Darcy; and although her use of a common colloquialism should offer him an affront to their respective stations in life, he found an allurement to the possibility of learning something new about Elizabeth Bennet. As casually as he could, he circulated about the room and took up a position where he could enjoy Elizabeth's musical turn, as well as take full advantage of observing her profile. Darcy could not believe her performance: The clarity of her voice sliced through him, and he found closing his eyes allowed him to enjoy it even more. Her singing was excellent, and although her performance on the pianoforte lacked faithfulness to the notes, her joy for life captivated him.

Regretfully, Elizabeth chose to end her performance even though others beseeched her with entreaties to continue. Mary, the plainest Bennet sister, succeeded Elizabeth at the instrument; Mary applied herself more completely than did Elizabeth to her practice and sought the gathering's appreciation, but Darcy felt if her sister spent more time in cultivating her taste rather than diligence in her application, she too might achieve Elizabeth's easy and unaffected manner.

The younger sisters, wanting their share of attention, interrupted Mary's concerto and demanded she play Scotch and Irish airs, more suitable for dancing with the officers. Darcy, having moved away from the instrument after Elizabeth's performance, looked on in disgust. He preferred an evening of conversation and, particularly, a chance to converse with Elizabeth Bennet. Engrossed in his thoughts, Sir William Lucas's approach took him unawares. "What a charming amusement for young people this is, Mr. Darcy! There is nothing like dancing after all. I consider it as one of the first refinements of polished societies"

With his usual outspoken bluntness, Darcy responded, "Certainly, Sir; it also has the advantage of being in vogue amongst the less polished societies of the world. Every savage can dance."

Darcy's reserve did not deter Sir William's conversation; he spoke of Bingley's affably joining the dancers, complimented Darcy's dancing at the assembly, inquired into how often Darcy danced at St. James, and finally queried about Darcy's house in town. Darcy, distracted by this babble, did not realize at that instant Elizabeth moved toward them, and Sir William, struck with the notion of doing a very gallant thing, called out to her, "My dear

Miss Eliza, why are you not dancing? Mr. Darcy, you must allow me to present this young lady to you as a very desirable partner. You cannot refuse to dance, I am sure when so much beauty is before you." Sir William took her hand and attempted to give it to Darcy.

Taken by surprise at this sudden turn of events, Darcy wanted to take advantage of this pleasant offering. The possibility of holding Elizabeth's hand uncharacteristically warmed Darcy's innards, creating an unfamiliar sensation. Although he was not unwilling to receive her hand, Elizabeth instantly drew back from him and said with some discomposure to Sir William, "Indeed, Sir, I have not the least intention of dancing. I entreat you not to suppose that I moved this way in order to beg for a partner."

"Miss Bennet, you would do me a great honor if you allow us to dance," Darcy responded gravely. The fact Elizabeth Bennet offered no pretense or traps to allure potential suitors appeared not wasted on his sensible nature.

However, Elizabeth would not agree; even Sir William's entreaties could not persuade her. "You excel so much in the dance, Miss Eliza, that it is cruel to deny me the happiness of seeing you; and though this gentleman dislikes the amusement in general, he can have no objection, I am sure, to oblige us for one half-hour."

"Mr. Darcy is all politeness," said Elizabeth, smiling. Yet, she continued her refusal and walked away.

Her briskness should offend him, but it did not do so; he still considered the beauty of the woman when Miss Bingley approached. "I can guess the subject of your reverie, Mr. Darcy," she began, close enough to nearly whisper in his ear.

Without turning his head toward her or taking his eyes from the figure of Elizabeth Bennet, he responded, "I should imagine not."

Not to be deterred, she continued, adding her usual censure of the gathering, "You are considering how insupportable it would be to pass many evenings in this manner—in such society; and, indeed, I am quite of your opinion. I was never more annoyed! The insipidity, and yet the noise—the nothingness, and yet the self-importance of all those people! What would I give to hear your strictures on them!"

She evidently expected Darcy to agree Hertfordshire society to be too full of self-importance. Imagine her surprise when he said rather distractedly, "Your conjecture is totally wrong, I assure you. My mind was more agreeably engaged. I have been meditating on the very great pleasure which a pair of fine eyes in the face of a pretty woman can bestow."

Miss Bingley, registering his unhinged attention, immediately realized his thoughts seemed elsewhere. With an underlying layer of urgency, she asked, "What lady creates such *pleasure* for you, Mr. Darcy? Is it someone I know?" Caroline hoped he meant the reference for her.

Darcy replied with resolve, "Miss Elizabeth Bennet."

Watching her hopes dissipate devastated Caroline. "Miss Elizabeth Bennet! I am all astonishment. How long has she been such a favorite?—and pray, when am I to wish you joy?" And although she continued to try to discredit Elizabeth in Darcy's opinion, concentrating her attack on Elizabeth's lack of suitable family connections, he never changed his focus.

The next morning as the Bingley party slept, Darcy decided to partake of the grounds on foot rather than on horseback. He spent an uneasy night; whenever he sought rest, a pair of fine eyes and an enigmatic smile haunted his dreams. Determined this morning to clear his mind of the thoughts of Elizabeth Bennet, Darcy hoped the pleasure in the walk would arise not from solitary thoughts of the woman but from being outdoors and from repeating some of the many poems that extol the beauty of autumn. Although he at first occupied his mind with thoughts of the weather, of the exercise, and of the beauty of the season, unfortunately, in no time, Darcy's mind drifted elsewhere: Elizabeth Bennet.

He wondered now, how were her sentiments to be read. Elizabeth's flirtations of late increased in their intensity and duration.

Before she forgave him, clearly, though, he should apologize for the assembly. He knew her to be a responsive person, one who would excuse his folly in not choosing to dance when they first met. Yet, on the other hand, a most disagreeable manner formed Darcy's opinion of the Bennets. Only the two eldest Bennets possessed any sense of propriety, and though he took an apparent liking for Elizabeth, his determination not to fall for her remained important. She would not make him a suitable wife; she did not fit his criteria of what a mistress of Pemberley should possess. He understood he should not encourage her interest; it would not be honorable to lead Elizabeth on. Therefore, did he then wish to avoid her? He thought all these things as he traversed the grounds. The chaos of his mind had him hating himself for the turmoil such thoughts created. Why did he question his motives? He knew what he should do in regards to his growing interest in Elizabeth Bennet, but what his mind told him to do and what his heart bade him do became two different things.

CHAPTER 3

" . . . to be really in love without encouragement . . ."

Darcy's thoughts fought each other as such for several days whenever he was alone and too often when he was not. Little of notice distracted him within the area except the arrival of the —shire in Meryton, and eventually, he and Bingley dined with the officers. Much to his friend's dismay, on the same evening, his sisters chose to engage Miss Bennet to Netherfield. He had not enjoyed Jane Bennet's company for several days, and Bingley's countenance showed the irony of the situation. "That beautiful angel dines here at my own table this evening, while you and I, Darcy, have the pleasure of dining with the local militia."

For Darcy's part, being away from Elizabeth Bennet the past few days solidified his newfound resolve to ignore her and to squash any aspirations she might have. Therefore, his response did little to allay Bingley's desire to cancel their engagement with the officers. After the dinner, the smooth brandy and the interesting conversation entertained Darcy. His interest in military history served him well during the evening, and several who originally found him proud had second thoughts about his congeniality. A continual downpour dampened his spirits some, but not enough to ruin the evening, while the rain and the travesty of the situation dramatically increased Bingley's discomposure.

Descending from their carriage upon their return to Nether-field, the gentlemen learned Miss Bennet took ill during dinner. She, evidently, rode the family horse to Netherfield from her home at Longbourn three miles away, and the downpour soaked her clothes. Miss Bingley and Mrs. Hurst insisted she stay the night. "Caroline, how is Miss Bennet?" Bingley pleaded with his sister when she exited the lady's room.

"The apothecary has come and gone, Charles. Miss Bennet has a fever. We offered her accommodations for the evening," his sister replied, a bit out of sorts with having to deal with this matter.

"Should we send to London for a physician?" Bingley said, pacing the floor.

"The lady has a cold. She will be better tomorrow. Sending for a physician would be preposterous for a cold! I warrant Miss Bennet will be better on the morrow, Charles." The whole matter fatigued Caroline. Although not thoroughly content with the answer, Bingley did not press his sister further. He would wait until the morning to assess whether Miss Bennet needed something else.

Satisfied he could do nothing to relieve his friend's tumult and seeing no other need for his service, Darcy retired to his rooms. Sitting before the mirror in his dressing room, he spoke aloud to the image of the man he had become. "So, Miss Bennet is here and ill. How convenient for her! I wonder who planned such a foolish venture—Mrs. Bennet, of course; she arranged this all. She sent her daughter out in the rain to *snag* herself a husband. Can one image such a mother—such connections—poor Elizabeth?" As soon as he said her name, a reverie of images of the woman overcame his senses. Every time he thought he rid himself of his desire to see and talk to Elizabeth Bennet, reminders resurfaced. *Elizabeth would never agree to such a clearly manipulated plot as this one was,* he mused. Should he warn Bingley? His friend became more entangled each day; could he allow Bingley to create an alliance with such a family? What was he thinking? He considered such an alliance himself on more than one occasion! *Elizabeth is still a Bennet;* he had to keep reminding himself of that fact and of the repugnance he felt for her connections.

Darcy undressed and prepared for bed. Leaning over to blow out the candle, another thought dawned on him. If Miss Bennet felt very ill, Elizabeth Bennet would probably come to Netherfield to take care of her sister. Darcy groaned with the realization that in such a case, Elizabeth would be here in the house with him. He would be forced to spend more time with her. Was the groan from pain or pleasure with the thought? He was not sure. Letting out the breath he did not realize he held, he blew out the candle, closed his lids, and welcomed the portrait of Elizabeth Bennet to his sleep.

Jane Bennet's fever worsened. In the morning the Bingleys dispatched a note to Longbourn for they decided whether to secure a physician should be one belonging to Mr. and Mrs. Bennet. Bingley realized the truth of the idea; he had no right to order a physician for Jane Bennet; yet, that fact did not soften his notice. A chaotic state overcame Bingley. "Please, you must calm down, Charles. Everything which can be done for Miss Bennet is being seen to." Darcy wanted to allay his friend's apprehension.

"I know, Darcy, but I feel I should be doing more for her." Bingley allowed his growing regard for Jane Bennet to show.

"Please, Charles, you are doing your best for Miss Bennet. She will recover soon; you will see. Let us join your family in the morning room. Your sisters are concerned for your well-being too."

Darcy's words lessened Bingley's anxiety, and he allowed himself to set aside his misgivings and to be led to the morning room. Although the rainstorm ended, and the land dried out, remnants of the downpour remained. Darcy knew they could not ride out today, and he too remained in a state of disorder; a ride on Cerberus would do him well. So, there they sat, partaking of the morning repast, making niceties, and each of them lost in his thoughts. Bingley worried for Miss Bennet's well-being; Caroline and Louisa wanted to rid themselves of the duty of caring for someone they only pretended to admire; and Darcy needed to free himself of the unexplained energy which thoughts of Elizabeth created in him.

Suddenly, the door swung open; a servant announced, "Miss Elizabeth Bennet," and she stood framed in the doorway. Her appearance took all of them by surprise. Mud steeped her petticoat, her hair windswept, and her clothes disheveled. The Bingley party sat in shock—in momentary suspension—at an unan- nounced visit so early. Simultaneously, both Bingley and Darcy recovered; they sprang to their feet to acknowledge the entrance of a lady into the room. Mesmerized by her image, Darcy stood dumbfounded; in all his nightly musings, he never envisioned Eliz- abeth to look as such; she was lovelier than ever.

Bingley, thankfully, had the good sense to leave the table to approach her. "Miss Elizabeth," he began, "please, join us." She mo- tioned his plea away. "You have come to see your sister. I am so glad to see you. Miss Bennet will benefit by having her loved ones close."

Sarcastically, Caroline said, "Miss Elizabeth, did you walk here?"

"I did, Miss Bingley. I was worried about Jane," Elizabeth reasoned.

"Three miles?" Louisa added incredulously.

Elizabeth smiled at their being astonished at her need to see Jane. "I believe so," came her simple reply. Then turning to Mr. Bingley she asked, "Would it be too much trouble for me to see Jane?"

"We will have someone show you to Miss Bennet's room," Bingley chimed in. "When you are able, please advise us on her condition; our apprehension grows. If Miss Bennet needs *anything*, we are your servants." Bingley turned to the doorman and indi- cated for him to take Elizabeth to attend her sister. During this exchange, Darcy did not move; the picture of Elizabeth, which he would add to his mental gallery of her, amused him.

When she was safely out of earshot, Caroline could not contain her distaste for the display made by Elizabeth Bennet. "Did you ever?" she began, but Darcy cut her short by removing her imme- diate audience. "Bingley, it appears we will be unable to ride out today and look at more of your holdings, but we still may address expenses for the renovations you have considered." Bingley looked relieved at the possibility. He needed to be away from his sisters and to contemplate what he should do in regard to Miss Bennet. They hurriedly retired to the study.

"Darcy, would it be inappropriate to bring a physician from London to attend to Miss Bennet?" Bingley began tentatively.

"It would be a break in propriety," Darcy responded in a halting speech. "May I suggest if Miss Bennet's progress is delayed, her sister should also be given accommodations so she may attend to Jane Bennet. From what I observe of Miss Elizabeth, I find her to be very sensible. She would never allow decorum to get in the way of her sister's health; Miss Elizabeth would ask, maybe demand, you do more if need be."

"Of course, why did I not think of that? When Miss Elizabeth joins us later, I will ask her to stay. Your good counsel never ceases to amaze me, Darcy." As Darcy turned back to the plans for Netherfield, he wondered whether he did the correct thing.

At three in the afternoon, Elizabeth entered the sitting room; she attended Jane all day, with the occasional help of the ladies of the house. The apothecary declared Jane to have a violent cold and in need of more care, and Elizabeth hated to leave her sister, but she must return to Longbourn as evening approached. Wanting to be rid of the competition, Miss Bingley, graciously, offered Elizabeth her carriage, which she accepted reluctantly and then prepared to take her leave. Bingley and Darcy entered the room as this last exchange occurred; Bingley shot Darcy a sideways glance, and Darcy nodded his approval. Bingley's affirmation could not be questioned. "I will not hear of it, Miss Elizabeth; you must stay and tend your sister. Miss Bennet will recover much faster if you are in attendance."

"Mr. Bingley," Elizabeth nearly gushed, "your kindness is most appreciated. I desire to stay with Jane if your offer is sincere."

"Then it is settled," Bingley added quickly. "We will send a servant to Longbourn to acquaint your family with your stay and to bring back a supply of clothes for your needs."

"I am in your debt, Mr. Bingley." Elizabeth curtsied and happily returned to her sister's room. This satisfied Bingley, but if he took note of his sister's face at the time, he would have seen displeasure. Caroline wanted the Bennet family out of Netherfield as soon as possible. She realized Charles favored Miss Bennet; she also recognized Darcy's growing interest in Elizabeth Bennet. She would need to be observant of the dynamics surrounding this household. Her plans for Charles's future and her plans for her future with Mr. Darcy were being challenged, and Miss Bingley never accepted defeat easily.

It was half past six before Elizabeth joined the party again, having been summoned to dinner. "I am afraid, Mr. Bingley, I cannot give you a favorable response to your inquiry. My sister shows no improvement."

"That is dreadful to hear, Miss Elizabeth," Caroline intoned, although she quickly returned to the needlework she held in her hand.

During dinner Darcy hoped for an opportunity to speak with Elizabeth, but Caroline strategically placed her next to Mr. Hurst. Darcy made conversation with Caroline. He split his attention, however, hoping for *gems* of Elizabeth's conversation, which he could use later.

Elizabeth returned to her sister's care after dinner, and Miss Bingley immediately began to abuse her. "Miss Elizabeth's manners, I find, are very bad indeed; they are a mixture of pride and impertinence. Did you notice, Louisa, she cannot hold a civil conversation; she has no style, no taste, and no beauty of which to speak. Country ideas of such appealing qualities must be far below those of refined societies." Darcy shuddered listening to her crassness; he wondered at how little he knew about Miss Bingley. He once found her to be dignified. *When was that exactly?*

Louisa Hurst joined in her sister's aspersion of Elizabeth Bennet. "She has nothing, in short, to recommend her, but being an excellent walker. I shall never forget her appearance this morning. She really looked almost wild."

Caroline cackled, "She did, indeed, Louisa. I could hardly keep my countenance. Very nonsensical to come at all! Why must *she* be scampering about the country because her sister had a cold? Her hair so untidy, so blowsy!"

"Yes, and her petticoat; I hope you saw her petticoat, six inches deep in mud!"

Bingley came to Elizabeth's defense. "I thought Miss Elizabeth Bennet looked remarkably well when she came into the room this morning. Her dirty petticoat quite escaped my notice." *Bless him,* thought Darcy. *Maybe he will be able to handle Caroline some day after all.*

Caroline turned her attention to Darcy. "You observed it, Mr. Darcy, I am sure, and I am inclined to think that you would not wish to see *your* sister make such an exhibition. To walk three miles or four miles, or five miles, or whatever it is, above her ankles in dirt and alone, quite alone—what can she mean by it? It seems to me to show an abominable sort of conceited independence, a most country-town indifference to decorum."

Caroline's references to the boorish behavior of the locals wore on Darcy's patience. "Her sister was ill; it shows an affection for her sister that is very pleasing."

"Mr. Darcy, you must agree, however, that this adventure has rather affected your admiration of her fine eyes." Caroline's voice displayed her desperation.

"Again you are mistaken, Miss Bingley. They were brightened by the exercise."

Darcy hoped his comment would stifle Miss Bingley's censure of Elizabeth, but it did not. "Did you know, Louisa, the Bennet family has an uncle who is a country attorney and an uncle who owns a warehouse in Cheapside?"

"I do not understand all this emphasis on material wealth when one judges a person's merit; even if the Bennets had enough uncles to fill *all* Cheapside, it would not make them one jot less agreeable." Bingley felt the need to defend his preference for Jane Bennet.

"Unfortunately, Bingley, other people will judge differently. It must very materially lessen their chance of marrying men of any consideration in the world." He hated to say it, but the facts were true. Men of fine society would not consider the Bennet sisters as probable mates, and although he found Elizabeth Bennet to be more than appealing, he knew he could not marry her.

Darcy's speech gave the Bingley sisters *permission* to continue their condemnation of the Bennet family's vulgar relations. Bingley, on the other hand, made no answer; he wanted to change the subject, but the reality of the situation did not allow him to open up another avenue of defense. Darcy, too, could not shake the uneasiness he felt each time Caroline mentioned Elizabeth in a negative light.

Eventually, the sisters ceased their *humorous* attack and removed to Miss Bennet's room for an update on Jane Bennet's condition. It was late in the evening before Elizabeth, however, rejoined the Bingley household. The party sat at loo when she returned; Darcy anxiously observed her again. During the day he decided he once more desired Elizabeth's company. Plus, he reasoned having her here would give him some time to really get to know Elizabeth Bennet. He had no one with whom he must share her responses. Darcy looked forward to once again engaging her in a verbal battle. Elizabeth would see him differently; she would increase her regard for Fitzwilliam Darcy. That idea played to Darcy's sense of pride; what woman would not desire his attention? No one Darcy met before refused his consideration.

"Will you join us, Miss Elizabeth?" Louisa asked graciously.

"I fear my sister may require my help; I would not wish to interrupt your game," Elizabeth begged off. "Pray, I will amuse myself with a book instead."

"You cannot tell me, Miss Elizabeth, you prefer reading to cards? That is rather singular." Mr. Hurst protested.

Miss Bingley seized the opportunity to disparage Elizabeth in front of Darcy. She offered a calculated cut. "Miss Eliza Bennet despises cards. She is a great reader, and has no pleasure in anything else."

Caroline's rudeness astonished Darcy. To call Elizabeth "Eliza" highlighted Caroline's way of showing her disdain. Miss Bingley's lack of proper manners mortified him. Turning to Elizabeth, he expected to see her taken aback as well; instead, he noted that same enigmatic smile, the one she gave him when she found his manners lacking. "Miss Bingley, you misjudge me. I deserve neither such praise nor such censure. I am *not* a great reader, and I have pleasure in many things."

Good for her, thought Darcy, *she held her own with Caroline.* How Elizabeth deflected Caroline's criticism impressed Darcy. Verbal attacks with her should entertain him nicely; he anticipated the pleasure of it all. As the evening progressed, Elizabeth, eventually, left her book and drew near the card table. Although she stationed herself between Mr. Bingley and his eldest sister, she played havoc with Darcy's well-being. Awashed with the fragrance of lavender, her nearness placed Darcy's every fiber on alert.

Caroline, aware of the changes in Darcy, tried to recover his attention. "How is dear Georgiana, Mr. Darcy? Is Miss Darcy much grown since the spring? Will she be as tall as I am?"

Darcy's eyes never left his cards, but his awareness of Elizabeth could not be described. "Actually, Miss Bingley, I think she will. She is now about Miss Elizabeth Bennet's height, or rather taller." He shot a glance at Elizabeth, and they momentarily locked eyes.

Caroline's exaggerated regard for Georgiana continued; she wanted Elizabeth to know how intimate she was with Darcy. "How I long to see her again! I never met with anybody who delighted me so much. Such a countenance, such manners. And so extremely accomplished for her age. Her performance on the pianoforte is exquisite."

"It is amazing to me," Bingley quickly added, "how young ladies can have patience to be so very accomplished as they are. They all paint tables, cover screens, and net purses. I never heard a young lady spoken of for the first time, without being informed that she was very accomplished."

Darcy's fondness for Bingley increased. Not only had his generosity placed Elizabeth within Netherfield, he opened up a mode of discourse of which Darcy knew Elizabeth would react. Challeng-ingly, Darcy asserted, "Your list of the common extent of accom-plishments has too much truth. I cannot boast of knowing more than half-a-dozen, in the whole range of my acquaintance, that are really accomplished."

Echoing his ideas, Miss Bingley said, "Nor I, I am sure."

Darcy's eyes rose to look Elizabeth squarely in the face; as predicted, she did not disappoint him. "It amazes me you have such an understanding of women's abilities, Mr. Darcy. Have you studied them thoroughly? You seem to comprehend a great deal in your idea of an accomplished woman."

Touché! Darcy had her now; he would let her see he was a worthy opponent for her verbal prowess. "I do comprehend a great deal in it. Just because I am a man, Miss Elizabeth, does not mean I am unaware of what qualities the ideal woman should possess," he began to lead her on.

Not wishing to lose his appreciation to Elizabeth Bennet, Miss Bingley recited her list of qualities for an accomplished woman. "A woman must have a thorough knowledge of music, singing, draw-ing, dancing, and the modern languages, to deserve the word; and besides all this, she must possess a certain something in her air and manner of walking, the tone of her voice, her address and expres-sions, or the word will be but half deserved." Caroline hoped she displayed her accomplished qualities to Darcy while amplifying Elizabeth's flaws.

Realizing this, he chose an area in which he knew Elizabeth excelled to add to the list: "All this she must possess, and to all this she must yet add something more substantial, in the improvement of her mind by extensive reading."

"I am no longer surprised at your knowing *only* six accom-plished women. I rather wonder now at your knowing *any*," Eliza-beth bantered.

Savoring the moment, Darcy parlayed his response, "Are you so severe upon your own sex as to doubt the possibility of all this?"

"I never saw such a woman," Elizabeth bristled. "I never saw such capacity, and taste, and application, and elegance, as you describe united. She would be something to behold!" Darcy smiled at the quickness of her mind. He never had a woman speak to him thusly; he found it intoxicating.

"Oh, Miss Eliza," Louisa protested, "you know not of which you speak. Hertfordshire cannot give you a basis to judge Mr. Darcy's sentiments."

"Are we going to discuss the merits of accomplished women all evening or do you believe, Louisa, you can concentrate on the cards in your hand?" Mr. Hurst's annoyance at such frivolous thoughts showed.

As all conversation came quickly to an end, Elizabeth felt it best she return to her sister's care. Her leaving disappointed Darcy. He felt exhilarated; *it was a beginning,* he thought; tomorrow could not come too soon.

"Eliza Bennet," said Miss Bingley, when the door closed on Elizabeth, "is one of those young ladies who seek to recommend themselves to the other sex by undervaluing their own; and with many men, I dare say, it succeeds. But, in my opinion, it is a paltry device, a very mean art."

Darcy found it amusing how Elizabeth's presence affected Caroline to the point she repeated herself. *If she could see herself as others see her,* Darcy mused. *Caroline criticizes Elizabeth for using wily ways to entice men when her flamboyant displays border on rudeness at times.* "Undoubtedly," replied Darcy, realizing Caroline made her remark for his address, "there is a meanness in *all* the arts which ladies sometimes condescend to employ for captivation. Whatever bears affinity to cunning is despicable." Caroline's countenance took on a disturbance and an agitation; her remark won her no new ground with Darcy. Meanwhile, Darcy thought Elizabeth's allurements genuine where Caroline's were purely for show.

Elizabeth made another brief appearance saying her sister felt worse, and she begged their pardon for she would not leave Jane again. Bingley once again urged Mr. Jones's being sent for immediately. His sisters, feigning true concern, said a dispatch for a more eminent physician should be sent. Elizabeth declined the offer for the time being, but she agreed to let Mr. Bingley send for Mr. Jones in the morning if Miss Bennet felt not more herself. This news made Bingley quite uneasy. Darcy noted although Bingley's sisters claimed to care about Miss Bennet's well-being, they consoled their unhappiness, however, with duets after supper. All these questions into what he accepted as appropriate behavior created more turmoil in Darcy; he could not rely on what he always assumed to be accurate portrayals of a person's character.

Darcy wondered if either Caroline or Louisa took ill, would they be concerned for each other or would they turn to the pianoforte instead. In his estimation, Elizabeth Bennet proved herself a remarkable woman. She traversed on foot the distance of three miles in poor conditions to give service to her sister. She refused to be intimidated by Miss Bingley's so-called social mores and his verbal challenges to her. She battled him with an unaccustomed quickness of mind. If Fitzwilliam Darcy chose a "sister" for Georgiana, he would choose the qualities displayed by Elizabeth Bennet over those of Caroline Bingley. As he slid his long limbs under the counterpane that evening, Darcy pictured Elizabeth Bennet standing on the staircase at Pemberley; it was the first peaceful night he had in some time.

Rested at last, finding Bingley up hours before his usual appearance in the breakfast room surprised Darcy. Bingley looked distraught; his concerns for Miss Bennet's health played havoc on his normal affability. "Bingley, please sit down. You are wearing a path in the flooring," Darcy teased, trying to distract his friend's distress over the woman.

"Darcy, what should be done for Miss Bennet's well-being?"

"Charles," Darcy switched his tone to one more soothing and intimate to help assuage his friend's fears, "one may trust Miss Elizabeth to do what is best for her sister. She will, I am sure, send you word shortly on Miss Bennet's progress."

Nearly as soon as the words left Darcy's mouth, a housemaid brought Mr. Bingley a response from Elizabeth. Miss Bennet's health appeared much improved, but Elizabeth wished a note sent to Mrs. Bennet to visit Jane and to form her own opinion on her eldest daughter's health. Bingley dispatched the message immediately. As he did so, Darcy's composure took a turn; he did not need to be reminded of Elizabeth's connections after finally getting a good night's sleep. He even worried Mrs. Bennet herself may choose to stay at Netherfield and send Elizabeth home to Longbourn. How intolerable that would be! Although he could not explain it even to himself, Darcy wanted Elizabeth to remain at Netherfield. Last night was a beginning; he did not want the dawn to bring an end—an end to what, exactly? He remained unsure, but being with Elizabeth took on a new importance to him.

Much to Darcy's amusement and to his horror at the same time, the two youngest Bennet daughters accompanied Mrs. Bennet. After spending the appropriate amount of time with her eldest, Mrs. Bennet and her daughters intruded upon the Bingley household in the morning room.

Darcy stood by the window, pretending to be taking in the prospect. In reality, he wanted to be away from Mrs. Bennet and the reminder she was Elizabeth's mother, as well as the fact if he developed affection for Elizabeth Bennet, he saddled himself to the family also. Such thoughts began to undermine the feelings he held for Elizabeth from the previous evening. Maybe he should consider her only as a diversion after all.

Mrs. Bennet's fawning over Bingley and his estate interrupted these thoughts. Darcy briefly wondered how well Miss Bennet would have to be before Mrs. Bennet thought her daughter should return to Longbourn. Clearly, having Miss Bennet ill and at Netherfield pleased Mrs. Bennet excessively. "Oh, Mr. Bingley, my Jane is a great deal too ill to be moved. Mr. Jones says we must not think of moving her. We must trespass a little longer on your kindness, Sir; our Jane is the kindest, sweetest soul God ever placed on this earth; she does not deserve such pain."

"You may depend upon it, Madam, that Miss Bennet shall receive every possible attention while she remains with us," Bingley added sheepishly.

"Oh, we do hope you plan to stay at Netherfield, Mr. Bingley; it is such a fine estate."

"I do like it here; I hope to stay a long time, but those who know me well will attest to my changeable nature." He gestured about the room.

"Mr. Bingley," Elizabeth began, "that is exactly what I should have supposed of you."

"Indecision, as they say, brings lamenting for lost days." Bingley enjoyed their banter. Darcy admired his friend's ability to be at ease in such conversations, and at this moment, he envied the attention Bingley received from Elizabeth. But Mrs. Bennet's reprimand of her daughter interrupted those thoughts. "Lizzie, do not forget your place, child."

Bingley enjoyed the exchange, though, and replied directly to Elizabeth, ignoring Mrs. Bennet's warning to her daughter. "So, Miss Elizabeth, you amuse yourself with a study of your fellow man—of his character? If I am correct, you begin to comprehend me, do you?"

With those sparkling eyes, of which Darcy found of late so compelling, she retorted, "I prefer to study intricate characters for they are the *most* amusing; in that they have all the advantage."

Despite his pledge to not get involved in any conversation involving Mrs. Bennet, Darcy could not help but to speak to Elizabeth, specifically, and engage her response. "If you prefer more intricate characters, Miss Elizabeth, the country can in general supply but few subjects for such a study. In a country neighborhood you move in a very confined and unvarying society."

He found Elizabeth's enthusiasm enchanting as she replied, "Luckily, Mr. Darcy, people themselves alter so much, that there is something new to be observed in them forever."

For a brief moment, Darcy and Elizabeth held each other's eyes, and both sported a hint of a smile. Unfortunately, Mrs. Bennet's voice shattered the flash of understanding between them. "I believe you are mistaken, Sir, country society is not lacking in anything of consequence."

Her affront to a man of Darcy's standing silenced the Bingley party. He started to respond, but a note of the mortification Elizabeth suffered at her mother's hand caused him to stifle his disfavor. The gentleman himself turned silently away, cursing himself for having paid any attention to Elizabeth Bennet and to her poor connections.

Elizabeth, however, softened the disdain he currently felt for her by coming to his defense while trying to smooth the indignity. "Mama, you mistake Mr. Darcy's intention," Elizabeth blushed for her mother's intrusion into the conversation. "He only meant that there was not such a variety of people to be met within the country as in the town, which you must acknowledge to be true."

Darcy turned slightly back toward Elizabeth during this speech. He watched as she resettled her shoulders and brought her chin up in an act of defiance. He discovered he developed a fondness for this temerity, and he rued the day he thought her not handsome enough to tempt him.

"Of course, Lizzie," Mrs. Bennet continued, wrapped in her own self-importance, "but we live in a large country neighborhood here in Hertfordshire; I know we dine regularly with four-and-twenty families."

Bingley wanted to respond to Mrs. Bennet's insipidity, but Elizabeth's obvious embarrassment concerned him; therefore, he kept his countenance. Caroline Bingley could not channel her disdain elsewhere; a roll of her eyes and a shift of her seat away from the offending woman became obvious. She caught Darcy's eye and offered him an expressive smile, which said, *"See what your appreciation of very fine eyes will earn you. Mrs. Bennet will be a regular guest at Pemberley if you pursue your interest in Elizabeth Bennet."*

The party found Mrs. Bennet impossible! Yet again, Darcy felt his back stiffen; she displayed such deplorable manners. Miss Bingley's distasteful taunt held little consequence; how Elizabeth felt mattered most at this time. No one seemed willing to breach the silence until Elizabeth herself plunged forward in hopes of changing her mother's conversational intent. "Mama, have you spoken to Charlotte?"

"She was by to see you yesterday, dear. Oh, the poor girl! There is an old maid in the making, for sure. Not that I think Charlotte so very plain, but she is our particular friend. Of course, my Jane is considered to be the most handsome woman in the county. One does not often see anybody better looking."

"Mama!" came Elizabeth's protest. The woman's audacity again amazed Darcy; he rarely experienced such boorishness. To think Elizabeth must live with this brought pity to his mind.

"When Jane was but fifteen, there was a gentleman at my brother Gardiner's in town so much in love with her that my sister-in-law was sure he would make her an offer before we came away. But, however, he did not. Perhaps he thought her too young. However, he wrote some verses on her, and very pretty they were," Mrs. Bennet lamented.

Darcy suspected the man withdrew with the knowledge of having Mrs. Bennet as part of his family rather than thinking Miss Bennet as too young. He turned to observe Elizabeth growing impatient with her mother; she actually interrupted this denigration of her friend and the overt promotion of her beloved sister by saying, "And so ended his affection. There has been many a one, I fancy, overcome in the same way. I wonder who first discovered the efficacy of poetry in driving away love!"

Darcy enjoyed how the quickness of her mind and how her wit allowed Elizabeth to take control of an embarrassing situation. He could not resist another response; he quipped, "I have been used to consider poetry as the *food* of love, Miss Elizabeth."

"Of a fine, stout, healthy love it may. Everything nourishes what is strong already. But if it be only a slight, thin sort of inclination, I am convinced that one good sonnet will starve it entirely away."

A broad smile of contentment spread over Darcy's face; he cared not that everyone's attention was now directed at him and Elizabeth. The connection between them resurfaced. After a few moments, he saw Elizabeth shudder as if she feared her mother would be exposing herself again. Instead, Mrs. Bennet took the more appropriate route of thanking Mr. Bingley for his diligence in caring for Jane and for his acceptance of Lizzy in the household as well. Bingley accepted her "thanks" with unaffected civility and even forced Caroline to respond in the same manner. Darcy stood to the side engrossed in the folly of the scene. The Bennet family circus seemed to be coming to a close; yet, before their departure, he witnessed another social faux pas, brought on this time by the youngest sister.

"Mr. Bingley, we do hope you will keep your promise of having a ball at Netherfield," Lydia Bennet abruptly reminded him.

"A ball at Netherfield would be the most pleasant of evenings," Kitty Bennet added to her sister's outrageous demand.

"And invite the militia," Lydia said dreamily. "They make excellent company."

"I am perfectly ready, I assure you, to keep my engagement; and when your sister is recovered, you shall, if you please, name the very day of the ball. But you would not wish to be dancing while she is ill," Bingley offered a diplomatic answer.

When Mrs. Bennet and her daughters finally left, Elizabeth returned to Jane's care. Instantly, the Bingley sisters took up their usual censure of the Bennet family, often calling upon Darcy to join them in their mirthful display; he could not engage in their suit even with all of Miss Bingley's quips on *fine* eyes. He was a man in turmoil, but Darcy would not befoul Elizabeth Bennet with disparaging remarks. Nothing, including his contempt for her relations, would allow him to do so.

CHAPTER 4

"You take delight in vexing me."

Leaving the others to their own entertainment, Darcy left the room, closing the door solidly behind him. He turned to ascend the stairs leading to his chambers; he found his ears still ringing with the witty remarks slung at Elizabeth Bennet. Standing perfectly still, closing his eyes, and breathing deeply, he hoped to rid himself of what he witnessed. Literally, sucking in air one last time, Darcy opened his eyes to find himself face-to-face with the image, which haunted his every private moment. Recovering quickly, he said, "Miss Elizabeth, I did not expect to see you here." He made the appropriate bow as an acknowledgment of her presence.

Returning a small curtsy, she replied only with his name and moved to go past him. It dawned on him Elizabeth carried a tray with an ewer of water and a large bowl. A bit taken aback, he stammered, "Miss Elizabeth, should not one of the maids be doing that?"

"It is true, such should be, but my sister needed fresh water to drink, and I must also bathe her feverish brow. I wished not to bother Mr. Bingley's staff; they have so much to do already. I fear my family a terrible imposition on his household."

"Nonsense," he began, and then he realized it might seem like a reprimand, so Darcy softened both his tone and his words. "Mr. Bingley would expect nothing else from his staff. It is the neighborly thing to do. Allow me to call someone to help you."

"No," she pleaded. "I would not want to embarrass myself or my family further in Mr. Bingley's estimation. Please, Sir, allow me to do this without his knowledge."

"Very well, then," he relented. "Would you allow my help? The pitcher is heavy, and the stairs are both narrow and steep."

He watched intently as Elizabeth dropped her eyes in assent. He stepped forward and took the water pitcher from the tray. Elizabeth paused briefly, not expecting such gallantry. They ascended the steps side by side. Darcy found he could not remove his eyes from her face encased in the auburn curls. At her sister's room, Elizabeth entered first to place the tray and bowl; Darcy waited at the door's threshold. Seconds later, she returned to retrieve the water pitcher from his hands. "Mr. Darcy, your kindness was most generous."

Her eyes did not meet his as much as Darcy prayed they would. "It is my pleasure to be of service to you, Miss Elizabeth." As she took the pitcher, her fingers touched his in the exchange; the sensation recoiled through his body, Darcy momentarily stumbling back from the shock. Automatically, he forced himself to bow while Elizabeth left him.

He hurried to his room—his mind racing—the brief warmth of her skin against his spreading throughout his body. He must find a way to clear his mind of thoughts of Elizabeth Bennet; he needed a distraction. He retrieved his sister's last letter from the desk in his bedchamber. Elizabeth's touch aroused him; he needed to read Georgiana's letter to refocus and calm his nerves. Of everyone, only Georgiana had that effect on him.

10 November

My dearest Fitzwilliam,

Your letters give me such great pleasure. The accounts of your activities in Hertfordshire are quite amusing. I do not mean to laugh at you my darling brother; I would never think of doing such an unattractive thing; yet, I do find it amusing how your affection for Mr. Bingley placed you in a position to be an observer of sundry activities; I delight at your retellings.

Sir William Lucas may be pompous, but I am sure he possesses a compassionate heart. His joy at giving pleasure to his neighbors showed through even your narration. Not all can be exposed to fine society; I admire Sir William for raising himself to the recognition he has been afforded at St. James. However, I was a bit surprised at your censure of Miss Bingley and Mrs. Hurst at the assembly. It must be poor behavior, indeed, for you to take such notice. I was happy you, at least, acted with decorum and gave credit to your dear friend. Bingley is much favored by having you as his commendable model. Your recollection of Miss Elizabeth Bennet's musical interlude at least brought you some pleasure that particular evening. From your description, Miss Bennet must possess true talent; I am sure such qualities make her all the more attractive to gentlemen. Being accomplished in music is a virtue to which many women strive.

Mrs. Annesley says my needlework needs a purpose. She has, of late, tried to convince me to help the poor in Derbyshire by creating pieces to be given to the children by the local vicar. He, when we attended church there last, preached about the need of the rich to help the poor. The lesson included the rewarding of such actions ten times over. I know my reward is having you as my brother; I am blessed those ten times. Last week in our lessons, I was introduced to the phrase "noblesse oblige," which you understand to be translated into the "likewise obligation." I took it to be as a mantra of what I should do. Although I am, admittedly, a bit shy about seeing my needlework given away to others, I hope I have your blessing in this endeavor. Dearest Brother, please give Mr. Bingley and his family my deepest regards and respect.

Your loving sister,
Georgiana

Darcy closed the letter and replaced it in the desk drawer; the missive brought him a sense of repose. He never felt as he did the past few weeks; he was a man of position—of control. It seemed of late he possessed no control; a pair of fine eyes and a wry smile sent him into turmoil. He wished for someone in whom he could confide and from whom he could seek advice. For now, he resolved he would answer his sister this very evening. If she found his narrative of the assembly and the dinner at Sir William's amusing, the change in the dynamics at Netherfield should bring her "great joy" indeed. Darcy wished he could find the simple pleasure in life Georgiana did. Of course, she was but a child. Such antics would not seem so amusing if his sister knew the extent of his involvement into Hertfordshire society. She might even pity her brother's position at the hands of a saucy maiden. Darcy wished Georgiana was older and could be his confidant; his "troubles" with Miss Elizabeth Bennet, however, were exactly that—his troubles. No one could resolve them but him.

The Bingley household gathered in the drawing room. Mr. Hurst and Mr. Bingley were at piquet, and Mrs. Hurst observed their game. As was his earlier intention, seated at the desk in the room, Darcy wrote his sister. Miss Bingley, finding nothing of her own for amusement, scrutinized his progress. Eventually, Elizabeth joined the group, taking up her needlework.

14 November

My darling sister,

I am happy my letters are of such an entertaining nature. This was not my intent, but I feel no offense in your finding them to be so. Our party at Netherfield Park increased by two of late. Bingley and I returned to Netherfield on the tenth after spending an invigorating evening with Colonel Forster and some of his senior officers to find Miss Jane Bennet took ill during her dinner with Mr. Bingley's sisters. Rather than sending her back to her home at the Longbourn estate in a consistent downpour, the Bingleys provided Miss Bennet accommodations at Netherfield. Miss Bennet is a favorite with Charles. A pretty face, which Miss Bennet does possess, often smites him; reputably she is the prettiest girl in the area. Bingley was secretly delighted at having Jane Bennet ill while at Netherfield, while also being extremely concerned about her health. He even considered sending to London for a physician.

Miss Bingley, my dear, wishes me to interrupt my letter at this point to tell how enraptured she is with your design for the table you decorated recently. Truthfully, not wishing to take away from Caroline's raptures, lately I find her placating compliments for everything relating to the Darcys and to Pemberley as being a reflection of her character. If not for Charles, I would disassociate myself from her.

The other member of our party is Miss Elizabeth Bennet, who has been asked to stay and attend her sister. Actually, I suggested this to Bingley. His having shown Miss Bennet to be his local "choice," it would not be proper for her to stay at Netherfield without a "chaperone." Propriety must be maintained. This is the same Miss Elizabeth of whom I spoke previously.

Miss Elizabeth and Mr. Bingley are both of a playful nature, and I, unfortunately, became the target of a recent rebuke. Bingley when speaking to Miss Elizabeth earlier in the day confided his tendency toward indecision. Then he insinuated his abstract handwriting to be a result of his thoughts coming too quickly for his hand to translate them properly. Miss Elizabeth found his humility endearing. I should have resisted the impulse to respond to Charles's rants and ravings, but I do so detest deceitful appearances. Of course, poor Bingley is too good of a friend; he often absorbs my criticisms and still considers me to be his partisan. Unfortunately, I listed in some detail a litany of Bingley's flaws, including his lack of attention to detail in his muddled script. I find Bingley's inconstancy to be troublesome where Miss Elizabeth believed in general and ordinary cases between friends, where one of them desired the other to change, the person would comply with the desire, without waiting to be argued into it. Her wit turned my argument in Bingley's favor. This is not the first time Miss Elizabeth and I verbally opposed each other. Although you probably think I find this to be offensive, I do not. It is such a contrast to Miss Bingley's fawning over my every move I admit I sometimes try to purposely engage Elizabeth Bennet's attention. The only thing I regret in the

exchange is an offhand remark by Bingley about my "dark" nature.
He insinuated I could be an imposing figure, especially of a Sunday
evening when I have nothing to do. The gravity of his statement was
an indignity I did not expect from my friend.

As far as my objecting to your giving needlework or other such
items to the poor in Derbyshire, you will hear no such complaint.
Giving to the poor has always been something our family embraced.
Our parents are warmly remembered for such generosity. How could I
object to your following their example? You are your mother's daughter;
she would be as proud of her daughter as I am of my sister.

Your loving brother,
Fitzwilliam Darcy

As the evening progressed, Darcy, having finished his letter, wanted
to relieve the earlier memories of the day. He applied to both Miss
Bingley and to Miss Elizabeth for some musical entertainment.
Jumping, literally, at the opportunity to do something to achieve
Mr. Darcy's favor, Miss Bingley was beside the pianoforte before
she realized her duties as the hostess. "Miss Elizabeth," she said
through gritted teeth, "would you favor us by going first?"

"Please precede, Miss Bingley," Elizabeth responded sweetly,
"your skill should take precedence to my pleasure."

Mrs. Hurst joined her sister as they took up several Italian love
songs to demonstrate their expertise. Elizabeth moved to the
instrument to peruse some music books found there. Enthralled
with her earlier performance, Elizabeth's deferment to Miss Bingley initially disappointed Darcy. Still, being given the comparable
pleasure of watching her figure from afar was nearly as intoxicating.
He mentally created a list of her mannerisms—the biting of her
lower lip when concentrating on her needlework, the creased forehead when she challenged him, and the curl, which often fell,
along her chin line in a caress of her neck. Fitzwilliam Darcy saw
little about Elizabeth Bennet, which did not fascinate him. Before
he realized what he did, Darcy moved up to stand beside her at the

instrument. He felt the air intensify around him. Miss Bingley, not wishing to have Darcy standing beside Elizabeth while listening to Italian love songs, varied the charm by now playing a lively Scottish air. In almost a hypnotic trance, Darcy turned to Elizabeth and said, "Do you not feel a great inclination, Miss Bennet, to seize such an opportunity of dancing a reel?"

As soon as he said it, annoyance filled him. He wanted desperately to say something, which would engage Elizabeth and would make her see him in a positive light. Instead, she could easily think Darcy laughed at her social origins. Those of refined and exacting taste did, after all, not prefer reels. Darcy did not mean it to be so, but Elizabeth could interpret his words as such.

She smiled, but made no answer. Her silence surprised him, and instantaneously, Darcy wanted to retract his words, but they were out there; he could not change them now so he repeated the question.

"Never fear, Mr. Darcy, I heard you before, but I could not immediately determine what to say in reply. You wanted me, I know, to say 'Yes,' that you might have the pleasure of despising my taste; but I always delight in overthrowing those kinds of schemes, and cheating a person of their premeditated contempt. I have, therefore, made up my mind to tell you that I do not want to dance a reel at all—and now despise me if you dare."

Darcy could not disengage his mind from thoughts of Elizabeth. She was resplendent! That was all he could think. "Despise you? Indeed I do not dare. No, Madam, I could never have such an opinion of you, Miss Elizabeth," he said, before bowing to her as he took his leave of the room; feeling her eyes piercing his back, he took refuge in the study. Pouring an abundant brandy, Darcy collapsed into a nearby chair. As he ran his fingers through his hair, he realized no woman ever affected him in such a way—he felt bewitched by her. Were it not for the inferiority of her connections, Darcy could easily imagine himself in some danger of falling in love with Miss Elizabeth Bennet.

Dinnertime found changes in the spherical makeup of the party at Netherfield; Miss Jane Bennet made an appearance in the drawing room upon the meal's completion. Darcy offered his congratulations regarding her recovery and watched his close friend stoking the fire to warm the room and to attend to Miss Bennet's every need.

Darcy found a chair where he could observe Elizabeth, who obviously delighted in the attention being given to her sister by the master of the house. Having no wish to play cards, he chose to read, with Miss Bingley following suit. Of course, Miss Bingley held no real interest in books; her pretense was for Darcy's sake, remembering his words: *All this she must possess, and to all this she must yet add something more substantial in the improvement of her mind by extensive reading.* In reality, Miss Bingley's attention strayed to watching Mr. Darcy's every move; she planned to interfere if he showed attention to Miss Elizabeth. She so desired for him to pay attention to her alone she tormented him with questions on what he read and what it meant; however, her design for his consideration remained fruitless. Darcy steadfastly continued to read his book choice. Quite exhausted by her efforts, she tossed her chosen book aside. Finally, Miss Bingley resorted to the one area in which she felt she excelled over Elizabeth Bennet—physical beauty, and she took the chance of being noticed by walking about the room. Darcy, upon whom she directed her attention, remained content to read, never even raising an eyebrow or looking her way. Desperation set in so Caroline turned to Elizabeth to say, "Miss Eliza Bennet, let me persuade you to follow my example, and take a turn about the room. I assure you it is very refreshing after sitting so long in one attitude."

Miss Bingley succeeded in one area: she received Darcy's attention; he looked up, surprised to see Elizabeth consent to such a devious plan. Why Caroline chose to invite Elizabeth to join her peaked his curiosity; Elizabeth, too, seemed wary of the invitation. Without knowledge of his actions, Darcy unconsciously closed his book. "Will you not join us, Mr. Darcy?" Miss Bingley nearly purred.

"I will decline your kind offer, Madam. I assume you have but two motives for choosing to walk up and down the room together, and I would interfere with either of them."

"What could he mean, Miss Eliza?" Miss Bingley queried, never able to decipher Mr. Darcy's double-meaning barbs.

Elizabeth, on the other hand, heard that tone before; she remained determined not to let Mr. Darcy win; she would match him wit for wit. Darcy recognized the resolve of her shoulders, the half-stifled grin playing about her lips, and the arching of an eyebrow. All these things sent sensations down his body; every nerve pulsed. Pausing briefly to make her point, Elizabeth turned slightly toward Darcy. It was all he could do not to walk over and take her in his arms. She taunted, "Depend upon it, he means to be severe on us, and our surest way of disappointing him will be to ask nothing about it."

Very good. It was exactly the kind of repartee he came to expect from Elizabeth Bennet.

Caroline Bingley would do nothing that might upset Mr. Darcy so she made it a point to ask, "Mr. Darcy, whatever can you mean by such a remark? You must explain as we are very anxious to know its meaning."

Darcy played with his response. "I have not the smallest objection to explaining them. You either choose this method of passing the evening because you are in each other's confidence, and have secret affairs to discuss, or because you are conscious that your figures appear to the greatest advantage in walking." At this point he left a pregnant pause to increase the drama of the situation. "If the first, I would be completely in your way, and if the second, I can admire you much better as I sit by the fire."

Take that, Elizabeth Bennet; the thought briefly slid across his mind. His eyes met Elizabeth's, burrowing deep into the green pools and locking in a secret desire. Maintaining his gaze, Darcy heard Miss Bingley's stunned response, "Oh! Shocking! I never heard anything so abominable. How shall we punish him for such a speech?"

Darcy waited with anticipation for Elizabeth's response. "Tease him—laugh at him. Intimate as you are, you must know how it is to be done." He never expected she would dare to laugh at him. As much as he hoped to maintain her gaze, Darcy experienced a momentary glint of uncertainty and dropped his eyes, breaking the bond.

Naturally, Miss Bingley could never speak ill of Darcy; she desired his good opinion too much to defy him on any subject. Elizabeth, carried away with the mirth of the situation, could not allow her love of nonsense to wane. "Mr. Darcy does nothing which might amuse his friends? I would not require many such friends for I dearly love a laugh."

Not able to abandon the serious armor, which served him well in the past, Darcy assumed an air of superiority as he said, "Miss Bingley has given me more credit than can be. The wisest and best of men—nay, the wisest and best of their actions—may be rendered ridiculous by a person whose first object in life is a joke."

Without thinking of its effect, Elizabeth, amused by her own cleverness, replied, "Certainly, there are such people, but I hope I am not one of *them*. I hope I never ridicule what is wise or good. Follies and nonsense, whims and inconsistencies, *do* divert me, I own, and I laugh at them whenever I can. But these, I suppose, are precisely what you are without."

Having spent his life hating any form of weakness, Darcy's affectionate gaze took on a steeled impalement; nearly biting the words, he said, "Perhaps that is not possible for anyone. But it has been the study of my life to avoid such weaknesses which often expose a strong understanding to ridicule."

"What sort of weaknesses, Mr. Darcy? Would, say, vanity or possibly pride be such a weakness?" she retorted.

Swallowing hard, Darcy steadied himself before giving a response. "Yes, vanity is a weakness indeed. But pride—where there is a real superiority of mind, pride will be always under good regulation."

Elizabeth's suppression of a smile surprised Darcy. He found nothing amusing in what he said; he meant his response to be a serious, diplomatic answer. He began to think she went too far. Amusing repartee was one thing, but he would not be her target, no matter what attraction he felt for this insipid miss. Miss Bingley regretted the beginning of this folly and begged an end to it. Elizabeth feigned innocence and coquettishly played down her affront. "I agree with you, Miss Bingley, Mr. Darcy has no faults; perfection is within his reach."

"No," Darcy snapped. "I have made no such pretension," he stammered. Elizabeth, obviously, knew nothing of superior society. "I have faults enough," he continued, "but they are not, I hope, of understanding. My temper I dare not vouch for. It is, I believe, too little yielding—certainly too little for the convenience of the world. I cannot forget the follies and vices of other so soon as I ought, nor their offenses against myself. My feelings are not puffed about with every attempt to move them. My temper would perhaps be called resentful. My good opinion once lost, is lost forever."

Earlier Elizabeth defended Bingley's appearing to be humbled, but she now attacked him! Darcy came to the speedy conclusion she knew nothing about him and cared not to recognize his worth. He misjudged Elizabeth Bennet's excellence! His full being pulled back from the woman to whom he gave his attention of late. "Your faults, as you define them, Mr. Darcy, are not open to scorn; possibly they are a bit too dark in nature, but they are not failings. I will not laugh at you, Mr. Darcy; you have nothing to fear from me."

She gave him a slight curtsy and started to turn away. *Wait this is not finished!* Before Elizabeth could take an exit step, he froze her in place by coldly saying, "There is, I believe, in every disposition a tendency to some particular evil—a natural defect, which not even the best education can overcome."

"And *your* defect is to hate everybody."

"And yours, Miss Elizabeth," he replied with a smile, "is willfully to misunderstand them." For a moment they held each other's application; then, Darcy nodded his head to allow Elizabeth to return to her sister. His emotional turmoil became difficult to conceal from the rest of the room. He discovered paying so much attention to Elizabeth Bennet dangerous.

Darcy fortified his resolve to banish his blossoming feelings for Elizabeth. She had been at Netherfield for only a few days, and he neared an obsession with her. Elizabeth appeared in his thoughts throughout the day and danced in his dreams at night. Today he would take no notice of her. He would not allow her hopes to develop, especially if his previous actions suggested his regard for her. What he did her last days at Netherfield would give weight in confirming or crushing those hopes. To that resolution, Darcy applied every fiber of his being as he entered the morning room. There he found Mr. Bingley trying desperately to persuade Miss Bennet she was not well enough to return to Longbourn so soon. Caroline Bingley made the obligatory civilities encouraged by her brother without much enthusiasm, fully realizing while Jane Bennet remained at Netherfield so would her sister Elizabeth. Darcy watched the scene between Bingley and Jane Bennet with a detached air, hiding his intense interest. He hoped Elizabeth would leave before long, and he could return to a more sensible existence. "Then it is settled; you may not consider leaving before tomorrow," Bingley half pleaded.

Miss Bennet nodded her agreement before abandoning the seat by the fire and returning to her room. *Finally,* he thought; an end to his upheaval was in sight. A little more than a day would put distance between him and his preoccupation with Elizabeth Bennet. He would steady himself, avoid contact with Elizabeth, and not engage in any unnecessary conversation. If he could confine himself to places of solitude, the hours would pass quicker. The woman frustrated Darcy beyond words. He never met a woman who so befuddled his mind. How many times over the past few weeks had he thought about Elizabeth Bennet? Almost from the moment he rejected the opportunity to escort her onto the assembly hall dance floor, her "fine eyes" mesmerized him; yet, he knew the inferiority of her connections would never be accepted by his family or his social circle. Darcy would become a mockery, a figure of ridicule if he chose Elizabeth Bennet. He could not let that happen to Georgiana, to his family name, or to the expectations for Pemberley. Fitzwilliam Darcy knew his duty to the Darcy name; his fascination with Elizabeth Bennet had to end today!

He found it relatively easy to escape close association with Elizabeth by taking a long, physically demanding ride on Cerberus. By the time he returned and properly presented himself to the rest of the party, Mr. Bingley and Mr. Hurst applied to him to join them for some shooting. As much as Darcy dearly loved the sport, his ride depleted his energy so he kindly begged off. The ladies took the carriage into Meryton to make some social calls. Elizabeth attended her sister, which meant Darcy could eschew all the trappings society would demand if everyone was together. He found a book in the Netherfield library in which he could, at least, pretend some interest if someone found him there. Settling back into the chair, he nearly fell asleep; his mind, despite his determination to evade thoughts of Elizabeth, clearly pictured her now in this pre-dream state. Her smile was there, and it was a smile directed toward him, the illusion so real he could not help but to utter her name aloud, "Elizabeth."

"Yes, Mr. Darcy." The word echoed through his whole body. With eyes fluttering and a mind grappling with the reality of what just happened, Darcy sprang to his feet, a rush of embarrassment at being found dreaming of the woman who now stood before him and who looked very quizzical about what transpired.

"I apologize, Miss Elizabeth," Darcy stammered, allowing his breeding to take over the situation. "May I help you find something in the library?"

"You are most kind, Mr. Darcy," she responded, still obviously amused by his response. "I thought you asleep; I wanted desperately not to disturb you; I tried reaching that book of poetry on the upper shelf. I fear my clumsiness brought you from your deliberation, and I foolishly interrupted your privacy. It is I who should apologize to you, Sir."

"Not at all, Madam," he quipped, making a quick bow. He stepped over to the shelf by which she stood. Reaching up to retrieve the book she desired, Darcy placed it into Elizabeth's hands. When she looked up to thank him, the thickness of her lashes consumed his senses, and Darcy found himself swimming in the scent of lavender. Elizabeth smiled briefly at him as she took a seat across from his chair. He considered excusing himself, but he feared in doing so her curiosity over his response would be compounded. Instead, he hoped by returning to his chair and his book, Elizabeth would think his blunder simply a lack of propriety at calling her by her first name rather than a realization he dreamed of her.

Pretending to read the historical account of William the Conqueror, Darcy peered over his book and watched Elizabeth as she devoured the words. She tapped her foot lightly as she read, evidently mimicking the rhythmic pattern of the lines. Darcy watched her so intensely he came close to closing his book in order to give her his full attention. Elizabeth bit her lower lip as she read, flitting glimpses of humor and sadness empathetically playing across her face. So they sat for half an hour; Elizabeth engrossed in the beauty of the lines; Darcy engrossed in the beauty of the woman. Noting the time, Elizabeth sighed deeply as she closed her volume. "Thank you, again, Mr. Darcy," she curtsied and left before he could acknowledge her remark or to stand upon her exit.

Darcy let out the breath he did not realize he held back for so long. His heart lodged in his throat. *How could I have been so foolish?* The thoughts fought for dominance. *I must not say anything else to her today; Elizabeth Bennet must be out of my life forthwith.*

At dinner Darcy devoted himself to Miss Bingley and Mrs. Hurst's trivial administrations. He barely looked at Elizabeth when she joined them. Steadying his voice as he spoke, Darcy kept ticking off the clock in his mind, praying Elizabeth would leave before it was too late for him to return to his familial allegiance.

Sunday brought the day of his redemption; in a few hours he would be free of Elizabeth Bennet. As much as Darcy rejoiced at his being able to return to himself, his friend felt despondent about the loss of Miss Bennet's company, and Darcy found he too would experience the deprivation of Elizabeth's presence if only he would allow the luxury of admitting as much. Reliving the last few days as he dressed for church services, Darcy acknowledged Elizabeth's power over him escalated to the point of distraction, and he felt obliged to struggle against his feelings. He could not—would not—entertain a design on Elizabeth Bennet. His prayer on this particular Sunday was to rid himself of the good opinion he formed of her. Putting distance between himself and Elizabeth Bennet could ease his distress; therefore, he resolved during the night to pretend business in town and to leave Netherfield.

Waiting on the ladies in the main foyer, Darcy paced with a renewed strength of resolve. Bingley, on the other hand, anticipated the pleasure of escorting Miss Jane Bennet to the morning's services. As Darcy contemplated how he could tell Bingley, without offending his friend, he chose to leave Netherfield, Jane and Elizabeth Bennet stood at the top of the stairs looking down at the gentlemen. Jane Bennet, still a bit pale, was dressed in royal-blue muslin, amplifying her blue eyes. Darcy thought he heard Bingley let out a low moan, but he could not be sure it was not his own response he heeded; for a few paces behind her elder sister, taking a supportive role, stood Elizabeth. The image hypnotized Darcy. Elizabeth was perfectly beautiful and perfectly insensible to the fact. Only moments before, he silently professed his desire to be away from the brilliancy of her eyes, and now he could not force his regard from Elizabeth's countenance. Clothed in a simple dress of muted rose trimmed with red stitching which complemented the auburn highlights of her hair, Elizabeth had no idea what inducements she created in a man of such esteem.

Mr. Bingley sprang up the staircase to attend to Jane Bennet's needs, taking up a position by her side and allowing himself the pleasure of bracing her unsteady motion. Pausing to give her sister distance and some moments of growing affection, Elizabeth nearly giggled with delight seeing Jane so singled out by Bingley's actions. Shortly, Elizabeth began her descent, and Darcy discovered himself compelled to meet her and offer her his arm. A bit embarrassed by his behavior, his gentility took control of his actions as he offered the incomparable Elizabeth Bennet his hand. She did not expect his chivalry, but propriety allowed her to permit him to do the proper thing.

Bingley, irritated with his sisters for being fashionably late once again, said, "Darcy, why do we not take the Miss Bennets in my carriage? My brother Hurst may bring my sisters in his." Darcy knew the folly of such an action. Two single gentlemen in possession of good fortunes escorting two single ladies to local church services could be viewed easily by society and by the ladies themselves as a declaration of the gentlemen's intentions. He wanted to say as much to his friend, but the slight pressure of Elizabeth's hand upon his wiped the idea away. He resolved to leave Netherfield in the next few days, and that would hinder any hopes Elizabeth may be contemplating. Darcy would allow himself the pleasure of her company one last time.

In the carriage, they found companionable silence. Both ladies kept their eyes down as Elizabeth fussed over Jane's comfort. Bingley and Darcy stared out the coach's windows, but Darcy's mind was anywhere but on the scenery; Elizabeth's lavender—her lush eyelashes—the flush of color on her cheeks—the shift of her shoulders—all these things consumed Darcy's being.

Alighting from the carriage, the ladies entered the church ahead of the gentlemen; Bingley grabbed Darcy's arm delaying their entrance momentarily. "Darcy, thank you for allowing me this deception. My sisters will take great offense, and we shall hear their rebukes this afternoon, but for me this will be well worth it."

Darcy tried to cover the deepest regard he held for Elizabeth. With a straight face, he said, "Bingley, although we should not have allowed decency to fall to the wayside, I do enjoy being in your company, and, by the way, is this *adventurous* enough for you?" he winked at his friend good-humoredly.

"You are a faithful friend," he shook Darcy's hand enthusiastically. "Let us find seats close to the Miss Bennets; I am afraid my attention may not be on the sermon today."

Darcy felt guilty for deceiving his friend, but how could he admit to Bingley his feelings for Elizabeth. He had not even vocalized to himself the disorder her presence afflicted upon him.

CHAPTER 5

"The talent of flattering with delicacy . . ."

Later in the afternoon, Bingley's carriage took the Bennet sisters from Netherfield. Part of Darcy hoped Elizabeth would show some reluctance about leaving, and part of Darcy felt relief at seeing her anxious to return to Longbourn. She did not indicate by her actions she expected him to pursue intentions he was not ready to give to her at this time. He was free to leave Hertfordshire and Elizabeth Bennet behind, taking his memories of her with him as a gauge for future romantic encounters. Darcy would tell Bingley tomorrow "pressing business" called him away. He hoped his friend was so enthralled with Jane Bennet the last few days to not take notice Darcy received no urgent communications.

Being left behind incensed Caroline and Louisa; Caroline desired to make her entrance on Mr. Darcy's arm; she could not fathom he gave Elizabeth Bennet his attentions instead. Caroline equipped and loaded her responses with venom. Bingley, too happy to care what his sister thought at the moment, found her display amusing. Darcy schooled his expression, trying not to duplicate the foolish grin plastered across Bingley's face, but it was hard to appear gracious to Caroline's shrewish exhibition. Forgetting Elizabeth's delicate touch as he assisted her into Bingley's carriage proved harder. He could not call her a woman of refinement, but Elizabeth's charm sheared his character.

Although he hated to deceive Bingley with the lameness of the lie he designed, Darcy knew if he did not escape Hertfordshire soon, he would likely discount all his breeding in favor of a high-spirited country miss. Glad to see Bingley up and taking his morning meal, Darcy joined him at the table and began his lament. "Bingley, I received unpleasant news. I have been called back to London on business. I am sorry to have to leave you here at Netherfield."

"Darcy, are you sure this is necessary? I just drafted invitations for the ball I am to give. I would never consider doing so without the knowledge you would be here."

Darcy took in the agitation that consumed Bingley. He possessed fleeting recollections of the first gathering he organized at Pemberley and remembered his own apprehensions. Of course, Darcy had a competent household staff used to such affairs as his support system; he regretted his lie and began to have second thoughts. "I could try to send my wishes in a letter rather than seeing to the arrangements in person, perhaps."

"Please, Sir," Bingley pleaded. "I know I will forget to attend to details. You are used to such gatherings; you probably forgot more than I currently know of such important social customs. I need your assistance, my friend. I will repay you ten times over if you aid me in this endeavor."

Darcy despised seeing Bingley in such a state; although Bingley was quite capable of handling all the necessary arrangements without Darcy's help, he lacked confidence, and it was that area to which Darcy applied himself. He prided himself as being Bingley's friend and his advisor. Reluctantly, he agreed to stay through the ball; he would just avoid Elizabeth Bennet. She left Netherfield so that should make the task easier; all he must do was what he always did; Fitzwilliam Darcy would do his familial duty, but as he confirmed his determination, a flash of color moving quickly along a country lane, which, ironically, now had a face, hopelessly beguiled him. His lack of sensibilities of late and his absence of self-control mortified his spirits. Could he rein in his admirations for Elizabeth Bennet and not betray his vulnerability?

Miss Bingley went out of her way to entertain Darcy during the evening. With Elizabeth's removal, Caroline's hopes and expectations resurfaced. Darcy noted the green-eyed monster no longer invaded her conversation, and she assumed a relaxed familiarity with him. Yet, the evening without Elizabeth was unpalatable. All the niceties Miss Bingley offered could not fill the void she left. The evening lacked passion, and as nonchalant as he tried to be, Darcy could not override his desire to be three miles from Netherfield and sitting in Longbourn's drawing room with Elizabeth Bennet.

On Tuesday, Bingley announced his notion to deliver a personal invitation to the ball to the Bennet family. Besides, it would give him a chance to inquire on Jane Bennet's health and recovery. He asked Darcy to accompany him, and although it was less than two days' passage since he forswore Elizabeth Bennet, Darcy welcomed the opportunity to glimpse her countenance. He could post letters in Meryton as a cover for his enthusiasm. Riding comfortably into town, the gentlemen espied several of the Bennet sisters in conversation with a militia officer and two other gentlemen. Darcy did not see Elizabeth among the group at first, but the officer turned slightly away, and there she was. Her conversation animated, as usual, and Darcy's face reflected the pleasure of seeing her. On horseback, they approached the group, with Bingley leading the way. Darcy heard the gurgle in Elizabeth's voice as she acknowledged Bingley. "Mr. Bingley, it is so good to see you so soon."

"And I you," Bingley responded. "We were on our way to Longbourn to deliver an invitation to my ball, and, of course, to inquire on Miss Bennet's health."

"I am nearly fully recovered," Jane Bennet extended her regard in his direction. "I am honored by your concern."

Elizabeth rejoined, "Gentlemen, may I present our cousin Mr. Collins."

Darcy totally focused on Elizabeth's face during this exchange, memorizing every line and every gesture. He now diverted his attention to those others in the party. There was Jane Bennet and two of the younger Bennet sisters; a militia officer, Mr. Denny, was in attendance too. The man identified as the Bennet cousin, Darcy noted, was a somewhat pudgy clergyman. Then his eyes fastened on the third male member of the group. Shocked, Darcy felt revulsion run through him. It was George Wickham! He was here in Hertfordshire—his former friend! The man whom he hated the most in this world stood on the streets of Meryton talking casually to the woman he found most exciting. What a twist of fate this was! How could God send him such a trial? The maligned feelings must have been obviously written on his face for he noted the surprise in Elizabeth's eyes as she observed Darcy's and Wickham's silent exchange. Wickham recovered from the initial revelation quicker than did Darcy. With a smirk, he tapped his hat in an extemporaneous greeting. Darcy's repugnance would not allow his returning the greeting; instead, he stiffened from the contemptible display and spun Cerberus away from the group.

Bingley's horse finally came abreast of his, but Darcy did not look at his friend for several minutes. "Darcy, what is wrong?" Bingley asked most gingerly.

Swallowing his anger, Darcy turned to his friend; speaking sternly, "Bingley, do you remember your promise to repay me ten times over if I stayed for your ball? Hopefully, you meant what you said for I am going to call in your debt. Please promise me the gentleman we met on the street just now with the Bennet sisters will not be a guest at your ball."

"Which gentleman, Darcy? Mr. Denny? The clergyman?"

"No, Bingley," Darcy steeled himself, "the other one, George Wickham."

"Anything, Darcy," Bingley considered his friend. "I planned to issue a general invitation to Colonel Forster's officers, and Mr. Wickham, according to Miss Bennet, will be joining the militia here in Meryton, but I will let the colonel know Mr. Wickham is not welcome at Netherfield."

"Thank you, Bingley," Darcy released some of the tension he felt upon the encounter. "I know this is an unusual request, and I am not at liberty to explain all of my objections to Wickham. I will only say I have known him since my youth. His father was my own father's steward, but Wickham betrayed my family's trust in him upon several occasions."

"Even without your explanation, Darcy, I would meet your request. Your objection to the gentleman would be enough censure for me. I respect your opinions on such matters."

In the solitude of his room, Darcy could not conceive how Wickham could be in Meryton. Every time he thought himself to be free of Wickham, the man rose from the ashes. It was unbelievable this spurious man could insinuate himself into Darcy's life once again. Was he here in Meryton because he knew Darcy was here? That was impossible! He could not have such knowledge. He was probably in the country because of some indiscretion he committed in the city. Leaving gambling debts and broken hearts in his wake, Wickham's infamous reputation followed him. *Broken hearts? Could Elizabeth be Wickham's newest triumph?* Darcy felt as if someone struck him in the stomach, the ache deep and painful. For once, Elizabeth's poor connections gladdened him. That might save her from Wickham's notice; normally, he preferred women with a substantial inheritance.

When Bingley and his sisters called at Longbourn later in the week to inquire once again on Miss Bennet's continued recovery, Darcy declined to accompany them. He feared because of the younger Bennet sisters' propensity for military officers he might find Wickham among the guests of Longbourn. No, he would bide his time until after the Netherfield Ball, and then he would quit Hertfordshire, Wickham, and Elizabeth Bennet.

Realizing today would probably be the last time he would see Elizabeth, Darcy began to feel his resolve fading all over again. He wanted to leave her with a positive regard for his behavior toward her; he could not stand to believe she would think poorly of him. With that thought, he decided to request a dance at the ball this evening. After all, he still owed her an apology for his snub at the assembly. Recognizing her worth by honoring Elizabeth with a dance—a dance with a man of his standing—should go a long way in making amends. Of course, having the opportunity to converse with Elizabeth for half an hour, to feel the warmth of her hand, and to gaze into her eyes had nothing to do with his decision. He convinced himself he simply wanted to apologize properly.

Darcy's anticipation increased dramatically as he waited impatiently for the Bennets' arrival. He debated whether to approach Elizabeth for the first dance set, but he decided against it. Bingley's neighbors could easily misconstrue his escorting her into the church and then requesting the first dance. He would wait until later in the evening.

Dressed in a white, Empire waist muslin gown, Elizabeth's appearance took on classical lines. Beaded hairpins reflected a halo quality, and Darcy gulped for air as he witnessed her entrance into the drawing room. He watched as she circulated about the room, obviously looking for someone in particular. Of course, he hoped the person might be he, but it was not to be. She briefly acknowledged his polite inquiries but quickly moved on to find her friend Charlotte Lucas.

As the dance began, the pudgy clergyman came forward to claim Elizabeth's hand. Darcy watched with initial amusement as Mr. Collins, who obviously thought himself to be adept on the dance floor, spent most of his time apologizing instead of attending and often moving wrong without being aware of it. Such a disagreeable dance partner should not be wished upon anyone. Collins's ineptitude would amplify Darcy's prowess later; however, Elizabeth's distress and mortification became so severe, it was all Darcy could do to not interfere and replace Collins in the set somehow.

Elizabeth next danced with an officer, and then she returned to Charlotte Lucas's company. Darcy decided it was now or never, and his approach took her by surprise. "Miss Elizabeth, may I apply for the pleasure of the next dance?" he said as he bowed to both ladies.

"Mr. Darcy, I . . . I . . . I would be pleased."

Not wishing to allow her the opportunity to change her mind, Darcy took his leave, but when the dancing recommenced, he returned to claim her hand. As they took their place in the set at the top of the line of dancers, a place of prestige, Darcy could not help but hope the uniqueness of the situation impressed Elizabeth; her neighbors recognized the honor he bestowed on her; he only danced with Bingley's sisters up until this point. Singling her out made a statement to the amazement of all who observed it.

As the dance began, Darcy planned to make amends for his earlier cut, but within her presence, he found himself to be embarrassed by those actions and was tongue-tied. She broke the silence first, commenting on the dance as they waited their turn. He replied and again fell silent. "It is *your* turn to say something now, Mr. Darcy. I talked about the dance, and *you* ought to make some kind of remark on the size of the room, or the number of couples."

He smiled. "Tell me what you most desire to hear, and I will happily comply."

"Very well. That reply will do for the present. Perhaps by and by I may observe that private balls are much pleasanter than public ones. But *now* we may be silent."

He nearly laughed out loud. She obviously demanded the long overdue apology, but he would make her wait a few more moments to take her by surprise when he did offer his amends. Instead, he said, "Do you talk by rule, then, while you are dancing?"

"Sometimes. One must speak a little, you know. It would look odd to be entirely silent for half an hour together; and yet, for the advantage of *some*, conversation ought to be so arranged, as that they may have the trouble of saying as little as possible."

So, she noticed his bias for silence. Was Elizabeth suggesting he did not enjoy their conversations? "Are you consulting your own feelings in the present case, or do you imagine that you are gratifying mine?"

Taking a jab at Darcy's haughty humor, she responded, "Both, for I have always seen a great similarity in the turn of our minds. We are each of an unsocial, taciturn disposition, unwilling to speak, unless we expect to say something that will amaze the whole room and be handed down to posterity with all the eclat of a proverb."

The verbal warfare was back. God, he missed this foreplay during the ten days since they last spoke! He would not let her win this skirmish, though. "This is no very striking resemblance of your own character, I am sure. How near it may be to *mine* I cannot pretend to say. You think it a faithful portrait undoubtedly."

They were again silent until they went down the dance. He did not like the coolness the turn of the conversation took. Wanting to lighten the tension their need for dominance created, Darcy tried to steer the interplay in a different direction. "Do you and your sisters often walk to Meryton?"

"Yes, we do," she added. "When you met us there the other day, we had just been forming a new acquaintance."

Darcy's heart stopped; she was speaking of Wickham. He knew Elizabeth saw the exchange between the two of them. Wickham had, most likely, spoken of their relationship to Elizabeth; of course, he would not tell her the truth of their dealings. Darcy discovered jealousy at Wickham's intimacy with Elizabeth after only a few days' acquaintance. He could barely control his feelings when he next responded to her. "Mr. Wickham is blessed with such happy manners as may insure his *making* friends—whether he may be equally capable of *retaining* them, is less certain."

"He has been so unlucky as to lose *your* friendship," replied Elizabeth with emphasis, "and in a manner which he is likely to suffer from all his life."

Darcy made no response. His anger came close to taking control of his tongue as well as of his mind; he searched for another subject. He did not want to spend his precious time with Elizabeth speaking of his worst enemy.

At that moment, Sir William Lucas cut through the set. "Mr. Darcy, may I compliment you on both your dancing and your choice of partner. It will be my pleasure to see you repeat your choice in the near future." Sir William gestured toward Bingley and Jane Bennet. Obviously, the Netherfield neighbors already spoke of the likelihood of upcoming nuptials. Sir William insinuated Darcy and Elizabeth would often, therefore, be thrown together.

Darcy barely heard what Sir William said, his attention drawn to Bingley and Miss Bennet. A force hit with the seriousness of the situation. Darcy realized he was so enamored with Elizabeth he did not try to stunt Bingley's growing attraction for Jane Bennet. He planned to leave Hertfordshire soon, but Bingley took up residence here. He could not allow Bingley to be so foolish; Bingley would quickly learn to regret Jane Bennet's bad connections.

The second dance approached; his time with Elizabeth grew short, and he still did not make his excuses to her. Recovering himself, he turned back to his partner and tried to reestablish some sense of dialogue. Elizabeth resisted his suggestions, decrying each hint of civility. Her thoughts wandered to their earlier conversation, and she exclaimed, "I remember hearing you once say, Mr. Darcy, that you hardly ever forgave, that your resentment once created was unappeasable." She did not wait for the reply. "Would it not behoove a person to then be accurate in his judgments if there is no room to change one's mind?"

When she repeated his earlier contentions, they took on a coarser tone than Darcy intended. "May I ask if you have a particular situation to which you refer?"

"Merely to the illustration of *your* character," she sallied; "I am trying to make it out."

Their parley took an unexpected turn. "And what is your success?" Darcy heard himself challenging her.

Elizabeth shook her head as if confused. "I do not get on at all. I hear such different accounts of you as puzzle me exceedingly."

Darcy wanted her to know the real him, but he had no way of changing the opinions she formed at the assembly hall; it was too late for that. Nor could he acquit her of the lies she heard without putting his sister's honor on the line too. Darcy would never betray

Georgiana. "I can readily believe that reports may vary greatly with respect to me; and I could wish, Miss Bennet, that you were not to sketch my character at the present moment, as there is reason to fear that the performance would reflect no credit on either."

"Unfortunately, Mr. Darcy, if I do not take your likeness now, I may never have another opportunity."

"I would by no means suspend any pleasure of yours. What you ask are not my answers to give at this time, Miss Elizabeth. I would ask you to trust your inclinations to know what is true." Their time together ended on this bitter note; they finished the second dance in silence and parted. The way things ended dissatisfied both of them. Elizabeth's natural curiosity initially told her things were not as they seemed, but she could not see past Darcy's earlier behavior to her to distinguish the truth from the lies. Darcy's hurt came from knowing he could never be anything more to her than he was at that moment; he forgave her for her disdain because he knew it was formed on half-truths. Instead, he directed all his anger on George Wickham.

Darcy left the dance floor in an agitated state; his performance left him wanting to say so much more to Elizabeth Bennet. He moved about the room oblivious to the civilities being offered on his behalf. He stood along the rim of a cluster of partygoers, pretending to be interested in their tales when the bow of the same pudgy clergyman who tormented Elizabeth with his "lightness of foot" interrupted his thoughts. Darcy could not comprehend the man's affront at first. Collins made him a low bow. "Mr. Darcy, I learned by a singular accident you are indeed the nephew of my esteemed patroness Lady Catherine de Bourgh; I wanted to assure you her ladyship was quite well yesterday sennight." This unsolicited address astonished him, and Darcy eyed the man with unrestrained wonder; and when at last Mr. Collins allowed him time to speak, he replied with an air of distant civility. Mr. Collins, however, set about an equally pompous second speech, which increased Darcy's contempt. Finally, he made the imbecile a slight bow and moved away. He thanked providence he was wise enough to not make a permanent alliance with Elizabeth Bennet. It seemed she possessed no shortage of poor connections. All he wanted at that moment was for the ball to come to a close so he could be rid of his promise to Bingley and to his time in Hertfordshire.

He moved with the others to take supper. Unfortunately, he found himself in close proximity to Mrs. Bennet and Mrs. Lucas. In an energized manner, Mrs. Bennet confided to Mrs. Lucas, "Mr. Bingley so honors our Jane with his attentions. He singles her out above all others. We expect a wedding at Netherfield very, very soon, and when Jane is so well placed, I told Mr. Bennet, we may cosign our other daughters to Jane's care in hopes of likewise excellent matches."

He watched while Elizabeth, realizing Darcy sat opposite them, tried to stifle her mother's enthusiasm and tone down her mother's voice. He felt sympathy for Elizabeth being plagued by such a family, but he found her mother's incivility intolerable. "What do I care what Mr. Darcy thinks, Lizzy. He is nothing to me." The absolute disdain he felt for her mother overrode his sympathy for Elizabeth. Finally, Mrs. Bennet said no more on the matter. Darcy hoped some sense of decorum might now return to the dining hall. Bingley, as the host, when the supper finished, called for singing and entertainment.

Darcy watched as Mary Bennet prepared to oblige the company. Mary Bennet's voice was weak and her manner affected. Darcy remained grave, but he witnessed the agony in which Elizabeth found herself. Elizabeth's eyes pleaded with her father to do something. Mary would not leave the pianoforte until someone forced her to do so. Mr. Bennet took his daughter's hint. As Mary finished her second song, he approached her at the instrument and closed the keys' door. Then he said loudly, "Mary, dearest, you have delighted Mr. Bingley's guests long enough; it is time to allow the other young ladies a chance to perform." Darcy sat in a state of astonishment while Elizabeth's countenance colored. The mortification she tried to stop with her father's intervention turned out worse than Mary's musical offerings. His bluntness with his daughter embarrassed all who witnessed it.

Mr. Collins then began to extol too loudly upon his own lack of musical ability. "If I were so fortunate as to be able to sing, I should have great pleasure, I am sure, in obliging the company with an air; for I consider music as a very innocent diversion, and perfectly compatible with the profession of a clergyman." He directed his speech toward Darcy for some unexplained reason. Darcy observed Mr. Bennet being openly amused by their cousin's silliness while Mrs. Bennet praised Mr. Collins for his ability to know his own talents. Darcy's indignant contempt changed to his usual formal hauteur. His silent contempt of the displays of Elizabeth's family could not be hidden from her or from anyone else.

He stood within a very short distance of Elizabeth, quietly disengaged from what he observed. He never came near enough to speak to her again. He replayed the whole evening in his head. Darcy saw her beauty and the thrill of escorting her onto the dance floor vividly, but those were doused by images of Mr. Collins's affront, Mrs. Bennet's allusions, Kitty's and Lydia's flirtations with the officers, Mary's poor performance, and Mr. Bennet's impropriety. The negatives of such a connection greatly outweighed the positives.

Bingley and Jane Bennet caught Darcy's attention. They were absorbed in their own conversations. They knew nothing of the spectacle Jane Bennet's family had become. Darcy knew he could save himself from such associations, but he realized he must also save his friend. He could not, in all conscience, leave Bingley to his own devices when it came to Jane Bennet. He must prepare himself to separate the two permanently.

CHAPTER 6

"My feelings in every respect forbid it."

The morning after the Netherfield Ball found Fitzwilliam Darcy pacing the bedchamber. The decision he made the previous evening would impact both his and Bingley's lives forever; it was not one to be taken lightly. The two gentlemen came to a country neighborhood, and both became infatuated with sisters. Darcy knew he could withstand Elizabeth's allurements by putting distance and time between them. Getting Bingley to likewise divorce himself from the situation might prove more difficult. Bingley wore his heart on his sleeve. He was more impetuous than Darcy, but he did trust Darcy's opinions implicitly; and he would use that influence to save his friend.

Luckily, Bingley left for London this very morning for a short business trip; this gave Darcy time to put his plan in action. It would mean a secretive alliance with Bingley's sisters, something to which he did not look forward, but his friend would thank them all later. Thinking so, Darcy left his chambers to speak to Caroline and Louisa.

"Ah, Mr. Darcy, you seem rested this morning," Caroline looked up from her morning meal.

"I am, thank you, Miss Bingley," he began, "but there is something about which I wish to speak to you."

The Bingley sisters held similar concerns regarding the attentions their brother showed Jane Bennet. They agreed Miss Bennet was a congenial young lady, and they were willing to have her as an acquaintance. Yet, the possibility of her becoming an intimate member of their family created a different story. They ridiculed the rest of the Bennet family's lack of civilities during the ball, but Darcy remained silent. He could not place Elizabeth among the offenders. Other than Miss Bingley loosely confiding Elizabeth ignored her warnings about Wickham's character during the evening, little was said against Elizabeth directly. Louisa even commented that "poor Elizabeth" appeared mortified with the actions of her family. Darcy was thankful they did not attack Elizabeth directly; he was still too vulnerable to her charms to allow that to happen.

"So, we are agreed. We will quit Netherfield immediately and follow your brother to town. There we will do whatever we must do to save Bingley from his own folly."

Louisa added, "It is of the utmost importance that we distract Charles from this recklessness. We must divert his thoughts from this woman by exposing him to society comprised of his equals or his superiors, thus eliminating those beneath him."

His sisters and Darcy's approach in his London hotel surprised Charles Bingley. He expected not to see them until the following day when he returned to Netherfield. Lying, Darcy reminded Bingley he too postponed business until after the ball. Of course, he could not leave Bingley's sisters at Netherfield unattended.

Bingley's sisters chimed in with excuses of many preparations to address before the Festive Season. They begged Bingley to stay in London for the holidays where they could enjoy the festivities at Darcy's London home.

"I told Miss Bennet I would be at Netherfield for the Festive Season," he protested. "I was to have dinner at Longbourn at the end of the week."

"But, Charles," Louisa inserted her voice, "you would not want to disappoint Georgiana. Mr. Darcy cannot spend the season at

Netherfield and neglect his sister. We have been their guests at Kensington Place since your friendship began. We cannot desert our friends now; it is tradition."

"I already sent Miss Bennet our regrets about the dinner invitation, and I indicated we will be spending Christmas in London." Caroline reassured him. "Miss Bennet's family circle will demand all her attention during the celebrations, would you not think?"

"You would not want to disappoint Georgiana, would you, Charles?" Darcy added. "She so loves your company. You are one of the few people who are able to draw her out of her shyness. She has practiced some special songs for a private concert. It is only for a few weeks."

"Of course, I would not want to disappoint Georgiana. I also suppose Miss Bennet's Festive Season is already planned with her own family traditions. It is only a few weeks, as you say."

"Good, you will stay as my guest at Kensington Place," Darcy added quickly. "I can bring Georgiana there sooner than I expected with both of us available to escort her to festive gatherings. She will be so pleased."

Once Darcy, Caroline, and Louisa had Bingley sequestered in London, they began their erosion of Bingley's feelings for Jane Bennet. Bingley, being young, was easy to convince. First, his sisters made casual comments about how women make fools of men by using feminine charms. Each "way" they ridiculed was a characteristic Jane Bennet possessed. Then Darcy added his concerns about whether Miss Bennet *really* cared for Bingley. "Bingley, she listens attentively to you, but I observed her doing the same in other conversations. What I did not observe," Darcy insinuated, "was an exclusive feeling in your respect. I believe she would accept your proposals; it would benefit Miss Bennet substantially, but you always said you would prefer a relationship which includes mutual affection."

"I do," Bingley added uncertainly, "but I thought she returned my regard."

"I have more experience than you, Bingley," Darcy continued, "in dealing with mothers trying to wed off their daughters to the first eligible bachelor who comes along. Miss Bennet appears to be *schooled* in such manners. You saw Mrs. Bennet's behavior. Do you suppose Mr. Bennet, a landed gentleman, would make such an inappropriate match if Mrs. Bennet at one time or another did not know how to rein in her enthusiasm and seem to be a genial young woman? Now, look at how Mrs. Bennet's behavior makes the Bennet family the laughingstock of the county. Their vulgar actions at your ball were a warning as to what you may expect if you align yourself with such a family. It is not acceptable to align oneself with a family whose poor connections affect others; you are not just making a choice for yourself, Charles; you are bringing all the Bennets into your family. Your family members are not used to such censure as what you may expect in this case."

Bingley became resigned to what he heard; he could have misjudged Jane Bennet's attentions. Although Bingley agreed with Darcy and his sisters, he did not welcome the news, and Darcy noted Bingley, when others were not looking, stared off and seemed to be elsewhere in his mind. Darcy knew Bingley's position well; he found himself ruminating over Elizabeth on more than one occasion. He replayed her accusations about Wickham; she only knew Wickham for a few days when she had known Darcy for nearly two months. Yes, Wickham had his charms, but how could she not see through to his character? Darcy was a man of standing. *I do not get on at all. I hear such different accounts of you as puzzle me exceedingly.* It did not take her so long to survey Wickham's attributes! She used Darcy ill, deserted and disappointed him; and worse, she showed a weakness in her own character, which upon reflection he could not endure. She gave him up to oblige others. She allowed herself to be persuaded by Wickham's "tales of woe." *How could she?* But Darcy would master his feelings for this auburn-haired miss; however, even in doing so, he would feel no triumph—only the pity at having loved and lost would remain.

The Festive Season in London never held the inducements for Darcy as those spent at Pemberley, but since the deaths of both of his parents, he could no longer bear to be at Pemberley at Christmas time. So, for the past five years, he and Georgiana spent their time at Kensington Place. This year, besides missing his parents, Darcy pined for Elizabeth Bennet. Even having Georgiana with him did not appease the emptiness he felt since leaving Netherfield, and try as he may, nothing erased the memory of her countenance.

After the Christmas celebrations, Darcy forced himself back into society. He still spent many evenings with Bingley and his sisters, but where he once thought of Caroline's civilities as refined, he now found them affected and boring. Darcy also made an effort to encounter other eligible young women in town, often calling on acquaintances and accepting more invitations than he was known to do. He once found a Miss Donnelly attractive, but then he was told her given name was "Elizabeth," and he was lost once again into a revelry of depression. Georgiana's company gave him some relief, but even she could not engage his attention with any degree of success. He finally gave up his pursuit of new social connections, allowing he just needed more time to find the solace he sought.

In mid-January, despite the weather and the terrible condition of the roads, Darcy made a brief trip to Scotland to see firsthand some of the new agricultural methods being utilized in the Americas. He hoped to try such methods at Pemberley this upcoming planting season. Darcy could easily read about the methods, but going to examine the type of soil and the crops involved lent him a good excuse to be alone with his thoughts.

Upon his return, he seemed more focused than he had been for months. Throwing himself into the business of improvements for Pemberley granted him relief from the contrasting memories, which haunted his idle hours.

One evening just Darcy and his sister settled in at Kensington Place. Mrs. Annesley had the evening off to visit a beloved nephew.

They took a light repast together and casually enjoyed each other's company in the drawing room. Darcy partook of more brandy than he should; he was not drunk, but the warmth of the liquid lowered his defenses.

"Will you travel to Kent to see our aunt at Easter?"

"I will; our cousin arranged a reprieve from his military duties so we will be able to tackle our aunt's many business issues together. It is not a trip to which I look forward. Our aunt can be so . . ."

"Demanding," Georgiana added maybe a little too quickly.

Darcy arched an eyebrow at his sister's response; Georgiana had become more opinionated of late although she never expressed those opinions beyond her brother's hearing. "Our aunt can be very solicitous. Has she said something to you, my dearest?"

"It is just her usual reproofs to practice my music and to maintain the proper manners. Sometimes I resent her constant remarks. I know I should not feel these things about a beloved relative, but, honestly, Fitzwilliam, her rebukes are very upsetting."

"Our aunt can irritate even the most devout. Do not bother yourself with Lady Catherine's many sentiments."

"Fitzwilliam," she changed the subject, "was not Mr. Bingley satisfied with his estate in Hertfordshire?"

"Why do you ask, my Dear?"

"It is he just quit the estate on impulse it seems. Did something happen?"

Darcy felt a bit uncomfortable knowing his part in removing Bingley from Netherfield. He shifted his weight, gulped down the last of the brandy, and poured himself another. "Bingley is such an impetuous young man," he extended an explanation.

"It is just," Georgiana began shyly, "he speaks well of his short time there and expresses a fondness for the company of Miss Jane Bennet."

"Does he now?"

"He seems so downcast. Is Jane Bennet not the sister of Elizabeth Bennet? Your letters from Netherfield mentioned her several times. I hoped when I read your letters if Mr. Bingley remained at

Netherfield I could visit there. I thought I might like to meet Miss Elizabeth. It would be nice to have a friend such as you described. Do you think Miss Elizabeth could have seen me as an acquaintance she might like to make?"

"I am sure of it," Darcy began slowly. "I often considered the possibilities."

Georgiana's interest perked up. Leaning forward and giving him her full attention, she asked, "Would you tell me about Miss Elizabeth?"

Darcy held his glass of brandy to his lips, but he did not drink. Impressions of Elizabeth Bennet came so easily to him, as if he saw her but five minutes ago rather than it having been nearly eleven weeks. He began slowly, guarding his words, fearing to betray his susceptibility to the woman. "I believe I described Miss Elizabeth physically previously. Miss Elizabeth's features are not as refined as her sister's, but they tend to be more classical. Her eyes are the key to her soul, a quick note of what she really thinks. She says she loves to laugh, and I find her humor to be teasing in nature at times. I have not found many women with a more agreeable character. Everything is united in Elizabeth Bennet: she possesses a superior intelligence and good understanding; generally correct opinions, which she often expresses without regard to the time or the situation; and a warm heart. She demonstrates strong feelings of family attachment, without calculating pride or insufferable weaknesses. Miss Elizabeth judges for herself in everything essential." Darcy stopped himself at this point, fearing he said too much.

Georgiana sighed heavily when he paused. "Miss Elizabeth Bennet seems like the perfect mixture of sense and judgment. I hope some day I have the opportunity to make her my friend. I always wanted a friend such as you describe."

"It would be nice to see Miss Elizabeth again," he said wistfully.

Images of Elizabeth Bennet and Georgiana together at Pemberley invaded his dreams that evening. The images instantly created happiness without the misery, but when awake, Darcy could only dwell on the misery of such happiness.

Those months also added to his duplicity against Bingley. Jane Bennet came to London to stay with her Cheapside relatives. She called unexpectedly on Caroline one afternoon. Caroline and Louisa were on their way out so her visit was short, but a like call upon her would be expected of the Bingley sisters. They agreed Caroline would wait several weeks before reciprocating, and even then, Miss Bingley would make Jane Bennet aware of her folly in pursuing Charles. Such incivilities ended Jane Bennet's hopes. Darcy hated himself for keeping the news of Miss Bennet's presence in London from Bingley. Obviously, from what Georgiana confided, Bingley's affliction of the heart was no more over than was Darcy's.

Late February brought signs of spring, and Darcy, Georgiana, and Mrs. Annesley returned to Pemberley. He spent these weeks with his steward explaining his plans to increase the production of crops among the tenants on Pemberley. The steward, Mr. Howard, was a respected overseer; the two spent many hours planning a four-crop rotation among the farmers. The system, developed by the Second Viscount Charles Townsend, had been successful in the Americas since the early 1700s. Pemberley used a three-crop rotation for many years, usually wheat, barley, and the third field left to fallow. Yet, the land was being used up too quickly, and production decreased, leaving many of Pemberley's tenants unable to maintain their farms.

Darcy hoped the four-crop rotation plan would save his estate and the livelihood of his tenants. Nitrogen-rich legumes would be used to put back into the soil the nutrients the grain crops used, and the grain crops put back the minerals the legumes used. They fed each other; it was a simple plan; now, he had to convince his tenants of the necessity of the changes. Mr. Howard would examine each farmer's soil makeup and decide who would plant which crops.

The excitement of getting back to the land relieved Darcy of the agitations of his mind. He had not thought about Elizabeth

Bennet more than a couple of times over the past few weeks. Then he received a letter from his aunt.

8 March

My dear Nephew,

I am anticipating your upcoming visit; your cousin Anne is most anxious to renew your relationship. Her health seems much improved; I am sure you will notice the difference. I hoped to introduce you to my new curate Mr. Collins and his wife, but much to my chagrin, I find you met them both while you were in Hertfordshire with Mr. Bingley.

Darcy's heart stopped. Mr. Collins married someone from Hertfordshire. Pictures of Mr. Collins's attentive behavior to Elizabeth flashed across his eyes. He danced with her at the Netherfield Ball, and after supper, Collins refused to leave Elizabeth's side, leaving her in misery and unable to dance with other gentlemen. *Please, God, do not let Elizabeth be married to Mr. Collins!* Mrs. Bennet would marry Elizabeth off to Collins just to be rid of one of her daughters at last. Collins kissing Elizabeth—the thought brought a murderous rage to Darcy's heart. With shaking hands, he returned to the letter.

Charlotte Lucas made Mr. Collins a reasonable match. Her temperament is most pleasing, and I assured Mr. Collins of my approval in his choice.

Darcy's breath came in ragged outbursts. Charlotte Lucas! It was not Elizabeth! He nearly cried with relief. Although Collins would provide Miss Lucas with a steady income and a protective home, he hated to see any woman's attentions wasted on such a supercilious ass, as was Mr. Collins. Darcy actually liked Charlotte Lucas, even without her being Elizabeth's special friend. He would not wish Collins upon anyone.

Mrs. Collins's father and sister have come to stay at Hunsford. Sir

*William spoke highly of you, as was natural, and of making your
acquaintance in Hertfordshire; the younger Miss Lucas is quite pretty,
in a plain sort of fashion, and I find her very attentive to my advice. I
am sure she gets no such direction at home, and I plan to spend some
time with her.*

Good! His aunt's reproofs could be directed toward someone
besides Georgiana. He made a mental note to speak to his cousin
about Lady Catherine's censure of Georgina; he did not like anyone interfering in his sister's life.

*There is another member of the Collins's party at the Parsonage.
Mrs. Collins's friend Elizabeth Bennet has also come for a visit.*

Darcy reread that line several times to be sure his eyes did not play
tricks on him. *Elizabeth? His Elizabeth?* Could she really be at Rosings Park residing within an easy walk of his aunt's house? Reading
on, Darcy realized his eyes did not deceive him. His aunt actually
spoke of Elizabeth. The irony of it all! Elizabeth Bennet stayed on
his aunt's estate.

*I understand you also made the acquaintance of Miss Bennet. My
pleasure in introducing you has been lost. I will forego that pleasure
with you, but, at least, it will still be my honor to introduce the
Collins's party to your cousin, the colonel.*

*Miss Bennet, I find, is a very outspoken young lady. She has been
allowed to run free with little reproach from her parents. She offers her
opinions without regard to station in life; this is most unusual for one
so young. I cannot say I approve of her manners or her upbringing. She
is one of five daughters, as you know. Her parents saw no benefit in
exposing any of them to the masters. None of them draw; Miss
Bennet's talents on the pianoforte are limited. I told her she could only
improve without more practice. Besides having no governess to
supervise her upbringing, the worst offense I find in her parenting is all
five daughters are out in society at the same time. The youngest are out*

before the eldest has married. When I expressed my disdain, you would not believe what Miss Bennet said.

Darcy laughed out loud for the first time in months. Without being told her response, he could just imagine Elizabeth's retort, accompanied by the "flash" in her eyes, a shift of her shoulders, and the hint of a mischievous smile. His sister could learn much from Elizabeth Bennet; he knew Lady Catherine did not intimidate her.

Her reply was very disrespectful. She seems to think having all five daughters out at the same time is perfectly acceptable. Miss Bennet believes her younger sisters deserve their share of society and amusement as much as does she and her elder sister. She indicated it was not fair to her younger sisters to be denied their share of fun and courtship just because neither she nor her elder sister have had the means or the inclination to marry. Miss Elizabeth does not feel it would be "very likely to promote sisterly affection nor delicacy of the mind." I was astonished by this response. I hope to temper her rough spirits before she leaves Hunsford.

His aunt may wish to temper Elizabeth's spirits, but he knew Lady Catherine was no match for Elizabeth Bennet.

Miss Bennet just needs an example of proper society to complement her undeveloped genteel attributes. Sir William, I am afraid, will depart before your arrival, but the ladies will remain another month. We will invite them to Rosings if you so wish to renew their acquaintances. Your cousin Anne and I look forward to your and Edward's stay at Rosings.

Lady C

Elizabeth, possibly the first to do so, obviously, dared to challenge the dignified impertinence of Lady Catherine. So, Elizabeth stayed at Rosings; he was glad to know prior to his arrival. It would be a good test of how well he recovered from her charms. In thinking so, Darcy did not acknowledge the swirl of his emotions when he feared Collins married Elizabeth as being anything more than a true concern for her well-being and happiness. He would be able to meet Elizabeth again as indifferent acquaintances; Darcy was sure of that fact.

His cousin Edward Fitzwilliam came to Pemberley on the nineteenth. He would spend a few days with Georgiana before they departed for Rosings. Along with Darcy, the good colonel served as Georgiana's guardian, and he adored her nearly as much as did Darcy.

"Cousin, Georgiana told me about Elizabeth Bennet," Edward teased. "Now, I am most anxious to meet our aunt's visitors. At first, I was not looking forward to meeting a 'country miss with poor manners,' but Georgiana seems to feel you hold Elizabeth Bennet in some esteem. If she impresses Fitzwilliam Darcy, she would be something extraordinary, I dare say."

"Pull in your tendrils, Edward," Darcy cautioned. "Miss Elizabeth is not for you. As the younger son of an earl, you need to find a woman of wealth to keep you in style. I am afraid although Miss Elizabeth is a gentleman's daughter, she has no wealth of which to make her a person of interest for a man in your position."

"I see," Edward began. "That is my bad luck. Some day I will find a wealthy woman with whom I might also find affection. I do not want to just marry for money; some level of love is not too much to ask is it, Fitz?"

"I never knew you felt that way." Edward's words stunned Darcy.

"Oh, well, at least," Edward shook it off, "Miss Elizabeth may help brighten our time at Rosings, can she not?"

"Miss Elizabeth, I found, can brighten most any room," Darcy whispered to himself.

CHAPTER 7

"This would be nothing if you really liked him."

As the carriage rolled toward the inevitable, Darcy tried to mask the restriction encompassing the core of his being. He hid behind the newspaper while his cousin snoozed in the seat across from him. His eyes looked at the newsprint, but none of the words penetrated his brain. In the next few days, he would be facing Elizabeth Bennet once again. He focused all his energies into forgetting Elizabeth. He went through the turmoil, chastising himself repeatedly for losing control when confronted with her. Darcy questioned himself: Why had he let Elizabeth speak to him as such? Why had he allowed her to possess him physically as well as emotionally? Why had he questioned who he was and what he valued? More importantly, why had he considered making her a part of his life? Yes, there was a physical attraction, but should he lay aside all his principles—all his values for physical beauty? Of course, he could have Elizabeth; Darcy never saw a woman he could not have, but he could not even think of making her the mistress of Pemberley.

It was funny; Darcy often visualized Elizabeth at Pemberley— the two of them together—Elizabeth and Georgiana; the images were always so clear! Yet, he never imagined making her his wife. That was the step in the equation he could not quite figure out. He instinctively knew Elizabeth belonged at Pemberley; she, naturally, fit into his plan for the estate, but marriage to Elizabeth could not be reconciled in his thoughts. It was not as if Darcy would ever dishonor Elizabeth Bennet; he did not think of her that way; his thoughts of Elizabeth were always honorable. He just could not accept actually professing his feelings for her and making a proposal. He could not marry her! Being a Darcy would never allow him to do so.

The splendid colors, which adorned Lady Catherine's estate, were lost on him. Staring out the carriage's window, a pair of thickly lashed watery-green eyes sparkled back at him. His cousin, being finally aroused from his journey's boredom, began a watch for Mr. Collins. "I understand," Edward laughed, "from our aunt that Collins's book room fronts the road. The chap dutifully watches for the carriages to come along. I want to see if he is watching for our arrival. You know our aunt apprised him of our visit. Look, Darcy, is that he? He resembles a windup doll; Collins is waving frantically. Wave, Darcy!"

"I do not think waving at our aunt's clergyman is in order," Darcy grumbled.

"Darcy . . . Edward, at last you arrived," Lady Catherine intoned. "Anne and I both expected you hours ago. Anne's health would not allow her to wait longer. She went up to rest. You will renew your relationship at dinner."

"We apologize, Aunt," Darcy bowed to his mother's eldest sister. "The roads were affected by last week's weather."

"We are most joyous at seeing you, Lady Catherine," the colonel added quickly. "I will be happy to see Anne feeling better and joining us this evening; it has been too long since we saw her."

"Excuse us, Lady Catherine," Darcy interrupted, "we will freshen from our travels and join you shortly for some tea."

As the two gentlemen left the blue salon, Darcy gave his cousin a wary glance. "What?" Edward queried.

"We look forward to seeing Anne?" Darcy began. "Why do you not just pronounce the vows while you are about?"

"Do you suppose Lady Catherine still expects a marriage proposal?" Edward teased.

"She has," Darcy moaned, "thought of nothing else since Anne and I were children. My father took up the practice of allaying her 'hopes,' but with his death, I have *no* protection, it seems." He shot his cousin a frustrated glance.

Edward spoke a bit too enthusiastically. "You do not wish to marry our cousin?"

"If I were to take a wife I did not love, I would want a woman whose health might withstand childbirth. An heir for Pemberley has to be one of my concerns," Darcy was matter-of-fact.

"Anne is just suppressed by our aunt. She has good manners and money. Her attributes are many," Edward cautioned.

Darcy could not believe Edward presented Anne as a reasonable proposition. *When did Edward take up Lady Catherine's cause?* "Anne is tolerable, but her wealth and station will not tempt me to favor her when she has been previously . . ." Darcy froze with the realization he recently said something very similar about Elizabeth Bennet; he changed his mind about Elizabeth's charms. Could Anne have charms of which he was not aware? He shook his head and said, "Never mind," and then excused himself quickly to his chambers.

Behind the chamber door, Darcy was angry with himself for allowing Elizabeth's memory to invade his being once again. He had not even seen her, and Darcy already had trouble ending his preference for the woman. He must master his romantic thoughts.

The first evening at Rosings passed slowly. Lady Catherine required divine attention; Darcy applied to her vanity although it vexed him most wholly to do so. His cousin Anne barely managed a greeting; the least effort seemed to drain Anne of her energies. Darcy noted she was a bit more animated when Edward plied her with humorous anecdotes of his military service. She smiled at Edward briefly for a fraction of a second. Yet, all Darcy could see was the futility of a match with his cousin. Even if affection was not a prerequisite for his marriage, Anne could not oversee Pemberley; the task would be too daunting for her.

On the morning after their arrival at Rosings, Mr. Collins presented himself to the gentlemen. Lady Catherine was making calls on some of her tenants. Collins fawned and preened as Colonel Fitzwilliam found amusing the obvious insincerity of the man.

"Do you return to the Parsonage?" Darcy asked, trying to sound nonchalant.

"Indeed, Sir, I do."

"Then may my cousin and I join you? I would like to give my congratulations to Mrs. Collins, and the colonel here has not had the pleasure of meeting your wife or your cousin."

Collins was beside himself. "You do my household a great honor, Sir. We would deem it our pleasure to share our humble abode with two gentlemen of such consequence."

"Then it is settled," Darcy bowed slightly. "Come, Edward, we are off to Hunsford to pay our respects."

Edward looked at Darcy in total disbelief. Never had his cousin considered it necessary to pay his respects to anyone of such asinine tastes before—he might have shown disdain, but respect—that was out of the question. "Yes, I am looking forward to the pleasure of the acquaintance," Edward added with some uncertainty.

The doorbell announced the three gentlemen. Collins led the way into the room, followed closely by Colonel Fitzwilliam; Darcy came last. He tried not to look directly at Elizabeth as soon as he entered the room; steadying his nerves, he took on his usual reserve and first offered compliments to Mrs. Collins, and then with an appearance of composure, which belied his actual thoughts, he likewise did the same toward Elizabeth. Their eyes locked momentarily, and he noted the usual flash of curiosity, but Elizabeth merely curtsied to him without saying a word.

Edward stepped forward saying, "Mrs. Collins and Miss Bennet, it is with great pleasure we finally meet. My cousin spoke most fondly of his time in Hertfordshire. It is nice to be able to put faces to some of his stories."

"Did he now?" Elizabeth began, and Darcy anticipated more,

but she was quickly stifled by her friend's grasp on her arm.

Edward let the tone of her brief remark pass. "Yes, indeed," he added quickly. "Mrs. Collins, your improvements to the Parsonage are duly noted. I never saw it look so much like a home. Do you not agree, Darcy?" he prompted.

"Yes, Mrs. Collins, the place, I find, took on new life," he stammered. "It is as if I am seeing it for the first time." Darcy could not recall ever being to the Parsonage before. He felt so foolish; could he not hold a conversation in the woman's presence without guarding his every word and thought?

Edward enjoyed the humor developing out of his cousin's presence at Hunsford. He knew Darcy never before would consider paying "respects" to Mr. Collins. He was not sure what the situation was, but he planned to find out. For right now, he continued his assessment of Darcy's behavior, wondering why he was so anxious to come to Hunsford if he was not going to say anything once he got here. Eventually, Elizabeth Bennet interrupted these thoughts. "Come, Colonel, tell us more about you."

Without realizing what was happening, Darcy's agitation increased; Elizabeth gave her attentions to someone else again. He allowed himself to appear in control as he watched his cousin engage Elizabeth with his usual readiness while Darcy made small talk with Mr. and Mrs. Collins, but, try as he may, Darcy spoke very little to anyone. He could not stop staring at his cousin and Elizabeth; his response dwelled on anger, but he really had nothing of which to be angry. Elizabeth did not belong to him; she was free to choose whomever she pleased, but he did not think he could tolerate her choosing his cousin. She would then be a part of *his* family, but she would not belong to him. In fact, the thought of her choosing anyone else repulsed him. *If Elizabeth could not be his,* he started, but he could not finish the thought. The sound of soft laughter came from the corner in which Darcy watched his cousin and Elizabeth. It was that delightful gurgle of hers, which he so enjoyed. Wanting to be a part of what they were saying, he found himself moving toward them. Not sure how to begin, he offered up the required pleasantries. "May I inquire, Miss Elizabeth, as to the health of your family?"

"My family was in health, Sir, when I left Hertfordshire," she answered in the usual manner. "Thank you for asking." Then he watched as a thought flashed through her eyes. "My eldest sister has been in town these three months. Have you never happened to see her there?"

Did she know his involvement with Bingley and her sister, or was she just making conversation? Either way, her words chilled Darcy to the bone. His attempt at engaging her in conversation diverted to his prejudice toward her connections. He faltered, "Regrettably, Miss Elizabeth, I did not have the good fortune as to meet Miss Bennet there." And as quickly as he moved to speak to her, Darcy withdrew. He could not speak to her on so delicate of a subject without betraying his part in her sister's separation from Bingley. With little else to discuss, Darcy and Colonel Fitzwilliam finally left for the great house.

Darcy cursed himself for getting caught up in the unknown that was Elizabeth Bennet. Being near her made him feel he was on trial; did she take such great joy in tormenting him? He nearly showed himself; he flirted with his own destiny. He vowed to be rid of Elizabeth; this was to be his test. Both his cousin and Elizabeth waited for his response. Could they read his face? He foolishly succumbed; that was decidedly brutal honesty; Darcy could not soften the truth. He *must* not let it happen again.

He spent a week buried in the paperwork of his aunt's estate. He passed his time sequestered from everyone else in the household and, more importantly, in the neighborhood. Mentally exhausted, he took some pride in having avoided Elizabeth. It did not mean she was not a consideration in his every choice, but he succeeded in placing some immediate distance between them.

While Darcy was busy with the estate's business, his cousin Edward either drove out with Anne in the carriage or paid a call on the Parsonage. Neither prospect appealed to Darcy. Spending time with his cousin would increase Lady Catherine's desire for a marriage proposal. Spending time at the Parsonage would only prove as much as he denied his feelings for Elizabeth, his heart had its own ideas. *She is not what I need in a wife. She cannot be!* Yet, he knew he cared for Elizabeth as he cared for no one before.

Lady Catherine oversaw Easter Sunday services with Mr. Collins jumping around and performing like a puppet. Because society demanded it, Lady Catherine asked the Collins's household to Rosings for tea in the evening. Darcy placed himself away from Elizabeth, but the distance could not prevent his attention being drawn toward her. He spent the last few days jealously listening to his cousin enumerate Elizabeth's charms, desperately wanting to hear the least fragment Edward offered. Yet, whenever Edward spoke of Elizabeth, he entertained images of tossing his cousin into the nearest pigs' sty for his obvious interest in the woman. Darcy summoned his habitual reserve, but as on the first evening at the Parsonage, Elizabeth's presence played havoc with his emotions. He could not draw his attention away from her.

Colonel Fitzwilliam seemed really glad to see them all; anything was a welcome relief to him at Rosings. The colonel enjoyed Elizabeth Bennet's company; she was the type of woman with whom a man could talk easily; they compared notes on Hertfordshire and on Kent; they discussed places they visited; and they considered the possibilities of new books and music.

Darcy tried to ignore the rest of the room and concentrate on his aunt's diversions, but his cousin and Elizabeth possessed so much life when they spoke it was difficult to ignore them. Even Lady Catherine could not draw her attention from them, and, as usual, Darcy was lost to the woman. His eyes strayed to where the colonel and Elizabeth sat, and he looked upon them with much curiosity. *Was Edward taken with Elizabeth?* The question he considered since coming to Rosings resurfaced. Could he lose her to his own cousin? Why not to Edward? Darcy did not want her, or so he told himself.

Eventually, Lady Catherine's scruples would not allow her to control her curiosity; she demanded to become part of their conversation. "I must have my share of the conversation if you are speaking of music. There are few people in England, I suppose, who have more true enjoyment of music than myself, or a better natural taste. If I had ever learnt, I should have been a great proficient. And so would Anne, if her health had allowed her to apply. I am confident she would have performed delightfully. How does Georgiana get on, Darcy?"

"Georgiana attends to her lessons studiously." Darcy waited for her reproof to his sister, but instead it was directed toward Elizabeth.

"I often tell young ladies that no excellence in music is to be acquired without constant practice. I have told Miss Bennet several times, that she will never play really well unless she practices more; and though Mrs. Collins has no instrument, she is very welcome to come to Rosings every day and play on the pianoforte in Mrs. Jenkinson's room. She would be in nobody's way, you know, in that part of the house." His aunt called out to her.

Darcy could not believe Lady Catherine offered Elizabeth such an example of rudeness and ill breeding at its height. He often, of late, found his aunt's continued rudeness shameful although he made no comment. He was a man torn between two worlds. Like Elizabeth, he clearly had his own connections sometimes lacking in propriety, but how could he criticize his aunt without criticizing his own standards? Did not Lady Catherine, because of her social standing, deserve some latitude in her opinions? He knew he often erred on the side of prejudice, especially when it was someone of impeccable ancestry; he admittedly had a value for rank and consequence, which blinded him a little to the faults of those who possessed them. So, where did the answer lie? He did not know how to accept one form of impropriety and condemn the other.

As the evening progressed, Darcy looked on as his cousin maneuvered Elizabeth to the instrument and drew a chair near to enjoy the music and her company. His heart ached with his cousin's treachery; Darcy wanted desperately to replace Edward, to be the one to whom she directed her attention, and to swim in the green pools of her eyes. Staring intensely, he visualized himself next to Elizabeth. Lady Catherine tried to engage him again in trivialities, but his mind rested with Elizabeth; only to Elizabeth did he pay his attentions. He rose from the settee and walked deliberately toward the pianoforte; commanded by his heart, he stood where he could have a full view of Elizabeth's countenance.

She could not help but observe this change in Darcy's attitude toward her; when the music allowed, she turned to him with her usual provocative smile and said, "You mean to frighten me, Mr. Darcy, by coming in all this state to hear me? I will not be alarmed though your sister *does* play so well. There is a stubbornness about me that never can bear to be frightened at the will of others. My courage rises at every attempt to intimidate me."

Ah, he thought. He so missed this playfulness. His heart jumped in his chest; the connection between them was still there. She teased him deliberately. He assured Elizabeth he had no design to alarm her. "I shall not say you are mistaken because you could not really believe me to entertain any design of alarming you; and I have had the pleasure of your acquaintance long enough to know that you find great enjoyment in occasionally professing opinions which in fact are not your own."

Darcy watched as Elizabeth enjoyed the picture he painted of her nature, and she was content with laughing at herself; he would gladly abandon his reserve for her lightness; he would gladly abandon his life for her love. Eventually, she turned to Colonel Fitzwilliam, but she still possessed Darcy. "Your cousin will give you a very pretty notion of me and teach you not to believe a word I say. I am particularly unlucky in meeting with a person so well able to expose my real character, in part of the world where I had hoped to pass myself off with some degree of credit. Indeed, Mr. Darcy, it is very ungenerous of you to mention all that you knew to my disadvantage in Hertfordshire—and give me leave to say, very impolitic too—for it is provoking me to retaliate, and such things may come out as will shock your relations to hear."

Darcy relished this moment; he missed her so; she had impertinence, true, but Elizabeth never excited angry annoyance in him. "Miss Elizabeth, you may speak as you see fit. I am not afraid of you," he said smilingly.

Colonel Fitzwilliam enjoyed the way Elizabeth affected his cousin, and he egged her on. "Pray let me hear what you have to accuse him of. I should like to know how he behaves among strangers."

"You shall hear then—but prepare yourself for something very dreadful. The first time of my ever seeing him in Hertfordshire, you must know, was at a ball—and at this ball, what do you think he did? He danced only four dances! I am sorry to tell you, but so it was. He danced only four dances, though gentlemen were scarce; and, to my certain knowledge, more than one young lady was sitting down in want of a partner. Mr. Darcy, you cannot deny the fact."

So, Elizabeth still desired an apology for his actions at the assembly hall. He could handle that; it was long overdue; Darcy planned an apology since her time at Netherfield. "I had not at that time the honor of knowing any lady in the assembly beyond my own party."

"True; and nobody can ever be introduced in a ballroom," Elizabeth retorted. Maybe in retrospect, the reason lacked soundness; Bingley offered Darcy an introduction, which Darcy refused. He owed her more of an explanation.

"Perhaps," said Darcy, "I should have judged better had I sought an introduction; but I am ill-qualified to recommend myself to strangers." There—that should allay her objections and tell Elizabeth he felt sorrow for his impolitic behavior.

Elizabeth enjoyed teasing Darcy's usual reserve, and she spoke to his cousin once again. "Shall we ask him why a man of sense and education, and who has lived in the world, is ill-qualified to recommend himself to strangers?"

"I can answer your question without applying to him," Edward offered Darcy a cut. "It is because he will not give himself the trouble." Darcy could not believe the colonel would say such provocative lies; he knew Darcy to operate as a gentleman; Edward, evidently, wanted to discredit him in Elizabeth's eyes.

Yet, those eyes still belonged to Darcy; they had not broken contact since this repartee began. He offered, "I certainly have not the talent which some people possess of conversing easily with those I have never seen before. I cannot catch their tone of conversation, or appear interested in their concerns, as I often see done."

That should allow Elizabeth an opportunity to see his cousin for the flatterer he is. Her eyebrow shot up, and Elizabeth's amusement flittered across her face. With a smirk of a smile, she said, "My fingers do not move over this instrument in the masterly manner which I see so many women's do. But then I have always supposed it to be my own fault—because I would not take the trouble of practicing."

At the moment, Darcy rationalized neither of them needed anyone else's approval and offered a compliment saying, "You are perfectly right. You have employed your time much better. No one admitted to the privilege of hearing you can think anything wanting. We neither of us perform to strangers."

Lady Catherine interrupted his revelry by coming to the instrument and once again criticizing Elizabeth's musical ability. Lady Catherine evidently did not appreciate his attentions to Elizabeth and planned to "remind" him of his duty to his cousin Anne by touting Anne's presumed musical talent. Ashamed for his aunt's behavior toward Elizabeth, Darcy assumed a haughty countenance. Elizabeth received Lady Catherine's remarks with all the forbearance of civility and unknowingly received Darcy's renewed regard. The colonel and Darcy took turns requesting her continued presence at the instrument until the carriage took her back to the Parsonage.

Darcy lay under the counterpane, stretching his limbs to relieve the tension the evening entertained. He spent the last few months declaring his freedom from Elizabeth Bennet, but the evening persuaded him to reevaluate his feelings once more. It seemed since Elizabeth Bennet entered his life, Darcy spent numerous hours debating about succumbing to her charms. He knew he was lost to her; Elizabeth would be the mark by which he would judge all other women. He still could not justify pursuing Elizabeth, but Darcy could also not give her up. Unless he did something soon, the quandary in which he found himself would further rob him of his sleep and his waking sanity.

If he could not rid himself of his obsession, then Darcy had to rationally plan how he could achieve Elizabeth's regard and not associate with her family. Of course, that would be impossible. He could tolerate the company of Miss Bennet and probably her father he supposed. Would regularly seeing them be enough for Elizabeth? Pemberley was a good distance from Hertfordshire; it would not be easy for Elizabeth's family to visit; he could arrange business in town when Mrs. Bennet and the younger sisters came to stay. He would have to guard against those connections having too much influence on Georgiana, however. The Bennets could be brought to Pemberley when others were not expected. It could be achieved; it would be worthwhile if Darcy could earn Elizabeth's love; a few moments of intolerable disdain would be pale indeed to all the pleasures of Elizabeth's company. Receiving Elizabeth's love and devotion was a prayer he recited more than once these last few months. "The prayer the Devil answers," he chuckled out loud as the darkness enveloped him. Images of Elizabeth at the pianoforte frequented his dreams, and her smile was all for his pleasure.

Dawn came early for Fitzwilliam Darcy; he found himself wrapped in the bedclothes and turned askew; his battle with himself and sleep took its toll on his resolve, but he made a decision during those long waking hours. Pushing himself from the mattress, Darcy swung his legs over the side of the bed and reached for the bell cord to call his man. Today he would seek out Elizabeth's company; today he would begin to win her heart; he knew Elizabeth to be at least aware of his interests although she probably was unsure of its depth; he gave her mixed signals up until this time. Now, Darcy would show Elizabeth despite his concerns with her family, he would apply himself to winning her love.

CHAPTER 8

"Proceed from the impulse of the moment . . ."

Today would be the first day of the rest of his life. Following his morning ablutions, Darcy dressed carefully trying to create an appearance of a gentleman open to new possibilities. He set out through the parklands surrounding Rosings, but he knew unconsciously his destination was not to be the park itself; he was to make a call on the Parsonage. The little over a quarter mile path was well worn, and its passage was short lived, and before he knew it, he stood outside Hunsford. He could not alter his choice; his entrance into the gate at the Parsonage would be well known. So noted, Darcy rang the bell and was soon admitted to the inner room. He expected the Collinses to be about, but he found only Elizabeth in attendance. Having planned to engage the household's occupants in conversation, his apprehension increased; although it was a pleasant surprise, he had to shift his emotional being to face Elizabeth one-on-one.

"Mr. Darcy, what a surprise!" she began, sounding a bit uncertain.

"Miss Bennet, I apologize for invading your privacy," he stumbled along trying to sound uneventful, but feeling aroused by her closeness. "I understood the Collinses were within. I pray I have not interrupted your solitary pleasures."

"An interruption does not necessarily have to be unwelcome, Sir," she curtsied. "I am afraid Mrs. Collins and her sister went into the village. I hope your appearance here does not mean your family at Rosings has taken ill. Are Lady Catherine, Miss de Bourgh, and your cousin, the colonel, all in health?"

"Thank you, Madame, their health is well," he returned her bow, while all the time thinking, *She welcomes my company!*

"Then, please have a seat, Mr. Darcy," she offered politely, while gesturing to a nearby chair.

Darcy stared at her so fascinated by her beauty he nearly forgot the need for conversation. He realized Elizabeth stared at him; so he cleared his throat and asked of her family and of the weather and of the road conditions during her journey to Rosings. It was a very disjointed conversation, definitely lacking in transitions, but he did not freeze completely in her presence. There were a few more awkward pauses than he would have preferred, though.

Eventually, that playful spark he so loved about her showed itself in her expression. He did not expect Elizabeth to bring up the subject of Bingley and Netherfield so quickly, but Darcy knew from her comment about her sister previously it would be a topic with which he would have to deal. Her inquiries dealt with the probability of Bingley's returning to Netherfield. As casually as possible, he assured Elizabeth of the unlikeliness of that situation. "I have never heard him say so; but it is probable that he may spend very little of his time there in the future. He has many friends, and he is at a time of life when friends and engagements are continually increasing." He hoped this explanation would temper her curiosity. Darcy changed the text of their conversation. "This seems a very comfortable house. Lady Catherine, I believe, did a great deal to it when Mr. Collins first came to Hunsford."

"I believe she did—and I am sure she could not have bestowed her kindness on a more grateful object."

"My aunt is an excellent benefactor for Mr. Collins; such improvements are the exception rather than the rule." Elizabeth simply nodded. Yet, it was not of the house he wished to speak; he wanted to know her thoughts on marriage. He began, "Mr. Collins appears to be very fortunate in his choice of a wife."

"Yes, indeed, his friends may well rejoice in his having met with one of the very few sensible women who would accept him, but in a prudential light, it is certainly a good match for her." Elizabeth did not seem to favor the match despite her friend's sensibility of marrying for monetary advantage. Darcy took her words to mean wealth was important, but Elizabeth wanted a loving relationship for herself. This was acceptable to him; he, too, wanted to replicate his parents' partnership in his own life; he had the necessary wealth, and he would wholeheartedly love Elizabeth if she would allow him to do so.

Darcy added, "It must be very agreeable to her to be settled within so easy a distance of her own family and friends."

A bit shocked, she replied, "An easy distance, do you call it? It is nearly fifty miles."

A challenge was before him; they would engage in their usual verbal swordplay. "And what is fifty miles of good road? Little more than half a day's journey. Yes, I call it a *very* easy distance," he remarked as he leaned forward in his chair.

Elizabeth shifted her weight, straightened her shoulders, and leaned in as she retorted, "I should never have considered the distance as one of the *advantages* of the match. I should never have said Mrs. Collins was settled *near* her family."

Darcy could detect the lavender; it was all he could do not to caress her face. "It is a proof of your own attachment to Hertford-shire. Anything beyond the very neighborhood of Longbourn, I suppose, would appear far." He smiled while thinking of her at Pemberley and realizing the additional distance between his home and her home and how it would give them relief from her connections.

Elizabeth argued one would need more fortune than the Collinses possessed in order for the distance to be an easy one. "It is comfortable for you to consider distance from a different perspective, Mr. Darcy. Where there is fortune to make the expense of traveling unimportant, distance becomes no evil. But that is not the case here. Mr. and Mrs. Collins have a comfortable income, but not such a one as will allow of frequent journeys."

Darcy had the financial stability to make her travel wishes a matter of choosing in which carriage she wished to traverse the distance. He could offer her so much; obviously, Elizabeth would learn to love him. Darcy drew his chair a little toward her and said, "*You* cannot have a right to such very strong local attachment. *You* cannot have been always at Longbourn." His feelings for Elizabeth caused his breath to be ragged and shallow; she locked eyes with him momentarily, and he saw an image of her uncertainty. He realized he must check himself; he moved too fast; he wanted to scoop her into his arms and carry her away to Pemberley, but, instead, he reluctantly moved his chair back. There was a newspaper lying on the table, and as he picked it up, he said coldly, "Are you pleased with Kent?"

Elizabeth leaned back casually in her chair. The intensity between them subsided, and small talk remained. Even this interchange came soon to an end as Mrs. Collins and Miss Lucas returned. Darcy explained he believed all the ladies of the house were at home when he called. After a series of civilities, he begged their leave and headed back toward Rosings Park. It was a beginning. Elizabeth must recognize his intentions; now he must determine if she would willingly accept him as her husband.

Over the next several days, Darcy continued to call at the Parsonage; sometimes he came with his cousin; other times he came alone. To his chagrin, his former reluctance to speak easily reappeared when others were about. He wished to find a way to engage Elizabeth privately again. Darcy noted Mrs. Collins's interest in his appearances at Hunsford, and although he could never make himself stop drinking in the beauty that was Elizabeth Bennet, he schooled his stare into an ambiguous, earnest, steadfast gaze. Eventually, eavesdropping on her conversations with his cousin, Darcy lighted on an idea. Miss Bennet chose a particular path at Rosings to be her favorite; he could arrange a rencontre. They could walk together and become more thoroughly acquainted; tomorrow Darcy would embark upon the second stage of his pursuit of Elizabeth Bennet.

He awoke early and left Rosings's warmth to brave a chilly morning and to wait for her company. He thought he knew which path she described to Edward, but after a half hour's stay, he questioned the information. To his relief, he spotted Elizabeth as she approached the roughly hewed clearing where he awaited her; he stepped back into the shadows, wishing the appearance of an accidental meeting.

Not expecting to see anyone along the pathway, Elizabeth started when Darcy appeared before her. "Mr. Darcy," she gasped, "I was not expecting to see you here."

"Miss Bennet," he feigned surprise, "nor I you. I did not realize you too preferred solitary walks. They are most pleasant, are they not?"

"You know me to be a person who is not afraid of a healthy walking distance," she appeared a bit unnerved by the mischance of their meeting.

"Are you nearing the end of your preamble?"

"Yes, Sir," she stammered. "I believe I will turn back."

"Then allow me, Madame," he said, doffing his hat, "to escort you back to the Parsonage. I would be remiss in my duty if I allowed you to return alone."

Elizabeth flashed a questioning look in his direction, but she accepted his extended arm as her support. Darcy resisted reaching out and placing his own hand on hers; the warmth of her fingers tantalized his senses. They walked for a few minutes in what he considered to be companionable silence; yet, he did not want to waste his time with her so he forced himself to offer up observations about the beauty of Kent. Elizabeth's response he barely heard, being so consumed by the moment, but he caught enough of the words to realize she found Kent to be very pleasant.

"Would you consider returning for another visit?" he ventured.

"Such would be a pleasurable sojourn," she turned to look up at him unexpectedly. Darcy glowed with the hopes she would find it more pleasurable if he were in Kent, as well.

"How do you find Rosings?" he questioned, engrossed in her closeness.

"It has a pleasant prospect when one first takes in its beauty," Elizabeth began. "Its many wings confuse me, however. Lady Catherine offered use of her library, but I must admit I found the billiard room instead. It is a bit amusing upon recollection."

Darcy caught the glint of a smile, and he joined in her ease. "I am sure if you were to return as a Rosings's guest, the likelihood of making such a mistake would be greatly reduced." The ambiguity of his words was not lost on Elizabeth. She glanced at Darcy briefly and shook her head. The movement of her bonnet caught his attention, and he partook of the flush of her cheeks and the thickness of her eyelashes.

The walk was coming to an end, and they drifted into silence once more. Approaching the gate, he reached out with his free hand to loosen the latch; he hated to part her company and walked with her to the door of the Parsonage. "Thank you, Mr. Darcy," her eyes rose to meet his.

"It was my pleasure, Miss Elizabeth. Your presence made the walk more agreeable." Before she could respond, he offered her a quick bow and strode away. Waiting until he was sure no one at the Parsonage could observe his reactions, Darcy finally gave himself permission to stop, lean against a tree, and replay the reflections of the last half hour.

It was another beginning. Darcy would like to think this was another step in his winning Elizabeth's regard when, in reality, most of his beginnings were faltering attempts. Accustomed to being the prey, not the pursuer, he knew what to do to sustain an interest once it began, but Darcy never met a woman such as Elizabeth Bennet and never initiated the relationship. Yet, he felt more hopeful; Bingley and especially his sisters thwarted his attempts at Netherfield; here at Rosings, his cousin frustrated his designs. Darcy knew he needed privacy to secure Elizabeth's affection; the solitary paths of Rosings permitted him the means and mode to win the lady's heart.

These were his thoughts as he sat in the high-backed chair in Rosings's library. The library was one of the places at Rosings where Darcy knew he would not encounter interruptions; besides his reputation as a lover of books, Darcy knew the other occupants of the house had little use for the precious volumes. Like everything else at Rosings Park, the library provided a showplace where Lady Catherine could proclaim expertise in the written form, as she did recently about music. Edward's military career left him little time for the improvement of his mind through pleasurable reading.

The light tread of his cousin entering the sanctuary disturbed his solitary moment; Anne de Bourgh was the last person he expected to find in the library. "Anne!" he blurted out, as he rose to his feet to greet her.

"Fitzwilliam," she returned his astonishment. Then she curtsied as if to leave.

Seeing her retreat from him so quickly, Darcy did the uncharacteristic thing, he gave "himself the trouble" of engaging his cousin. "Please join me, Anne."

"Fitzwilliam, I did not mean to disturb your solitude."

"You have no cause for censure, Anne," he coaxed her toward a close chair and returned to his own seat. "It seems we see so little of each other."

Anne blushed briefly, but a sense of resolve permitted her the luxury of speaking openly to Darcy. "If I may speak candidly, Cousin," she began; he nodded his assent, "I avoid your company because my mother would perceive her plans for our marital felicity as progressing."

"I see," said Darcy slowly, unaccustomed to such honesty from his cousin. "I am ashamed I never realized you felt as such. Edward tried to counsel me as to your true feelings, but I fear I trusted him not."

"Actually, it was Edward who convinced me to let you know my feelings. I sought you in here today, but when I saw you, I nearly left before I began. I wanted to say so much for so long I blurted out without thoughts of civility. Edward assured me you do not wish us to marry either." The last line was more of a question than it was a statement.

Anne opened a discussion which he did not anticipate, but which he welcomed. Darcy was taken aback by the speed with which she broached the subject. Clearly, Anne felt the pressure of getting everything out between them before Lady Catherine discovered them. "Cousin Anne, I am astounded to hear such protests, but it seems Edward is a reliable courier. Without wishing you harm or reproof, I do not feel your mother's wishes would serve either of us well. Our dispositions are too much in contrast."

"That is a relief, Fitzwilliam," she nearly whispered. "I fear your dark, brooding nature. Did you know I have been afraid of you since we were children?" He looked a bit shocked at her words. "My mother will be looking for me; I will leave you now. Thank you for allowing me to speak in earnest and in haste. It will give the situation ease when we both choose to look elsewhere for our mates," and as quickly as she entered, Anne took leave of the room.

Darcy shook himself in disbelief; Edward told him recently Anne was not what she appeared to be. Obviously, his cousin did have "charms" of which he was unaware; he always thought himself to be an astute observer of others; then how could he not have seen Anne as she was? It had really been a day of new beginnings—first with Elizabeth and now with Anne.

On the third day Darcy so met Elizabeth, he encountered some resistance on her part, but he prepared himself for her reluctance. "Miss Bennet," he began upon meeting her "accidentally" again, "I have purposely come to meet you here." His words registered a mild shock upon Elizabeth's face. "After leaving you yesterday at the Parsonage, I recalled a particularly pleasant prospect I believe you would enjoy. I came here today in hopes of having the pleasure of showing it to you."

"Thank you, Mr. Darcy," she stammered, "that will not be necessary."

"I understand if you are too tired. I should have thought better than to intrude myself on your time again," he said apologetically. "The walk was one of my late mother's favorites. I forgot about it until Lady Catherine reminded me of it," he lied. "I simply thought you might find it a pleasant choice for a solitary walk."

Elizabeth hesitated briefly and then assured him if it was not too far, she would take pleasure in seeing it. She took his proffered arm. Walking along the narrow, winding path, she often moved in closer to Darcy for support, as the footing was a bit bumpy with tree roots. He would gladly pick her up to carry her, but he resisted any rash impropriety. In less than ten minutes' walk, they emerged from the thick-trunk tree-lined path into a clearing painted by the sun. Darcy pushed aside some branches and allowed Elizabeth to step into a field of vibrantly colored wildflowers—primroses, blue-bells, wild hyacinths, and anemones. He enjoyed the gasp she emitted upon seeing what the clearing had to offer.

"Mr. Darcy," she exclaimed, "this is magnificent!"

He could not stop the smile erupting from inside him. Elizabeth stepped away from him and nearly ran toward the field. He watched as she stopped suddenly, spread her arms full wide, and turned around and around, looking skyward with joy. He did not expect such unencumbered pleasure, but he did not find anything critical about Elizabeth's actions. She walked through the field at several angles, stopping to enjoy the various flowers; then she strode purposely back toward him. "Mr. Darcy, you honored me by sharing this clearing with me. I cannot understand why you chose to do so, but it will be a treasured memory of my trip to Rosings."

"My mother loved nature, Miss Elizabeth. I believe she would have been pleased to know you approved of her favorite refuge," he offered. "Are you ready to return to the Parsonage?"

"Yes, Sir, I believe I am." He extended his arm, and she took a firmer grip than previously, anticipating the pathway's unevenness. Her rich, mellow eyes sparkling as she turned around and around in the field filled Darcy with happiness. He loved Elizabeth Bennet; the realization of admitting his feelings flashed through his being; no more would he say he loved her eyes or loved how she spoke her mind; no longer would he think of his feelings being only a strong attraction; Darcy loved Elizabeth. It was as simple as that: he loved Elizabeth. Finally openly acknowledging his devotion for her to himself, Darcy wanted to scream it to the world. Instead, he forced himself to swallow hard and say, "I am pleased my intrusion was not unpleasant, Miss Elizabeth."

"I believe I told you earlier not all intrusions are unwelcome, Sir."

"Our acquaintance has been long enough for us to know something of the other's preferences." She looked at him with questions hidden behind her eyes; Darcy knew Elizabeth would now expect him to make known his intentions—he shared his mother's favorite refuge with her—he told her of his wishing to share precious parts of his life with her; he realized fully Elizabeth could no longer doubt his purpose. The companionable silence returned between them, broken only by small civilities about the weather *and* their respective families *and* books recently read. He left her at the Parsonage's door, but this time as he strode away he allowed himself the pleasure of turning for a final look at her; Elizabeth stood transfixed and looking toward where he brought up; he touched the brim of his hat to bid her farewell and strolled away. After he turned, he did not see her grimace, nor did he observe her perplexed stare.

Tomorrow—he thought as he walked to Rosings; tomorrow he would offer his hand to Elizabeth. He would leave Rosings in two days; therefore, tomorrow would be the day. *The prayer the Devil answers,* he reminded himself. *Let the Devil beware,* Darcy thought. He would declare his love for Elizabeth; she would accept; and then Darcy would deal with those whose censure would surely come. Tonight he would prepare a proper proposal; he would tell Elizabeth how his regard for her grew despite their differences. He imagined her happiness at his declaration. That evening Darcy slept well with the knowledge on the morrow Elizabeth would be his.

When he found his way to Elizabeth's favorite pathway, reality dashed his hopes. Edward walked with her, and they conversed intimately. He could hear her soft laughter and see his cousin's animated gestures. Darcy felt as if someone ripped his heart from his chest; his plans for the proposal not only ruined, but he witnessed her enjoyment of his cousin's company; the green-eyed monster known as jealousy ricocheted through him. Darcy withdrew without their seeing him and returned to Rosings unnoticed.

He watched from the study's window as his cousin returned to Rosings. He tried to note any changes in Edward, but none of any consequence were found. Darcy stepped back from the window and moved to where anyone going by the door would think the room to be empty; he could not check his emotions to converse with Edward or any other member of the de Bourgh household at this time. He needed to find another opportunity to engage Elizabeth, assuming Edward had not offered intentions of his own to her.

The longer Darcy sat and examined the situation, the more reasonable he became. Edward as a second son could not afford to marry Elizabeth; he said as much to Darcy before they came to Rosings. Edward may find Elizabeth attractive, but he talked to everyone, just like Bingley, both amiable gentlemen. As his reason returned, Darcy knew he could see Elizabeth tomorrow. What would four and twenty hours change?

Much to his surprise, he discovered from one of his aunt's maids Lady Catherine invited the Collins's household to Rosings for tea. At least, Darcy would have the pleasure of Elizabeth's company this evening, and although Edward liked to monopolize her time, tonight Darcy would spoil his cousin's plan. Tonight, Elizabeth's attentions belonged to him.

The Collinses' arrival came at last, but to Darcy's dismay, Mr. Collins offered Lady Catherine his sincerest apologies for his cousin had taken ill. *How could Elizabeth be ill? She seemed in health this morning when he observed her in the park.*

Darcy went through the motions society demanded, but he

could not separate his mind from the thoughts of Elizabeth Bennet. If she was ill, he must do what he could to comfort her. Now, he fully understood how Bingley felt when Jane Bennet took ill at Netherfield. Possibly her illness was a sham; she expected his offer this morning only to find Edward in the park in his stead. Of course, did they not congenially meet in the park each morning? Her distress of not seeing him today created her illness, or it could be a means of their being alone; yes, it must be so.

Convinced of the latter, Darcy excused himself from the party using the pretext he and Edward would depart in six and thirty hours, and some business still needed addressed. Edward, he assured the gathering, better entertained than did he. Returning to his chambers, Darcy retrieved his greatcoat, hat, and walking stick, and not wishing to be seen by his aunt's guests, he took the back stairway of the servants' quarters. He had to be to Elizabeth, and he had to be there now. He had a purpose—a purpose that would ironically change his life forever. He rang the bell, and a servant admitted him to the inner room where he found Elizabeth agitated and flushed. His hope sprang from the depths of his love for her; obviously, she awaited his appearance. He came forward and immediately inquired about her health although in countenance, Elizabeth appeared more flustered than unwell. "I came with a wish of hearing you are not suffering," he extended his excuse.

Coldly civil, Elizabeth answered him. "As you may see, Sir, I am well."

Naturally, his coming not to her earlier upset her. Darcy tried to recall exactly what he wished to say to her this morning; he planned his speech carefully, drafting it several times. He accepted the seat she offered, but his nerves would not allow such constraint; he had to move, and within a few moments, he paced about the room. Elizabeth's eyes followed him, but she knew not what bothered him. Finally, he turned to her, and he stood with agitation building, knowing he must say the words soon or lose his opportunity. Silence ensued for several minutes before he could compose himself; eventually, he approached her and blurted out, "In vain have

I struggled. It will not do. My feelings will not be repressed. You must allow me to tell you how ardently I admire and love you."

Elizabeth remained silent, and Darcy convinced himself she waited only to hear of his deep regard for her; so, he continued. "Miss Elizabeth, my regard for you began when we first met in Hertfordshire. I was, admittedly, foolish to not seek out a proper introduction at the assembly, but my station in life does not allow me the luxury of associating with those of inferior society, and I was at first blind to your worth. At Netherfield, I found worthy your devotion to your sister, as well as your kindness to Maria Lucas and others who sought your good wishes. Of course, I struggled for several months as to my feelings for you. One must realize the superiority of my family's connections had to be a concern for our alliance; the censure and disdain we are likely to encounter with such an unequal match was another consideration, but after much self-reproach, I accepted the inferiority of your family's connections, and I offer you my hand in matrimony."

Fully expecting her acceptance, Darcy watched as a gamut of emotions flashed across Elizabeth's face; most of which he could not read. When she spoke, he froze with the vehemence lodged in her words. "Mr. Darcy," she began slowly, "in such cases as this, it is, I believe, the established mode to express a sense of obligation for the sentiments avowed, however unequally they may be returned. But I cannot—I have never desired your good opinion, and you have certainly bestowed it most unwillingly. I am sorry to have occasioned pain to anyone. It has been most unconsciously done, however, and, I hope, will be of short duration." *How could he have so misread her mind?* "The feelings which you tell me have long prevented the acknowledgment of your regard can have little difficulty in overcoming it after this explanation."

His ears deceived him; Elizabeth refused his proposal. Disdaining any visual form of weakness, Darcy worked hard to compose his thoughts and control his rage before speaking to her again, but his hurt and anger showed clearly visible, and he did not speak for what seemed to be an infinite moment. At length, in a voice of forced calmness, he said, "And this is all the reply which I am to have the honor of expecting! I might, perhaps, wish to be informed why, with so little *endeavor* of civility, I am thus rejected. But it is of small importance."

She turned on him angrily. "I might as well inquire why with so evident a desire of offending and insulting me, you chose to tell me that you liked me against your will, against your reason, and even against your character? Was not this some excuse for incivility, if I *was* uncivil? But I have other provocations. You know I have. Had not my own feelings decided against you—had they been indifferent, or had they even been favorable, do you think that any consideration would tempt me to accept the man who has been the means of ruining perhaps forever, the happiness of a most-beloved sister?"

So, she knew his part in separating Bingley from Miss Bennet. From where had Elizabeth heard it? Edward—Edward unknowingly told Elizabeth of his deceit. How she must hate him—although what he did, he would do again—he did it for Bingley's own good.

Her continued condemnation of his actions interrupted his thoughts. "I have every reason in the world to think ill of you. You dare not, you cannot deny, that you have been the principal, if not the only means of dividing them from each other—of exposing one to the censure of the world for caprice and instability and the other to its derision for disappointed hopes and involving them both in misery of the acutest kind. Can you deny that you have done it?"

Darcy pretended to be unmoved by her words. "I have no wish of denying that I did everything in my power to separate my friend from your sister, or that I rejoice in my success. Towards *him* I have been kinder than towards myself." He showed her no remorse for his actions, and he even looked at her with a smile of affected incredulity.

The shift of her shoulders and a rise of her chin should have warned Darcy there was more to come, but he doubted her defiance. He could claim his allegiance to Mr. Bingley in the affair with her sister, but she knew of other offenses, which turned her opinion against Darcy; and she began to attack him with the plight of Mr. Wickham at Darcy's hands. "But it is not merely this affair on which my dislike is founded. Your character was unfolded in the recital which I received many months ago from Mr. Wickham. On this subject what can you have to say? In what imaginary act of friendship can you here defend yourself?"

Wickham's name—she spoke Wickham's name. Jealousy crushed his heart; his worst fears confirmed. George Wickham, the man whom he most detested in the world, smote Elizabeth. *How could that be?* Coming in close to let his true feelings be known, he approached her. "You take an eager interest in that gentleman's concerns." Darcy's tone changed, and his color heightened.

With fervor, Elizabeth closed the distance even more as she challenged, "Who that knows what his misfortunes have been, can help feeling an interest in him."

Nearly spitting out the words, Darcy replied contemptuously, "His misfortunes! Yes, his misfortunes have been great indeed!"

Energized by their encounter, Elizabeth's response accused Darcy of reducing Wickham to a life of poverty by depriving him of his rightful income. "You have done all this! And yet you can treat the mention of his misfortune with contempt and ridicule."

"And this," cried Darcy, as he walked with quick steps across the room, "is your opinion of me! I believed if anyone knew me it would be you, Miss Elizabeth, but according to you, I am a calculated manipulator. I thank you for explaining it so fully." Darcy turned to face the woman to whom he foolishly gave his heart. "But perhaps these offenses might have been overlooked, had not your pride been hurt by my honest confession of the scruples that had long prevented my forming any serious design." Yet, he could not stop at that; he was angry; he was devastated; his own pride hurt—attacked and destroyed. Darcy never sought favors from another; he never needed to do so; being reduced to applying for adoration and respect offended every fiber of his being. He taunted Elizabeth satirically by describing how he could have applied for her hand with false compliments, but he prided himself on always speaking the truth; and truthfully, he had qualms about an alliance with Elizabeth. "Could you expect me to rejoice in the inferiority of your connections?—to congratulate myself on the hope of relations, whose condition in life is so decidedly beneath my own?"

If Darcy thought Elizabeth would accept his words as the voice of reason, he greatly mistook her. His rebuke infuriated her, placing her motives for preferring Wickham as being superficial. Unaccustomed to being questioned on her judgment, she prided herself on being an "observer" of society. "You are mistaken, Mr. Darcy, if you suppose that the mode of your declaration affected me in any other way, than as it spared me the concern which I might have felt in refusing you, had you behaved in a more gentlemanlike manner."

Darcy stiffened at these words; he prided himself the most upon being a gentleman, and she called him on this matter; his color paled as she continued her ridicule. "You could not have made the offer of your hand in any possible way that would have tempted me to accept it. From the very beginning—from the first moment, I may almost say—of my acquaintance with you, your manners, impressing me with the fullest belief of your arrogance, your conceit, and your selfish disdain of the feelings of others. I had not known you a month before I felt that you were the last man in the world whom I could ever be prevailed upon to marry."

Darcy could stand it no more: "You have said quite enough, Madam. I perfectly comprehend your feelings, and have now only to be ashamed of what my own have been. Forgive me for having taken up so much of your time, and accept my best wishes for your health and happiness." And with that said, he hastily quit the room and the house; yet, he could not do so without one last wistful glance at her.

Leaving the Parsonage, Darcy momentarily did not know where he was; this was a nightmare from which he must awake. *Elizabeth!* He wanted to scream her name; a knife through his heart would have been less painful; at least, from the stab wound he would die; living without Elizabeth's love would haunt him for the rest of his life. *The last man whom I could ever be prevailed upon to marry*—those were her words! She always hated him. Darcy thought of the many women he thwarted or ignored; he knew the slightest nod of his head would secure their attentions, but the one woman he desired found him to be arrogant and conceited. The memory of the last few months recoiled and bounded forward into an empty vault.

His gait drove him toward Rosings; surprisingly, his legs worked even though his heart lay shredded by Elizabeth's words. *If you behaved in a more gentlemanlike manner.* Darcy ran his hand through his hair and tried valiantly to steady himself. He totally lost his perspective. Nearly staggering up the stairs, he made his apologies to his aunt and retreated to the sanctuary of his chambers.

CHAPTER 9

"I do comprehend a great deal."

Elizabeth! Her name echoed through his head; disbelief, anger, and empathy fought for control of his emotions. As a man, he must answer the charges she laid before him, but the prospect of seeing the contempt in her eyes again was not something he could do. *Then how? How could he respond to her attacks? He would write her an explanation;* Darcy would tell her what his resentment and dismay would not allow. He realized addressing Elizabeth's sentiments about Bingley and her sister would be easily portrayed as an innocent misunderstanding, but what of those of Wickham? He must share Georgiana's shame. Wickham poisoned Elizabeth's mind against him; he had to trust her with the knowledge of his sister's near indiscretion in order to clear his own name.

Darcy paced the room, trying to compose his mind before taking up the quill. He would maintain a formality and choose his words carefully. Lashing out at Elizabeth's words would lessen her chances of reading his missive; he spent several hours selecting the right words—ones which would encourage her to read the entire letter and maybe be less repulsed by his attentions to her. Darcy had no illusions such a letter might restore Elizabeth to him; he knew he lost her forever, but he could not, even now, have her in the world and thinking poorly of him.

Be not alarmed, Madam, on receiving this letter, by the apprehension of its containing any repetition of those sentiments or renewal of those offers which were last night so disgusting to you.

117

She could never be prevailed on to marry him. The words haunted his memory each time he closed his eyes. Leaning back in the chair, he forced himself to swallow the bile-like anguish invading his chest.

I write without any intention of paining you, or humbling myself. The effort which the formation and the perusal of this letter must occasion, should have been spared had not my character required it to be written and read. You must, therefore, pardon the freedom with which I demand your attention; your feelings, I know, will bestow it unwillingly, but I demand it of your justice. Two offenses of a very different nature were last night laid to my charge. The first was that, regardless of the sentiments of either, I detached Mr. Bingley from your sister, and the other that in defiance of various claims, ruined the immediate prosperity and blasted the prospects of Mr. Wickham. It is my wish with this letter to offer you some explanation and, therefore, be in the future secured.

I had not been long in Hertfordshire before I saw, in common with others, that Bingley preferred your elder sister to any other young woman in the country. But it was not till the evening of the dance at Netherfield that I had any apprehension of his feeling a serious attachment. I had often seen him in love before. At that ball, while I had the honor of dancing with you, I was first made acquainted by Sir William Lucas's accidental information, that Bingley's attentions to your sister had given rise to a general expectation of their marriage. From that moment, I observed my friend's behavior attentively; and I could then perceive his partiality for Miss Bennet was beyond what I had ever witnessed in him. Your sister I also watched. Her looks and manners were open, cheerful, and engaging as ever, but without any symptom of peculiar regard and I remained convinced from the evening's scrutiny, that though she received his attentions with pleasure, she did not invite them by any participation of sentiment. I did not believe her to be indifferent because I wished it; I believed it on impartial conviction, as truly as I wished it in reason.

How could Darcy say what he must next convey without hurting Elizabeth? Even after all her vehemence, he could not bear to see her in distress. How could he explain his objections to Elizabeth's family applied to Bingley, as well as himself; yet, he distanced himself from the Bennets' improprieties? Darcy could not explain his objections to her connections because in retrospect, they made little sense to him. The Bennets' vulgarity appalled Darcy when he came face-to-face with it; he easily acknowledged his objections then because he had not allowed himself to love Elizabeth at that time; now those exceptions paled in review. If he allowed himself to love Elizabeth, why could not Jane Bennet reciprocate Bingley's affections?

> *My objections to the marriage were not merely those which I last night acknowledged, although the want of connection could not be so great an evil to my friend as to me. The situation of your mother's family, though objectionable, was nothing in comparison to that total want of propriety so frequently, so almost uniformly betrayed by herself, by your three younger sisters, and occasionally even by your father.*

Darcy explained his criticism did not apply to Elizabeth or to her elder sister. He told of observing the Bennets and Mr. Collins at Netherfield and how he and Bingley's sisters separated Bingley from Miss Bennet. He would like to place his actions as being aboveboard, but if Elizabeth's evaluations were true, he wronged Miss Bennet. However, Darcy made few ill decisions and had an innate reluctance to admit such a shortcoming. So, with some trepidation, he continued his letter.

> *Upon reflection, my motives for trying to spare Bingley I would take up again as a way to protect my friend, but there are two parts of the situation of which I feel dissatisfaction. While protecting Charles, I duplicitously lied to him about your sister's visit to London. I knew she was in town, and I did not share that information with him. Neither*

Miss Bingley nor I told him, and he is currently ignorant of the fact. If I have wounded your sister's feelings, it was unknowingly done; and though the motives which governed me may to you very naturally appear insufficient, I have not yet learnt to condemn them.

Maybe he should change that last sentence and show more humility; of course, if he crossed out the idea, it would emphasize it; he hoped to convey that although he may have erred, Darcy did so in the service of a friend, and in so doing, he could find no real fault with his actions. Now, he faced the daunting task of addressing Elizabeth's opinion of George Wickham. Darcy knew he could trust Elizabeth with the truth, but relating the pain of Mr. Wickham's deceit filled him with regret—regret of failing his sister and, ultimately, failing the trust of his father.

With respect to that other, more weighty accusation, of having injured Mr. Wickham, I can only refute it by laying before you the whole of his connection with my family. Mr. Wickham is the son of a very respectable man, who had for many years the management of all the Pemberley estates. My father supported Mr. Wickham at school, and afterward at Cambridge.

Darcy's letter relayed how his honorable father had the highest opinion of Mr. Wickham although Darcy himself knew otherwise. He never betrayed Mr. Wickham to his father, and Mr. Darcy died thinking well of George Wickham and intended to provide the man with a living in the clergy. Trying to fulfill his father's wishes, Darcy offered Wickham the living as soon as it became vacant. He worded the next passage most carefully; he felt anger at Wickham's betrayal and jealousy that Wickham earned Elizabeth's acceptance when he could not. His words told of Wickham's refusing the living upon his own father's passing and of his lie about a wish to study law. Wickham accepted three thousand pounds and gave up all claims to assistance in the church.

All connection between us seemed now dissolved. In town I believe he chiefly lived, free of all restraint, his life was a life of idleness and dissipation. Upon hearing the living had once more become available, Mr. Wickham wrote to me applying for the presentation. He assumed to play on my dear's father's name.

Darcy confided to Elizabeth how he chose to refuse Mr. Wickham's request, knowing him to be a man of discredit. He shared the depth of Wickham's abuse of the Darcy name and his revengeful vow. It now came time to share Georgiana's story with Elizabeth. This part would be more difficult to write because it involved someone innocent.

But last summer he was again most painfully obtruded on my notice. I must now mention a circumstance which I would wish to forget myself. Having said thus much, I feel no doubt of your secrecy. My sister, who is more than ten years my junior, was left to the guardianship of my mother's nephew, Colonel Fitzwilliam, and myself. About a year ago she was taken from school to Ramsgate; and thither also went Mr. Wickham, undoubtedly by design; for there proved to have been a prior acquaintance between him and Mrs. Younge, my sister's companion, in whose character we were most unhappily deceived. Georgiana was persuaded to believe herself in love with the man and to consent to an elopement. She was then but fifteen.

Darcy recounted how he discovered Mr. Wickham's duplicity and how Georgiana grieved for offending a brother to whom she looked up to as a father. She also pined for what she perceived as lost love. Mrs. Younge was dismissed at once, and Mr. Wickham, having been foiled in his plans, left the place with haste.

Mr. Wickham's chief object was unquestionably my sister's fortune, which is thirty thousand pounds; but I cannot help supposing that the hope of revenging himself on me was a strong inducement. His revenge would have been complete indeed. This, Madam, is a faithful narrative of every event in which we have been concerned together; and if you do not absolutely reject it as false, you will, I hope, acquit me henceforth of cruelty toward Mr. Wickham.

Darcy finished the letter by excusing Elizabeth for being fooled by Wickham's falsehoods. He offered Colonel Fitzwilliam as a witness to the truth of his plea. He would ask his cousin to confide in Elizabeth his knowledge of the events if she so wished. He finished with,

I shall endeavor to find some opportunity of putting this letter in your hands in the course of the morning. I will only add, God bless you.

Fitzwilliam Darcy

It was over; he did all he could do to change Elizabeth's opinion of his worth. He would return to London and then to Pemberley, and he would try to get on with his life without the hope of earning Elizabeth's love. The depth of his sorrow he would mask in reticence and a perverse hauteur. Now the middle of the night, Darcy's actions exhausted him; howbeit pale and although he tried to convince himself he neither sought nor deserved pity, tears welled in his eyes as he reached to put out the candle. Sometime during the next few hours, he stumbled to the bed and sprawled in despair upon it. Sleep came slowly; abhorring the self-indulgence of his loss, he summoned defiance and accepted blame.

The light of a new day streamed in through the window as Darcy dressed; he wrote Elizabeth three pages in a very close hand and sealed it with the Darcy insignia; now he must see her one last time and implore Elizabeth to read it through. He hoped she would stay with her routine and choose to walk her favorite path. Darcy waited along a section of the trail where he might espy Elizabeth before she knew he was there. After a wait of five and thirty minutes, he saw her approach. Darcy's heart leapt from his chest when she hesitated at seeing him there, but he steadied himself and approached her respectfully and formally.

"Miss Elizabeth, I have been walking in the grove for some time in hope of meeting you. Would you do me the honor of reading this letter?" Then he handed her the message he wrote and made his parting obeisance, walking away briskly. However, he could not resist the urge to stop and look at her one last time; she filled his senses, and tears came to his eyes again; finally, he turned and left her there.

Returning to Rosings, Darcy found his cousin alone in the morning room enjoying a second helping of the breakfast repast. "Edward," Darcy's voice came out heavier than he intended. "I am glad to find you without company at this time. I have something for which I must beg your assistance."

The brusque manner in which Darcy spoke surprised Edward. "Pray tell me there is nothing wrong with Georgiana."

"There is no fear there, but of what I wish to speak does relate to my sister. May we be seated?"

"Certainly," Edward's concern played across his face, but he gave Darcy his full attention.

Darcy took a deep breath and began slowly. "Edward, there was something I shared with no one about my time in Hertfordshire. George Wickham is stationed with the militia in Meryton, and I was nearly thrown into his company there."

Edward cut in, "Darcy, you jest. Wickham! How can that be? He lacks the discipline for such a life."

"I would not argue with you there, Cousin, but I have other tales to share. Miss Elizabeth's sisters favor the company of officers, and she has been often in Wickham's company. As we both are aware, Wickham has his charms, especially when it comes to the ladies. He filled Miss Elizabeth's head with lies about his relationship with my family; and I, with much deliberation, shared the story of Wickham's betrayal of Georgiana with her." Edward's shock could not be hidden. "I assured Miss Elizabeth you will verify my story; would you please make yourself available to her if she so wishes? Elizabeth respects your worth."

"Darcy!" Edward exclaimed, "Are you sure Miss Elizabeth can be trusted with Georgiana's future?"

"Implicitly," came his simple response.

"If you say so, Cousin," Edward shook his head. "Elizabeth Bennet must be a remarkable woman for you to risk Georgiana's reputation as such."

Darcy did not answer; he feared his heart would betray him if he spoke of Elizabeth's worth.

Before taking their leave of Rosings, Darcy and Edward called upon the Parsonage to pay their respects. Elizabeth did not return from her walk, and Darcy was not sure whether he rejoiced at the idea or whether he trembled from the anticipation of her return. He had no pretense to hold him there so he bid the Collinses adieu and left his respects for Elizabeth with them. Edward waited upon her return for nearly an hour, but Elizabeth, evidently, did not desire his proof for Darcy's secret; he, too, bid those at Hunsford a fond farewell. Joining Darcy, Edward took time to appease their aunt and lingered some time with Anne before stepping into the carriage to return to London and his military duty. *At least,* thought Darcy, *Edward has something to distract him;* Darcy was not sure anything could make him forget Elizabeth Bennet.

CHAPTER 10

"The folly which he must have witnessed . . ."

Darcy stayed in London for less than a fortnight, but he did not spend his time well. He roamed from room-to-room at Kensington Place, standing for hours staring out the window or sitting at his desk, his work left unattended; nothing gave him pleasure. Although Georgiana joined him at his London home, Darcy was still alone, wanting no one's company, their conversations limited to the barest of civilities. His sister knew nothing of his pain, and she took on a countenance laced with guilt; however, Darcy took no notice of Georgiana's believing she disappointed him. Being lost unto himself, he did not see her apprehension.

Edward, at Georgiana's insistence, joined them for dinner one evening to assess his cousin's change of demeanor. Darcy's haggard looks shocked Edward, and Darcy's reserve, even with his relatives, created an unclear picture of what his cousin thought. "Fitz," Edward began tentatively, "I thought you might want to know Miss Elizabeth is in town."

Darcy's whole being reflected his discomposure at his cousin's tidings. He forced himself to swallow and to sound uninterested. "Miss Elizabeth, you say? Pray tell where you might have encountered her in London."

"I did not speak to her directly. She, Miss Lucas, another young lady, and an older couple were in a drapers shop in Pall Mall, near Harding and Howell, last Tuesday. I just finished training some new recruits and was not presentable to greet the rest of her party; I assumed, Cousin, you would know how to reach Miss Bennet here if you so wished."

"I am not that intimate with Miss Elizabeth to know her affairs!" Darcy nearly snapped. He downed a large glass of brandy and softened his tone. "The mercantile district, you say?"

"From the window, I observed that she chose some lace, even going back to it several times, but she did not purchase it," Edward added. "I thought you might be interested."

"Miss Elizabeth is no consequence to me," is what Darcy answered, but the fluttering around his heart belied his words. "Edward, I have some matters to address in my study. Why do you not join Georgiana? She would appreciate company more pleasant than I have been of late." And with that, he left the room.

Several hours later Edward knocked lightly at Darcy's study, but no response came from within. He rapped again before opening the door gingerly; he saw papers all over the floor and Darcy slumped over his desk, the remnants of a glass of brandy clutched tightly in his hand. As he came forward to rouse his cousin, Edward at first thought Darcy slept, but he soon discovered Darcy was clearly inebriated. The colonel had helped more than one of his military acquaintances in similar situations, but to find Darcy so was uncharacteristic. He could not recall of a single time when Fitzwilliam allowed himself to lose control and to take too much drink. For his cousin to be in such a condition concerned the colonel.

"Come, Cousin," he lifted Darcy to his feet, "let me help you to your chambers."

"Ah, Edward," Darcy swayed as he stood. "My good cousin— you know I was very jealous of you—in fact, did you know I wanted to be you?" The words were slurred, and Darcy could barely stand upright.

"Why, Darcy?" Edward positioned his cousin's arm around his shoulder. "You have so much more than I."

"You could have had Elizabeth," slouching, Darcy turned to speak directly to his cousin's face. "She liked your company so much better than she did mine."

Not completely taken by surprise, Edward led Darcy toward an overstuffed chair, which sat close by; he watched Darcy vie for Elizabeth Bennet's attention at Rosings so Edward was aware of his cousin's interest in the woman. What he did not know was the extent of Darcy's regard. With that purpose in mind, he tested Fitzwilliam's feelings. "Miss Elizabeth had her charms, but, as you kindly pointed out, her connections are low; I cannot imagine anyone we know who would align himself with the likes of Elizabeth Bennet. She has nothing to make her a suitable choice."

Deeply intoxicated, but still incensed by Edward's words, Darcy pulled himself up straight and faced his cousin indignantly. "Sir, I will beg you not to speak so of Miss Elizabeth. Your censure is most unwelcome."

Edward's smile went unnoticed by Darcy as the man collapsed into the colonel's arms. "I apologize, Cousin," he began. "Let me call for some coffee, and maybe you can tell me of Elizabeth Bennet's many allurements."

Clinging to Edward, Darcy lurched forward, reaching for the arm of the chair. As he nearly fell into the seat he murmured, "Elizabeth Bennet is an incomparable woman, and I am the last man in the world she could be prevailed upon to marry." Thus said, Darcy passed out from the effort of reaching the chair, but his cousin's disclosure suddenly alerted Edward to Darcy's dilemma. His curiosity piqued, he wanted to know of what his cousin referred; Edward knew Darcy showed some preference for Elizabeth Bennet, but even he did not realize the depth of the relationship.

It took more coffee and more time than anticipated, but Edward, eventually, brought Darcy back to some semblance of his normal self. Darcy sat with his head in his hands, propped on elbows based on his knees. It was very late, but Edward pressed on. "Cousin, we should talk. You have become a shadow of the person you once were; you withdraw from Georgiana and your friends; your work lays untouched upon your desk; and you made a reference to Miss Elizabeth we should address."

Darcy sat up and looked vaguely about him; he reached out and took the coffee cup from the tray on the side table as a ploy to forestall what he must face; he held the cup from which he sipped to his lips and hesitated, trying to get his mind in order. "I guess I owe you some explanation, but I am not sure I can speak the words."

"It is Georgiana to whom you owe an explanation. Have you not noticed your sister blames herself for your current misery? She believes she disappoints you."

"How is that so?" Darcy began, but he stopped short knowing his conduct of late was contemptible.

"You have fallen for Elizabeth Bennet, have you not?"

"Am I that obvious?" Darcy asked reluctantly.

"Fitz, we have been more like brothers than even my own brother is to me." Darcy chuckled as he acknowledged Edward's words. "I knew before we journeyed to Rosings your interest in Elizabeth Bennet was more than a passing fancy. When the great Fitzwilliam Darcy mentions a woman twice, I notice. When he mentions her repeatedly, I know something is amiss."

"Miss Elizabeth thinks nothing of me; she said as much when I offered her everything I had."

"Elizabeth Bennet refused you? This cannot be. You are perfect for each other; she makes you laugh, Fitz; no one has ever made you laugh." Darcy smiled at the image. "Darcy, you must tell me what happened?"

"Mr. Wickham poisoned her mind to me. I am lost to her," Darcy nearly moaned. "Plus, in my pomposity, I tried to control things over which I should have taken no notice. I wronged Elizabeth by hurting her sister."

"How could you have hurt Elizabeth's sister?"

"Do you remember my bragging about separating Bingley from an inappropriate connection?"

"Not Elizabeth's sister?"

"Unfortunately," Darcy nodded.

"Darcy," Edward's realization shot across his face, "I fear she heard of this from me. No wonder she suddenly took ill that day in the park."

"Do not worry yourself, Cousin. I realized from whom she heard the news before we left her at Rosings; Elizabeth would have discovered my deceit sooner or later; she is a clever woman. Elizabeth settled against me before I convinced Bingley to leave Netherfield; I treated her poorly, and then professed my love for her; my duplicity only encouraged her contempt for me."

"Then I am to assume you actually offered Miss Elizabeth your hand in marriage?" astonishment covered Edward.

"Well," Darcy hesitated, "I did request Miss Elizabeth's assent, but I fear I did not articulate my feelings well. I planned what I wished to say, but in her presence, my mind could not recall the words I wanted her to know."

Edward chuckled, "What, may I ask, did you say?"

"I explained the torment of my decision, my qualms about her lack of connections, and the impropriety shown by her family ..."

Edward laughed loudly as he filled his cousin's cup. "Only you, Cousin, would tell a woman you loved her by telling her how repugnant you found her family to be. Is it not surprising Elizabeth did not find this to be endearing?"

Darcy blushed, recognizing his foolishness; what seemed so reasonable at the time now played as absurdly insipient. A sough escaped his throat indicating the sorrow of his struggle, and he again buried his face in his hands. "It appears," he said at last, "I have been a simpleton when it comes to Elizabeth Bennet; my folly does not speak well of my intentions, does it?"

"Men, in love, are often foolhardy," Edward added quietly. "Let us finish this tomorrow, Darcy. Do you think you can make it to your chambers now?"

Darcy nodded his compliance. The colonel rang for Henry's assistance, and together they got the master into his bed. Henry left to prepare a room for Edward. Thinking Darcy's labored breathing indicated he slept at last, Edward moved quietly to the door to take his leave. With his speech muffled by the pillow in which he buried his face, his cousin called out from the bed, "Edward, which shop in the mercantile district did Miss Elizabeth frequent?"

"There is no need for concern, Cousin; I am way ahead of you," he chuckled knowingly, "I will send a servant around tomorrow for the lace; some day you will give it to Miss Elizabeth yourself."

Darcy's arm waved his acceptance, and Edward slipped from the room.

Breakfast came late at Kensington Place, but neither Darcy nor the colonel cared. Both men had affairs of the heart with which to worry.

"Well, Darcy, where do you go from here?"

The words choked him. "I know my duty; the Darcy name and Pemberley must survive; I must forget Elizabeth Bennet and find a suitable match. I am a rich man, and I will settle on an appropriate woman as soon as I am tempted by her charms; I am now ready to marry with all speed; I have a heart ready to accept the regard of the first pleasing woman to come my way." *Excepting Elizabeth Bennet. This was his only secret exception to his declarations.* "A woman with a little beauty and some words of flattery will have me as her own, whether she be fifteen or thirty or somewhere in between. I am perfectly ready to make a foolish match."

"Then you mean to have our cousin Anne?" Edward had difficulty saying the words for he feared Darcy's response.

"As much as I respect and admire Anne," Darcy said seriously, "she is not the woman I envision as the mistress of Pemberley. Despite Lady Catherine's wishes, Anne will not be the object of my search even after Elizabeth's refusal. The woman I want will possess a handsome countenance, a lilt figure, and a quickness of mind. I must find a woman who can help me run Pemberley; her character must be an adventurous one; she may not be easily intimidated. I may choose to settle for something a bit less, but I will not compromise my standards; I thought about this for a long time."

Edward let out a ragged sigh of relief, which caught Darcy off guard. "What troubles you, Edward?" he asked finally quitting his own revelry and giving his cousin full note.

"I," Edward stammered, "I wish to marry Anne." Edward's eyes came slowly to face Darcy head on.

Initially stunned, Darcy did not take long to realize he should have recognized Anne's interest in Edward; she always enjoyed Edward's company more; Anne said as much to him at Rosings. "Your confession took me by surprise, Edward, but upon reflection, I realize you were always the person for Anne. I wish you well if Anne is your desire."

"We cannot address Lady Catherine until you marry, Darcy," Edward stated. "Our aunt would never agree as long as there is a possibility of your changing your mind. I will never convince Anne to stand up to her mother until she knows Lady Catherine will have no other choice but to agree. My happiness hinges on you, Fitz."

"I shall not change my mind, Edward, but our aunt can be stubborn. Although you wish me to expedite my choice, please allow me some time to choose wisely."

"Of course, Darcy," Edward blustered, "your happiness is our utmost desire. We will not push you into making a poor decision just to satisfy our own hopes; you are, after all, our cousin, and we wish your life to be filled with love. I believe I will go, Fitz; give Georgiana my love. I will check with you in a few days."

So saying, the colonel left the room. Darcy sat for some minutes contemplating the events of the past two days. Admitting his love for Elizabeth he hoped would allow him to move on; the madness would no longer consume him, and he could once again set about being Fitzwilliam Darcy, the master of Pemberley. He had only one other thing to clear up before he began his life anew so Darcy sought his sister.

He found Georgiana in the music room listlessly stroking the keys of the pianoforte; she sprang to her feet when he entered the room. He strode over to her purposely, took her hand, and said, "Come with me, Georgiana; we need to talk." She tentatively followed him as he led her to the settee; they sat down together, but he never released her hands. She dropped her eyes, afraid to face him, but Darcy cupped her chin gently with his fingers, forcing his sister to look him directly in the face. "Georgiana, my girl," he began, "I have dealt you a disservice, and I beg your forgiveness. You did not deserve the treatment you received from me of late."

Uncontrollably, the tears rolled down his sister's cheeks, and he reached up to gently brush them away; she caught his hand and kissed the palm. "Fitzwilliam, you never forgave any fault of your own while you forgave many of those around you, especially me." He started to protest, but she shushed him with a touch of her finger to his lips. "Please, let me finish. You are always there for me, Fitzwilliam. You accepted my sorry and made it your own. Edward told me of your hope and your loss; now I must be there for you."

"Georgiana, our father left you in my care."

"No, Fitzwilliam," she contradicted him. "Our father left you as my guardian, but we are left to care for each other. How can you hurt so without my feeling it?" Darcy could not believe his sister's transformation; she was still the shy, innocent girl he always cherished, but she had emotional strength of which he was not aware. He could never think of George Wickham's betrayal without loathing, but his sister matured from the experience; she knew the rebukes of love. "Our parents were of superior birth," she continued. "We learned to be proud of being a Darcy, but we have not learned to look at the true worth of others. Mrs. Annesley has given me a 'mother's' look at the world. Fitzwilliam, there are so many who need our help; helping the poor in Derbyshire is persuading me to care about myself. If we do not love ourselves, how can we expect others to love us?"

"When did you become so wise?" he whispered and stroked her hair away from her face.

"You taught me these things, Fitzwilliam. You just never listened to your own lessons," she giggled.

"Today, you are the teacher and I, the student." He pulled her to him and kissed her forehead, holding her next to him for a long time.

Darcy threw himself into London's society, trying to forget Elizabeth Bennet and Hertfordshire. He became a regular at his gentleman's club; he escorted Georgiana to concerts and the theatre; he dined with old acquaintances and made new ones. Yet, try as he may, it was too soon to forget Elizabeth. Darcy knew he could truly love none but her. She could not be replaced in his mind as the woman he was meant to love; he could not believe himself to see her equal. Unconsciously, he allowed himself such thoughts: he would remain constant to Elizabeth; he meant to forget her and believed it to be possible; he imagined himself to have no preferences; but, in reality, he was only angry—angry at her and angry at himself. Her character became fixed in his mind as perfection itself; at Hertfordshire he learnt to do her justice, and at Hunsford he began to understand himself.

In his attempts, attempts of angry pride, to attach himself to another, he felt it to be impossible; he could not forget the perfect excellence of Elizabeth's mind or the way she possessed him. From her he learned the steadiness of principle, and he had to admit to admiring her for standing up to him in favor of George Wickham. Although it hurt him to think she favored Wickham's side of the story, Darcy finally recognized if he opened himself up to her before he did, Wickham would not have stood a chance of addressing Elizabeth. His desire to protect Bingley was not really protection at all or else he could not have abandoned those same objections to secure his own happiness. Darcy could not be happy without Elizabeth, and he could not see Charles with Jane Bennet and not think of what he lost. He told himself he wished to protect Charles, but now he realized he wished only to protect himself.

Eventually, Darcy realized if he yielded to what he thought to be his duty and married a woman indifferent to himself, all risk would be incurred and all duty violated. So, after a month of futile attempts, he and Georgiana prepared for an early return to Pemberley. Both felt the solitude of home would allow them time to refocus; Darcy would take care of his estate and wait for acceptance to come; Georgiana would continue her maturation; together they would safeguard each other's love.

A few evenings before their departure, Edward returned to Kensington Place; he traveled to Bath and then to Brighton; the military buildup kept him busy preparing the troops. He and Darcy lingered in the dining room while Georgiana and Mrs. Annesley prepared to entertain them in the music room.

"Am I to understand you have been in Kent again, Edward?" Darcy asked pouring them both a brandy.

"Indeed," his cousin began. "I expect to be away for several months; I wished to bid Anne a farewell; of course, that is difficult when our aunt is in attendance, but she does leave us to our own *diversions* occasionally."

Darcy smiled and nodded his approval. "I am happy my absence from Kent benefits you, Cousin."

"When you marry, Lady Catherine will lose control of Anne; she will not be pleased," Edward lamented.

"What will not please her, Edward," Darcy stated, "is not losing Anne but the loss of Rosings Park. She will become Dowager de Bourgh. Surely, you thought of that."

"My interest in Anne is not Rosings," he sounded a bit offended.

Darcy warranted, "You told me once you needed to marry for money, but you wanted love also; I assumed you found both in Anne."

Edward accepted Darcy's insights as a means to settle what tension lay between them. "I do bring news from Kent, but I dare not speak of someone of interest there," Edward ventured.

Darcy fixed his countenance, hoping to not belie his interest in the subject. "Edward, you may speak Elizabeth Bennet's name; I cannot avoid her forever; my best friend has an estate in Hertfordshire; her best friend is married to Lady Catherine's cleric; I must harden myself to her memory and my former feelings."

Edward still hesitated about telling Darcy what he knew. "Anne shared some news of Miss Elizabeth. We were having our own amusement at Mr. Collins's expense, I am afraid." Darcy rolled his eyes at Collins's name. "Did you know, Fitzwilliam, prior to marrying Charlotte Lucas, Mr. Collins proposed to Elizabeth? Evidently, that was the day after Mr. Bingley's ball at Netherfield." Just the mention of the ball brought exquisite memories to Darcy; holding Elizabeth's hand and looking into her eyes were some of his fondest memories of her. "Miss Elizabeth's mother demanded she save the family estate by marrying Collins; her father refused and supported his daughter's not accepting. The estate is entailed to Collins, it seems. We wondered how Collins came to marry Charlotte Lucas—it is all so clear now. Can you imagine Elizabeth Bennet's vitality in the hands of a superfluous ass such as Collins?"

He tried to play it off as nothing, but the thought of Collins kissing Elizabeth and taking husbandly privileges with her caused Darcy to redden with abhorrence; a shudder of disdain racked his body, and even a large shot of brandy did not deaden the distaste filling his judgment. Georgiana's musical interlude was as superb as ever, but all Darcy could see were Elizabeth's eyes and smile and then the horrifying image of Mr. Collins placing his arms around Elizabeth and preparing to kiss her.

The month they spent at Pemberley brought both Darcys some peace. Georgiana called on the tenants and helped the new rector administer to the villages surrounding the estate. Darcy rode out on Cerberus daily, usually with his steward, Mr. Howard. The siblings walked the paths surrounding the lake, read, and reenergized. They were to meet Bingley in London the first week of July; Bingley's sisters and Mr. Hurst were to join them in London, and they all would return to Pemberley for several weeks. The Bingleys would then travel on to Mr. Hurst's estate for the rest of the summer.

Walking arm-in-arm through the rose garden, Georgiana smiled up at her brother. "I know it is not practical, but I wish we could remain here forever. I hate to be away from Pemberley."

"Pemberley flows through our veins; it is the source of our life. I, like you, cannot imagine any place more beautiful," he said. They walked on in silence.

Each evening, in the privacy of his chambers, Darcy replayed his time with Elizabeth; he pictured her at Pemberley so many times, but the knowledge of how his prideful behavior placed him in disfavor with the lady laced his reproofs. He assumed Elizabeth would accept his proposal; it never occurred to him she would not *settle* for security. Collins could give her a pleasant home and living, but she wanted more. He offered her *more money*, but that was not what would earn Elizabeth's love. Elizabeth could not love a man she could not respect; therefore, she did not love him. Brought up in opulence, he learned superiority at his father's knee; had he not been warned repeatedly of those who would flatter him to become an intimate? When he remembered his time with Elizabeth, Darcy saw himself as proud and leaden. Elizabeth accused him of not only arrogance but of conceit and disdain for others.

He often wondered how he would feel if someone spoke to Georgiana as he spoke to Elizabeth. Even if he and Georgiana had no more than what Elizabeth had to offer, Darcy knew he would have called the dastard out, and a duel would have ensued. His place in the world had been unthreatened until there was Elizabeth; now he became more pensive and introspective—his life a quandary—he wanted to once more try to make Elizabeth a part of his life. He wanted to show her he changed, but first, Darcy would need what his sister said; he would have to find value in himself; he would alter how he spoke to people and how he thought of people and how he treated people. If he could do so without *glory*, but because it was the right action, then maybe he could someday present himself to Elizabeth Bennet again.

So, the transformation of Fitzwilliam Darcy began. Always undeniably attractive, he possessed an air of confidence and an aristocratic demeanor; Darcy could command a room just by walking into it. Even still, he never knew himself until he encountered Elizabeth Bennet. He questioned so many things about his life now. Why had he, for example, never recognized Georgiana as an intelligent, benevolent young woman? His often-shy sister, he recently discovered, had a hidden strength, strength of character others saw as pride or naïveté. Georgiana Darcy possessed so much more than sweetness and beauty; she possessed a superior intellect, a loving heart, and an open mind.

Why had Darcy not recognized his own nature? He had Pemberley; he had respect; he had wealth, but Darcy did not have contentment. He knew he could find another woman with whom he could share tenderness and even moments of passion; but, much to his frustration, Darcy knew Elizabeth was his other half; with Elizabeth Bennet he could share his innermost self. She charged him to be a better person than he was; even without her by his side, Fitzwilliam Darcy would be attentive to her rebukes and live up to her accolades.

The deception to which he exposed Charles Bingley created an issue he needed to address immediately. When he saw Bingley again in London, he would observe his friend; if Charles still felt strongly for Jane Bennet, Darcy would move heaven and earth to bring them together. It would probably cost Darcy his friendship with Charles, but his comfort was secondary to Charles's happiness.

Bingley came to stay at Kensington Place; he had the same easy manner, but something was missing. Darcy originally hoped Bingley and Georgiana would find each other, but although they got along well enough, no romantic attraction ever developed. Bingley's heart, like Darcy's, was lost to a country miss in Hertfordshire.

Somehow, Darcy must ascertain whether Jane Bennet found another suitor; if Elizabeth turned to George Wickham and the younger sisters to other officers, it would be possible for Miss Bennet to have found someone else in these last five months. Briefly, Darcy allowed himself to think of the possibility of George

Wickham's embracing Elizabeth; the pain of it crushed his soul. He could possibly accept Elizabeth's finding happiness with another because for him her happiness would be the utmost, but if that person was George Wickham, he did not think he could survive the injustice of it all. Then again, maybe his letter impacted her thoughts on Wickham. He could not allow himself to think of having a chance with Elizabeth; he must accept the inevitable. Putting those thoughts aside, Darcy returned to his first concern, the future of Charles Bingley and Jane Bennet. Without their reconciliation, Elizabeth would forever consider him to not be a "gentleman"; she would never find forgiveness.

He considered hiring someone to secure the information in Meryton, but he quickly realized how foolish that would be. If he needed information on the Bennet family, a reliable source could be found on his aunt's estate; surely Mr. Collins could be manipulated into providing the necessary facts. Darcy would wait; if Bingley's interest in Miss Bennet persisted, he would find a way to return his friend to Netherfield.

CHAPTER 11

"If she does not help him on . . ."

———◦◦◦———

"Bingley," Darcy began, "the club will be a nice diversion this evening; do you not think?"

"If you say so, Darcy."

"You do not seem to find pleasure in it though."

"The club will be," Bingley paused, "amusing enough."

"What is it, Bingley? Let me be of service to you."

Bingley sighed, "It is nothing . . . It is just . . . I cannot really explain it."

Darcy watched as his best friend turned away and was lost in his own reverie; he knew what Bingley felt; he felt it himself at least once per day since that fateful autumn night in Meryton. The empathy Darcy felt for Bingley increased his own pain. He did Bingley a disservice, one he would rectify.

"Your sisters will arrive in London tomorrow?" Darcy began again. "When do you anticipate leaving for Pemberley?"

"My sisters expressed an interest to be at my brother Hurst's estate by late-August. Of course, Caroline would hear nothing less than spending a fortnight at Pemberley." Bingley left his chair and walked about the room distractedly. "I suppose the first part of next week would be the most logical time. However, as our host, we wait on your happiness."

"Monday next would serve Georgiana and I well," Darcy said. "Is that acceptable to your travel schedule?"

"I will tell my sisters to be prepared for early Monday morning. It will be good to be out of London; the weather is getting sultry."

"As for me," Darcy said wistfully, "I, too, look forward to leaving London. I would be content to spend the rest of my days at Pemberley."

"I hoped," Bingley hesitated, "Netherfield was to instill such longing in me." Darcy waited for his companion to finish his thoughts, but there was no more. Finally, Darcy looked away to avoid the hurt evident in Bingley's eyes.

On his last evening at Kensington Place before returning to Pemberley, Darcy reflected on the past ten months. Before Elizabeth, he thought his life was perfect; he lived well by the standard of the day, but he knew so little about what was important in life. Now he understood how to love, but it was too late to give his love to Elizabeth; however, the things he learned would give him the chance to learn to love again. Darcy realized he spent his whole life trying to replicate his father, but he lost himself along the way. His father, unknowingly, formed his son in his own image, but his father lived in another lifetime. Darcy became a shadow of his father's greatness for he forgot giving service to someone did not mean the person was one's servant. From his mother, he learned about tradition and duty to family. She gave him his identity; his name Fitzwilliam came from a line of noble earls, and his father's name of Darcy came from a respectable, honorable, and ancient family. She gave him a conscious awareness of his own social position.

From Georgiana, he learned courage, as well as humility, and even though she had doubts at times, his sister achieved a sense of independence, a palatable truth hidden behind a façade of shyness. Her gentle chastisement to him forced Darcy to look at the society to which he was born with the same discerning eye he often used on others.

Elizabeth showed him his ideas on the state of marriage were insignificant ramblings. It was not man's inevitable fate; instead marriage was a complex blend of spirits, each needing respect and acceptance to flourish. Elizabeth challenged Darcy; unlike other women, she never flattered his ego, and with Elizabeth he learned to not assume anything. For Elizabeth, he abandoned thoughts of his own well-being; protecting and loving her would have been a privilege.

When Elizabeth first refused him, Darcy blamed everyone but himself. Mr. Wickham poisoned her mind; the Bennets' inferior society created problems; his honest report offended her; his cousin misspoke. All these and many more served as excuses for her behavior, but, finally, he faced the deficiencies in his character, which she enumerated at Hunsford. She gave him a more equal relationship with his sister; her words brought him to an understanding of what he should value in his life. He had been too proud; he had been too confident; Darcy had been too concerned with his own reputation to truly love anyone, as *real love* requires. Although memories of his loss shaped mortifications of self-revelation, they no longer frightened or confused him. The disorder of his mind no longer forced him to struggle to master his faults; instead, he discovered acceptance and a truthful resolve—the advantage of intimately knowing his own nature.

Darcy, Georgiana, Mrs. Annesley, and Bingley traveled to Pemberley under the Darcy livery while the Bingley sisters and Mr. Hurst made the journey in an accompanying carriage. Darcy preferred to travel on horseback or alone in his own carriage; he absolutely hated having to stop every few hours or so for Caroline to "stretch her legs." Since his return from Hunsford, he avoided interacting with Caroline; if it were not for his regard for Bingley, Caroline would be relegated to a bowing-only acquaintance. The distance between Darcy's house in London and Pemberley could comfortably be covered in two days even with the coaches laden with multiple trunks, which were principally owned by the Bingley sisters. Mr. Hurst used his largest coach while Darcy made use of a slightly smaller one, which would seat four comfortably. The hours crawled by in cordial civilities; Bingley's sonsy nature appealed to all, and the conversations centered mostly on music and literature and occasionally on the politics of the day. The party broke for a midday meal at one of Darcy's favorite inns before proceeding on to where they would rest for the evening, an establishment some miles more than equidistant between London and their destination.

The condition of the road was deplorable between some of the villages, and they were about five miles from their evening's stop when Hurst's coach came to an abrupt halt. Darcy's driver noted the problem and pulled up the horses. Everyone disembarked to find the crank neck of Hurst's coach broken in two. If Darcy brought his larger coach, the problem would have been easier to resolve, but the party would need to squeeze together to make it to the next village, where the crank neck needed to be addressed. The coach would still operate without the crank neck, but it would be a bumpy trip.

Mrs. Hurst and Caroline shuffled into Darcy's coach, and Mr. Hurst crawled into the seat of the driver's box. Darcy and Bingley moved as many trunks as possible to the benches inside Hurst's coach to avoid losing any of them. Darcy climbed into the driver's box with Hurst's man; the rest of the day's trip would be slow and uncomfortable, but they would arrive safely. Bingley and Darcy, upon their arrival, made arrangement for the repair, but the trip would be delayed until it was finished.

Over the evening meal, Darcy explained he would leave them the next day, taking a horse from the local stable for the trip. The group protested, asking him not to leave. "Bingley, when we discussed our leaving on Monday, it was because of pressing business I had to address with my steward," he explained. "By taking my leave early, I may be rid of the business before you arrive, giving me more time to be a congenial host."

"I understand," Bingley began. "We are being selfish by wishing you to remain with us."

Darcy simply nodded, indicating their fraternity; there was no comment necessary. He knew Bingley loved his sisters but often found their company to be trying; he took sympathy on both his friend and on Georgiana when he said, "Bingley, I charge you with delivering my sister safely to Pemberley. As my friend, I trust you with her care."

Both Bingley and Georgiana gave him a sigh of relief; his charge to Bingley in front of the rest of the party gave them both a reason to spend their time in each other's company and as traveling companions. No one would question their choosing to do so; it relieved both of them of having to share Caroline's company. Bingley's response was almost too enthusiastic, and Georgiana mouthed "Thank you" to him when no one else looked her way.

Georgiana joined him for a light breakfast before his departure. "I envy your ride this morning, Brother," she teased. "I wish my escape was so easily achieved."

"At least," he grinned, "Charles will be *devoted* to you today."

"I thank you again for that, Fitzwilliam."

"I will see you at Pemberley tomorrow, my Dearest," he took Georgiana into his arms and gently kissed her forehead. "By addressing my business with Mr. Howard today, I can be at your disposal tomorrow."

"Be safe, Sir," she pushed his hair out of his eyes. "It is just we two. I will plan our time at Pemberley carefully," she laughed.

Darcy gave her one last hug and left the inn. The sun burned off the morning dew as he mounted the horse he secured from the stable. He would prefer Cerberus, but to be alone in the saddle delighted him. He turned the animal toward Pemberley and rode away; he stopped several times to rest the horse, not sure of the animal's dependability. He stayed to the roads until he drew closer to Pemberley; by taking the rolling hills surrounding the parkland, he knew he could save valuable time; plus, the prospect of the house coming from the far side of the lake always took his breath away. No one on the estate expected him until late evening and being alone on his lands brought him peace.

He rode into his stables at midmorning, scattering servants

surprised to see the master. The ride left Darcy covered in road dust and perspiration, but he dismounted the horse with the self-confidence he always displayed. Handing over the reins, Mr. Howard's approach from the back of the house startled Darcy.

"Mr. Darcy, Sir, we did not expect you until later today at the earliest," he stammered.

"The rest of the party will arrive tomorrow," he offered, shaking hands with his steward. "I hoped we could address our business later this afternoon; then I can be at my sister's disposal to help with our guests."

"Yes, Sir," Mr. Howard offered. "Whenever you are ready, Sir."

"I will send word once I freshen my clothing," Darcy turned toward the house.

"Mr. Darcy, Sir," Mr. Howard continued, "Mrs. Reynolds reports there are visitors in the main house."

"Visitors—I will try to avoid them. Thank you, Mr. Howard," Darcy stared toward the house trying to see where the visitors might currently be. "I am not quite attired for social calls, am I?"

"No, Sir," Mr. Howard mumbled.

Darcy thought the visitors would still be in the main corridors of the house so he followed the road from behind the stables to make a side entrance. Coming forward from the road, he encountered the visitors standing on the lawn leading down to the stream; they still looked toward the house, and, at first, he thought he would step back into the bushes until they passed him by when his eyes alighted on a figure he many times envisioned standing in this exact place; it was Elizabeth, and she was within twenty yards of him. His heart leapt at the sight of her, and Darcy momentarily froze. Her eyes met his, and they both blushed with the initial embarrassment of seeing each other for the first time since he left her at Hunsford.

Darcy's prayer was answered; Elizabeth was here at Pemberley, and he had a second chance. He recovered quickly and advanced to where her party stood; she instinctively turned away from him, but when he called her name, she stopped and received his greetings. Although not as composed as he wanted to be at that moment, Darcy made a point of speaking calmly and with civility. "Miss Elizabeth, what a surprise to find you at Pemberley," he blurted out while trying to steady his voice and his composure. He made her the obligatory bow, but he could not take his eyes from her face. It had been months since he had seen her, and he *had* to observe how she reacted to his presence.

Blushing, she curtsied and addressed him, her voice more composed than his. Elizabeth did not raise her eyes but said, "Mr. Darcy, we understood you were away."

"No, no, I am not," he answered as evenly as his composure would allow.

Elizabeth did not respond; obviously, her embarrassment was intense; she was a woman who was never at a loss for words. Darcy realized how she must feel at his finding her at Pemberley; she would *never* be here if she thought he was here. He had to let her know her choosing to come to *his* house pleased him. "I returned early; I have business with my steward. None of the household staff knew of my change of plans."

"Your housekeeper assured us of as much," she nearly whispered.

"Forgive me," he said haltingly, "are your parents in health?"

She half smiled, "They are, Sir. Thank you for asking."

The start of the smile sent his mind spinning with hope for some renewal of their acquaintance. She continued to be embarrassed, but no disdain showed in her being.

"And your sisters are in health, too?"

"They were, Sir, when we left Longbourn," her voice had more volume.

"How long have you been in Derbyshire?" he must keep her talking; Darcy could not walk away from her.

"Two days," she stumbled over the words.

"Your parents are in health?" he chuckled at his own discomposure. "Where are you staying?" *Oh, God, should he have said that?*

"In Lambton—at the Royal Crown," her uneasiness still

remained. She lifted her eyes briefly to him, evidently still expecting him to take some sort of revenge for their last meeting, but Darcy's mind was more pleasantly engaged. "We should not have disturbed your privacy, Mr. Darcy," she faltered. "I can only offer my apologies."

"Miss Elizabeth," he stammered through the words, "you are always welcome at Pemberley." He wanted to say more, but he realized how his unkempt appearance must betray the sedateness he hoped to present. "Please enjoy the grounds at your leisure." With that, he made his bow and left her standing on the lawn.

He walked away quickly knowing once he propelled himself forward, he could not stop. If he paused even briefly, Darcy thought his legs would buckle under him. *Elizabeth was here at Pemberley.* If Hurst's carriage had not broken down, Darcy would still be in a village twenty miles away keeping Caroline Bingley company. Instead, he had a chance, although slim it may be, to show Elizabeth Bennet he learned from her accusations; Darcy was not the same man she refused at Hunsford.

Entering Pemberley, he took the staircase two steps at a time. He knew not what he would do, but he knew he must engage Elizabeth again before she left the grounds. Servants rushed about as he barked out orders for fresh water to be brought up to his dressing area immediately. He luckily sent Henry ahead last evening with some of the trunks to lighten the load of both coaches. He prayed as he ascended the stairs he would find Henry and fresh clothing awaiting him in his chambers.

At the top of the stairs, Darcy nearly ran into Mrs. Reynolds. "Mr. Darcy," she exclaimed. "You were not expected."

He did not acknowledge her remark, but he made his inquiry. "Mrs. Reynolds, the visitors—were they treated well?"

"Yes, Sir, I showed them the house myself."

"Send word to the gardener to delay their leaving as long as possible. I wish to greet them properly," he rushed by her.

"The young lady said she was an *acquaintance,*" the housekeeper added as he started toward his chambers.

Darcy stopped dead in his tracks. "Did she say anything else, Mrs. Reynolds? I mean—about me?"

"She agreed she found you to be handsome," she looked at the young master questionably. His contrary behavior to expectations made her unsure whether what she said was appropriate. "And she spent some time looking at your portrait in the gallery, returning to it several times. I thought that was unusual. Should I have not shared those areas with her party?"

Darcy's smile unmistakably showed his happiness. "Mrs. Reynolds, the young lady should *always* be welcomed at Pemberley." Then he turned and rushed off to his chambers.

"Henry, I am glad you are here," he called to his valet.

"Mr. Darcy," the man hesitated, "what do you desire, Sir?"

"I want fresh clothes, Henry. There are visitors on the grounds I want to greet properly. I must be quick. They are acquaintances from my time in Hertfordshire."

The man set about helping his master off with his boots as warm water was brought in for Darcy's bath. "The water is only warm, Sir—not hot."

"It will do, Henry. Please hurry."

"Yes, Sir," Henry snapped into action, and in less than half an hour, Darcy exited one of Pemberley's side doors and headed toward the parkland. *Elizabeth!* Somehow Darcy must show her, as if she did not already know, the power she had over him. He was affectionately attached to her and would never see a woman whom he thought her equal, but he must not rush things. However, he had but a limited time; she may not be in Lambton long. One of the gardener's apprentices pointed the way the visitors took, and Darcy set out toward an abrupt rise. The apprentice apprised him of the whereabouts of the visitors; they entered the woods and ascended some of the higher ground and neared part of the stream. Darcy knew the gardener would lead them around the outskirts of the area; he would cut across the less traveled pathways to intercept them.

As he approached, he noted Elizabeth tried to compose herself; he saw the setting of her shoulders and the raising of her chin. There would be no more surprise for either of them for each had had a few moments of preparation since he left her on the lawn. His emotions felt the gamut of sensations; there was pleasure, pain, agitation, delight, and even a bit of misery. For her, it was obviously purely embarrassment—not disdain or contempt—just embarrassment at being found by him at his estate.

"Mr. Darcy," she began, "Pemberley is *delightful* and *charming.*" Suddenly, she stopped as quickly as she began. At first, this confused Darcy, but then he saw the "horror" flash upon her face; she feared he might think her motive might be to regain his favor with praise of his home.

It amazed him to think she did not know he would give anything to be pursued by her. He assigned importance to her opinion so he asked, "Then you approve?"

Elizabeth blushed. "What type of person would not approve of such a home? It is so well situated—I never saw such an estate."

"Your opinion is valued, Miss Elizabeth," he said earnestly. His voice betrayed his anxiousness and the intensity he felt; yet, he maintained an elevated politeness, which seemed to confuse her. "Miss Elizabeth," he faltered, "please excuse my manners—would you do me the honor of introducing me to the rest of your party?"

He detected a hint of a smile as she moved past him. "Mr. Darcy, may I present my aunt and uncle, Mr. and Mrs. Gardiner. My sister Jane stayed with them on her recent trip to London."

Darcy, a bit astonished, had taken the couple for people of fashion. He understood her hint of a smile; these were the same people he criticized at Hunsford. Although the folly of his earlier opinion stunned him, he did not turn away as she obviously suspected he might do. Instead, to her surprise, he began to walk with them and to converse with her uncle. Admittedly, he did not expect Mr. Gardiner to be the man of intelligence, taste, and good manners he was, and he did not expect to notice "hints" of his own father in the man's phrasing and gestures. He discovered he enjoyed the short-lived conversation with Elizabeth's uncle, and as they came up on the stream, Mr. Gardiner paused to observe the trout. "Mr. Gardiner, do you enjoy fishing?" he asked cordially.

"Indeed I do, Sir."

"Then please feel free to fish the stream, or the lake, for that matter, at any time you choose. I will have my man furnish you with tackle; let me point out some of my favorite spots." He led her uncle toward the stream and began to point out secluded alcoves for the sport. "I hope you will fish at Pemberley before you leave the area." Darcy could feel Elizabeth's gaze upon him; his actions a compliment to her earlier censure of his manners, he hoped she saw the changes. Curious about some water plant, Elizabeth and Mrs. Gardiner walked down to the brink of the river while Darcy spent his time with Mr. Gardiner, but as luck would have it, Mrs. Gardiner found Elizabeth's arm inadequate support when they turned back toward their carriage.

Mrs. Gardiner turned to her husband for his arm, allowing Darcy the luxury of taking a position next to Elizabeth. They walked on in silence with the lady speaking first. "Mr. Darcy, again I must apologize for disturbing your privacy. Your housekeeper informed us that you would certainly not be here until tomorrow. Indeed, before we left Bakewell, we were informed you were in London and not in Derbyshire at all. I feel horrible at your having found us here; it seems so inappropriate; my aunt had her heart set on showing me Pemberley, and I had no way of denying her that pleasure without a complicated explanation." Neither of them wanted to openly discuss their last conversation so they talked in circles without acknowledging the obvious.

"Miss Elizabeth," he started, "please do not stress over my finding you here. I am pleased to see you again. As I said before, business with my steward precipitated my coming forward a few hours before the rest of my party." At this point, he hesitated, but he knew some reference to their acquaintances could not be avoided forever. "Among those who travel from London with me are several of whom you are familiar—Mr. Bingley and his sisters."

Elizabeth lowered her eyes but gave a slight nod of the head as an acknowledgment of what he said. Darcy worried about the images of Bingley's name besetting her. There were scenes of their time in Hunsford such as the sharing of his mother's favorite walk, which brought them both joy, but there were also moments of pain, which affected their ease with each other even now. Yet, Darcy felt the pain softening, and he hoped for friendship and reconciliation; anything beyond that was a distant dream. They walked on, both embarrassed by the realization of their folly.

After a pause, he continued, "There is also one other person in the party who more particularly wishes to be known to you. Will you allow me, or do I ask too much, to introduce my sister to your acquaintance during your stay at Lambton?"

Although her voice came out in not much more than a whisper, Elizabeth acceded to his request, "Mr. Darcy, I would be honored to meet Miss Darcy." Whether she realized it or not, Elizabeth agreed to be in his company again; Darcy's happiness could barely be contained.

Silence prevailed with each of them deep in thought. Elizabeth still did not appear to be comfortable, but the tension eased. There was so much he wanted to tell her, but he simply had to find a way to extend her stay in Derbyshire so the words could all be spoken. At the moment, it was enough that he would see her again, and, finally, Georgiana would meet Elizabeth. They soon outstripped the others, and when they reached the carriage, Mr. and Mrs. Gardiner were nearly a quarter of a mile behind. "Would you care to step in the house, Miss Elizabeth, for some refreshments?" he offered, trying to prolong their time together.

"I am not tired, Mr. Darcy," she started. "I hope it will not offend you if I ask we remain here and enjoy the view."

"Not at all," he responded, finally getting a long look in her eyes. They both wanted to talk about their relationship, but neither knew what the other was thinking; therefore, she, finally began a discourse of her travels, telling him about Matlock and Dove Dale and also of Oxford, Blenheim, Warwick, Kenelworth, and Birmingham.

Shortly, her aunt and uncle appeared. "Mr. and Mrs. Gardiner," Darcy offered, "may I persuade you to join me in the house for some refreshments before returning to Lambton?"

"We thank you, Mr. Darcy," her uncle began, "but my wife made arrangements for us to dine with friends in the area."

"I was unaware of your knowing others in the area. How good it will be for you to renew acquaintances," he said, hoping Elizabeth understood his double meaning. He chanced a quick glance and saw her suppressing a smile.

"I grew up in Lambton, Mr. Darcy," Mrs. Gardiner stated, bringing his attention from her niece.

Again a bit surprised, he never showed it to his guests. "It is a delightful village."

"I am afraid I filled Elizabeth with tales of Derbyshire before our trip. I find it to be the finest county in England," Mrs. Gardiner beamed.

"You will find no contention on my part," Darcy guarded his words. "Derbyshire offers the best of everything."

Elizabeth and Mr. Gardiner chuckled at this cordial exchange. "The two of you have something in common," Mr. Gardiner offered. When it was time for them to leave, Darcy helped the ladies into the carriage, taking the liberty to hold Elizabeth's hand momentarily.

"Mr. and Mrs. Gardiner," he acknowledged them with a bow. He bowed separately to their niece. "Miss Elizabeth."

"Mr. Darcy," she nodded to him, but her stare bolted him in place.

"I look forward to presenting my sister to you," his voice was hoarse.

"And I to meeting her," she mouthed as the carriage pulled away. They watched each other for a few brief fleeting seconds, and then Darcy turned and walked slowly toward the house.

Entering his home, Darcy knew he should send for Mr. Howard as he promised, but he also knew he would not be able to do so.

Exhilaration overwhelmed his ability to concentrate on mundane matters right now. He entered his study, closed the door, and sank into one of the more comfortable chairs. The chaotic condition of his mind sent sensations flashing through his body; he ran his fingers through his hair and realized his hands were trembling.

Not knowing how long he sat in isolation, a light knock on the door roused Darcy. "Come," he called, automatically adjusting his posture.

He was a bit surprised to see Mrs. Reynolds bringing him tea and biscuits; normally, she was too busy overseeing the house to serve him personally. "I thought you might enjoy some tea, Sir," she began as she set the tray on a low table. "Would you like me to pour, Mr. Darcy?"

He acceded with a flick of his wrist. Mrs. Reynolds handed him a cup, but after he took it, she remained waiting his recognition. "Mrs. Reynolds, is there something else?"

"Mr. Darcy," she vocally stumbled, "I hope you are not angry with my behavior with your visitors. If I offended the family in any way, I am most apologetic."

So becharmed with the memory of Elizabeth's being at Pemberley, for a few seconds, he did not comprehend what his housekeeper said. He looked stunned and then said, "Mrs. Reynolds, you have been a part of the Pemberley household for nearly five and twenty years; I trust you implicitly. I assume you said no more to Miss Bennet than you would to other visitors."

"Yes, Sir, I have only praise for the Darcy family; yet, sometimes I may show too much pride in being chosen to oversee Pemberley, I fear."

At the mention of the word "pride," the master actually chuckled with the irony of what she said. He looked to the woman he entrusted with maintaining his household and saw the discomfort in her face. "Do not concern yourself, Mrs. Reynolds," he said softly. "I found no offense."

"Yes, Sir," she said as she curtsied to leave. "Thank you, Sir."

The woman was nearly to the door when he called to her, "Mrs. Reynolds."

"Yes, Mr. Darcy," she turned from the door.

"Would you come sit with me for a few minutes?" he uttered his request. "Please join me with some tea." Although most uncharacteristic of Darcy, she consented. When she was settled in the chair directly across from him, he anxiously took a deep breath and nearly pleaded, "Would you please tell me everything said by Mr. and Mrs. Gardiner or their niece Miss Bennet? It is important I know the words and the tone they used in speaking them." Mrs. Reynolds realized these were more than just travelers interested in the beauty of Pemberley; Mr. Darcy's keen interest in the recitation of the household tour renewed his gratitude for her loyalty and a sense of peace.

Darcy busied himself first with checking on the delivery of the pianoforte he ordered for Georgiana. A surprise gift, it spurred him to return to Pemberley early. He also called in Mr. Howard to conduct the estate's business and only occasionally did not focus on the task at hand. Mr. Howard repeated when the master's attention became distracted and waited patiently when Darcy's mind replayed the scenes of the day. With the financial books approved, Mr. Howard left Darcy alone once more. He leaned back in the chair, interlaced his fingers, and closed his eyes. Elizabeth's staring back from the carriage filled his wonder; the words, the elation, the marvel, and the anticipation jostled for dominance; he felt sweet agony.

With Elizabeth only five miles away, he could not divorce himself from thoughts of the woman. He wandered into the garden and took a seat; he took off his jacket and enjoyed the late summer breeze. How he wished to know her sentiment! Could he be mistaken? Was he looking for more than was there? Elizabeth apologized for being found at Pemberley, but Darcy did not believe her disliking the place; his finding her here simply made her uncomfortable. In fact, she offered compliments on the estate. Elizabeth accepted his trepidation over mentioning Bingley; she also accepted his request to meet Georgiana. No, he did not make a mistake; Elizabeth no longer felt disdain for him, but what did she feel?

Georgiana would finally be able to meet Elizabeth; Georgiana deserved someone such as Elizabeth in her life. So many times his sister expressed a desire to meet Miss Elizabeth Bennet; now, she would be able to establish that acquaintance; the prospect overjoyed him. How often he imagined the three of them at Pemberley. Such thoughts led him to another plan. Elizabeth would not expect Georgiana to call until Thursday, but maybe he could convince his sister to call on Elizabeth tomorrow; then they could invite her party to Pemberley for dinner on Friday. Darcy wanted her to be relaxed and to enjoy Pemberley and to see him in his element as its master. Any chance of her feelings for him changing would happen at Pemberley. Encountering her outside his estate would mean having to share her attention, but at Pemberley he could shower Elizabeth with his attentions, and he cared not who saw. Mr. Gardiner confided as they walked the park today that he, his wife, and his niece would return to Longbourn soon. Darcy had only a few days before Elizabeth would be gone again.

The morning seemed to crawl by with Darcy checking the clock repeatedly, anticipating his sister's return. When the carriages appeared, he nearly sprang from his chair, meeting the party in the courtyard. Hurst lumbered out of his coach, groaning from having to move his indolence; he turned and helped Mrs. Hurst and Caroline Bingley to alight.

"Ladies," Darcy bowed in acknowledgment.

"Mr. Darcy," Caroline intoned. "Finally, we have reached Pemberley. Of course, one would suffer much to spend time here."

"I am sorry you have suffered, Caroline. Perhaps you need time to rest and recoup your energies. Mrs. Reynolds will show you to your usual rooms," he said as he stepped by her and sought his sister's company.

"Bingley," he said, "I see you survived the journey!"

"In the comfort of your coach and in your sister's company, the journey was far from insufferable," Bingley beamed.

"Your chambers are ready, and there is something to wash away the road dirt." Darcy shook Charles's hand. "Would you be so kind as to escort Mrs. Annesley into the house?"

"Gladly, Darcy."

Darcy then turned to help his sister from the coach. He literally lifted her from the coach's steps and set her down several feet away.

"Fitzwilliam," she giggled, "you are certainly in a good mood. What brings such a smile to your face?"

"Is it that apparent?"

"You have a secret. This is just what you used to do when I was a child. Oh, please tell me now."

"You will just have to wait until we are in the house," he feigned innocence.

"Come then," she pulled on his hand in anticipation, her laughter contagious.

Once inside, he said, "I actually have more than one surprise."

"Brother, please stop teasing me. I can wait no longer," she pleaded.

"If you will look in the music room, something may take your notice."

Georgiana grasped the lapels of his jacket, pulled him toward her, and kissed his cheek. Then she nearly skipped through the hallway to the music room. She came quickly to a halt, and he heard her gasp as he strode into the room behind her. "Well, what do you think of your first surprise, Dearest One?" he asked as if he expected her to object.

"Fitzwilliam," her voice was breathy, "it is magnificent." She ran her fingers lightly along the keys of the new pianoforte. "When ... I mean, I do not deserve this."

He came forward to embrace her; tears misted her eyes. "Do you not know it gives me pleasure to see you happy?" he whispered as he stroked her face. "Now you know why I left you in Charles's care yesterday."

"I should rebuke you, Sir, for deserting me, but I believe you are absolved of guilt," she picked up on his mirth. "But you said there were two surprises."

"You are a greedy girl, are you not?" he tapped her on the chin with his finger. Georgiana laughed as he pulled her to the settee. He took her hands in his, looked into her face in earnest, and took a slow, deep breath. "The second surprise," he began, "is actually one for both of us." Georgiana giggled as she watched his apprehension. "How would you like to meet Miss Elizabeth Bennet?"

"Oh, yes . . ." she started and then checked her enthusiasm. "I always wanted to make Miss Bennet's acquaintance but not if it hurts you, Fitzwilliam."

"I appreciate your concern, my Dearest One," he continued the smile, "but even if there was no hope for my regard, I would still wish you to meet Miss Elizabeth. She is the kind of person you should have as a friend." He thought *sister* rather than *friend,* but he would not voice such hopes.

"How may I meet Miss Elizabeth? Do we travel to Hertfordshire?"

"She is here," he blurted out. "Actually, Miss Elizabeth is in Lambton at the Royal Crown."

"How?" she tried to comprehend the incoherency of his explanation.

"Let me start at the beginning," he unraveled the details. "Miss Elizabeth travels through Derbyshire with her aunt and uncle, Mr. and Mrs. Gardiner. When I returned to Pemberley yesterday, they were here visiting the estate."

"Oh, Fitzwilliam," she consoled him. "How awkward for both of you!"

"There were moments of disbelief for both of us," he recalled. "I stumbled through inquiries, often repeating myself, trying to engage her in conversation. She blushed often, but she was civil, and there was none of the disdain from before. I was a mess, covered in road dirt, so I left her on the lawn."

"Is that all you said to her? Please, Brother, tell me there is more."

"There is more," he reassured her. "I sent servants scattering as I hastened to make myself presentable. Then I went to find her on the park's pathway. We spoke again, and I was more composed. Her aunt is from Lambton; her aunt and uncle, I found, were people of taste and fashion. I, finally, got enough nerve to ask her permission to present you to her."

"What did Miss Elizabeth say?" Georgiana doubted her own worth.

"Miss Bennet is looking forward to forming an acquaintance." His sister squeezed his hand with joy.

"When shall we meet?"

"I hoped," he began more slowly, "you would agree to go as soon as you freshen your clothes."

"Oh, Fitzwilliam," she said, "so soon?" He saw the fear slip into her composure.

"Georgiana," he patted her hand, "I would not ask if there was time, but Miss Bennet will leave Derbyshire in a few days."

"Of course," she said unsurely, "I will be happy to go with you today." She stood up and straightened her dress. "Let me freshen my clothes; I will return in fifteen minutes."

"Thank you, Georgiana," he stood and held her at arm's length. "Elizabeth Bennet will love you as I do." She smiled weakly and turned to leave. "Georgiana," he called, "let us keep this our secret for now. A private introduction will be more comfortable for us all." She nodded and left the room.

While his sister was gone, Darcy paced the room wondering about this decision; Elizabeth would receive Georgiana cordially. Of that, he was sure, but how would she see his impetuous actions? He assured Georgiana of Elizabeth's goodness of spirit, but it was his own self-confidence that needed shoring up. He ordered his curricle to be brought around and waited on Georgiana's return in the front foyer when Charles Bingley came down the steps only seconds ahead of his sister.

"Darcy, are you going out?" Darcy debated whether to tell his friend his plans, but with the appearance of Georgiana in a fresh pelisse and bonnet left him no other choice.

"Bingley, Georgiana and I are going into Lambton to call on a friend."

"But, Darcy, we just traveled through Lambton on our way here," Bingley conjectured.

Darcy looked at his sister; Georgiana's uneasiness at the meeting showed; having to lie to Bingley would play havoc on her gentle nature. "Bingley, the friend is Miss Elizabeth Bennet, and she is in Lambton. She travels with her aunt and uncle; I happened on her yesterday here at Pemberley. She agreed to make Georgiana's acquaintance. We will make a short morning call today."

"Georgiana, you will like Miss Elizabeth." He turned toward her. "She is a delightful young lady. I understand your desire for a private introduction, but I would very much like to see Miss Elizabeth again myself if you would have no objections."

Georgiana's eyes pleaded with her brother, and Darcy, reluctantly, agreed, but he asked Bingley to wait downstairs at the inn until after Georgiana's introduction. Bingley readily agreed, saying he would saddle a horse and follow them to Lambton. Darcy then hinted as politely as possible for Charles to keep this from his sisters. "I understand," he grinned, "Caroline would be an *impediment.*"

CHAPTER 12

"A man who has one agreeable quality . . ."

As the curricle pulled away from Pemberley, Darcy reached for his sister's hand again. "Your kindness is unfathomable," he smiled at her. Georgiana guessed how important this meeting was to her brother, the magnitude of his request not lost on her. However, although she was more than ten years his junior, Georgiana knew something her brother did not: one cannot control the heart; when *real love* is ready, it will find its own way. Therefore, she looked forward to meeting Elizabeth Bennet; she was still nervous, but the nerves were selfish ones—she desired a female friend. Having no mother, Georgiana had questions she could not share with either her brother or Mrs. Annesley. Miss Bingley was just "too"—well, she would not do. Elizabeth Bennet's "free spirit" could contain the answers she sought.

Pulling the curricle to a halt in front of the Royal Crown, Darcy slid quickly out of the seat and helped his sister down. He thought he caught a glimpse of Elizabeth at the window. Their appearance in the village created a stir, and as they entered the inn, villagers sought their favor. As they waited to be announced, brother and sister held hands but were silent, both lost in thoughts of what the next few minutes would hold, Elizabeth Bennet's approval elevated in the estimation of both. When the time came for their entrance into the Gardiners' quarters, Darcy placed his sister's hand on his arm and covered it with his own hand after lightly chucking her under the chin and giving her a smile. He mouthed "Thank You" as the door opened to them. Stepping into the room, Darcy briefly broke contact with Georgiana as he bowed to the Gardiners and Elizabeth.

"Mr. Darcy," Mr. Gardiner came forward, bowed, and then offered his hand.

"Mr. Gardiner, Mrs. Gardiner, Miss Bennet, please excuse our intrusion. My sister and I have come a day earlier than expected; we apologize."

"Think nothing of it, Mr. Darcy," Mr. Gardiner continued the civilities. "We are happy to see you again so soon."

"Yes," said Mrs. Gardiner, "we are honored by your attentions." As she said so, she turned toward her niece and smiled. Darcy's eyes could not help but follow her lead.

"You are very kind," he nodded his head to all three. "I have come to introduce my sister. Mr. Gardiner, Mrs. Gardiner, Miss Elizabeth Bennet, may I present my sister, Miss Georgiana Darcy." As he said this, Darcy stepped behind to bring his sister center stage.

Georgiana made her curtsy. Mr. and Mrs. Gardiner came forward and offered appropriate welcoming remarks, but it was Elizabeth's actions he wished to observe. When her relatives finished their niceties, Elizabeth stepped forward and curtsied, "Miss Darcy, I am so pleased to finally meet you."

"And I you," Georgiana returned the courtesy. Darcy's heart leapt as he noted the genuine smile on Elizabeth's face as she engaged his sister's company. Hoping to leave them time together, Darcy asked the Gardiners about their previous evening's engagement. He tried desperately to listen to both conversations—the Gardiners' and the one between Elizabeth and his sister. He heard Elizabeth ask about Georgiana's studies and his sister's monosyllabic responses. Finally, he turned to them and suggested Georgiana share her "secret" with Miss Elizabeth. Georgiana's eyes replied her thanks, and they sparkled as she told of her brother's gift.

"You are fortunate to have such a loving brother," Elizabeth observed. He did not hear his sister's reply or what was said after, but light laughter occurred, and the nature of the exchange seemed pleasant.

Darcy remembered his promise to Bingley so when there was a lull in the conversation, he said, "Miss Bennet, Mr. Bingley is awaiting the opportunity to renew his acquaintance with you. May I summon him?"

"By all means." Darcy asked a servant to inform the gentleman, Mr. Bingley, of his company being desired, and then he stepped to his sister's side.

In seconds, they heard Bingley's step on the stairs, and in a moment he entered the room. His unaffected warmth and cordiality brought forth Elizabeth's good opinion of him. He inquired in a friendly way after her family. Darcy observed how Elizabeth looked at Bingley and Georgiana together; he knew enough of her disposition to realize she suspected his and the Bingley sisters' separation of Bingley and Jane Bennet anchored in hopes of an alliance between the two. Bingley's sisters may still hold out such hopes, but Darcy abandoned any such notions long before there was a Jane Bennet. Time would prove Elizabeth's conjectures wrong.

The half hour stay passed too quickly for Darcy's pleasure, but when they rose to leave he called upon his sister to invite the Gardiners and Miss Elizabeth to dinner at Pemberley before they left Lambton. The day after tomorrow was decided upon among the group, and plans were made for their arrival at his estate. "Yes, please, Miss Bennet, I would love for us to play together," Georgiana added quickly.

"I am not sure my talents merit a new pianoforte," she teased while looking only at Darcy, "but I would enjoy sharing some of your favorite music."

Before departing, Bingley expressed great pleasure in seeing Elizabeth again. He asked of her sisters, without mentioning Jane directly, and reminisced about their time at Netherfield and gave her to know he hoped to speak more of those not mentioned previously. Darcy observed all this and realized he too must secure information on Jane Bennet's inclinations toward his friend. Finally, he renewed his invitation to Mr. Gardiner to join the gentlemen at Pemberley for some fishing; Mr. Gardiner would join them by noon on the morrow. Unwillingly, the Darcys and Mr. Bingley left the Gardiner party with promises to meet again soon; the day and the meeting went better than he anticipated. Elizabeth smiled with momentary flashes of the connection they once possessed.

Darcy's smile could not be contained on the return trip to Pemberley. Finally, he asked, "Georgiana, did you like Miss Elizabeth?"

His sister's smile was nearly as large as was his. "I was so frightened at first, but Miss Elizabeth is one of the most pleasant people I ever met. I felt foolish for being so apprehensive."

"You were enjoying yourself, then?"

"Miss Elizabeth was telling me tales of your acquaintance."

"Is that what you found so amusing?" His eyebrow shot up.

"Actually, she was telling of her mortification at having to dance with Mr. Collins for the first set at Mr. Bingley's ball," his sister confided while continuing to chuckle.

"It was a display to which I would not wish to subject anyone," Darcy reflected. "I nearly stepped in to rescue her."

"Then she spoke of the honor of dancing with you, Fitzwilliam," Georgiana added cautiously, not wishing to give her brother false hopes for she too could not determine the lady's regard for her brother. "I was most touched when she talked of your showing her a glade at Rosings which was a favorite of our mother. I was a bit jealous."

Darcy felt his sister's hurt and apologized immediately. "I feared it would distress you, Dearest One." He caught her eye. "I would love to show you the path the next time we are at Rosings. We should speak more of her."

"I have no memories of our mother, Fitzwilliam," she whispered.

"Then we should share my memories. If I realized you felt as such, I would have done so before now. I thought," he stumbled, "I was protecting you."

"Miss Elizabeth says I am fortunate to have a loving brother, and I agree." Georgiana smiled up at him.

"Mr. Gardiner appears to be a real angler—a real sportsman. I am anxious to spend time with him tomorrow."

Georgiana interrupted, "I agree; Mr. and Mrs. Gardiner are most amiable."

"It is likely, my Dear, while Mr. Gardiner partakes of the sport, his wife and Miss Elizabeth will return your call. Are you comfortable with being their hostess or would you prefer my early return?"

"I have no experience in serving as the hostess." The thoughts of it obviously agitated her. "I suppose I can count on Mrs. Annesley, Miss Bingley, and Mrs. Hurst if I can think of nothing of interest."

"Mrs. Annesley," Darcy cautioned, "will be most helpful, and, of course, Mrs. Gardiner and Miss Bennet will be congenial. However, I do not believe Miss Bingley or Mrs. Hurst will be more than barely civil with Miss Elizabeth."

"I do not understand," she questioned. "Do not Mr. Bingley's sisters hold Miss Elizabeth in as high regard as their brother?"

"Bingley's sisters will not, I believe, be happy to remind their brother of Hertfordshire and Miss Jane Bennet. They do not share his regard for that particular lady. Plus, I foolishly showed Miss Elizabeth more attention than I should have. Miss Bingley took note of my actions."

"I see," was his sister's only reply at first, but then she added, "Do you think you might make an appearance, Fitzwilliam?"

"If you so wish." Darcy was relieved; he knew if Elizabeth was at Pemberley, he could be nowhere else. They finished their journey with Georgiana's retellings. At last, she looked at her brother and said, "Miss Jane Bennet must be very lovely, indeed."

"I do not understand," he turned to her.

"If Miss Jane Bennet is more beautiful than Miss Elizabeth, then she must be very beautiful; it is no wonder Mr. Bingley found her beguiling." His sister sighed.

"Miss Bennet," her brother added, "is beautiful, but I once told Charles I thought she smiled too much." His sister stifled her laughter. "Miss Elizabeth," he continued, "has beauty of both body and mind."

"Her eyes—I remember you once saying—are the secret to her soul."

"It was my comment on Miss Elizabeth's *fine eyes* which set off Caroline Bingley's antagonism. I am afraid Miss Elizabeth suffered rebukes because of my faults."

"Miss Elizabeth, I believe, can handle someone as shallow in her opinions and her own consequence as is Miss Bingley."

"Miss Darcy," he smirked, "you continue to amaze me. Where was I when you became a young lady of such astute opinions and discernments?" Georgiana did not answer, but she found she liked the new freedom she shared with a brother who always was so reserved and who until a few months ago saw her as a *pesky* little girl for whom he was responsible.

When they returned to Pemberley, Caroline Bingley and the Hursts were having tea and a light meal in the morning room. "Ah, there you are, Mr. Darcy," Caroline delivered a statement more in the form of a question.

Neither Darcy nor Georgiana responded. Instead, they moved to the serving tray; handing her brother a cup, Georgiana rolled her eyes and grinned while his response included a light tap of his finger on her chin, a gesture he often used with his sister when he wanted to show he cared for her; others did not understand it, but they knew the unspoken truth. Finally, Darcy turned back to his houseguests, "We have been to town, Miss Bingley."

"What?" she exclaimed. "Why would you submit your sister to the discomfort of traveling again so soon?"

"I assure you, Miss Bingley," Georgiana came to his defense, "my brother never asks more of me than I am willing to give."

"Yes, of course," Caroline stumbled, not wishing to offend her hosts, "but what could take you out on the road again so soon?"

As she asked her question, Caroline's brother joined them from his ride and provided the answer. "We have been to Lambton to see Miss Elizabeth Bennet; is it not fortuitous she is in Derbyshire at the same time as we are at Pemberley?" If he looked at his sisters during his response, Charles Bingley would have observed their shared duplicity.

Louisa Hurst recovered her voice first. "Miss Elizabeth Bennet! Are all the Bennets on holiday in Derbyshire?"

"No," Charles brought his tea and scones over to join the party. "It is just Miss Elizabeth and her aunt and uncle."

"Please tell me," Caroline pronounced the words slowly, "this is not the uncle who is a lawyer in Meryton." Louisa guffawed.

"Of course, not," Darcy snickered, "it is the uncle from Cheapside."

"Heavens, help us," Caroline gasped.

Standing quickly, Darcy added before he exited the room, "I hope the planets are aligned, and the heavens are favorable for we dine with Mr. and Mrs. Gardiner and Miss Elizabeth the day after tomorrow. It will give you a chance to renew your acquaintance." With that, he took Georgiana's hand and said, "Come, Dearest One, I am in need of your soothing music, and I am anxious to hear how well the new instrument sounds." Georgiana and Darcy left the insipidity of the breakfast room to find privacy in the music room. Their exit spoke volumes to those who professed fine manners but greatly lacked even common civilities.

Mr. Gardiner took full advantage of Mr. Darcy's invitation to fish his stream and found great pleasure in joining the master himself, as well as Mr. Bingley and Bingley's brother, Mr. Hurst. Eventually, Darcy and Gardiner isolated themselves from the other two. The former, as true sportsmen, understood patience and quiet time brought success to an angler. They spent nearly an hour in peaceful companionship when Mr. Gardiner turned to Darcy and said, "Mr. Darcy, I do not know when I spent a more pleasant morning. Some may find this waiting for the fish to bite boring, but with a house full of children and servants and a business, which demands much of my time, tranquil contemplation is a luxury. Although I enjoy your company, please, Sir," he added, "if you have business at your house, I am content to entertain myself."

Darcy wondered if the man recognized Darcy's admiration for his niece. By now, Darcy did not hide his feelings for Elizabeth. "I did promise my sister, Sir," he remarked casually, "to check on her this afternoon."

"My wife and niece are probably with Miss Darcy as we speak." Mr. Gardiner seemed to be expecting Darcy to look shocked by this information, but Darcy's eyes only reflected the urgency of his desire to leave. "A call of such honor as your sister bestowed on my family requires a like response."

"If that is the case, it is prudent on my, at least, making an appearance." Darcy bowed. "I will return shortly."

He walked away quickly and headed for the house. Elizabeth was here at Pemberley, and he would not waste any time they might share together—to hell with what the rules of propriety may call upon his actions. God gave him a second chance to keep Elizabeth Bennet in his life; he wanted her here with him at Pemberley, but, more importantly, Darcy desired her happiness and her friendship. He found the ladies in the salon; his entrance brought a veil of silence as all eyes fell on Darcy and Elizabeth. Everyone in the room knew why he came there; Elizabeth blushed slightly, but unlike the other ladies, her eyes locked on his face. Georgiana had enough composure to serve her guests light refreshments of cake and fresh fruit, but she struggled with the conversation. Her awareness of Miss Bingley's vehemence for Miss Elizabeth and her brother's desire for her and Elizabeth to be friends took its toll on her abilities to play hostess.

Darcy assessed the scene quickly, and moving to his sister, he took her by the hand and said, "Come, Dearest One," and he seated her next to Elizabeth on the settee. He took up a position next to Mrs. Gardiner. "Your husband, Mrs. Gardiner, is a superb fisherman," he offered. "I may need to restock the stream after today." Mrs. Gardiner reached out and lightly patted the back of his hand and chuckled softly.

Elizabeth managed to offer her thanks. "My uncle graciously allowed my aunt and me all the pleasures on this trip. We are most thankful for your providing him time to enjoy himself in an avocation he so loves."

"I am gratified to see him so content." Darcy did not take his eyes from her face. After an awkward pause, he added, "I bet, Miss Elizabeth," trying to bridge the lull, "you brought something with you to read for your travel time. Reading seems to give you great pleasure."

"I did, Sir," the lady smiled in that mischievous way which told him to expect some sort of barb. "I hope to improve my mind with extensive reading."

Darcy nodded at her remembrance of what he said at Netherfield, telling him he was in her thoughts at least some of the time. Georgiana turned to Elizabeth, "What, Miss Elizabeth, do you prefer to read?"

Her brother wanted to add his own memories to the mix. "I recall Miss Elizabeth to prefer poetry. Is that not what you chose to read the last day in the library at Netherfield?"

"Oh, Miss Darcy," she turned to his sister, "your brother wishes to reproof me for disturbing his privacy that day. I thought him engrossed in a volume on William the Conqueror, but I fear, I caught him napping instead."

"That is difficult to believe, Miss Elizabeth. My brother devours books," Georgiana giggled.

"I was reaching for a volume of poetry on an upper shelf," Elizabeth explained to Georgiana, but she really spoke to Darcy, "and I knocked over something which caught your brother's attention. He retrieved the collection for me, however. He was actually very chivalrous." Then she pursed her lips in that all-knowing challenge he came to recognize.

"Which poets do you prefer?" asked Georgiana.

"I believe that particular day," Elizabeth added, "it was William Cowper I chose to read."

"No Lord Byron for you then?" Georgiana continued. Darcy showed his surprise at his sister's mentioning of Byron, often considered controversial, especially for a schoolgirl to be reading.

"Cowper or Scott is more to my liking," Elizabeth confided. "When I was with the Collinses at Hunsford, I had little to read besides Fordyce's *Sermons to Young Women*. Lady Catherine was kind enough to allow me access to her library, though." Darcy saw the glint of mirth creep across Elizabeth's face before she added, "I thought Mary Wollstonecraft's *A Vindication of the Rights of Women* might be found there. I hoped to share it with Mrs. Collins."

Georgiana laughed out loud and reached out for Elizabeth's hand, which Elizabeth offered willingly. Mrs. Gardiner stifled a laugh of her own; Elizabeth feigned innocence and gave Darcy that smile which possessed him from the first time he saw it.

Miss Bingley, who offered little to the conversation up until this time and who, secretly, wanted the visit to be a failure, moved beyond curiosity to desperation. Caroline was astute enough to see how Darcy anxiously wanted Georgiana and Elizabeth to become friends and how he encouraged the conversation on both sides. In the imprudence of anger, she took the first opportunity of saying, with sneering civility, "Pray, Miss Eliza, are not the —shire militia removed from Meryton? They must be a great loss to *your* family."

Darcy froze, and Georgiana dropped Elizabeth's hand, gathering her own hands nervously into her lap. He could little believe Miss Bingley could be so cruel; she knew nothing of Georgiana's distress; Caroline's comments were to serve as a reminder to Darcy Elizabeth once preferred Mr. Wickham to him, and the rogue's lies unreasonably influenced her. Darcy, obviously agitated, earnestly looked to Elizabeth. *Georgiana's reputation is in your hands.* She offered him a slight nod as if to say I will protect your sister as my own.

He saw her straighten those formidable shoulders and raise her chin. Then Elizabeth spoke both sweetly and calmly, "On the contrary, Miss Bingley. We will miss the *intelligent* conversation the officers brought to all the gatherings, and I suppose the community may feel more vulnerable without the military's protection. I also assume many merchants feel the deprivation of the additional income, but my father brought up each of his daughters to be self-sufficient enough to entertain herself. We need no outside source of diversion." As she said these lines, Elizabeth's hand reached across the settee to retrieve Georgiana's hand into her own grasp. Darcy watched her give his sister's hand a little squeeze and saw Georgiana's eyes follow the motion of her hand toward Elizabeth and how she raised her eyes reluctantly to look tentatively into Elizabeth Bennet's face. Elizabeth offered up a gentle smile, and Georgiana started to drop her eyes, but a breathy expulsion gave her the fortitude to stare at Elizabeth. Elizabeth turned her attention back to Georgiana. "I apologize for losing my thoughts, Miss Darcy; I wanted to ask your reading preferences."

Georgiana's voice, initially barely a whisper, gained volume as she continued. She never took her eyes from Elizabeth during the exchange, putting all of her trust in the woman she hoped would become her friend. "In my studies, I read Oliver Goldsmith's *The Vicar of Wakefield.* I have also lately enjoyed the prose and verse found in *Elegant Extracts,* as well as Frances Burney's *Cecilia.*"

"How about Mrs. Radcliff's *The Romance of the Forest* or *The Children of the Abbey*? My father's library held such schoolgirl favorites for my sisters and me," Elizabeth encouraged.

"I have enjoyed them both, Miss Elizabeth."

Darcy watched as his adorable, but shy, sister struggled to maintain the conversation, realizing he never appreciated Elizabeth Bennet properly before now; he observed Elizabeth leading others before—Maria Lucas's needlework flashed before his eyes—but even when he thought he loved her, this moment with Georgiana sealed his regard for her forever. In the background, Caroline Bingley droned on, often directing her comments to the room, but more often to the tittering sighs of her sister Mrs. Hurst. The rest of the party, generally, ignored them, however.

"Have you been able to attend the series of concerts being commissioned by the Prince Regent?" Mrs. Gardiner interjected, hoping to channel Georgiana along a familiar line of conversation.

"Yes, Mrs. Gardiner," Georgiana smiled briefly. "The last one was the most magnificent I ever heard; was it not, Mrs. Annesley?"

"I agree most wholeheartedly, Miss Georgiana. The room was filled with an indescribable essence."

"This sounds so thrilling, Miss Darcy. Would you be willing to acquaint me with the pieces you most enjoyed?" Elizabeth coaxed the girl.

Darcy marveled at how Georgiana's whole body changed as she spoke to Elizabeth and Mrs. Gardiner. Her voice became fuller and less breathy, and Georgiana's very posture became one of a well-bred lady, rather than a timid schoolgirl.

"Oh, yes, Miss Elizabeth, I would love that. When you come to dine, maybe we can find time to play together. Mrs. Annesley helped me select some interesting pieces, and my master, Mr. Steventon, taught me some of the difficult cords."

"My goodness, they sound challenging, but I must admit I can think of few things I would find to be more pleasurable than spending time with you in learning what pieces you chose, although I am sure your talents are so superior to my own, Miss Darcy."

Georgiana's eyes sparkled as she looked at Elizabeth. *At last,* Darcy thought. *At last, Georgiana found someone who sees her for what she really is.* Of course, Elizabeth Bennet had a way of seeing people—she saw his many flaws. Could he imagine she might see him in other ways some day? Dare he let himself believe it might happen?

Elizabeth said something about regrets but having the need to take her leave.

"Miss Bennet, Mrs. Gardiner, please tarry a few minutes more," Darcy interjected, "and I will have your carriage brought around." Darcy said this to both women, but his eyes remained on Elizabeth, trying to memorize her every expression.

"Thank you, Mr. Darcy," Mrs. Gardiner offered, noting Elizabeth could not look away from his intense stare.

Coming to himself, Darcy, making a quick bow and averting his eyes to his sister, rose quickly. "Georgiana, while I see Mr. Shepherd about the carriage, why do you not show Miss Bennet and Mrs. Gardiner the conservatory?"

"Mr. Darcy, thank you again for your courtesy toward my uncle," Elizabeth discovered her voice. "I cannot remember seeing him as contented as he was when contemplating the pleasure of fishing your lake, Sir."

"Then I am well satisfied, Miss Bennet," Darcy replied and quickly left the room to find Mr. Shepherd.

"Please follow me, Miss Elizabeth, Mrs. Gardiner," Georgiana offered as she stood to lead them toward the conservatory.

"Happily so," Elizabeth said as she also stood. Then interlocking her arm into Georgiana's, Elizabeth smiled brightly at Darcy's sister. "Pemberley is a magnificent home. Its elegance comes in its simplistic sophistication."

"That is ironic," Georgiana gasped as they headed toward the door.

"What is, Miss Darcy?"

"Your description of Pemberley," her nose wrinkled a bit showing she was still a schoolgirl at heart. "It is what Fitzwilliam says about Pemberley when he describes our home—simple sophistication."

Elizabeth turned to make sure Mrs. Gardiner followed close behind but also to conceal the blush overtaking her face.

Entering the conservatory, the beauty of the place awed Elizabeth and Mrs. Gardiner, but it also had a calming effect on them. "I hope you love this place, Miss Elizabeth," said Georgiana, "for it is one of my favorite rooms at Pemberley. I feel my mother here. Fitzwilliam says she would spend hours tending the plants."

"Each part of Pemberley seems to override the previous, Miss Darcy," Elizabeth gushed, "but this room would be one of my favorites also. It speaks of the magnitude of your mother's character. A woman who loved flowers and nature so to replicate this atmosphere could have no less children than you and Mr. Darcy."

Darcy came back to escort Elizabeth and Mrs. Gardiner to their carriage. He stood in the shadows of the doorway watching his precious sister and the woman who possessed him completely. He could barely breathe while watching the two of them together. Could they become friends? Georgiana deserved these happy moments. Elizabeth strolled aimlessly, looking at the exotic flowers and the shrubbery. She stopped at a yellow boxwood rose plant, touching its leaves lovingly, nearly caressing the petals. Georgiana, walking now with Mrs. Gardiner, looked back and beamed. "You discovered my mother's favorite flower, Miss Elizabeth. My brother reportedly fought to keep the cuttings alive after my mother's death. I felt often he did so to keep my mother's memory alive too."

"I can imagine so, Miss Darcy," Mrs. Gardiner entered the conversation. "Your brother took on many responsibilities at a young age. I would imagine the plant gave him comfort." Darcy could hardly believe his ears. These people whom he once shunned because of his misplaced pride understood him better than many of his close acquaintances.

He watched Elizabeth in Pemberley's conservatory, deeply inhaling the fragrance of his mother's boxwood rose. He could barely breathe; his heart lodged again in his throat. He knew at this moment he must make Elizabeth Bennet a part of his life. If she could learn to love him, Fitzwilliam Darcy would not hesitate or question himself again. Yet, even if all they ever had was the quiet repartee they enjoyed since he found her on the grounds of Pemberley two days ago, then he would settle for that. He would protect Elizabeth. He would love Elizabeth from afar if necessary, but he would do everything in his power to secure her happiness even if that meant finding Elizabeth a suitable romantic match. *Oh, God, could he do that? Could he stand to see her with another man?* He could not stand a life without seeing Elizabeth; that much he did know; making her happy took on new importance. Maybe she would consider becoming a traveling companion for Georgiana. Mrs. Annesley gave Georgiana refinement, but Elizabeth Bennet could give her confidence. What was he thinking? He thought of Elizabeth being a part of his life. He thought about Elizabeth Bennet as he had thought since his days at Netherfield. Darcy cleared his voice and stepped into the room. "Mrs. Gardiner, your carriage is without."

"Thank you, Mr. Darcy, for a most pleasant afternoon."

"Yes," hurried Elizabeth. "You and Miss Darcy have a most well-suited home here at Pemberley. I will never be able to think of either of you without picturing you here at this great estate. This has been a most unexpected pleasure." Elizabeth colored slightly, but only Darcy noted the change.

"You are to be our guests at any time you so desire," Georgiana said with a glow of confidence she was learning to like; Darcy marveled at the change.

"I see you prefer the yellow boxwood rose, Miss Elizabeth," Darcy could not help himself; he wanted to speak to her again. When she talked, he heard the same voice and discerned the same mind.

"It is a cherished plant, is it not, Mr. Darcy? Or has your sister exaggerated its importance?" Elizabeth's enigmatic smile overspread her face as her eyes drifted to Darcy's passionate stare.

"Oh, no, Miss Elizabeth," Georgiana began.

"Georgiana," Darcy stopped her in mid sentence, "you will find Miss Bennet likes to test my mettle with her responses some times." As he said so, a wry smile turned up on the outline of his lips as if he and Elizabeth just shared a private joke. The "attitude" displayed between her brother and Elizabeth Bennet and the intensity of their stares amused Georgiana. Mrs. Gardiner simply smiled as she took Georgiana's arm to head toward her waiting carriage and to allow Georgiana to return to her other guests.

Elizabeth fell into step with Darcy, both of them in a quiet state of chaos, not admitting their need to be with each other. With her eyes down so Darcy could not see her face, Elizabeth said at a barely audible level only Darcy listening with his whole being could hear. "I meant no disrespect, Mr. Darcy. I just meant yellow is my favorite color of flower, especially the yellow rose. Some say yellow represents jealousy. I say it demonstrates a constancy of spirit; like the sun, it lasts forever."

As he handed Mrs. Gardiner and Elizabeth into the carriage, Darcy could not resist the impulse to hold Elizabeth's hand a moment longer than propriety would allow. Elizabeth glanced down at his hand and slowly withdrew hers from his, prolonging the sensation. Darcy's heart beat so loudly he was sure everyone must have heard it. He could not remove the smile from his face as he watched Elizabeth's carriage leave the grounds.

CHAPTER 13

" . . . tormenting a respectable gentleman."

With reluctance, Darcy returned to the salon; he could not leave Georgiana to deal with the Bingley sisters alone. As predicted, Caroline Bingley's disdain for Elizabeth Bennet overflowed with criticisms of Elizabeth's person, behavior, and dress. To no avail, Georgiana and Mrs. Annesley tried to redirect Caroline's censure. When Darcy entered, he found Georgiana in nearly as much distress as when Miss Bingley earlier made references to George Wickham. "Georgiana, my dear," he said as he entered, "do you not have lessons to which to attend?" Darcy shot his sister a secretive glance.

"Yes, Brother, I do, and then I have some letters to write." She returned a wink of "thanks," made a quick curtsy, and left the room. Georgiana felt relief at being away from Miss Bingley's comments about Elizabeth Bennet. Her brother favored Miss Bennet, and as for Georgiana, his judgment could not err. Yet, even if her brother did not speak so highly of Miss Elizabeth, Georgiana would have found her to be lovely and amiable. Elizabeth Bennet won Georgiana's heart also.

When Georgiana left, Miss Bingley repeated to Darcy what she said to his sister. As jealousy consumed Caroline Bingley, she forgot to check her sharpened tongue before Darcy's hearing, and he, at first, tolerated her comments for Bingley's sake. She began with renewed disapproval of Elizabeth's looks, noting she believed Elizabeth's face to be "brown and coarse."

Darcy tried to warn Miss Bingley of her being too forward by saying coldly, "Miss Elizabeth travels in the summer months; it would make sense for her to be tanned. Other than that, I perceive no great change in her looks."

Needless to say, this did not satisfy Caroline; determined, she reminded Darcy of his initial dislike for Elizabeth Bennet. The tirade included a profound dislike for Elizabeth's thin face, lackluster complexion, and unattractive features, including her nose, teeth, and "her fine eyes." Caroline referred to Elizabeth as having an air of self-sufficiency without tolerable fashion.

During this, Darcy tried repeatedly to restructure his composure; it took great constraint not to order Caroline Bingley to leave Pemberley at once; he even considered helping the servants pack her trunks to be rid of her in a timelier manner.

Caroline, unfortunately, did not realize she stepped across the line of his patience; she desired to remind him he, too, once found Elizabeth Bennet and her family to be intolerable. "I remember, when we first knew her in Hertfordshire, how amazed we all were to find that she was a reputed beauty; and I particularly recollect you saying one night, after they had been dining at Netherfield, '*She* a beauty! I should as soon call her mother a wit.' But afterwards she seemed to improve on you, and I believe you thought her rather pretty at one time."

Her voice sent revulsion through Darcy's body; he did not recall saying such things about Elizabeth, but he did not doubt he could have been that pompous at one time. Steadying his voice, he turned a look of steel upon Miss Bingley. She gasped at the intensity of his stare and dropped her eyes quickly as he delivered his cut. "Yes," he snapped, "but *that* was only when I first saw her, for it is many months since I have considered her as one of the handsomest women of my acquaintance." He then went away, quitting the room; he must be away from the venom Caroline Bingley spread. He needed the companionship of intelligent, genteel people. Darcy returned to the stream to find Mr. Gardiner still leisurely enjoying the pleasures of the day in sport. He turned his attentions to getting to know the man whom Elizabeth admired and found his day improved by the effort.

Dinnertime drew near, but Darcy found he lost his taste for both the food and the company awaiting him in the dining room. The fragrance of roses filling his senses wafted over him, followed closely by the light scent of lavender. Sitting in the conservatory, he pleasantly recalled the last three days, praying he still had a chance with Elizabeth Bennet. Deep in these thoughts, his sister eventually interrupted him by saying, "Fitzwilliam, here you are."

Darcy looked up as the haze of his memories retreated to be called forth again on a moment's notice. "I apologize, Dearest One, I neglected you since our visitors departed. Please sit with me for a few minutes before we must go into dinner."

"Are you not well, Fitzwilliam?"

"I am well, at least, physically."

"Is it Miss Elizabeth of whom you are concerned?"

"Dearest One, how could it be you have become so wise?" He smiled as he kissed her hand and then held it to his cheek. "I fear Miss Elizabeth is rarely far from my thoughts."

"I do like her, Fitzwilliam, just as you said I would. I find Elizabeth Bennet to be one of the most amiable people of my acquaintance."

Darcy smiled down at his sister's face overspread with happiness. "I am delighted you found her to be so; she is uncommon."

"Fitzwilliam, tomorrow evening—I would hope to extend an invitation to Miss Elizabeth to spend some time at Pemberley, but I do not wish to pain you. If it would hurt you, I could possibly ask her to come to London with Mrs. Annesley and me instead."

"Georgiana, you recognize my prayer of one day earning Miss Elizabeth's regard and bringing her to Pemberley, but even if those hopes are never achieved, I have come to realize I must have her in my life; I could not bear never seeing her again. Having Miss Elizabeth here at Pemberley as your special friend would give me nearly as much pleasure as having her here with me."

"Fitzwilliam, I know little about love except for what I read in novels and poetry, but the greatest fool can see you and Elizabeth Bennet belong together."

"From your lips," he whispered, "to God's will, but even if Miss Elizabeth never returns my affection, she already gave me a new life; she opened the door for me to come out of the shadows of a prideful existence, without abandoning my ideals, and she created a new understanding between us two. It pains me to think I once offended the woman I most respect. Now I have sought Miss Elizabeth's acquaintance again, any effort I might now make to shun her presence would create suspicion, would it not? You may invite her to Pemberley if you so wish."

"Fitzwilliam, if Miss Elizabeth finally realizes what an honorable man you are, she will possess a great love—a different kind of admiration, but I am a foolish school-girl," she added, thinking she said too much for his serious sensibilities. After an awkward pause, she began again, "I know I disappointed you when I turned to Mr. Wickham." She felt him stiffen at the mention of George Wickham's name. "I knew nothing of interpreting character then; now I see what superior affection really is." Darcy realized his sister was not as naïve as he once thought her to be; she was a young lady looking for love and for her own way in the world. Of course, he was not anxious to let her leave him anytime soon, but he felt he understood her better since he showed himself to be vulnerable. "Did you see what Miss Elizabeth did today when Miss Bingley broached the subject of the —shire in Meryton? I was mortified; my first thoughts were Caroline knew about Mr. Wickham, but, of course, she did not."

"No, Miss Bingley's directed her comments to my memory of Elizabeth once preferring Mr. Wickham also; it seems you and Miss Elizabeth were both fooled by his façade of caring."

"Obviously, Miss Elizabeth knows my secret; you told her. Is that not so?"

"At Hunsford in an impulsive act, I ludicrously proposed—a *droit du seigneur*, so to speak; but, when I professed my love for Miss Elizabeth, her reproofs included charges of my abuse of Mr. Wickham. I was angry, at first, and wished to defend my actions, and then I wanted to protect Elizabeth from George Wickham's deceit. I am afraid I betrayed you, but I did not do so lightly. I knew enough of Miss Bennet's character to realize she would never use the knowledge against you. You saw her strength of character today."

"The strength of her grasp on my hand gave me the ability to raise my eyes and look in her face. Her face told me I had nothing to fear from Elizabeth Bennet."

"Yes, my dear," Darcy nearly at a loss for words continued, "we hold mutual admiration for Miss Elizabeth, it seems. But we must put these thoughts aside and attend to our guests. Come, Sweet One." He offered his sister his arm; both paused before the boxwood rose before leaving the conservatory.

Darcy retired to his chambers early that evening. Hope and a bit of confidence flowed through him; his sister's words involving his and Elizabeth's futures rang in his memory, but Darcy needed to discover the whole truth about his chances, and only one person could accurately supply the information: Elizabeth. He must see her, and he must see her alone.

The master of the house rose early. He wanted to be away from his guests. He thought only of Elizabeth and of finding out if she could learn to love him. If her wishes changed, Darcy would renew his proposal and face the consequences of his choice later. The ride into Lambton took a little over a quarter of an hour. It was early, but not unreasonably so. He would simply ask Elizabeth for permission to call upon her in advance of the rest of her party; he would bring a curricle, and they could take a drive around the grounds of Pemberley before dinner. Darcy would make his intentions known again and let fate take its course.

Upon reaching the inn, he learned the Gardiners left only moments before. Disappointed, he first considered seeking them in the village when the servant told him the young lady remained behind in her quarters. Darcy's eyes glinted with pleasure when he instructed the servant to announce his presence to the young woman. As the servant knocked on the door and opened it to the sitting area of the guest rooms, coming face-to-face with Elizabeth startled Darcy. Her pale face showed her to be in a clearly agitated state. She barely saw him, so great her discomposure, and before he could recover enough to speak, she started past him by saying, "I beg your pardon, but I must leave you. I must find Mr. Gardiner this moment, on business that cannot be delayed; I have not an instant to lose."

He knew not the source of the anguish in which he found Elizabeth, but he knew he must protect her. Propriety would demand he let Elizabeth pass without interference, but Darcy's love for her could not allow him to ignore her. "Good God! What is the matter?" He wanted to take her in his arms to comfort her. "Miss Elizabeth, I will not detain you a minute; but let me, or let the servant, go after Mr. and Mrs. Gardiner. You are not well enough; you cannot go yourself."

He stayed close because Elizabeth seemed to sway under the distress of the situation; she took his advice, and the servant was recalled and commissioned to find Mr. and Mrs. Gardiner and have them return immediately.

With the servant on his way, Elizabeth took a seat, as she could control her trembling legs no longer. Her distress caused Darcy to fear news of the death of her mother or father. Without being asked to stay, he pulled a chair close to her for he could not leave her in such discontent, and he momentarily reached for her hand, stroking her palm with his thumb as he gently held her fingertips. He inquired of what he might do to help her, and although Elizabeth requested nothing of him, she did, finally, turn to him with her dilemma—she had dreadful news from Longbourn. Darcy began to think of ways to care for her well-being if the death of a parent was of what she spoke. The acknowledgment of the situation brought tears to her eyes, and her sobs held Darcy in desolate anticipation. He offered her comforting words and then observed her in sympathetic silence.

When she finally spoke, the words spilled out in clusters of ill happenings. "I have just had a letter from Jane, with such dreadful news. It cannot be concealed from anyone. My younger sister has left all her friends—has eloped; has thrown herself into the power of—of Mr. Wickham. They are gone off together from Brighton. *You* know him too well to doubt the rest. She has no money, no connections, nothing that can tempt him to—she is lost forever."

Darcy tried to control first the contempt, then the anger, and lastly, the empathy he felt; astonishment fixed him in place. Elizabeth blamed herself for not letting others know of Mr. Wickham's low character, but it was his secret—his sister's secret—she kept. Darcy's pride would ruin the woman he loved. Lydia Bennet's folly would not only mark her as a "fallen" woman, but it would taint the reputations of all of her sisters as well. "I am grieved, indeed—grieved—shocked. But is it certain—absolutely certain?"

"Oh, yes! They left Brighton together on Sunday night, and were traced almost to London, but not beyond; they are certainly not gone to Scotland."

Darcy fought the urge to touch her shoulder, but instead he lightly touched her fingertips once more. Elizabeth continued to sob, but he noted her shoulders no longer shook. He asked, "And what has been done, what has been attempted, to recover her?"

Even before asking the question, Darcy knew where this conversation led. He grappled for something to say which could change the situation; although he listened to Elizabeth's response, he attended to it only for the details for he swam in the disgust he now felt for Mr. Wickham, as well as himself. His forswearing her to secrecy caused Elizabeth's distress; loaded with self-reproach, he became determined to find a way to remedy the situation for only two days ago Darcy vowed to protect Elizabeth no matter what the consequences. Elizabeth lamented the inevitable outcome of her sister's alliance. Mr. Bennet went to London, but he needed Mr. Gardiner's help, and she would leave shortly to help comfort her family. Mr. Wickham's character, as he knew, could only be easily swayed with monetary inducements, and her family could offer him no such sums. Again, she blamed herself for the lack of foresight in seeing George Wickham's true nature and Lydia's idolized ideas of love.

Darcy stood during this last passage and began to pace the room in solemn reflection; the intensity of his anger pulsed hard along his temples. He wondered if Elizabeth recognized the effect she had on him. Her tears pierced his heart, and every time she dabbed at her eyes, Darcy's agony crescendoed. He needed to be free of this room; he needed to find Wickham and stop this madness; he needed to take action. With compassion he finally spoke, "Miss Elizabeth, I am afraid you have been long desiring my absence, nor have I anything to plead in excuse of my stay, but real, though unavailing, concern. Would to Heaven that anything could be either said or done on my part that might offer consolation to such distress! But I will not torment you with vain wishes, which may seem purposely to ask for your thanks. This unfortunate affair will, I fear, prevent my sister's having the pleasure of seeing you at Pemberley today."

"Oh, yes," she stumbled with embarrassment, "be so kind as to apologize for us to Miss Darcy. Say that urgent business calls us home immediately. Conceal the unhappy truth as long as it is possible, I know it cannot be long."

Demonstrating as much decorum as he could muster, he readily assured her of his secrecy. "I pray for a happier conclusion to this matter than there is at present reason to hope. Please give my regards to Mr. and Mrs. Gardiner." He made her a quick bow, which she acknowledged with a sorrowful nod of her head. Stepping to the door, Darcy gripped the handle and with only one serious parting look went away.

Emerging onto the streets of the village, he leaned back against the inn's outer wall and gasped for air. *How could it be?* He was so close to winning Elizabeth's heart. To have her snatched away from him again seemed unthinkable. He knew, or, at least, he hoped for an honest chance of Elizabeth's wishes changing in regard to him; now all possibilities of love appeared in vain. *What made the situation worse was George Wickham created it. He always wanted revenge on Darcy; if Wickham knew the irony of the situation, he would be pleased with what he started.* Darcy climbed upon Cerberus's back and turned the reins toward Pemberley, but he remembered none of that—all he remembered was Elizabeth's "fine eyes" lost their glow.

Darcy arrived at Pemberley as his houseguests finished their breakfasts; he mumbled his apologies about having urgent estate business, which caused him to ride out early this day and to which he would now need to devote some time alone to work through. He waited not for their civilities but made an exit to his study and quickly secured the door behind him; he wanted no interruptions until he sorted things out.

Several hours later a light tap at the door roused his attention—the tap so delicate Darcy had no doubt it came from Georgiana; otherwise, he would have ignored it as he had the offers from servants for tea and refreshments. He crossed to the door and opened it quickly to find his sister half turned to go. Darcy spoke not a word, just offered his hand, and led her to the settee; he seated himself next to her, but he did not speak—no words necessary for her to share his anguish. After several excruciating minutes, Georgiana reached up to brush the hair from his eyes. "Has something happened to Miss Elizabeth?" she asked while gently stroking his cheek.

"Why would you ask that? Am I that transparent?" he snapped.

She withdrew her hand from his face and dropped it into her lap. Georgiana enjoyed the new level of respect her brother gave her of late, but his restraint and that stern look sometimes made her still feel like a foolish little girl. Darcy noted she flinched from the tone of his voice; he forced gentleness into his manner when he spoke again. "I apologize, Georgiana, you deserve none of my anger. Allow me to collect my thoughts, and then I will try to explain what has happened." Her eyes rose to meet his as she tried to read the turmoil found in his face. "I do not know where to begin," his voice was hoarse. "I arose this morning with hopes sowed by your words in the conservatory last evening. I decided I would woo Miss Elizabeth, and I rode to Lambton to ask her to ride out with me this afternoon before dinner. I know it was rash, but ..."

Georgiana reached out to squeeze his hand. "Fitzwilliam, please tell me she did not refuse your attentions again."

"No, Miss Elizabeth did not refuse me; I found her in too much distress to even accept my compassion. Miss Bennet received dreadful news from Longbourn." Darcy heard Georgiana gasp. "I am going to tell you quick what must be said, but the news will play hard on your sensibilities, Dearest One; remember I mean to give you no harm. In short, Miss Elizabeth's youngest sister ran away—gave her heart—to George Wickham." The news clearly caused agitation for Georgiana, but she did not look away; she waited for him to continue. "Lydia Bennet has nothing but her affections to attract Mr. Wickham. He will use her ill and then abandon her. Her folly will destroy her reputation, which will, ultimately, reflect upon Miss Elizabeth and her sisters."

Georgiana's eyes filled with tears. "Poor, Miss Elizabeth! Poor Mr. Bingley and his love for Miss Bennet!" She consciously omitted a touch of empathy for her brother to her list. "What will you do, Fitzwilliam?"

"What would you have me do, Georgiana?"

"Brother, you love her; you cannot cast Miss Elizabeth aside, even if she cannot be yours; you said as much last night. Our pride in dealing with Mr. Wickham allowed him to prey on others. We never concerned ourselves with their destruction, only with our own, and now God brought Mr. Wickham's evil back to someone we both affect."

Darcy actually laughed out loud. "Georgiana, you continue to amaze me. How little I know about you! I already decided I must resolve this situation, which means I must deal with George Wickham. I wondered how to tell you without causing you grief. Instead, you give me permission and demand my speed in these negotiations."

"We have always been of the same nature," she nearly teased.

"You spend one afternoon with Elizabeth Bennet, and you already 'pain' your brother with your taunts."

"What is your plan?" She turned more serious, but only after giving him a brief smile.

"I will go to London tomorrow to find Mr. Wickham and Lydia Bennet. I know things about George Wickham's nature Mr. Bennet has yet to learn. I hope to convince the girl to return to her family; they could then hush up her indiscretions. Her journey began in Brighton so most in Hertfordshire will have little knowledge of her folly, assuming Mrs. Bennet controlled her tongue for once. I will tell the Bingleys estate business calls me back to London, but that means you must entertain them while I am away. Are you up to it, Sweet One?"

"I will do what is necessary to protect Miss Elizabeth."

"Miss Elizabeth must never know of my involvement; it would not be proper to inject myself into so private a matter. Besides, although I desire Miss Elizabeth's regard, I do not want her to bestow it upon me out of gratitude. I want her love."

"As our first dealings with Mr. Wickham were our secret so will this one be."

"Let us go and play our parts as good hosts to our guests." Darcy stood with refreshed confidence. Georgiana stood by him and then kissed his cheek gently. "For luck," she said. They exited the study to find the Bingleys and initiate their plan.

That evening over dinner, Darcy informed Charles Bingley and his sisters of his regrets at having to return to London on pressing business. He led them to believe the estate business also cancelled his plans to entertain the Gardiners and Elizabeth Bennet. This gave the Bingley sisters some perverted pleasure. "It grieves me, but it must be so," he added. "Georgiana will serve in my stead. We both thought you might enjoy an overnight trip to Nottingham or to Cromford. Georgiana and Mrs. Annesley both desire to visit those areas to the north. I shall be only a week or so. What say you, Charles?"

"I would be honored to escort your sister in your absence, Darcy." Darcy detested his own deceit, but it would be best if Bingley knew nothing of this crisis, which could ultimately affect both their futures.

CHAPTER 14

"On an affair of importance . . ."

———◦∞◦———

Darcy, consumed by what he must do to save Elizabeth, left early for London. Riding in the comfort of his favorite carriage, he began to reflect on how far he would go to "persuade" George Wickham to marry Lydia Bennet or to "persuade" the foolish flick of a girl to abandon her folly and return to Longbourn. What if he found no success in either endeavor? He loved Pemberley, not just for its beauty but because it held the traditions of his family. He loved the society to which he was accustomed. The wealth and his reputation created a sense of worth, a part of his being. He felt willing to sacrifice some of both for Elizabeth's love; but, now, he might also be faced with the Bennet sisters' loss of respectability or even worse having George Wickham as a brother. Which would be harder to overcome? Could he seriously still consider Elizabeth to be a viable mate in either case? The resolution of the current crisis would not necessarily solve Darcy's dilemma.

On Monday morning Darcy set off to a seedy part of the city. He hired a public cab, not wanting to attract too much attention; he planned to find Mrs. Younge, Georgiana's former governess. Mr. Wickham, as Darcy warned Elizabeth at the Netherfield Ball, had a reputation for being able to make friends, but keeping friends was a different issue. Mr. Wickham "used" people, ill-abused them, leaving most in his wake. In Darcy's estimation, Mrs. Younge was of the same lot; if Mr. Wickham was in London, Mrs. Younge would know where he could be found. He knew where Mrs. Younge lived; he had an address in his London ledger—an address to which the last of her wages were delivered when Darcy dismissed her for her part in Wickham's seduction of Georgiana. From what he ascertained, Mrs. Younge let rooms from her home on Edward Street.

Calling on the house, a dirty-faced snit of a child evidently working as a servant admitted Darcy to the sitting room. When she entered to find him there, Mrs. Younge hid her surprise well. "Mr. Darcy . . . what brings you to this part of town? Did you decide to try slumming for the day?" Anger laced her sarcasm.

"Mrs. Younge," he kept his voice calm and steady, "I have come to your home on business."

She looked him up and down, measuring the merit of his words. Her training as a governess allowed the woman to maintain an image of a refined lady even in the midst of the squalor in which she now found herself. She motioned Darcy to a nearby chair and crossed to one to his right. "I thought any business we might have was settled some time ago. Do not tell me you are once more in need of my services."

Darcy accepted the double meaning of her words with a slight nod of his head and then said, "I appreciate your offer, Mrs. Younge, but that was not the business I had in mind."

"Then what may I ask are you doing here, Mr. Darcy?"

"I come seeking news of Mr. Wickham," Darcy's reply showed no change in his composure, but hers relayed the information he sought.

"Mr. Wickham? Mr. George Wickham? Why would I know of Mr. Wickham's whereabouts?" she protested.

"Mr. Wickham is in London. He has with him the daughter of a friend; that friend, knowing of my connection to Mr. Wickham, asked me to assist in finding the daughter." The words sounded stilted and a bit ambiguous even to him. Darcy did not like the deceit; but, at least, this was not a total fabrication: he and Elizabeth were certainly *friends*.

"It appears you have been misinformed, Mr. Darcy," Mrs. Younge stood to take her leave. "I have not seen or heard from Mr. Wickham since that unfortunate time at Ramsgate."

Darcy stood slowly and slipped on his gloves. "I see," he began as he walked leisurely around the room. "This is an interesting place, Mrs. Younge. I will have to remember this address; it will be an important fact when I tell the constable about . . . let us see . . . which tale do you think the constable will most believe? After all, I am Fitzwilliam Darcy, *a man of impeccable reputation*. I would not want to relate a tale which would be unbelievable." He could not help but smirk as he walked back toward Mrs. Younge. To her credit, she showed no signs of cracking. "I am sure your tenants will *love* having the constable call here on a regular basis with a litany of complaints. I am also sure I can secure other gentlemen of *impeccable reputations* to lodge similar *complaints* to mine. The constable could be here so often you may want to let him one of your rooms. Farewell, Mrs. Younge." Darcy tipped his hat as he started toward the door.

As predicted, Mrs. Younge's voice halted his exit. "Mr. Darcy."

"Yes, Mrs. Younge," he turned, having a hand on the doorknob.

"If I could remember where Mr. Wickham might be, would it stop the visits from the constable?"

"It would, indeed, Mrs. Younge."

"Call tomorrow, and I will see what I can do for you."

Darcy said no more but turned to go back to his waiting cab. A sense of satisfaction rested on his face.

Darcy came again to Edward Street. Mrs. Younge's information was not easy to come by, but for a promise of no visits from the constable and thirty shillings as a bonus, the woman provided Darcy with an address for George Wickham. He took the public carriage again today, and he gave the driver the address. "Are you sure, Sir, you want to go to this place?" The driver looked confused. "I beg your pardon, Sir, but a man of your obvious standing would not regularly be found there." Darcy just nodded to the driver as a sign of his determination to go. Inside the carriage, Darcy's contempt for the situation he must enter nearly made him tell the driver to turn around, but the memory of the misery found on Elizabeth's face forced him to push onward. He discovered George Wickham let a room above a tavern on a bustling, inner city street frequented by a diverse clientele. Having already asked the proprietor for a private table, a bottle of brandy, and two glasses, he paid the man extra to tell Mr. Wickham that Mr. Darcy waited on him in the tavern.

In a matter of minutes, George Wickham strolled into the public room. "Well, Darcy, what a happy occasion this must be to bring us together again."

"Have a seat, Mr. Wickham." His reply had the intonation of a command rather than a request.

Wickham slid casually into the seat. "May I?" he indicated the brandy. Darcy did not break his stare, nor did he verbally respond, but Wickham poured himself two fingers of brandy from the decanter, tossed it off, and quickly poured another before he turned back to his former friend. "I seriously doubt this to be a pleasure call, but I am confused as to why of all people you are here, Darcy."

"I have come for the girl, Mr. Wickham."

"What girl? Can you not get your own girl, Darcy? With all your money, do you need my help in finding a girl?" Wickham snickered at his attempt at humor.

"I have come to see Lydia Bennet." Darcy's voice led Wickham to realize he meant business.

"Oh, her! You are welcome to her; she has lost her usefulness, if you know what I mean," Wickham sneered.

Darcy flexed and released his fists several times under the table, but he never flinched although Wickham's words disgusted him. "Then I am to assume you have no intention of marrying Miss Lydia." He measured each word carefully.

"Why would I want to marry such a silly girl as is Lydia?" Darcy's contempt grew by the second, but he kept his anger in check. Wickham had no intention of doing the honest thing by Lydia Bennet; that much was guaranteed.

"May I see the girl?"

"Of course," Wickham replied, "once you tell me how you became involved in this matter. Why is the great Fitzwilliam Darcy here in this place asking about an insignificant girl like Lydia Bennet? Do you fancy her for yourself? No, she is not the type for you, but I cannot figure your connection."

Darcy hoped the story he had *practiced* would be believable although it possessed holes in it. If Wickham knew Darcy's real motivation, Wickham would use it against him. "During my stay in Hertfordshire, I became intimate with Mr. Bennet; we share common interests—love of the land and, of course, books. His cousin upon whom Longbourn is entailed is my aunt's cleric, a man whom she respects. My connection to you was known by your own words to anyone in Hertfordshire who would listen. All of these factors led Mr. Bennet to swallow his pride and to ask for help in this matter. He has no sons to aid him, and he is not familiar with London. I am the logical person. Mr. Bennet simply wants a resolution to this matter."

"I am not sure I totally believe you, Darcy," Wickham began, "but I will send the girl to talk to you."

Darcy commanded, "We will need to speak again after I have time with Miss Lydia."

Wickham said nothing, but one could easily tell he enjoyed the drama of Darcy's request. He left the table, and Lydia Bennet shortly replaced him. She flounced to the table like a spoiled child being sent to stand in a corner. "Mr. Darcy," she did not even make him the courtesy of a bow, "my dear Wickham says you wish to speak to me, Sir."

"Please have a seat, Miss Lydia." He tried to use the voice he used to use with Georgiana when she did not want to practice her music or to complete her studies. Lydia sat down, but she tried to let him know by her actions she did not do so willingly. "Miss Lydia, I have been asked to bring you back to the safety of your family," he began softly.

"Why, Lordy, would anyone in my family ask you to do any such thing? You snubbed Lizzy; no one there likes you." Her words stung Darcy's pride, but he relied on the restraint of his emotions before; he did so now.

"Your family and friends are concerned for you, Miss Lydia. A person would turn to the Devil for help in order to bring a loved one home. I am far from being the Devil even in your sister's estimation. My connection to Mr. Wickham made me a logical choice for this task."

Luckily, Lydia Bennet's shallowness kept her from seeing through this deceit, but her shallowness also made her immovable. No matter what Darcy offered as a logical reason for her leaving, Lydia Bennet's determination remained with Wickham. She wanted nothing to do with "boring old Longbourn" or with "sisters who never wanted to do anything that was fun." She believed Wickham planned to marry her as soon as his "luck" changed, and they got a little cash flow. She wanted nothing to do with any of her "so-called" friends. Lydia Bennet could not be persuaded to leave; that meant Darcy would have to *break* Wickham's resolve.

When Wickham returned to the table, he helped himself to another drink before he addressed Darcy's demand. "So, the girl prefers me to you, it seems," he started. "I guess I win this battle."

"The girl expects you to marry her," Darcy's voice had not changed since he began this ordeal. "I realize you must be in dire straits or else you would not be here, Mr. Wickham."

"I do not know where she got the idea we would marry," he protested. "I promise I never made such overtures."

"Your promises are well known, Mr. Wickham." Darcy wanted to deal with him physically, but he continued what he started. "I am not the betting man who you are known to be, but I would think it to be a sure bet you left Brighton because your debts were coming due. Miss Lydia probably had some ready cash—at least, enough to get you this far. Am I getting close?"

"As far as Lydia is concerned, it was her choice to come along. I offered her no encouragement," Wickham swore. "I will admit to being short of cash, however."

"As I suspected," Darcy stated. "Mr. Bennet is not a rich man, Mr. Wickham, but I am sure he would bestow something suitable on Lydia upon her marriage."

"I would prefer a woman with a larger purse, if you do not mind."

"It is not as if an heiress is likely to find you in this *fine* establishment; now is it, Mr. Wickham? At my count, you lost the last two with whom you tried to make an alliance. A man should seriously consider his options."

"If Lydia Bennet is my only option, then I am in more trouble than I first imagined."

Darcy stood; he had all of George Wickham he could take for one day. "I will give you some time to think on it; I will call on you again tomorrow."

"I may no longer be here," Wickham looked agitated.

"I would not try to leave if I were you," Darcy said calmly. "I found you easily; the law would not be so kind as to buy you a bottle of brandy. I understand debtors' prison is worse than this if one can imagine such a place." Thus said, he took leave of the tavern, but before he left the area, Darcy paid a street urchin to keep his eye on Wickham. He told the boy he would pay him each day to keep tabs on Wickham's comings and goings. He was to send word to Darcy if Wickham tried to leave for good.

Sitting in his study at Kensington Place, Darcy planned how far he would go to secure Lydia Bennet's marriage to George Wickham. He would have to bribe the man—that was evident. Wickham, he knew, would ask for more than he could get. Darcy determined a reasonable figure, one he would expend on two worthless individuals such as George Wickham and Lydia Bennet. The thoughts were repugnant, and only images of Elizabeth on the grounds of Pemberley sustained him through these musings.

Wickham seated himself at the same table upon Darcy's arrival. A fresh bottle of brandy sat on the table, along with two glasses. Darcy removed his gloves and started to sit down. "I hope you do not mind, Darcy," Wickham smiled, "but I told the proprietor you would pay for the brandy when you arrived." Darcy tossed a coin on the table, and the tavern owner hurried over to claim it.

"I have pressing business today, Mr. Wickham. I do not have time to play games. Have you thought more about marrying Miss Lydia?"

Wickham launched into the negotiations, "How much do you believe Mr. Bennet will bestow on Lydia?"

"I cannot say for sure. I have not discussed this with him directly. I would be willing to contact him on your behalf if you so desire." Darcy hoped Wickham would not call him on this; he did not want Mr. Bennet, whom, in reality, he barely knew knowing how he went beyond good society in this matter. For if Mr. Bennet knew, Elizabeth would also know the extent of his involvement. "You will need," he continued, "a fresh start. I would, personally, be willing for old times' sake, as part of my dear father's memory, to pay your debts in Meryton and Brighton. Mrs. Bennet's brothers offered to cover me on any such expense, if necessary. As a lawyer in Meryton, one of Mrs. Bennet's brothers has been approached by several residents with complaints of your *shortcomings*."

Wickham pondered, "All my debts would be cleared?"

"Of course, I am assuming you have a full accounting to whom you owe funds," Darcy offered. "Do you have any idea of the extent of your debt?"

"I would be able to determine that information for you, I believe," Wickham stumbled on.

"Then we are agreed," Darcy started.

"Wait . . . I may need a way to support my new wife. I can no longer return to the militia."

"I have considered that. What say you to a commission in the regulars? Miss Lydia has a preference for men in uniforms. It would be best if we find you a regiment in another part of the country where your reputation is not known; that would aid your fresh start. Colonel Fitzwilliam could help us."

"It seems you planned my life for me, Darcy," Wickham faltered. "It is so out of character for you to be taking all this on. What is the true nature of your concern?"

"I told you of my connections to Hertfordshire previously, but I also admit some shame in how our relationship deteriorated. Your father served my father most faithfully. Although I still find what you did to Georgiana and now to Miss Lydia to be abhorrent, I do understand your desperation. For my father's sake, I wish you another chance to be successful."

"That is generous of you," Wickham stammered. "Let me think on it; you may buy me another bottle of brandy tomorrow." He slugged down the alcohol in his glass, took the bottle with him, and climbed the stairs to his let rooms. Darcy left the tavern, stopping to pay his "spy" along the way. He knew by tomorrow Wickham would be his.

On the third day of their meetings, Darcy found Wickham made a more presentable appearance; he abandoned his previous unkempt look, and he spent time with his ablutions. The tavern keeper brought over the brandy without being asked, and Darcy dutifully paid him. So far, Wickham was too easily persuaded, and Darcy knew him well enough to know when he took an accounting of his debts, Wickham would not sell out so quickly; therefore, when Wickham began a renegotiation of the previous terms, this did not surprise Darcy.

"I have been thinking, Darcy, about what you said yesterday about your father and mine. They were good friends, were they not?" He reached for the brandy again. It seemed to give him something to do with his hands for Darcy noted although Wickham's voice and countenance portrayed him to be calm, the trembling of his hands betrayed his lie. Darcy simply shot Wickham a complementary look of calm. "We were great friends, too, Darcy, in our youth."

"What is your point, Mr. Wickham?" Darcy asked, knowing where the conversation led.

"I was thinking about the living your father's promise intended on my having," Wickham began. "Do you think it might ever be available to me?"

"I can never say *never*," Darcy began, hoping to keep Wickham's plans alive without promising him anything definite, "but I cannot see that as a possibility in the near future. It would be several years off at best. Your immediate future would be best spent as we discussed yesterday. The colonel helped me locate an available commission in the North if you are willing to accept it. It appears to be a perfect match for your temperament; you need only to resign your current position as an officer in the ——shire. The paperwork for such a transfer can be complete in less than a week according to the colonel."

Wickham mulled over Darcy's words; Darcy saw glimpses of the desperation Wickham experienced displayed in his manner. "Mr. Bennet," Wickham still pressed for more, "will give Lydia her share of her mother's inheritance, but that may not be enough for us. I am afraid my intended has expensive tastes; I do not think I can afford her."

"Of what are you thinking?" Darcy asked although he knew what to expect.

"If I chose to leave Lydia and found someone else, I could probably use my *charms* to find a more lucrative match. I was thinking an extra ten thousand pounds might make me more amiable to the Bennet offer."

"Mr. Bennet, as you well know, cannot afford such a demand, and although I am one of his friends, I cannot assume so many of his debts. Between Mr. Bennet and Mrs. Bennet's brothers, reasonable demands will be met, but ten thousand pounds is not a *reasonable* idea. They would be more willing to turn you over to the constable and use their money to hush up the issues of Miss Lydia's spoiled reputation. They could easily purchase her an appropriate match for a lot less. I would not press for so much if I were you; the

Bennet offer is the best one on the table for you at this time. If you and Miss Lydia economize her spending and your gambling, the two of you may live quite well on your commission and her inheritance. I will, however, pledge an additional two thousand pounds, but that is my last offer. I will not return here after today if you do not accept the Bennets' agreement." Wickham shifted uncomfortably in his chair as he weighed the situation. After several minutes of fretful silence, he agreed with Darcy's demands. An end was near, but Darcy did not let down his guard too soon. "You agree, Mr. Wickham, to the following: a resignation of your current position, an acceptance of a commission in the regulars, a payment of all your current debts in Meryton and Brighton, and a settlement of three thousand pounds total on Miss Lydia."

"I agree, Darcy." He extended his hand; Darcy did not move, however.

"If you do not mind, I would prefer my attorney draw up the agreements and obtain your signature rather than accepting your handshake."

Wickham conjectured, "Do you not trust me?"

"It is not personal, Mr. Wickham; it is business. Where I might accept your word, I am sure the Bennet family would prefer something more binding."

Wickham's laugh held elements of sorrowfulness, but he made his decision and with a resiliency Darcy once envied, he stood to take his leave. "Before you go, Mr. Wickham, I need for you to approach the local clergyman and make arrangements for the wedding. Miss Lydia cannot return to Meryton for the service after having been here with you for so long. She must be married here in London. I will contact her aunt and uncle; she should stay with them until the marriage vows take place. St. Clements Church is the closest parish; please see the clergyman there about the reading of the banns; you are looking at a fortnight, at least, before the vows. I am leaving you ten shillings to pay the minister and additional funds to maintain your room here. Do not spend it unwisely."

"As usual, Darcy, you have thought of everything," Wickham's smile suggested the sarcasm his tone did not betray.

"It has been my lot in life," Darcy also stood. "My attorney will call on you tomorrow for your signature. I will see Miss Lydia's uncle as soon as possible, and he will make arrangements for her removal to his residence. He will allow you, I am sure, appropriate time with her as you wait for the nuptials."

"Then there is nothing left to do; I will tell Lydia she is soon to be Mrs. Wickham." He took the brandy once again and poured himself a quick drink before he headed for the stairs that led to the room where Lydia Bennet awaited his return.

Friday brought Darcy a short letter from Georgiana. They traveled to Nottingham, and she told him of a few items she purchased from the local merchants. The most important part of the letter was the last paragraph.

Now that Miss Bingley walked away from examining how much my handwriting resembles my brother's, I can say what I wanted to tell you. Your sister, my darling Fitzwilliam, is proud of your efforts to save Miss Elizabeth, especially considering the mortifications you must be suffering at Mr. Wickham's hands. You see, I have no doubt you have found him, and a resolution is at hand. I await your return and news of your success.

With love,
Georgiana

Darcy realized the blessing of having someone such as Georgiana as a sister rather than someone like Lydia Bennet. He knew Georgiana would gladly suffer the public humiliation of her brief relationship with Mr. Wickham in order to save Elizabeth where Lydia Bennet cared not for anyone but herself. Lydia Bennet and George Wickham deserved each other; Wickham married an embodiment of Mrs. Bennet; maybe Darcy would have the final revenge after all.

In late afternoon, Darcy made a trip to Cheapside to see Mr. Gardiner, but he found upon calling about business Mr. Gardiner met with his brother Mr. Bennet. Darcy did not wish to see Mr. Bennet so he made his exit, telling the servant he would call again the following day. The servant told Darcy Mr. Bennet planned to depart on Saturday, and Mr. Gardiner would be available then.

When he made his call on Mr. Gardiner the next day, he received a genuine welcome although he surprised the man. "Mr. Darcy, it is so pleasant to see you again so soon. When Emily said I had a visitor yesterday, I had no idea it was you; Mr. Bennet and I would have received you had we known."

"It is of no consequence, Mr. Gardiner," Darcy stated as he accepted the seat being offered. "My business is of a *delicate* nature, and I purposely avoided Mr. Bennet's knowledge of it."

Mr. Gardiner said seriously, "You have my undivided attention, Sir."

"As you are aware, I was with your niece Elizabeth when she received the news from Miss Bennet which has distressed your family of late."

"Elizabeth told us of the comfort your presence provided her then, but I do not understand how that affects you, Sir."

"Mr. Wickham's relationship with my family has been a tenuous one, but my many dealings with him gave me knowledge of his habits, which you and your brother did not have. My knowledge of George Wickham came from his father being my father's steward. Mr. Wickham and I were at Cambridge together, and I have dealt with him in such nefarious matters as this one before. I took that knowledge, and I followed you to London. I realize I took on more than is acceptable, but I hope you will forgive my intrusion into such a private matter when I tell you I found them and spoke to them on several occasions about their folly."

"You found them!" Mr. Gardiner's relief showed on his face. "I would gladly forgive your intrusion for such happy news. Where are they? Are they married?"

"They are not married," Darcy saw Gardiner's happiness fade, "but I presented myself to both Mr. Wickham and to Miss Lydia as being your family's agent in this matter. I concocted a lie, which I hope you will also forgive, to achieve an agreement with Mr. Wickham and your family. He applied for an ordinary license with the minister at St. Clements Church yesterday. They will be married in a little over a fortnight."

"Mr. Darcy, my sister's family will be ever in your debt."

Darcy then told Mr. Gardiner of the financial arrangements he made with Mr. Wickham. Although Darcy's news astounded him, his niece's lack of concern for her family, however, did not surprise the man. "I fear only the two eldest Bennet sisters possess good sense, Mr. Darcy. They are our favorites, as you can imagine." Darcy could easily imagine Elizabeth; he had done so every day since the assembly at Meryton, but he made no comment. Mr. Gardiner, he was sure, knew of his affection for Elizabeth; why else would he have gotten involved in such a situation as this one if he did not care about Elizabeth Bennet; he no longer tried to deny his feelings for her.

Mr. Gardiner agreed Lydia should be married out of his home, and he would make arrangements to bring her there the next day. Mrs. Gardiner returned to London then, and they would go together to bring Lydia to Gracechurch Street. Gardiner soon learned of Darcy's good business sense. Getting Mr. Wickham to marry Lydia Bennet for so little was a stroke of genius. Although it would be a strain on the Bennets' finances, Mr. Gardiner would share the expenses with his sister's family. That is when he learned Darcy's full plan. Darcy would assume all the expenses of the wedding, but he wanted none of the credit for doing so.

"I will hear of no compromise. It is my conviction if George Wickham's worthlessness was better known, it would be impossible for him to persuade any young woman of character to leave with him without proper bonds. I knew of his low character, but my foolish pride would not allow me to make known the extent of his depravity. I once thought myself above his actions. However, I came to realize if I did something before, none of this would be possible. I cared only for my own private matters and did not consider the ramifications of Mr. Wickham's evil on other people." Darcy never spoke directly of his sister's shame, but he gave Mr. Gardiner to know Mr. Wickham betrayed Darcy's family. He was obstinate about his involvement and would not relent, no matter how much Mr. Gardiner tried to change his mind.

"Well, Mr. Darcy," Mr. Gardiner offered, "it seems you have Mr. Wickham's life planned."

Darcy laughed conspiratorially. "He said something similar."

"Will you join me for dinner, Sir?"

"I cannot, Mr. Gardiner, I have other obligations this evening."

"My wife returns tomorrow. I wish to discuss your proposal with her. Will you join us tomorrow evening as our guest?"

"It would be a pleasure to spend time with you and Mrs. Gardiner again."

The men parted, each with a degree of satisfaction. Mr. Gardiner would see an end to the troubles Lydia brought on the family; Darcy would preserve Elizabeth's respectability and maintain his slim hopes she would one day change her mind and marry him.

"I will not change my mind, Mr. Gardiner." Darcy renewed his contention to be the sole benefactor in the Wickham matter again on Sunday for Mr. Gardiner had second thoughts about taking credit for Darcy's triumph; but Darcy's obstinacy won out.

Mr. and Mrs. Gardiner finally agreed to his demands, but they did so with an ulterior motive, realizing Darcy's preference for their niece, a preference Darcy hoped to one day make public. "I must tell you, Mr. Darcy, we will be forever in your debt," Mrs. Gardiner began. "We accept your offer reluctantly in hopes by doing so we maintain the respectability of Lydia's more deserving sisters. They should have fulfilling lives despite their youngest sister's folly."

The Gardiners had the pleasure of his company that evening for dinner, and Darcy had the pleasure of listening to them tell stories of Jane and Elizabeth as children and as young ladies growing up in the Bennet household. Those tales of Elizabeth's precociousness most interested him, but he also took delight in learning more about Jane Bennet. He misjudged her nature, and he knew making amends to Bingley must come soon. "Those two girls," Mrs. Gardiner was laughing so hard at the story she told that tears came to her eyes, "would look at you and maintain their innocence, which was usually true for Jane, but not so much for Lizzy. Even when you were mad at what they did, you could not be mad at either of them. Their goodness made you love them even when your favorite vase lay in a hundred pieces on the kitchen floor."

The Gardiners' own children showed interest in Mr. Darcy because he was a "favorite," according to their parents of both "Cousin Jane" and "Cousin Elizabeth." Having children in the house made Darcy fancy Elizabeth even more than usual. It was a perfect way to end a most pleasurable evening.

On Monday, Darcy finalized the plans for the church, the transfer of funds to Lydia Bennet, and the purchasing of the commission. Calling on the Gardiners one last time, he found they sent a dispatch to Longbourn with news of the impending marriage. *Finally,* he thought, *Elizabeth will be free of all these provocations: she will be able to laugh again*; he dearly missed that laugh. Lydia was coming to Gracechurch Street that day, and he would return to Pemberley on Wednesday. He would come again to London for the actual wedding; Mr. Wickham had no one else to stand up with him; plus, Darcy's need for meticulous planning required he be there to assure nothing went awry before the nuptials.

All were happy to see his return to Pemberley, with his sister most anxious to seek his company privately; but that would wait; today Darcy served as the "good" host. "Mr. Darcy, you were grievously missed on our trip to Nottingham," Caroline called to him.

He answered her politely, "I am sorry to cause you grief, Miss Bingley."

"Has your urgent estate problems been resolved?" Bingley implored.

"Generally so," Darcy lied, "but I will need to return to London for a day or two at the end of the month. Then everything *will be finalized*." He emphasized the last words to give Georgiana some peace while she waited to learn the whole story.

"I would have wished to be of service to you, Darcy," Bingley offered. "You do so much for my family."

"Your caring for Georgiana was of service to me, Bingley. I could not leave her in your care if I did not value your friendship. She means more to me than does Pemberley." Georgiana blushed with his words, and her eyes misted with emotions. He was the finest man she knew; finding a mate who could live up to her brother's image could be difficult in her estimation. "In fact," he continued, "I hoped to keep you at Pemberley when your sisters depart for Scarborough. Besides wishing you to care for Georgiana in my absence again, I would wish to spend some time with you as gentlemen."

"I would enjoy that, Darcy," Bingley smiled from ear-to-ear.

Later that evening, Georgiana tapped lightly on his study door. "I wondered when you would make your way here, Dearest One," he teased.

"I wanted to make sure our guests retired for the night," Georgiana came forward to have a seat across from his desk. "Please tell me what happened in London. Did you find Mr. Wickham?"

"Are you sure you want to hear all the unsavory details?"

"Besides knowing Miss Elizabeth is going to be well, your story can only confirm how lucky I am to have you as my older brother. Although it would probably upset me to ever see Mr. Wickham again, I do want to know his fate *and* your advantage."

Darcy summarized the events of the last ten days, accenting the squalor in which he found both Mrs. Younge and George Wickham, but he assured Georgiana Mr. Wickham would marry

Lydia Bennet; Darcy would attend the service at St. Clements Church along with the Gardiners.

"Then you will be able to pursue Miss Elizabeth again," Georgiana encouraged.

"Have you considered the ramifications of that, Georgiana?" he started. "If I earn Elizabeth's love, it would mean Mr. Wickham would be my brother—our brother."

"Fitzwilliam, we have many relations we rarely see. Mr. and Mrs. Wickham will be in Newcastle; I am sure Miss Elizabeth would understand Mr. Wickham would never be welcomed at Pemberley. You could not have done all these things and then give up. You must find a way to win Miss Elizabeth's heart; you deserve her, and although she does not know it yet, she needs you."

"Georgiana, the man who earns your heart will be winning a true romantic." He chuckled while she blushed. They finished the evening with his relating some of the more amusing Elizabeth Bennet stories shared by the Gardiners; they laughed and talked into the late hours.

As promised, he returned to London to witness the exchange of vows and to finalize the money matters. The wedding took place on a Monday at eleven o'clock in the morning. A month had passed since Mr. Wickham and Lydia Bennet left Brighton, and finally to be rid of the chaos gladdened him. In Lydia Bennet, Darcy saw the same effusive, immature girl from Hertfordshire; the results associated with her actions meant nothing to her. Instead, she babbled on about whether Mr. Wickham should wear his blue coat for the ceremony. Mrs. Gardiner tried to caution the girl, but silence could not be attained.

Darcy dined with the Gardiners on Tuesday, but they spoke more of Lydia's insolence rather than of Elizabeth and Jane; he would prefer to hear about the latter. One of the Gardiner children, Cassandra, gave him a crayon picture of himself, Jane, and Elizabeth walking in a garden and holding hands. Although the likenesses were not accurate, the sentiment touched his heart in a way he never knew. He took the drawing back to Pemberley and placed it in a special spot in his study.

CHAPTER 15

"The usual practice of elegant females . . ."

———◦◦◦◦———

Returning to the security of Pemberley, having both Georgiana's and Bingley's company brought him comfort. Yet, being with Bingley constantly reminded Darcy he must make amends for his duplicity in separating Bingley from Jane Bennet. One early autumn day, although the season was yet to open, they went out shooting. "I believe the last time, Darcy, we were shooting was at Netherfield," Bingley said wistfully.

"You are right, Bingley," Darcy paused as he planted the idea. "That was a pleasant time, was it not? By the way, have you made a decision on Netherfield? It seems a waste of money to let an estate one never uses."

Bingley, not sure he heard Darcy accurately, seized on the idea. "Not having stayed through the winter, I am still unsure of the house's soundness. Maybe I should consider returning to Netherfield and make my decision based on what I find."

"That seems to be a logical manner of making a judicious decision, Bingley."

"Would you consider joining me, Darcy? We could shoot, ride, and enjoy my estate. I would like for you to come with me."

Darcy chuckled with the success of his ploy. "I would enjoy that, Bingley."

"Capital! I will send servants to open the house. We can go to Hertfordshire next week."

Darcy's heart leapt. He would see Elizabeth again. Could they continue what they began at Pemberley? At dinner that evening,

Bingley told Georgiana of his plan to return to Netherfield. "Your brother consented to join me," he shared. Georgiana smiled knowingly at Darcy, but she said nothing. She knew him well enough to know the uncertainty he felt in returning to Elizabeth's home. Everything could change in the next few weeks.

She hugged him a bit longer than usual and reached up to caress his cheek when they departed for Netherfield that mid-September morning. "I will say a prayer for your happiness, Brother." He smiled weakly at her as he boarded the coach; Darcy could think of nothing but Elizabeth.

"Darcy, we have been at Netherfield for two days now," Bingley mused, "and Mr. Bennet has not called. Do you think we should call on him instead?"

"Let us wait until tomorrow to see if the situation changes. If not, then, we can offer our own civilities."

"Tomorrow it is then," Bingley stared out the window.

There were few places at Netherfield where images of Elizabeth did not dance through Darcy's head. He saw her on the staircase as she was on that last Sunday; he saw her carrying the water to her sister's room; he saw her reaching for the book of poetry in the library; the image haunted his waking and his sleeping hours. *Tomorrow*, he thought, *tomorrow will tell whether I declare my love to Elizabeth Bennet again.*

Riding next to Bingley as he entered the pathway leading to Longbourn, both gentlemen were silent, deep in the wonderment of what the next hour would bring. Bingley wondered could he renew his relationship with Jane Bennet; Darcy wondered how Elizabeth would welcome him. Of course, this was not Pemberley. The excellent company he found in Mr. and Mrs. Gardiner would be replaced by the simple-mindedness of Mrs. Bennet, but what Mrs. Bennet said did not interest him. Darcy had a dual purpose for this visit: assess Jane Bennet's feelings for Bingley and Elizabeth Bennet's feelings for him.

Upon being announced and entering the room, Darcy's eyes sought only Elizabeth. Weeks had passed since he saw her; the last time she cried over Wickham and Lydia, and relieving her distress became his only concern. He observed her for weeks last fall, memorizing her every gesture and the full gamut of her emotions; therefore, immediately, he recognized her uneasiness—the source of the uneasiness questionable. Was it his presence here at Long-bourn? Was it that others might find out about Hunsford and Pemberley? Was it embarrassment of his knowing about Lydia? *Let me first see how she reacts to my presence; then I will decide my next step.*

On their appearance, Elizabeth blushed, but she made both gentlemen a curtsy before returning eagerly to her needlework. Mrs. Bennet warmly welcomed Bingley, offering him her favorite chair and refreshments. Barely civil, she acknowledged Darcy only by name. He moved to the side where he could see both Elizabeth and her elder sister. Jane Bennet looked a little paler and more sedate than he expected; but she received them with tolerable ease and appeared to be accepting of Bingley's presence at her home. If Jane Bennet held no resentment, Charles stood a chance with her. Darcy wished her sister would show him some preference. As far as he could tell, Elizabeth ventured only one glance in his direction. He wanted to be alone with her, to hear her voice, to see her smile; he wanted only to profess his continuing love. Instead, he swallowed hard and forced himself to say, "Miss Elizabeth, may I inquire about the health of your aunt and uncle?"

"They are well, Sir," she stammered.

"I am pleased to hear it."

"They were," she tried to look at him, but, in reality, she spoke to the floor, "so pleased with Pemberley. My uncle still speaks fondly of enjoying the sport he found there."

"He will always be most welcome there."

Before the conversation could continue, however, Mrs. Bennet interrupted with a declaration of the benefits of having a married daughter so well situated. The mention of Wickham's name sent a shiver down Darcy's spine with the remembrance of the circumstances in which he found Wickham and Lydia. Too mortified to look at Darcy, Elizabeth notably stiffened as Mrs. Bennet asked Mr. Bingley if he read the wedding announcement in the news; however, Darcy could not force his eyes from her.

"I did see it; may I offer my congratulations," Bingley replied. Darcy did not join the conversation for fear his tone would betray his thoughts of George Wickham.

Mrs. Bennet lamented Wickham's removal to Newcastle. "Mr. Wickham has been stationed in the North. I have no idea when we might see our dear Lydia again." Darcy, had she known, rejoiced in Wickham's removal. The commission he purchased for his former friend was under a very strict commanding officer, and Darcy hoped the officer would break Wickham's insolence. Mrs. Bennet's next remark offered another cut leveled at Darcy. "Thank Heavens, he has *some* friends, though perhaps not so many as he deserves!" *If Mrs. Bennet only knew what Wickham truly deserves.*

Her words forced him to once more turn his back on Elizabeth's family in order not to respond to the woman, but if he looked at Elizabeth, he would have seen her shame. His having to bear her mother's feeble command of social graces made her miserable, and she could hardly keep her seat. Seeing him thus treated forced her to exert herself and speak, "Mr. Bingley, do you plan to stay long in the country?"

Her words reached Darcy as nothing else could; even the simplest phrase added to the image he drew of her. The words she said did not fascinate him; it was the way she responded to each situation—how she knew him—had known he needed her at that moment to deflect her mother's attention. He turned back to add to *his portrait* of Elizabeth Bennet.

Nervousness echoed in Bingley's response; Darcy for a moment forgot he should also observe Miss Bennet's reaction to Charles. "I hope to stay several weeks, Miss Elizabeth—for the shooting. Several weeks would be most gratifying." Bingley hesitated as he shot a quick glance at Jane Bennet.

Both Elizabeth and Darcy saw how Bingley's response to Elizabeth's question affected Jane Bennet. Darcy wondered why he never saw the admiration she held for Bingley before. Elizabeth glowed with seeing the spark between Jane and Bingley being rekindled. Darcy wished she would look at him with such persuasion. Elizabeth tried to protect him from her mother but was that because she feared further censure of her family or because she had feelings for him?

When Bingley and Darcy rose to take their leave, Mrs. Bennet issued an invitation to Mr. Bingley for dinner in a few days' time. "You are quite a visit in my debt, Mr. Bingley, for when you went to town last winter you promised to take a family dinner with us as soon as you returned. I have not forgot, you see." A less civil invitation was also issued to Darcy. "Of course, you may join us too, Mr. Darcy." The gentlemen were shown to the door. As the Bennet family gathered around, there was no way for Darcy to speak to Elizabeth again. His bow and her curtsy were all they could manage.

Arriving back at Netherfield, Bingley felt ecstatic, his hopes secretly coming true. Jane Bennet did not turn from his attentions as he successfully engaged her over and over. She smiled at him, laughed lightly at his attempts at humor, and made eye contact with Charles repeatedly.

Darcy, on the other hand, felt misery. Elizabeth appeared uneasy from the beginning; she answered his questions, and her voice got stronger with each response, but she barely looked at him and offered him no encouragement. His hopes were overturned as scenes from previous encounters at Netherfield and Hunsford flashed before his eyes. *You were the last man in the world whom I could ever be prevailed upon to marry. . . . I hear such different accounts of you as puzzle me exceedingly. . . . I have every reason to think ill of you. . . . Had you behaved in a more gentleman-like manner . . . .* All the old insecurities returned. Would he never be able to make her love him? He thought positively when they were alone at Pemberley, but here she was so different. How was he to judge her sentiment? Maybe he should leave. The feel of the hand she offered him to be helped into her uncle's carriage said otherwise; the backward stare as they departed said she cared; the touch of the petals of the boxwood rose said she believed in constancy. Which images? Which images should he believe about Elizabeth Bennet? He would wait until after the dinner. Possibly, it was the shock of his being at Longbourn. Possibly, she was embarrassed by her mother's actions. Possibly, she was more concerned with Jane's welfare. All of these possibilities were characteristic of Elizabeth. He would try to be calm and allow things to take their course. Darcy would wait to see if she was different at the dinner; then he would decide whether to leave or not. Besides, he could assess Jane Bennet's estimation of Bingley before he confessed his deceit. He told himself all these things. Surely, if Elizabeth cared for him as he hoped she did, their hearts would find each other before long.

Several of the Bennet sisters welcomed Bingley and Darcy upon their entrance to Longbourn. Elizabeth took their greatcoats and briefly greeted Darcy with a hint of a smile and an obligatory curtsy. When they repaired to the dining room, Darcy hoped to be seated close to Elizabeth, but finding himself seated instead close to Mrs. Bennet dashed those hopes. Bingley found his seat near Jane Bennet; oh, for such pleasure with Elizabeth! He could hear nothing of what she said. Only once did he notice her attentions toward him. It was when Bingley placed himself next to Jane; Elizabeth gave Darcy a triumphant look, and he bore it with presumed indifference. The dinner included venison and soup. Darcy attempted to make conversation with Mrs. Bennet by complimenting her on the serving of partridge as part of the meal. She clearly made a statement with the menu, and his good breeding required he take notice, but he would rather take notice of her second daughter's eyes. Generally though, Darcy spoke very little to anyone at the table.

He hoped for the opportunity of some conversation with Elizabeth as the evening progressed; all he needed was a few moments alone. He would ask her to meet him privately, and then he would ask her once again to marry him. Useless and mundane time was spent in the drawing room with the gentlemen; he was anxious to return to the ladies. When the gentlemen entered the drawing room, Darcy planned immediately to approach Elizabeth, but she served coffee to the guests and was surrounded by ladies who appeared to be protecting her for they stood close by. He moved toward her, but one of the girls moved in closer, taking on a conspiratorial stance. He, therefore, took his cup and walked away to another part of the room.

The evening went badly, but, eventually, Darcy brought back his coffee cup. Elizabeth, thankfully, seized the opportunity of saying, "May I inquire about Miss Darcy?" She even forced herself to look at him.

"Georgiana is at Pemberley with Mrs. Annesley. She will remain there until the Festive Season."

"Then her friends have gone to Scarborough?"

"They have, Miss Elizabeth." Darcy was barely able to utter the words; her beauty enthralled him.

"I am sorry we could not dine at Pemberley as we had planned." She struggled to express her regrets.

"Georgiana and I *both* regretted your sudden departure. We hope to see you at Pemberley again." *Did she understand the double meaning of his words?*

The conversation staled at that point. Searching for something more to say, he stood by her, but what he wished to tell her could not be done so in public. He wanted only a few minutes' conversation with Elizabeth again, and he would be satisfied if only the opportunity occurred. The girl still listened in, and Darcy eventually walked away.

That was the last of their conversation for he was relegated to a table of whist at Mrs. Bennet's insistence; Elizabeth sat at a different table. Darcy's mind always searched for her rather than paying attention to the game, making him play poorly. When the others began to leave, Mrs. Bennet tried to keep them for supper, but their carriage was ordered, and Bingley and Darcy were soon on their way to Netherfield.

Bingley rejoiced in the progress he made with Miss Bennet although he guarded his feelings from Darcy; memories of Darcy's censure of Miss Bennet required Bingley to be cautious. He wanted to retain Darcy's friendship, but Bingley also desired Jane Bennet's affection. Despite his own misery, Darcy knew the time for telling Bingley the truth neared, but he could not do so this evening. His own heart was breaking as he wrote a quick passage to his sister.

22 September

Georgiana,

I return to London tomorrow; my time at Netherfield has been most disheartening. I wished to send you good news, but instead, I fear my expectations were unreasonable. Mr. Bingley, however, will be more successful. I told Bingley I will return to Netherfield in ten days, but those plans may change; my heart may not be able to withstand it. I am sorry Elizabeth will not be returning to Pemberley with me. I know this was your wish as much as it was mine. I know not what else to do.

Fitzwilliam

When Bingley entered the morning room, finding Darcy dressed for a journey surprised him. "Darcy, do you plan to leave Netherfield today?"

"I do, Charles."

"Why? Are you not satisfied at Netherfield? I know country

society does not appeal to you, but I hoped you would find it more pleasurable this time."

"Charles," Darcy established the tone of what he had to say, "would you please join me at the table? I have something important to tell you."

"Darcy, you sound so serious." Bingley walked cautiously to the table and slid into a chair.

"Charles, I am not leaving Netherfield because of country society. In fact, I learned my lesson; some parts of the country can be very appealing." The ambiguity of Darcy's speech confused Bingley. "I do have business to address in London, but that is not my main reason for leaving. After I say what I have to say to you, you will desire my going."

"Darcy, this speech lacks sensibility; I could never turn away a friend such as you have been to me."

"I have been a poor friend, indeed, Charles. You trusted me unwisely."

"Darcy . . .?" he began, but his friend stopped him with a raise of his hand.

"Please, Bingley, I must say this while I still have my nerve. I gave you a disservice." Bingley sat unresponsive, not sure where this conversation led. "I conspired with your sisters last fall to separate you from Miss Bennet; I did so because I considered you to be my best friend, and I believed at the time Miss Bennet was indifferent and did not desire your affection, but that is no excuse for what I did to you."

"Darcy," Bingley got up to pace the room, "am I to understand you kept me from Miss Bennet with some sort of lie or deceit? How could you? You knew how I felt about her. You hurt me, and what is worse, you hurt her!"

"Bingley, you are right to be so upset. I am without reason; my conceit at thinking I knew what was best for you is unforgivable." Darcy, eyes lowered, sat dejected, realizing he ruined his relationship with Charles Bingley. Several minutes passed before Bingley spoke again.

"Darcy," Bingley tried to steady his voice, "I am not sure how I will be able to forgive you, but I must assume some of the blame, this much I know. My nature is too changeable. What you did, you did for me, and I allowed it to happen. I should have returned to Netherfield as I planned to do; I have known that for a long time."

Darcy let out a deep sigh, knowing how much he hurt his friend, but his conscience would not allow him to tell his friend only half-truths. "Bingley, you are good to offer your absolution; yet, I have something else to confess."

Bingley's face showed he was seeing Darcy for the first time. Turning back and gritting his teeth, he said, "Please continue."

"Miss Bennet was in London last winter for nearly three months; she stayed with Mr. and Mrs. Gardiner. Miss Bennet sent word to Caroline and even called one day. Caroline, with my permission, gave Miss Bennet a cut by not returning the visit for many weeks. She led Miss Bennet to believe you were interested in Georgiana. I was aware of her being in London, but I told you not. Again, I saw you fall in and out of love so often I did not judge your affections to be so constant. Since the time I realized you and Miss Bennet were meant to be together, I have tried to bring you back to one another."

"Darcy, you overextended your influence on my life. Is it no wonder Miss Bennet sees me as being a lothario."

"Bingley," Darcy laughed, "Miss Bennet, if I may be allowed one last judgment, loves no one but you."

"She cannot! She must think me a cad—to be indifferent to her!"

"Charles, there are not many things of which I am absolutely sure, but the constancy of Miss Bennet's feelings for you is one of the few things. Miss Elizabeth reprimanded me at Hunsford for my misgivings; the Gardiners showed me how thoughtful Miss Bennet is. I came here to observe her reactions to your renewed entreaties; her love still rests in you, Charles, if you are willing to ask her."

"Ask her? Ask her what?" he nearly shouted.

"Ask her to marry you, Charles," Darcy said softly. "She will accept you."

"How can you be so sure? I am not, and it is I to whom you reportedly believe she directs her attentions!"

"You are too close to see the look in her eyes when you walk into the room. Most men would give their life for one such glimpse. She stirs your soul, Charles; with Miss Bennet you can share your innermost self with respect and dignity. You can wait; you can postpone, but if I were you, I would grab 'happiness' with both hands and ask Miss Bennet to marry me."

"She will say 'yes,' will she not, Darcy?" Bingley was awestruck.

"Miss Bennet will say 'yes,' Charles."

Bingley began to pace, to spin, to stop, and to start all over again. "If Miss Bennet agrees, Darcy, then you will be completely forgiven." Bingley laughed.

"Then I am forgiven," Darcy smiled. "You will send me news of your happiness, but pray write *legibly*."

"I will send you my fate," Bingley could not control his thoughts; but then he recalled his sisters' parts in his misery.

"I hope you predicted Miss Bennet's response accurately, Darcy, for it will offer me a chance for revenge when I *demand* Caroline and Louisa give Jane her proper due as my wife. They believe me to be with you at Pemberley. What I would give to see their faces when they read I am at Netherfield, and I asked Miss Bennet to accept my hand."

Darcy came forward. First, he shook Bingley's hand and then slapped him on the back. "I must leave you now, Bingley."

"When will you return? If Miss Bennet accepts, you will stand up with me?"

"It would be my honor, Bingley, although I do not deserve your honest consideration. I will try to return within a fortnight; your *fate* should be decided by then."

Darcy picked up his hat and walking stick and headed for the waiting carriage. Bingley followed close behind. At the carriage, Darcy turned, and Bingley extended his hand. "Friend," he said. Darcy grasped the offered hand. "Friend," came his thankful reply.

There was little to do in London, but Darcy did not care; his mind could not be happily employed. He went to the theatre one evening, for his spirits wanted the solitude and silence, which only numbers could give. A protégé of David Garrick performed magnificently, but the drama *The Chances* reminded him of Elizabeth for like the character's jealousy, Darcy remained jealous of the possibility of anyone else having Elizabeth as his wife.

At Longbourn, they did not speak beyond common civilities. He once believed their hearts were intertwined, and nothing could come between them. Their natures so similar—their understanding so perfect—he could never imagine their not finding each other. It was impossible for him to forget how to love Elizabeth, but the fact was when they last met, she did not seem to want to be near enough for conversation—near enough to him. Elizabeth did not return his regard; he had no choice but to put distance between them. The distance between Pemberley and Longbourn was one kind of distance, but he would also have to build a wall around his heart. Darcy was Bingley's friend; Bingley would marry Jane; Darcy could not avoid seeing Elizabeth . . . but he could force himself to be indifferent.

When he was in London a week, a dispatch arrived from Bingley. It read,

28 September

Darcy,

You are forgiven. Miss Bennet said "yes." My fate is sealed! We await your return to Netherfield. Your friend forever . . .

Charles Bingley

The letter brought Darcy relief, but he envied Bingley's chance for happiness. Bitterness and lost opportunities marred his chances;

if he realized how much a refusal to dance at an assembly would change his life, he would dance with Elizabeth the first time he met her; if he . . . He could not live with all these regrets—with the ache of lost love.

Colonel Fitzwilliam called on him on Thursday, and they agreed to dine together on Saturday. "I want to know about the commission you bought, Darcy. You were very secretive. I warn you—I will have the truth, Cousin."

On Saturday he returned from an afternoon outing to discover his aunt's chaise and four before Kensington Place. "Mr. Darcy," his butler approached and took Darcy's hat, gloves, and greatcoat, "your aunt, Lady Catherine de Bourgh, insisted on being admitted although I told her you were not at home. She demanded, Sir, to wait on your return."

"You were right to admit her, Mr. Thacker. Would you have tea brought to the drawing room?"

"Yes, Mr. Darcy."

Darcy did not like visitors to come to his home without a proper invitation; his aunt knew his dislike of such intrusions upon his privacy. Something must be amiss. *Could something be wrong with Anne?* He strode into the drawing room expecting to find his aunt in tears. Instead, she was agitated; she was angry; she was demanding. "Lady Catherine, what brings you to Kensington Place? I was unaware of your plans to travel to London. Please tell me my Cousin Anne has not taken ill again."

"Darcy, you came at last; I am so distressed—such an inconvenient situation!"

"Aunt, I could possibly empathize with you if I knew of what you speak."

"Then you have no knowledge of it? I suspected as not." Her voice rose in volume with each subsequent phrase.

The tea arrived at that precise time. After the servant placed the tray on the table, Darcy poured his distraught aunt a cup and then fixed himself one. "Let us have some tea and allow me the opportunity to ascertain what most disturbs you."

Lady Catherine tried to sip the tea, but her discomfort overwhelmed her, and she decidedly placed the saucer on the table to emphasize her agitation.

"Please tell me what brought you here today."

"That girl!" His aunt spit out the words.

"What girl, Madam?"

"Miss Elizabeth Bennet, of course!"

Darcy froze. Had he heard his aunt correctly? "Miss Elizabeth Bennet?" he tried to sound nonchalant. "What could Miss Elizabeth have to do with our family?"

"She is an insincere young lady, one not to be given proper address!"

Darcy's mind raced; *about what could his aunt be talking?* "I thought Miss Elizabeth was a favorite, Aunt."

"She most certainly is not! She spreads scandalous falsehoods, and I came here to demand you deny her report."

Darcy stood and forced himself to walk casually to the mantel. "What falsehood has Miss Elizabeth spread which caused you such torment?"

"That girl," she began again, "let it be known she intends to be united in marriage with you, Nephew."

Darcy's heart leapt at the words. He never thought Elizabeth could spread such a rumor; it was beyond her. "Are you sure, Aunt? This seems uncharacteristic of what I know of Miss Elizabeth. From whom did you hear this rumor?" He tried not to show his own turmoil.

"From Mr. Collins, of course," she exclaimed. "He is Miss Bennet's cousin! I have it on his good authority, and I expect you to publicly contradict this braggart."

"No one, I am sure," he started slowly, "of any consequence will repeat such stories. The Lucases are a gossipy lot. These are only Collins's assumptions based on Charles Bingley's plans to marry Miss Elizabeth's eldest sister. Mr. Collins exaggerates the situation.

There is nothing for me to contradict."

"First the girl will not retract the rumors, and now you refuse to contradict them!" she lamented.

"Lady Catherine, have you spoken to Miss Elizabeth?" He could not believe his aunt confronted Elizabeth with these accusations; Elizabeth must hate him for bringing such censure into her life!

"I have, Sir. I am almost your nearest relative, and I will expunge your reputation even if you will not!" Her haughtiness showed her true nature.

Darcy gripped the mantel for support; he must keep his aunt talking to know what happened, but at the moment he wanted to drive the woman from his house for attacking Elizabeth. "May I ask what you so kindly told Miss Bennet?"

"I confronted her, demanding she contradict the rumor she started. Of course, Miss Bennet feigned innocence, claiming my coming to Longbourn would only give merit to a rumor if it existed."

"She makes a reasonable point, Lady Catherine."

"Nonsense! I asked her if she could declare there was no foundation for the rumor, and that impertinent young lady told me I may ask questions which she may choose not to answer! Can you imagine such insolence?"

Imagining Elizabeth's brazen confrontation of his aunt, Darcy stifled an ironic laugh. "Go on, your Ladyship," he encouraged for he must know whether Elizabeth spoke of him positively or not.

"When I told her as your aunt I had a *right* to know all your dearest concerns, Miss Bennet claimed I had no *right* to know hers. Her arts and allurements are many; I fear you have succumbed to them, Nephew."

Darcy could not respond; all he could think of was although Elizabeth did not say she loved him, she refused to say she did not love him. "What else happened, Aunt?" He tried to control the chaos of his mind by steadying his voice and encouraging his aunt's retelling of the events.

"I reminded her of your engagement to my daughter and how it was your mother's wish for it to be so; and I told her as a young woman of inferior birth, she had no claim on a man of your standing. I reminded her of propriety and delicacy."

The gentleman gritted his teeth and bit the words as he said them, but miraculously, Darcy controlled his ever-building anger. "What was Miss Elizabeth's answer?"

"The response reeked of more insolence! She said although she heard it before you were to marry Anne, that fact would not keep her from marrying you if neither your honor nor inclination confined you to your cousin. She said if you were to make another choice, and she should be that choice, she had the right to accept the proposal."

Darcy's breath came in short bursts. Elizabeth did not say she would accept his proposal; only she had the right to accept it. He had to know more; he forced his mind and his being to appear in tune with Lady Catherine's sentiments, but she waited not for his response. "I told Miss Bennet such an alliance would bring her only disgrace; she would never be recognized or accepted by your family and friends. She is so obstinate and headstrong Miss Bennet claimed being your wife would have its own attached happiness, and that happiness would be great enough to keep your wife from feeling any regret in her choice."

Again, Darcy heard Elizabeth thought being married to him could bring a woman happiness. *Was it possible to bring her happiness?* Hope grew again in him. "I assume that was the end of this confrontation," he added, hoping it would keep his aunt talking.

"It most certainly was not! I reminded her of your noble lineage of your mother's family and that your father was from a respectable, honorable, and ancient, though untitled, family. I told Miss Bennet if she was sensible of her own good, she would not wish to quit the sphere in which she was brought up."

Darcy cringed with his aunt's lack of prudence and decorum. "Miss Elizabeth probably did not appreciate your bringing this to her attention."

"She was livid! She said by marrying you, she would not be quitting *her* sphere because she is a gentleman's daughter. I had her there, Nephew! I had her there! I told her I knew of her mother's low connections, but she insisted if you did not object to her connections, it was nothing to me."

Much to his regret, Darcy remembered saying something very similar to his aunt's words at one time to Elizabeth. Now, however, he came to a new realization: his aunt repeatedly abused Elizabeth, and Elizabeth had a right to deny any connection to him. If she had, Lady Catherine would have stopped her tirade, but even with all Lady Catherine said to her, Elizabeth never said she would not marry him. He walked toward the window; he feared if his aunt could see his face at the moment, it would betray how happy this conversation made him.

"I demanded to know if you were engaged." Darcy's back stiffened with anger directed toward his aunt's intimidation of someone lower in standing. "Thankfully, she confirmed you were not engaged, but Miss Bennet refused to promise she would never enter into such an engagement." *Elizabeth would not promise to refuse him.* "I told her I would never give up this mission. Being wholly unreasonable, Miss Bennet claimed my application to be ill-judged and my arguments to be frivolous, saying even if she refused your hand, it would not make you turn to Anne."

"Madam, do you not think you overstepped your bounds? This is my life of which you speak."

"I have not, Sir. Family resentment will follow such a union."

"I doubt our family would dare resent any woman I chose."

"Miss Bennet said something similar. She said she would not let her decision to marry you be affected by duty, honor, *or* gratitude. Resentment from your family or indignation from the world would mean nothing to her if you were excited by being married to her; the world, according to Miss Bennet, would have too much sense to join in the scorn!"

"Miss Elizabeth is correct, Madame. If I chose her, your disapproval would mean nothing; I would regret the loss of your affection as my aunt, but it would not alter my decision." He did not turn to face her.

"Darcy, you cannot mean as such. Have you forgotten your mother's wish for you to marry Anne?"

"My mother never expressed such a desire to me, and I will not let it control my heart nor my choice. As much as I respect Anne, she is not the woman for me. I need a mistress for Pemberley; I need a mother for my children, Pemberley's heirs. Anne and I have spoken; she and I are of a like mind in this matter."

Lady Catherine stood abruptly. "So, you intend to make *this girl* your wife despite my objections?"

Darcy turned back to face his aunt head on. "If Elizabeth Bennet will have me, my life would be complete."

"It is her arts and allurements," she said as she headed toward the door, "which make you speak so foolishly. I will give you one week to come to your senses; if not, you will never be welcomed at Rosings again." With that, she walked brusquely through the hall and out to her carriage, shooing servants out of her way as she went.

When she left, Darcy collapsed into the chair she vacated. Lady Catherine gave him hope; where days before he resolved to put distance between him and Elizabeth, now he thought only of returning to Netherfield and to her. He would have done so immediately if he was not to dine with Edward this evening; also he reasoned he needed time to reflect on what his aunt said and what he should do next. Edward was the perfect person with whom to discuss this encounter for besides Edward's clear thinking, what Darcy chose next would affect both of them.

Darcy most welcomed Edward's arrival at Kensington Place that evening. He needed his cousin's advice because his own emotions were far too out of control for him to think sensibly. The gentlemen took dinner leisurely, stopping several times for intense conversation and then returning to the meal to "chew" over the ideas as much as to consume the food. Darcy updated Edward on the pleasure of finding Elizabeth at Pemberley, sharing many of the intimate details and asking for Edward's astute interpretation of what Elizabeth said and did. When Darcy told how Elizabeth thwarted Miss Bingley's attempt at a cut and maintained Georgiana's secret, the news astounded Edward. "I always found Miss Bennet to be most engaging," he said with a smile.

Next came the story of George Wickham and Lydia Bennet's "arranged" marriage. "Now you understand why I purchased the commission," Darcy related.

"In some ways I wish Miss Elizabeth realized the depth of your love, Darcy. Only a man as good as you would help his worst enemy to secretly save the woman he loves. My estimation of you has increased substantially, and it was always of the highest regard."

This brought Edward to the news of Darcy's return to Netherfield. "I went with Bingley when he called on the Bennets the first time. I hoped to be able to talk to Elizabeth, but she barely looked at me. Her needlework was never as beloved as it was that day."

"Darcy, she had not seen you since sharing her sister's shame with you. She must be confused. Why would you come there? Elizabeth has to know how you feel by now, but she must wonder how you could renew your affections to her with George Wickham as her brother."

"What you say is so reasonable when you say it but not when I am living it," Darcy chuckled ironically. "But things did not change at the dinner two days later. I spent the meal seated next to Mrs. Bennet; she spent the evening surrounded by other ladies, and we were unable to talk at all."

"Again, Darcy, was that Elizabeth's doing or Mrs. Bennet's?"

"Why would Mrs. Bennet want to keep me from Elizabeth? If she threw Elizabeth at Mr. Collins, my wealth should earn me a right to court her daughter. The woman may dislike me, but her only goal is to marry off her daughters to well-suited matches. She would not keep me from Elizabeth!"

"Mrs. Bennet, I doubt, realizes your interest in Elizabeth. If what you say about the woman is true, and she knew how you felt, Elizabeth would be sitting *on* your lap. Instead, I think Mrs. Bennet was trying to keep you from Mr. Bingley. The Bennets must know of Miss Bingley's cut in London of Miss Bennet by now. You and Caroline are intimates in the Bennets' opinions. Keeping you from stopping her plans to marry off Jane Bennet to Mr. Bingley seems a more likely explanation of what happened. Did Miss Elizabeth not say anything?"

"She only asked about whether Georgiana was at Pemberley."

"Cousin, Miss Elizabeth asked about Pemberley because it was the place where you shared something *special*. If you do not stop second-guessing everything, you will lose this woman." Ashamed at how easily Edward saw what he did not, Darcy dropped his head. "Now," Edward rubbed his hands together in anticipation, "tell me what our dear aunt had to say today. If she said what I hope, both of our loves may be soon achieved."

"Our aunt heard from her favorite gossipmonger Mr. Collins that Elizabeth started a rumor of our impending marriage, and Lady Catherine demanded it be universally denied. Lady Catherine went to Longbourn to confront Elizabeth."

"That must have been some conversation! I cannot imagine Lady Catherine displaying much civility."

"Our aunt was quite frank about what she said to Elizabeth. I kept myself in check to ascertain the extent of the accusations and the exact discourse, but it was difficult. She reminded Elizabeth of her connections, berated her for her insolence, and demanded Elizabeth honor my pledge to Anne."

Edward emitted a moan. "Please tell me Elizabeth withstood Lady Catherine's demands. She is the only person who could be so defined."

"Elizabeth refused to say she would not marry me if I asked, but she also never said she would accept my proposal. How do I know she desires my affections? She could have been obstinate and disagreeable because of our aunt's interference in her private affairs. I know the words Elizabeth said, but I still do not know the tone of those words."

"Darcy, she could have simply promised Lady Catherine to never marry you, and her ordeal would have been over. Instead, Elizabeth withstood all our formidable aunt issued to her rather than to promise she would not marry you. Darcy, do you not see Elizabeth will accept you this time?"

"I am afraid to think as such; my heart cannot take such disappointment again."

"Then do nothing, but are you not the one who told Bingley his fate would be the same whether he chose to wait or not? You should heed your own advice, Cousin."

"I already told Lady Catherine I would not marry Anne even if Elizabeth refuses me. You need not push me toward Miss Elizabeth in order to earn your own love, Edward."

"It is true I wish you to no longer be an embracement in Lady Catherine's mind, but it is truer I wish you happiness, Cousin. Elizabeth will be yours if your temperament will take the chance."

"I apologize, Edward; I should not have spoken so harshly; my emotions race about unchecked. You are right; I cannot give up my chance. If I am successful, I will send you word, and you may attend to our aunt's vexations and plead for Anne's hand before Lady Catherine realizes your title may be enough for Anne, but it will mean the dower's house for her."

"It would be a pleasing vindication for both of us, Darcy."

They settled things; Darcy would return to Netherfield on Monday. His fate was in his own hands. As they parted that evening, there was genuine respect between the two gentlemen. Their lives had been intertwined since their youth, and if things went well in Hertfordshire, their lives would be changed but still bound to one another. As he left, Edward embraced his cousin and reminded Darcy, "Take the package of lace with you, Cousin. Miss Elizabeth will need it for her wedding attire."

CHAPTER 16

"It jumps from admiration to love ..."

When Bingley returned to Netherfield on Monday evening, he found Darcy's livery on the carriage in front of the house. Upon entering, he discovered Darcy in the library. "Darcy, you came back; I am so pleased to see you."

"I apologize for not sending ahead of my return; I hope I have not offended you by my presumption to be welcomed."

"Of course, not," Bingley crossed the room to shake hands with his friend. "You did read my letter, did you not?"

"I do not call four short lines a letter, Sir," Darcy teased.

"That is the length of my legible content." The levity between them helped to alleviate the apprehension Darcy felt since leaving London.

"Come, I want to hear what you said, what Miss Bennet did, and all the details of your upcoming nuptials," Darcy led Bingley to a nearby chair. "You may even bore me with all Mrs. Bennet's *nerves* if you so choose." Bingley laughed at the references to his future mother's silliness, but his happiness allowed him to find no fault even with Mrs. Bennet. Darcy's true interest lay only in his friend's happiness and in any references to Elizabeth's reaction to the proposal.

"Miss Elizabeth," Bingley offered, "keeps her mother and sisters attending to other things so Jane and I may talk privately. Now you are here, you can help me entertain Mr. Bennet. We have agreed to go shooting later in the week; you are twice the sportsman as I; you could impress him, and maybe Mr. Bennet will not notice I am generally a terrible shot." Darcy laughed, but undercurrents of shattered nerves hid in the layers.

"You will join me at Longbourn tomorrow, Darcy? Miss Elizabeth deserves someone other than her mother to which to speak, and you and she got along well at Pemberley. Would you mind spending some time with Miss Elizabeth? Jane and I want to make plans for Netherfield without her mother's input and before the arrival of my sisters. What say you, Darcy? We can walk out together—Jane and I can talk over what we need to discuss, and you can talk to Miss Elizabeth and maybe her sisters." Darcy would not mind seeing Elizabeth alone. That would be perfect for what he planned. That evening images of Lady Catherine and Anne standing along the road to Meryton disturbed his sleep, and a clear likeness of Elizabeth's face could not be had.

After breakfast, Darcy and Bingley rode to Longbourn. As usual, tender words of his worth greeted Bingley; Darcy, on the other hand, received a cold welcome; yet, he did not care what Mrs. Bennet said or did; his eyes searched Elizabeth's face, trying to see what she must be thinking about him after being so chastised by his aunt. Before Mrs. Bennet had time to tell Darcy of Lady Catherine's calling upon the family, Bingley said, "It is a beautiful day. May we take a walk and enjoy the weather?"

"Oh, I am not in the habit of walking about, Mr. Bingley," Mrs. Bennet fussed, "but the girls are quite good walkers."

"I would prefer to stay here, Mama, and address my studies," Mary intoned.

"Do be quiet, Mary," Mrs. Bennet was quite rude. "No one cares whether you go or not." She turned back to the others. "Girls, go find your outside things."

Soon the five set off together; Bingley and Jane lagged behind, allowing the others to outstrip them. Little discourse occurred between the three; Kitty remained in awe of the "haughty Mr. Darcy." Darcy and Elizabeth each formed a resolution to speak what had not been said before.

When they reached the path leading to Lucas Lodge, Kitty asked to be excused to visit Maria Lucas. Elizabeth agreed but warned her sister not to stay too long. After Kitty's exit, they walked on in silence for a few moments. He tried to get the courage to approach her when she found her voice, "Mr. Darcy, I am a very selfish creature; and, for the sake of giving to my own feelings, care not how much I may be wounding yours."

What was she saying? She did not care if she hurt his feelings? His aunt's rebukes combined with his earlier insecurities showed her she wanted nothing of him.

"I can no longer help thanking you for your unexampled kindness to my poor sister."

She was not talking about his aunt's attack, but Elizabeth knew about his involvement in Lydia Bennet's marriage. Now, as was customary, she would be obligated to marry him.

"Ever since I have known it, I have been most anxious to acknowledge to you how gratefully I feel it. Were it known to the rest of my family, I should not have merely my own gratitude to express."

There it was—the dreaded word "gratitude." I do not want her gratitude; I want her love. What can I say to her now? I never wanted her to know of my part in the wedding. Darcy stopped and turned toward Elizabeth. She stopped, too, and they faced each other for a few infinitely long seconds. Without planning to say so, her words of "gratitude" drove him forward. "I am sorry, exceedingly sorry, that you have ever been informed of what may, in a mistaken light, have given you uneasiness. I did not think Mrs. Gardiner was so little to be trusted."

Elizabeth glanced up briefly at him; the tension was so thick. Both knew what needed to be said, but neither could broach the subject. She tried to explain how Lydia's foolishness let the news of his attending Wickham's wedding slip out. Then she added, "You must not blame my aunt. Lydia's thoughtlessness first betrayed to me that you had been concerned in the matter; and, of course, I could not rest till I knew the particulars. Let me thank you again and again, in the name of all my family, for that generous compassion which induced you to take so much trouble, and bear so many mortifications, for the sake of discovering them. It truly befuddles me why you would put yourself through all that trouble."

Elizabeth left him the opening. She could not understand why he troubled himself with Wickham. *He loved her; that is why. His sister demanded it; that is why.* "If you *will* thank me, let it be for yourself alone. That the wish of giving happiness to you might add force to the other inducements which led me on I shall not attempt to deny. But your *family* owe me nothing. Much as I respect them, I believe I thought only of *you*."

Silence enveloped them; he wanted her to say something or do something to let him know if he overstepped the limits. *Yet, Elizabeth was never silent,* he thought. If he offended her, her temperament would be to reprimand him. Dare he believe she would willingly listen to him? When he looked closely at her downcast face, he saw her embarrassment but not her disdain. He could contain it no longer, and he added, "You are too generous to trifle with me. If your feelings are still what they were last April, tell me so at once. *My* affections and wishes are unchanged; but one word from you will silence me on the subject forever."

Darcy waited, frozen in time, forgetting even how to breathe; his eyes searched her face, anticipating her answer. An eternity passed as he waited; finally, she raised her eyes to his. "Mr. Darcy," she said the words slowly as if to convince herself as much as him, "my feelings . . . my feelings are so different from what they were last April. My sentiments have gone through a full array of emotions since the period to which you allude; I willingly receive your present assurances. The fact you still seek my love gives me great pleasure."

The conviction with which she said the words made the dream real, and he slowly lifted her hand to his lips and kissed it tenderly. "Elizabeth, I have imagined this moment so many times, but never once did I feel such contentment and exhilaration at the same time." Transfixed, they stayed that way for a long time fighting the urge to smother each other with kisses. "You are beautiful, Elizabeth." She started to drop her eyes, but he lifted her chin with his finger. "If you plan to drop your eyes each time I tell you how much I love you, my dearest Elizabeth, you will forever be looking at the floor. You need never to look down again." Elizabeth rested her hand on his chest; he wondered if she felt the faint trembling and the erratic beating of his heart. He closed his eyes, and her nearness consumed him. "Elizabeth, you have stolen my heart; I cannot live without you. Please say you will be my wife."

"I can think of nothing more perfect than our matrimonial felicity. Being forever known as Mrs. Darcy would be my happiest desire." Darcy's breath caught in his throat; Elizabeth was finally his. Now so close he could feel her breath on his cheeks, his arms enveloped her as she offered her mouth for their first kiss.

"I have been waiting for you," he whispered into her ear. The passion in his voice made her body tremble, and Darcy instinctively moved in closer to support her. They separated reluctantly and started to walk; only this time she wrapped her arm through his. He cupped her hand with his free hand. The realization of the last few minutes sustained them at first, but they both possessed a nature to analyze every aspect, which brought them to their present understanding.

Elizabeth paused briefly and looked up at Darcy; he was lost in the revelry of their combined touch. "Mr. Darcy," she stumbled over the words, "the honor you bestowed on me today cannot be expressed in words. I feared you would not renew your proposal; I thought I lost your love forever."

Darcy took both of her hands in his and held them next to his heart. He turned and said, "At Pemberley, I hoped to show you how much I changed. I came to Lambton that last day with the intention of asking you to ride out with me before dinner. I wanted to take you around the grounds; I decided within a few moments of finding you on the lawn of my estate, I would not be able to live without you in my life."

"When you left the Royal Crown that day," she nearly whispered, "I told myself I would never see you again. My chances of your renewing your proposal I hoped of once we were together at your home, but when you left so suddenly, I believed you could never love me after the shame Lydia brought on our family. The realization of Mr. Wickham becoming your brother, I thought, would keep you from me. I could not fathom why you followed them to London; I hoped I was the source of your action, but I could not believe my heart."

"I did talk to Georgiana before I left, not for her approval but out of respect for her guidance; but, from the moment I departed the inn, I had no other purpose in mind than to protect you." Darcy reached out to gently stroke her cheek. "Images of your face sustained me when I negotiated with Mr. Wickham for your sister's wedding. I concocted a lie of how your family sent me there. If Mr. Wickham knew my real purpose, he would have extricated a larger payoff."

"Then it will be pleasurable to send my sister news of our engagement. Besides placing her family's reputation in jeopardy, Lydia flaunted her 'well placed marriage.' She even demanded to take Jane's place in our home. She and Mr. Wickham are of the same mind; when Mr. Wickham realizes you did all for me, it will be a punishment for their follies."

As they continued to walk along a path leading through a wood, Darcy told her, "Sending Mr. Wickham to Newcastle to a hard-nosed commanding officer was part of my revenge."

Elizabeth laughed, "He deserves worse than that," she taunted, and he marveled at the irony of the similarity of their minds. "Will Georgiana be able to manage having Mr. Wickham as a brother? She has a delicate temperament."

Darcy smiled down at the concern in Elizabeth's face. "As you misjudged me when we first met, I fear my dearest Elizabeth, you misjudged my sister. She is a true romantic! When she found out Mr. Wickham ran off with Lydia, Georgiana *demanded* I do something to protect you. You will make great friends, and I will pay the price of having two spirited females under my roof," he chuckled. "Georgiana wanted to protect you even if her reputation was brought under close inspection." Elizabeth could not hide her surprise at having earned Georgiana's respect in such a short time period.

They found a place where they could sit and rest for a while. Darcy liked the feel of her hand in his. Elizabeth looked him squarely in the eyes. "When you left Netherfield, I believed you decided against me." She still could not believe they were here at last. "A man who has been once refused is not likely to risk such censure again."

"Your temper," he laughed, "is not something I wish to encounter often," remembering the heated confrontation of his first proposal. "When I left Netherfield a fortnight ago, I was convinced *you* were decided against me!"

She smiled brilliantly at him when she said, "We are a destructive pair, are we not? We need no enemies for we serve both roles." He kissed her fingertips and brushed the hair from her face. "If you were convinced of my disdain, what brought you back to Netherfield?"

"My aunt," he started.

"Yes, she was here," Elizabeth rolled her eyes.

"How can I apologize to you for Lady Catherine's behavior? Her manners were abominable."

"I would welcome her barbs repeatedly if I knew they would bring me to this moment." Her voice was breathy with anticipation.

"Her coming to London did not achieve the effect she expected. I remained calm as was humanly possible to do because I wanted to know your response. Her words taught me to hope as I had scarcely ever allowed myself to hope before."

Elizabeth smirked as she said, "Lady Catherine so prefers to be of use to everyone; she should be pleased she was of use to us."

With a tone of sarcasm, Darcy assured her Lady Catherine would be *most displeased*. "My cousin Anne will think otherwise, however. Do you know, Elizabeth, you were not the only one at Rosings who refused to be my wife? Anne and I met in the library, and she informed me I was quite a 'frightening' figure; then she said she did not wish to be my wife. In fact, I need to send Edward news of our engagement; he hopes to catch Lady Catherine when she is most vulnerable and then secure Anne for his own."

"Edward and Anne?" He shook his head in affirmation. "Why did I not see that relationship? I once thought myself to be a keen observer of people, but since I met you, Mr. Darcy, I have come to second-guess my opinions."

"Will I continue to always be *Mr. Darcy* to you, Elizabeth? May you not call me *Fitzwilliam* or, at the least, *Darcy?*"

"Once you receive my father's consent," she teased, "then you will no longer be *Mr. Darcy*. Until then, I shall call you thus."

"You are a stubborn woman, Elizabeth Bennet. Maybe I should rethink the offer of my hand," he returned the joviality.

"I am afraid it is too late, *Mr. Darcy*," she emphasized his name, "because I already am in possession of your heart."

"You are, indeed, Madam," he bent to kiss her cheek, "you are indeed." Darcy let his lips linger, and she could feel his breath on her neck. His voice was raspy when he spoke again. "My aunt's retelling inspired me to action. I knew enough of your disposition to be certain that, had you been absolutely, irrevocably decided against me, you would have acknowledged it to Lady Catherine, frankly and openly."

Elizabeth offered a ghost of a grin as she chastised herself. "Yes, you know enough of my frankness to believe me capable of *that*. After abusing you so abominably to your face, I could have no scruples in abusing you to all your relations."

For the next few minutes, they each belabored themselves for the foolishness of their earlier wrongs. Darcy, who prided himself on being a man of scruples, criticized his first proposal for its poorly worded sentiments. He showed mistaken pride, and he proved himself not worthy of Elizabeth's love then. He admitted the memory of his conduct, his manners, and his expressions of love pained him for their inappropriateness. "I shall never forget your challenging me with 'Had you behaved in a more gentleman-like manner.' Those were your words. You know not, you can scarcely conceive, how they have tortured me—though it was some time, I confess, before I was reasonable enough to allow their justice."

Elizabeth, being of a lighter temperament, blamed them both for the many misunderstandings, which occurred that evening. "I was certainly very far from expecting them to make so strong an impression. I had not the smallest idea of their being ever felt in such a way."

Darcy was not willing to abandon his self-reproach so easily despite the fact Elizabeth was now his; the pain was difficult to surrender, but Elizabeth now understood his nature and first gave him his moments and then redirected his passions. She begged him not to recollect in so much detail how they misread each other for so long. "We will be happy now—the happiest couple to ever be married."

Darcy chuckled lightly as they stood to continue their walk; they caught each other's eye, and shades of their present tranquillity insolently demanded admittance. "The letter," he embarked, "did it soon make you think better of me? Did you, on reading it, give any credit to its contents?"

Elizabeth told him the letter was a revelation. "It gradually removed all my former prejudices. I came to know myself as I never had before."

"I am sorry if it gave you pain. I was angry at your rejection; I was jealous of your attentions to Mr. Wickham; I was lost to loving you," his countenance dropped.

"Mr. Darcy, we will have no more melancholy," she emphatically said. "You will not be the Prince of Denmark for if you recall I dearly love to laugh. If the letter brings you recompense, it shall be burned. The feelings of the person who wrote the letter and the person who received it differ greatly now." The subject needed airing without distraction, but Elizabeth would not have him sad today. "I want you to remember only the pleasant things from the past. We will have no sadness today."

Darcy gave her credit for having acted well in all their dealings. He, on the other hand, realized his life created a double man—the man the world saw and the one Elizabeth now loved. He told her his parents were loving people and taught him what was right; but they allowed him to act prideful with others, never correcting his disposition. "Unfortunately an only son, for many years an only child, I was spoiled by my parents, who, though good themselves, allowed, encouraged, almost taught me to be selfish and overbearing; to care for none beyond my own family circle; to think meanly of all the rest of the world. Such I was, from eight to eight-and-twenty; and such I might still have been but for you, dearest, loveliest Elizabeth! What do I not owe you. You taught me a lesson, hard indeed at first, but most advantageous. By you, I was properly humbled. I came to you without a doubt of my reception. You showed me how insufficient were all my pretensions to please a woman worthy of being pleased."

"I never meant to deceive you," she stammered and looked deep in his eyes. "If I was not blinded by my own prejudices, I would have seen the man you really are. Our pride and our prejudice are a dust from the past; dust must be wiped away, leaving a clean surface. You spent your life ignoring others; I spent mine constantly censuring them; we will learn and offer forgiveness to each other." She gently stroked his jawline. "May we not talk of something more pleasant?"

Darcy conceded easily. They would have a lifetime to vanquish those ghosts. They unknowingly leisurely walked several miles, and upon looking at their watches, they realized it was time to be home. Elizabeth looked around sheepishly. "I totally forgot about Jane and Mr. Bingley. They will wonder where we have gone . . . . Tell me true, Mr. Darcy, did you give Mr. Bingley permission to court my sister again?"

"Bingley needs not my permission," he claimed his innocence. "What I did give him was my sincerest apology for interfering in his life."

"Did he forgive you?" Elizabeth teased.

"His letter announcing his engagement to your sister told me I was forgiven."

"Then you changed your mind about Jane?"

"I knew I was wrong last April. Your insights allowed me to see Miss Bennet as I never saw her before. Then Mr. and Mrs. Gardiner spoke of her affable nature. What could I do but to rescind my judgment? How could I keep Bingley from Miss Bennet and justify my feelings for you? I simply told Bingley he could wait or he could offer his hand; either way, the result would be the same. I watched Miss Bennet in your home, and I knew her regard for Bingley had not diminished."

Elizabeth thought it to be amusing how easily he could manipulate Mr. Bingley. As they neared Longbourn, they knew they would have to part until Darcy could secure her father's consent. He felt her conviction as he moved up behind her and rested his hands on her shoulders. Elizabeth turned toward him, captured by his nearness. "Mr. Darcy, you are an exceedingly handsome man." Her fingers traced his lips.

He caught her hand and kissed her fingertips; Darcy's eyes danced with the passion he could no longer conceal. "Elizabeth, you gave me the world today. I will spend my life trying to make you happy." They walked next to each other the rest of the way to Longbourn; they did not need to touch to be connected. Their love was there; that was enough for now.

Entering Longbourn, Jane turned and asked, "My dear Lizzy, where can you have been walking to?"

"Yes," Kitty added, "we feared something happened to you."

"I am sorry to plague your sensibilities. We wandered about until I was beyond my own knowledge," she offered an explanation. Darcy noticed she blushed, but no one else took note of her nervousness. Elizabeth shot Darcy a quick glance, and he gave her back a reassuring smile.

Dinner awaited them, but they purposely sat at opposite ends of the table. Neither could look at the other without betraying the love now openly declared. Darcy, seated next to the man, turned his attentions to her father. "Mr. Bennet, I understand from your daughter you are considering some changes at Longbourn. I am also trying to address concerns at Pemberley; would you consider sharing some of the changes of which you are thinking?"

Mr. Bennet's interest in Darcy increased. "Well, Mr. Darcy," he began, "what are you considering?"

"A four-crop rotation is one of the prevalent changes my steward Mr. Howard and I have put in place. It is widely used in Scotland and the Americas."

"A four-crop rotation, you say?"

Throughout the dinner, Darcy's effort to engage her father pleased Elizabeth. She knew thanks to her earlier censure of this man she now loved, except for Jane, the Meryton Assembly set her family's opinion of Darcy. Tomorrow she would admit her error in judgment and tell them how much she now esteemed him. Jane and Mr. Bingley talked and laughed together; everyone easily accepted Bingley. Happiness did not take an open path in Darcy's case, and although she knew him to be so, others would not; plus, Elizabeth feared even with his fortune and consequence, her family may not accept him.

"Are you up for a game of billiards, Darcy?" Charles Bingley called to his friend when they returned to Netherfield.

"Truthfully, Bingley, I would prefer some of your pleasant conversation; that is, if you have anything left to say after spending the day with Miss Bennet," Darcy smirked.

"She is the most beautiful woman. Do you not agree, Darcy?"

"I am afraid I prefer something with a little darker coloring, but Miss Bennet is perfect for you, my friend."

"A little darker coloring, you say?"

"Yes, I do say." Darcy avoided the question as he watched Bingley pour them both drinks.

"You are being mysterious this evening, Darcy." Bingley handed him a glass of port as they found chairs across from each other in the drawing room. "I noticed you and Mr. Bennet had what appeared to be an enjoyable conversation at dinner. Thank you for trying to be cordial to Jane's family. You are a dear friend."

"The conversation with Mr. Bennet was enlightening, but I must admit it was not totally for your benefit, Bingley."

"Do tell, Darcy." Darcy's words peaked Bingley's interest.

"Bingley," he began, not sure if he dare say the words, "I asked Miss Elizabeth to be my wife."

"Darcy, this cannot be! I saw how you showed her preference at Pemberley, but I also saw you do so at Netherfield last fall. Then you two would be nearly in an altercation the next moment. You seem to always be in contention rather than in love."

Darcy laughed; Bingley's assessment of his relationship with Elizabeth Bennet was accurate. "I cannot explain it; I have been in constant turmoil since I beheld her at the Meryton Assembly."

"But you refused to even dance with Miss Elizabeth then!"

"An act for which I will always owe her an apology," Darcy chuckled ironically. "I have been a fool in love; everything about the woman went against my principles, but, much to my chagrin, I found Elizabeth was exactly what I needed. She is the only woman who dared to challenge me—to humble me."

"Remarkable!" Bingley exhaled loudly.

"That is a true estimation of Miss Elizabeth—remarkable!" Darcy mused.

"Tell me more. When did this love begin? She did accept you. Of course, she did," Bingley reasoned.

"I wish I could tell you when it began. First, I noticed her; after all, you kindly threw the two of us together in your pursuit of Miss Bennet." Bingley laughed lightly as he recalled his early infatuation with Jane Bennet. "I thought her to be a *diversion* for the lack of society I found in Hertfordshire; but then, I found, I could think of little else but Elizabeth Bennet. I concocted ways to engage her in conversation—what you interpreted as our verbal battles. Think about it—in all our time in Hertfordshire, besides your sisters, to whom did I show any attention other than Elizabeth?" Again, Bingley chuckled with the realization. "And Miss Elizabeth *has* accepted my proposal of marriage *this time.*"

"Wait a minute! This time? I do not understand, Darcy."

"I proposed to Elizabeth last April at Hunsford, and she sent me packing."

"Darcy, you jest. She refused you?"

"Most emphatically! I treated her poorly, and she *rewarded* me with her disdain. In reality, my interference in your life, plus Mr. Wickham's deceit colored Elizabeth's opinion of me. All my wealth could not persuade her otherwise; but her understanding of the real situation allowed her to finally love me."

"This explains the changes I have seen in you, Darcy. Elizabeth Bennet allowed you to be the man I always saw as your friend, but rarely saw in public."

Darcy took a sip of the port as the changes came slowly but predictably to mind. "I will ask for her father's consent tomorrow so please do not say anything, Bingley, until then."

"I may tell Miss Bennet, may I not, Darcy?"

"If I know Miss Elizabeth, your Jane knows by now; Elizabeth and Jane are more than sisters; and now, Charles, we will be more than friends; we will be brothers."

The joy on Bingley's face was evident. "We shall be brothers, Darcy," he laughed aloud. "What say you to another walk in the country tomorrow, Brother? This time you and Miss Elizabeth may get lost legitimately."

"Bingley, you read my mind perfectly."

The rest of the evening they spent in intimate conversation, each man extolling the merits of his perspective bride. As they prepared to retire for the evening, Bingley looked at Darcy and said, "Darcy, may I have the pleasure of telling my dear sister Caroline not only am I to marry Miss Bennet, but you are lost to Miss Elizabeth? It will be a fitting revenge for her intrusion into my private affairs."

"I would not want to be in the room with Miss Bingley when she receives that letter," Darcy weighed. "Pity the poor servants."

"After you receive Mr. Bennet's consent, I will write a *most legible* letter to her. I would not want my renowned poor handwriting to keep this important news from Caroline." Both men found the image of Caroline Bingley reading the letter to be very amusing.

Entering Longbourn the following day, Darcy's eyes went immediately to Elizabeth, and she rewarded him with a purse of her lips and a smile. He could tell from her expression his appearance vexed Mrs. Bennet, and the remark pained Elizabeth. He also realized his earlier behavior would be hard to explain away to Mrs. Bennet and the others. Bingley could not totally control his enthusiasm for upon their entrance, he looked at Elizabeth so expressively and shook hands with such warmth, she knew immediately Darcy informed Bingley of their engagement. Bingley turned to Mrs. Bennet and said aloud, "Mrs. Bennet, have you no more lanes hereabouts in which Lizzy may lose her way again today?"

Mrs. Bennet laughed lightly at his humor. "I advise Mr. Darcy, Lizzy, and Kitty to walk to Oakham Mount this morning. It is a nice long walk, and Mr. Darcy has never seen the view."

"It may well do very for the others," replied Mr. Bingley, ironically, enjoying his new role of controlling Darcy's life, "but I am sure it is too much for Kitty. Won't it, Kitty?"

"If it is acceptable, Mama, I would rather stay home," Kitty acknowledged.

Darcy offered, "Mrs. Bennet, Oakham Mount sounds interesting."

Elizabeth could hardly help laughing at so convenient a proposal, but she silently consented. Mrs. Bennet followed her upstairs with epithets about Darcy, which truly vexed her daughter so by the time she started out, Elizabeth's temper was aroused. At the fork in the road, the couples parted to find their own way and their own privacy. Darcy and Elizabeth took the steeper pathway, both needing the exercise to relieve the tension. They walked along in silence for a quarter of a mile; finally, Darcy caught her hand to stop her progress. She turned back to look at him, and he held her stare; eventually, Elizabeth chuckled at herself, which made him feel good. Darcy held her there with a look of barely restrained passion. "I know that look," she teased.

"What look?" he pretended to misunderstand.

"There was a time when I thought with that look you disdained me and found fault with me. Then I saw the same expression on your face in your portrait at Pemberley," she sashayed closer to him. She placed her hands on Darcy's chest, "and I wanted nothing more than anything to see you look that way at me again." Elizabeth went up on her tiptoes to nibble on his lower lip.

"Mrs. Reynolds," his voice was breathy and ragged, "tells me you find me to be handsome," he teased her by brushing his lips over hers.

"Did I not tell you so last night?" Her mouth was near his.

"I am a vain, prideful man, as you have so often pointed out." He smiled down at her face tilted toward him. "I need for you to feed my vanity with your praise."

"Then you must reciprocate with praise of my good qualities." Their breathing caused a sudden flush of heat to rise to Elizabeth's cheeks.

"My dearest Elizabeth, you are so beautiful." The warmth of his kiss smothered the words. Elizabeth now realized it was a look exclusively reserved for her; she was the one person who brought passion to his being. They parted unwillingly and started their walk again, but now it became more leisurely and more loving. "Georgiana will be so pleased when she hears; if it was not for her, I may have given up my hopes of our reconciliation. She is more intelligent and astute than I once gave her credit for being; I am afraid I spent so much of my time being her guardian I forgot she is my sister."

"It will be pleasant to have Georgiana as a sister. Losing Jane is something about our future to which I am most dreading; Georgiana and I will be great friends."

"I dreamed of you at Pemberley so often."

"I dreamed of it last night," she stammered. "How will I ever manage to be its mistress? I am frightened; how will I survive?" Anxiety showed in her manner of speaking.

"Elizabeth, there are servants to manage Pemberley. It could run by itself. You will be my wife; you have nothing to fear. If you can win my heart as easily as you did, there is no one at Pemberley you have to fear." Then he quickly changed the subject, not wanting her to dwell too long on the transition to her new life. "I would ask your father's consent this evening. How will he react?"

"Papa, I am afraid, will be very surprised. I told him nothing of Hunsford or of Pemberley. I fear my earliest impression of you is the only one of which he knows."

"Does he dislike me so much?"

"Your refusal of his favorite daughter at the assembly colored his opinion of you, Mr. Darcy," Elizabeth needled him about his once haughty behavior.

"I believe I still owe you an apology for such bad behavior." Darcy reached out to caress her face.

"By starting over, My Love, we can get some place else," she said decidedly, and the beauty and wit of this *remarkable* woman again overwhelmed him.

"Do you have a preference for when to set our wedding date? I suppose we will have to wait until after Charles's and Miss Bennet's nuptials."

"I have a suggestion . . ." She hesitated not knowing how he would react. Darcy waited patiently for her to finish her thoughts. "Jane and I stumbled on an idea last night when I told her of our engagement. At first we thought it to be a lark, and we laughed at it; but, the more it was considered, the more reasonable it sounded."

"Do you plan on sharing this idea, or must I guess your mind?"

"What say you to a double wedding?"

"You and Miss Bennet and Bingley and I?" He seemed stunned.

"Is it a bad idea?" She was unsure of how to read his reaction.

"Will Bingley agree to this?"

"Jane will ask him today," she offered. "We would not have to wait so long. You do not want a long engagement do you, Mr. Darcy?"

"I believe we waited long enough to start our life together." He kissed her with renewed ardor.

"I will tell Mama about our engagement once you secure my father's consent." She planned this part of what she would say to him today. Elizabeth feared her mother's reaction to the news of her daughter's choice of a husband. Mrs. Bennet was not known to be tactful; one never knew what she would say. "Jane and I will then tell her our plans. Mama's *nerves* will only have to go through the planning of one ceremony and one wedding breakfast." She said no more, but Darcy knew her sentiments. "There is only one thing more of which we should speak before you address my father this evening," Elizabeth hesitated again. "My father received a letter from Mr. Collins the day Lady Catherine paid her visit. It actually warned me not to accept your proposal. Papa finds anything Mr. Collins writes amusing. He had no idea how I felt about you. When he finished his humorous diversion, I questioned whether you could love me."

"I will take the time, Elizabeth, to allay your father's fears. Everything will go well, I promise." They walked back toward Longbourn with plans of their life together.

After dinner, Mr. Bennet made his usual retreat to his library, and Darcy followed. "Mr. Darcy," seeing this guest in his library surprised Mr. Bennet, "may I help you find something to read or would you care for a glass of port?"

"Thank you, Mr. Bennet," Darcy cleared his voice, "but I would like to speak to you on a matter of importance."

"Of course, Mr. Darcy, please have a seat. What may I do for you? It would give me pleasure to be of service to you."

"Mr. Bennet," Darcy paused, wondering how to tell Elizabeth's father of his love, "I asked your daughter Elizabeth to be my wife, and she accepted my proposal. I come here tonight seeking your permission for our union."

Mr. Bennet sat bolt upright in his chair and gripped the handles tightly. The color drained from his face, and he was momentarily speechless. "Mr. Darcy, are you sure? This is not some joke the family is playing, is it?" Mr. Bennet seemed to be looking for an explanation.

"Mr. Bennet, I realize you are unaware of my relationship with Miss Elizabeth. We have been more secretive than my friend Mr. Bingley. Our natures are not so open, but, I assure you Elizabeth and I are deeply in love; she agreed to be my wife." Darcy's voice sounded calmer than his body felt.

Her father got up and walked to the window before he spoke again. "Mr. Darcy, I do not wish to offend you, but Elizabeth is my favorite of all my children. Her nature will not be dictated to; Elizabeth has a spirit I would not wish to see caged by your society's rules and regulations."

"Mr. Bennet, I am well aware of your daughter's spirit; she humbled me; I learned about myself thanks to her. I realize I offended Elizabeth at the Meryton Assembly, and from that you drew your opinion of me." All this frankness made Mr. Bennet uncomfortable, but it also made him see Darcy in a different light. "When I saw Elizabeth care for Miss Bennet at Netherfield, I realized she was the type of person I would want to be a friend to my own sister Georgiana. We spent time together at Hunsford and most recently at my estate in Derbyshire. I did not fall in love with Elizabeth overnight; even when I thought we would never be together, my love for her stood the test. I adore Elizabeth."

"Mr. Darcy, I understand your affection for my daughter, but you must understand as her father I want to be sure she is protected. You can provide for Elizabeth, no doubt, but I would like to speak to my daughter before I give my final consent. If Elizabeth loves you as you say, my consent will be yours immediately and willingly."

Darcy thanked the man and said he would send Elizabeth to him shortly. "When you satisfy your inclinations, we may meet again regarding Elizabeth's settlement, but please know I already decided to create a jointure for Elizabeth as part of the marriage articles; even without an heir, Pemberley will be hers."

"Mr. Darcy, your being able to provide for Elizabeth is not my concern. Elizabeth will choose with her heart; if you own her heart, you are an incomparable man indeed."

When Darcy returned to the drawing room, her increased attention to her needlework spoke volumes of her anxiousness. When he stepped into the room, her eyes shot up searching his face for reassurance; Darcy offered her a smile, giving her some relief. He walked casually about the room, talking specifically to Bingley and Miss Bennet, and, eventually, coming to stand beside Elizabeth.

"May I see your work, Miss Elizabeth?" he asked, wanting to talk only to her, but knowing he must wait.

"What do you think, Mr. Darcy?" she asked, holding out the needlework for his inspection; but his nearness ignited her passions, and she allowed her eyes to drift up his body just a little too slowly.

He bent down as if to inspect her work, but it was to her eyes he spoke. "Beautiful, Miss Elizabeth, absolutely beautiful," he spoke from his heart. She blushed slightly. Then in a whisper he said, "Your father wishes to speak to you in his library." Thus said, he stood and walked casually back to the settee across from Bingley and Jane and joined their conversation. Soon Elizabeth left the room.

Darcy's attention to the conversation was minimal at best; of course, Bingley and Jane were happy just to be together; they were the acknowledged lovers. When she did not return right away, the more consternation Darcy felt. Had her father refused? Was the initial dislike for him enough to sway Mr. Bennet's decision? After nearly an hour, Elizabeth reentered the room, giving him a great sense of relief; she came to sit beside him on the settee; and although she did not speak to Darcy directly, Elizabeth engaged Bingley, Jane, and Darcy in a lively conversation. They spoke of the rooms at Netherfield, Georgiana's musical talent, and the neighbors, the conversation secondary to Darcy. What was important was he was sitting beside Elizabeth in her home. Tomorrow they would be acknowledged lovers also, and soon he would be sitting beside Elizabeth in *their* home. It was enough for now.

When it was time to leave, Elizabeth stepped into the foyer with Jane as the gentlemen put on their greatcoats. Handing Darcy his hat and gloves, their fingertips intertwined for a few brief seconds. Elizabeth whispered, "I will tell Mama tonight. All will be known tomorrow."

He leaned in as near as he dared. The familiar lavender overtook his senses. "As I said before, I have been waiting for you. Tomorrow cannot come soon enough." Darcy reached out and squeezed her hand; they could not take their eyes from each other.

The ladies stepped out into the early fall evening as the men mounted their horses. Jane said a loving goodbye to Mr. Bingley while Elizabeth stood a bit apart staring up at the man she chose as her husband. Desire charged the air between them. Darcy looked at her as he always did; the stare so intense it used to make Elizabeth uncomfortable. Now it seemed so natural—so him. He leaned down from Cerberus's back and touched her cheek lightly. "Elizabeth" was all he said. She caught his hand and kissed his palm. "Darcy" was her reply. Nothing else needed to be said; there was no more "Miss" or "Mr." Their names were bound together as were their hearts and their minds.

CHAPTER 17

"Everything in his favor . . ."

———————

At last came the day he was welcomed at Longbourn. In such awe of Darcy, Mrs. Bennet kept her comments in check except to offer him any attention or to mark her deference for his opinions. Mrs. Bennet was beside herself to have two daughters so well-placed; having Jane at Netherfield was one thing, but having Elizabeth at Pemberley would be an honor for the whole family. Mr. Bennet sought Darcy's opinion again on the estate. They walked out over some of the property, and Darcy's sharp eye for details impressed Mr. Bennet. They also spent some time discussing the marriage articles, and Mr. Bennet took note of Darcy's good business sense.

"Mr. Darcy," he said, as they sat in the library at Longbourn, "Elizabeth told me of your part in saving my other daughters' reputations and your dealings with Mr. Wickham. It is my intention to repay you, Sir, for your efforts."

"Mr. Bennet, Sir," Darcy knew this conversation was inevitable, "my part in Mrs. Wickham's marriage was nothing I could not afford. I freely admit to doing so for selfish reasons. To give relief to Elizabeth was my motivation. I never wanted the Bennet family to feel an obligation to repay me. I desired Elizabeth's love, not her gratitude. You repaid me tenfold by giving me your daughter, Sir. Give me your respect as Elizabeth's husband and keep your money, Mr. Bennet."

Mr. Bennet chuckled. "Elizabeth also tells me you took great amusement in choosing Newcastle for Mr. Wickham's commission."

"It was the best I could do on such short notice," Darcy smirked.

"Mr. Darcy, your value as a son is increasing by the moment. Of course, you will have to go some to catch up with Mr. Wickham. I am afraid I have a propensity for choosing amusing characters such as our own Mr. Collins and Mr. Wickham as my *favorites*. The only foolish thing I can say of you is you gave your money to two of the most frivolous people in England, but you made up for it by falling in love with my Lizzy." Darcy was not used to such tongue-in-cheek teasing from a gentleman, but he found nothing offensive in the conversation as he settled into the comfort of Elizabeth's home.

In early afternoon Darcy and Elizabeth finally found themselves alone; they sat together in the copse holding hands. Darcy reached behind him and brought out a simply wrapped package. He handed it tentatively to Elizabeth. "I brought something with me from London for you."

"Fitzwilliam," she started, and then he saw the quizzical look cross her face. "How did you know I would accept you? Would you give me this package if I refused you?"

"There are many things I plan to give you, Elizabeth, but what is in this package, I could not bear for you to share with anyone else."

She looked at him suspiciously as she unwrapped the string and turned back the paper. Elizabeth's fingers caressed the delicate lace, and he watched her eyes well up as she rubbed her hands gently over the package. Without warning, she hugged his neck tightly. "How did you know?" she whispered in his ear.

Darcy held her for a few minutes, gently stroking the back of her head as she collapsed against him. Finally, he moved her back away from him so he could look at her and tell her how he came by the lace. "Last April, Colonel Fitzwilliam saw you in London with Miss Lucas and Miss Bennet. He did not approach because he trained recruits all day and was not presentable, but he observed your choice of this lace. That night the good colonel came to Kensington Place because Georgiana feared I would go mad if I did not talk to someone." He stroked each of her delicate fingers as he spoke softly to her. "My cousin teased me with tales of seeing you; I was in such turmoil I did the unthinkable—I drank a decanter of brandy and then confessed my love for the beautiful Elizabeth Bennet." He smiled briefly at her for he rarely remembered seeing her so somber. "I told him everything—the proposal—the letter; as I literally crawled into bed that evening, I called out to him to ask from which merchant I could find the lace; Colonel Fitzwilliam laughed and told me he would make arrangements for me to have the lace. The good colonel knew I would want it; Elizabeth Bennet chose it but did not buy it for some reason. The colonel knew I loved you even then; I kept it for you."

"Fitzwilliam, when I saw the lace in London, I kept thinking you were somewhere close by and thinking ill of me. By that time, I read your letter at least a dozen times, and I knew if not for my prejudices, I could be choosing this very lace for my wedding. I went back to the lace several times, but I did not buy it because I thought you were lost to me forever. I was discovering myself— how I judged people—how I judged you. You offered me an honor with your proposal. I foolishly threw your love away. It was the first time I admitted to myself I carried any feelings for you."

"Then the lace was meant for you, Elizabeth," he whispered as he moved a strand of hair away from her face.

She reached for the hair at the back of his neck, rubbing her finger along the shirt line. "I used to tell Jane the problem with our parents' marriage was Mama always waited for Papa to make the *grand* gesture. She is a very foolish woman, but as much as I adore my father, I believe she wants only some of his attention—the things he showed her when they were first married. They forgot what brought them together. You, Fitzwilliam Darcy, gave me more today than my parents have given to each other in years. You obtained the lace for a woman who thoroughly abused you and refused you. What did I ever do to deserve your love? You made the grand gesture without ever knowing I would love you in return."

Darcy took her hand and brought it to his lips. "Elizabeth," he too hesitated before saying what he now realized, "you will be—we will be wiser—my parents loved in a manner appropriate for their time and station, but they only showed regard for our family circle, leaving me with all my false pride. You admire your father's abilities and are grateful for his approval, but you understand although you love his wit, it has its limitations. Do not second-guess; being his daughter does not mean you will make Mr. Bennet's mistakes any more than I will make those of my father. We are not our parents; our love will be freer, more open—more hopeful. There is no guarantee, Elizabeth; you are more vulnerable than is your father because you love life. That is one of the many reasons I fell in love with you."

She nodded as he spoke, and Darcy watched as she shook her head as if to shake off the desperation she felt. The shift of her shoulders and the glint of her eyes told him she was ready to face their life together devoid of the apprehension she just experienced. In due time, playfulness rose again. "When, Love, did you know you cared for me? How could you begin? I can comprehend your going on charmingly, when you had once made a beginning; but what could set you off in the first place?"

"I cannot fix on the hour, or the spot, or the look, or the words, which laid the foundation. It is too long ago. I was in the middle before I knew that I had begun."

"My beauty you had early withstood, and as for my manners—my behavior to you was at least always bordering on the uncivil, and I never spoke to you without rather wishing to give you pain than not. Now, be sincere; did you admire me for my impertinence?"

"I believe it was your wit—the liveliness of your mind of which I first took note."

"You may call it impertinence, my Love, for it was very little else. The fact is, that you were sick of civility, of deference, of offi-cious attention. You were disgusted with the women who were always speaking, and looking, and thinking for your approbation alone. I roused and interested you because I was so unlike them. There—I have saved you the trouble of accounting for it. To be sure, you knew no actual good of me; but nobody thinks of that when they fall in love."

Darcy loved the quickness of her mind, and he picked up on her playfulness. "I pray thee now, tell me for which of my bad parts didst thou first fall in love with me?"

Elizabeth recognized the familiar Shakespearean lines offered up by Benedick and Beatrice. "For them all together, which maintained so politic a state of evil they will not admit any good to intermingle with them. But for which of my good parts did you first suffer love for me?"

Darcy's laugh resonated; the woman stirred him in unfamiliar ways. He took a countenance of false hurt. "Suffer love! A good epithet! I do suffer love indeed, for I love thee against my will."

"In spite of your heart, I think, alas, poor heart!" Her hand rested on his chest.

He touched her chin with his finger; it was the same gesture he used with Georgiana. "Thou and I are too wise to woo peaceably." He pulled her to him once again. Then they both found happiness in such shared moments. Taking a more serious tone, he then said, "I told your father, Elizabeth, your affectionate behavior for Jane when she was ill at Netherfield touched my heart. I wanted a person such as you to be Georgiana's sister."

She turned to him. "Why when you came to Longbourn were you so shy and did not speak to me? Even when you dined here you looked as though you did not care about me."

"I tried to read your countenance, and you were grave and silent; you gave me no encouragement."

"I was the same as when you first found me at Pemberley. I was embarrassed."

"And so was I."

"You might have talked to me more when you came to dinner."

"A man who felt less might."

"You are very lucky, Mr. Darcy," she teased, "your answer is so reasonable, and I am reasonable enough to accept it."

He took her hand. "Let us walk for awhile. I love being outdoors."

"I am anxious," she said looking up at him, "to see Pemberley again. I wish to walk its many pathways."

"I have much of our home I wish to share with you, Elizabeth."

"Despite our contentious times at Rosings, our walks produced some fond memories. The field of wildflowers was beautiful!"

"You were beautiful, turning around and around in it. I could barely contain my ardor! That image lulled me to sleep on many a night."

"You thought me not foolish?"

"Elizabeth, you have no idea what effect you had on me."

"*Had,* Sir?"

He scoffed, "I am not the man I was then."

"Thank goodness, neither of us is what we were then."

They walked on in silence for a few moments. Finally, she tentatively began again. "I was anxious to go to Hunsford; Charlotte's marriage to Mr. Collins placed a wedge in our relationship; I missed my friend, but I dreaded seeing Mr. Collins again."

"Because of his proposal?" His knowledge of her private affairs surprised her. "I cannot say, Elizabeth, it gave me much pleasure to know I was in the same category as the colorful Mr. Collins. The only pleasure I received from its knowledge was you would not *settle* in a marriage. I would have to earn your love."

"My mother wished me to marry Mr. Collins no matter how unsuitable a match."

"Then how did you avoid it? Did your father, too, not insist?" Darcy asked the question although he knew Mr. Bennet allowed Elizabeth the choice.

Elizabeth remembered fondly her father's support against Mrs. Bennet's will. "No, Sir, he did not. He simply said if I did not marry Mr. Collins, Mama would never speak to me again, and if I did agree to marry Mr. Collins, he would never see me again."

Darcy laughed softly. "Hopefully, he did not say something similar to you about me, but I must thank your father for his insight. When I heard of the proposal, Elizabeth, I . . . I cannot explain . . . the revulsion of the idea . . . Mr. Collins and you brought about murderous thoughts." His features darkened suddenly with the words.

Elizabeth reached up to soothe his brow with her fingertips; fortunately, the approach of Bingley and Miss Bennet interrupted his apprehension. "We were going to the house for some refreshments," Jane began. "May we all go together?"

"Yes, it seems we have some mutual plans to discuss."

The couples sat together in the drawing room at Longbourn. Mrs. Bennet graciously went to town to spread the news of Elizabeth's "conquest" to her sister Mrs. Phillips and to Mrs. Lucas. She took both Mary and Kitty with her so the intendeds served as each other's chaperones, allowing them to speak openly. Jane Bennet served the tea and the afternoon cakes and fruit. When she finished, she turned to her sister's choice for a husband. "Mr. Darcy, I cannot tell you how happy Charles and I are you and my sister have finally found each other. We often spoke of the possibilities, but we never thought it would happen. We wish you the same happiness we expect for ourselves."

"Yes," Bingley added with a smirk, "Miss Elizabeth, we are relieved you are putting my friend out of his misery."

Elizabeth smiled. "It is my true pleasure, Mr. Bingley." She sipped on her tea.

"I offer you similar congratulations, Miss Bennet," Darcy began. "Everything has come about so quickly, none of us have had time to reflect on our good luck."

"Darcy," Bingley began, calling his friend's attention back to him, "it seems our brides landed on an idea which needs our mutual approval."

"They are artful women." Both ladies blushed slightly, but it was Elizabeth who recovered her voice first.

"Jane and I are so close. Fitzwilliam, you and Mr. Bingley are such good friends. Our idea was for us to share our wedding day."

"Elizabeth," Darcy began, "I can think of nothing more pleasant than to marry you as soon as possible, but as Charles is my dear friend, I would not want to intrude on his day with your sister."

"Nonsense, Darcy," Bingley broke in, "I can think of nothing I would like more. We are friends; we will be brothers on the same day."

"If you are sure, Bingley," Darcy leaned forward to shake Bingley's hand. "I fully accept; it is settled then."

"May we set a date then?" Jane put in shyly, not used to asserting herself in company.

"I would like to do so before the festive days," Elizabeth added. "I know this sounds impetuous and probably a little demanding, and I do not mean it to seem so." She lowered her eyes, realizing how boldly she spoke. Darcy reached across the seat and took her hand in his, bringing it to his lap and pulling her closer to him.

Jane Bennet reiterated her sister's opinion, but not so boldly. "It is the first week of October," she began. "The earliest date we could consider with a proper reading of the banns is early to mid-November."

"November," Bingley thought about it for a few seconds, "will come soon enough."

"Fitzwilliam," Elizabeth turned to him, "I wanted to ask you something privately, but this conversation leads me to it sooner than I intended."

"Go on, Elizabeth," he encouraged her. "You need only to ask, and if it is in my power, it is yours."

"I am ashamed to speak so in front of your friend," she stammered.

"Miss Elizabeth, you are to be my sister soon," Mr. Bingley responded. "I will not judge ill of you for what you say among us four."

"I really do not know how to broach the subject without seeming greedy or prideful." Darcy's light chuckle sustained her nerves, and she went on. "When Mama heard of my marrying Fitzwilliam, you can imagine her surprise."

Jane Bennet snorted with suppressed laughter. "You will be happy to know, Mr. Darcy, the news literally silenced our mother for some time." Darcy smiled at the playful wit of his new sister; it was something he did not expect to find.

Elizabeth began again. "Anyway, Mama in her ravings said something I did not consider before, but I will ask if it is possible. Mama suggested a special license."

"Elizabeth!" Jane gasped.

Darcy's eyes could not be diverted from the anxious look on Elizabeth's face. "Is that what you want, Elizabeth?"

"The honor of a special license means nothing to me; I do not see it as a symbol of status, and I care not for a large wedding; family and a few friends are all I need besides you, Fitzwilliam. A special license just means we would not have to wait so long."

"I would wish for no more either, Charles," Jane Bennet added.

"What say you, Charles?" Darcy turned to him.

"A special license—can we arrange such a convenience, Darcy?"

Darcy turned to Elizabeth. "If Elizabeth wishes a special license, I will apply for one immediately."

"I would want to be your wife, Fitzwilliam, as soon as possible."

"Then we will apply for a special license," Bingley added in reassurance. "What date will we choose?"

"Monday—a fortnight," Elizabeth offered.

"Our poor mother," Jane began. "Her nerves will be such a flutter."

Realizing her mother preferred her other sisters, Elizabeth offered, "But she will only go through it once."

"I must make arrangements for Georgiana to join us. I may bring her to Netherfield; may I not, Charles?"

"Of course, Darcy, you need not ask."

Darcy turned back to the man whose friendship he never valued properly until of late. "It seems our days are numbered, Charles." Darcy laughed lightly, but he squeezed Elizabeth's hand to reassure his speech was in jest. "This evening at Netherfield, you and I will take care of the legal matters, the marriage articles, the application for the special license, and the church. I will send for Georgiana to come to your home. Are your sisters on their way?"

"They come at the end of the month. I will wait to tell them of the change in plans. Their arrival will be soon enough." Charles Bingley's face showed the angst he felt concerning his sisters' arrivals. Jane Bennet, sensing his discomfort, interlocked her arm through his.

"Miss Bennet," Darcy offered her a slight nod of the head, "you have earned the love of one of the finest men I know."

"Thank you, Mr. Darcy," she smiled as Charles Bingley caught her hand in both of his.

Elizabeth then showed her sister the lace Darcy gave her. "Is that not the same lace you wanted in London?"

"It is one and the same. Is it not a pleasant surprise?" Elizabeth gifted Darcy with a seductive pout of her lips.

"I tried to talk Lizzy into buying the lace, but she refused. Mr. Darcy, how do you know my sister so well?" Jane Bennet showed her dismay.

"Elizabeth is my other half." The explanation spoke for itself; he took Elizabeth's hand and kissed it tenderly.

At dinner that evening, Darcy received the pleasure of sitting next to Elizabeth; Mrs. Bennet added several special dishes to the meal in hopes of pleasing the gentleman. Although they were too *rich* for his taste, he complimented his future "mother" several times. Under the table when no one looked, Elizabeth rewarded him with a squeeze of his leg just above his knee. Although all too brief, the warmth of her hand on his leg burnt his flesh, and Darcy needed several slow, deep breaths to not betray his passion to the rest of the table. Elizabeth giggled softly knowing the effect she had on this man.

Jane Bennet finally opened the discussion of the wedding with her mother. "Mama, while you were in town today, Lizzy, Mr. Darcy, Charles, and I made some decisions about our wedding."

"Of course, dear, go on, Jane. Your father and I are most anxious to see our daughters portrayed in the best light on their special days."

"*Day*," Jane corrected. "Elizabeth and I chose a double wedding. We shall share our wedding day with friends who will then become brothers."

"That is such a romantic idea," Kitty sighed.

"Quiet girl," Mrs. Bennet shushed her daughter with a wave of her hand while Kitty blushed from the needless censure. "Oh, my dears, how exciting this is! Think of it, Mr. Bennet; we will have both daughters married on the same day. They were always so close."

Mr. Bennet looked at his two eldest daughters with a look of a heavy heart. "I will miss you, Jane. I will miss you, Lizzy. The house will seem empty without you." Elizabeth reached out and squeezed her father's hand and then looked at Darcy for support. He stroked the back of her free hand with his fingertips and smiled at her; she returned him a weak smile, which said *I hate to hurt my father*.

Jane turned to Charles to take the lead on the next part of their shared news, realizing her mother would act out less if Mr. Bingley approached her. "Mrs. Bennet, Mr. Darcy and I decided to apply to the archbishop for a special license. None of us wish to have a large wedding; a few *select* family and friends will suffice for our tastes."

"Oh, Mr. Bennet, did you hear—a special license? What an honor! Our daughters to be married under a special license! Mr. Darcy! Mr. Bingley! Jane! Lizzy! I am so happy—oh, Mr. Bennet!"

"I hear, Madam. I am sure the whole village has heard or will hear shortly."

Darcy's more formal manner of speaking brought everyone back to the conversation at hand. "Mr. and Mrs. Bennet, Elizabeth and Miss Bennet chose a date: Monday—a fortnight. We hope this is acceptable; your daughters express a desire to celebrate the Festive Season in their new homes."

"Of course, Mr. Darcy," Mr. Bennet began, "but that leaves very little time for settlements and marriage articles."

"This is true, Mr. Bennet, but Mr. Bingley and I are capable of handling all the legal matters in a short period if you will give us some time with you after dinner. Charles and I can meet with you separately or the three of us may address common concerns together."

"Naturally, Mr. Darcy," Mr. Bennet said reluctantly, knowing finalizing such plans would mean his two eldest daughters would soon be gone.

"But, Mr. Bennet," his wife interrupted, "our daughters will be married by a special license! I did not know I could be so happy."

Elizabeth added, "Mama, Jane and I only need a few new things for our wedding clothes. We should be able to manage with careful planning."

"My only concern," Bingley added, "is Jane will not have an opportunity to make all the changes she wishes to Netherfield before the wedding."

"Charles, that is of little concern. The changes may be made after the wedding. We have time—all the time we need." She sparkled with love.

"What of Pemberley, Elizabeth?" Kitty asked.

"I would not wish to change it at all."

"What is it like?" Kitty continued. "Is it as beautiful as reported?"

Darcy turned to Elizabeth, interested in her description of his home. She stammered a bit at first, but her description reflected her vision of her future with Darcy. "Pemberley is perfection. It is a handsome, stone building backed by high woody hills. It sits on rising ground, and every detail of it reflects the natural beauty of the estate. I truly never saw such a place! The house reflects Fitzwilliam's heritage but also his taste; the interior is simple sophistication." Darcy's smile could not be contained; Elizabeth saw Pemberley as he did; she did not speak of its wealth; she spoke of its natural beauty.

"Pemberley is magnificent," Bingley added. "I hope some day Netherfield is a shadow of its splendor. Mr. Darcy's family left him a great legacy; Miss Elizabeth will be living in what is considered to be one of England's finest homes."

Darcy acknowledged his friend's accolades. "Netherfield has the

potential for greatness, Charles. No place happens overnight." Then he turned to Elizabeth, "Do you not wish to change something in your new home?"

"Fitzwilliam, I would not be so presumptuous! Georgiana and I may choose little things once we all are settled and have time to know what we want. Pemberley is perfect the way it is." Darcy gave her that look with which she was now so familiar and which created a tumultuous state in both of them.

When the gentlemen left that evening, Jane and Elizabeth walked out with them. Bingley and Darcy completed the settlements with Mr. Bennet, and plans for the ladies' clothing needs were well underway. Jane and Bingley were to the side with their heads together when Elizabeth came forward and boldly wrapped her arms around Darcy's waist. He enveloped her in his arms, both uncharacteristically brazen for a newly engaged couple.

"Elizabeth Bennet, you take my breath away," he whispered down to her. "It is difficult for me to conceive we are finally going to be together."

"Fitzwilliam, I can think of nothing but being your wife, but please, Love, do not fret so about the past. Any arbitrary turning we might take along the way would bring us to some place else and to someone else. The journey we made brought us to this time and this place. This is where we were always meant to be."

"Do you know to what I look forward?" Darcy had a mischievous smile.

"Pray tell." Elizabeth was just as vexing.

"Being able to kiss you whenever I choose to do so." With that said, he leaned down and claimed her mouth with his.

The next day, Darcy and Bingley made their way from Netherfield to Longbourn to spend their time with their betrotheds. Being rainy, taking a long, leisurely walk was out of the question. Both couples found residence in their respective parts of the drawing room. Darcy and Elizabeth chose a secluded alcove, affording them some privacy although the other Bennet family members and the household servants were in and out of the room. A holding of hands was the most passionate act allowed with so many about.

"Have you written to Georgiana?" Elizabeth asked. "If not, I wanted to add my own lines to the letter; I do look forward, Fitzwilliam, to having Georgiana in my life. I really did not know what to expect, but she is so much more than I conceived her to be; she has your same fine mind and quick wit; you two are very much alike."

Her references to his sister pleased Darcy; he wanted them to be close. "Georgiana would enjoy hearing the news from you. Should we write the letter together?"

"I will get the paper," Elizabeth scrambled to the desk. There they sat together.

9 October

Georgiana,

I returned to Netherfield, and you will be happy to know Miss Elizabeth finally agreed to be your sister and my wife. I am in a state of euphoria; I have waited so long for this to happen; it is definitely a dream come true. Thank you, Dearest One, for always believing this day would happen. When I was at my lowest, it was your love, which sustained me. You never allowed me to give up hope, and you allowed me to see I could be the master of Pemberley and still love Elizabeth— a choice between the two was never necessary. You are still the teacher and I the student when it comes to matters of the heart. I just wish our parents were here to see this day; I am sure next to our births, this day would be one to bring them both great pleasures. Elizabeth will be a fine mistress for Pemberley, and the two of you will bring life to the walls of our home again; the house has been silent too long. I will make arrangements to bring you to Netherfield next week so you and Elizabeth may renew your friendship. I know you wanted to come to Netherfield for some time, and this is a joyous event to celebrate here. It seems now that Miss Elizabeth agreed to marry me she cannot wait to do so. We will be wed in a double ceremony with Mr. Bingley and Miss Bennet. I am looking forward to introducing you to Miss Bennet. You heard so much about her from Mr. Bingley. Can you believe Charles and I will become brothers? The date has been set for a little over a fortnight. Elizabeth and I await your presence to share in our joy.

Your loving brother,
Fitzwilliam

Georgiana,

 Your brother is mistaken; I am in no hurry to be his wife; I am only anxious to have you as my new sister. In reality, your brother has honored me, and I am truly blessed to have earned his love. Fitzwilliam has told me of your part in bringing the two of us together, and for that reason you have won my heart. Even when I was foolish, you saw I needed him in my life, and you did not allow him to turn away. Our love is because of you; your brother says you are a true romantic, and now I believe him. I am the happiest of God's creatures. We will share Pemberley as our home—you and I.

Your sister,
Elizabeth

Looking over her shoulder, Darcy teased, "You are not anxious to marry me?"

"Why would I wish to marry such a dark figure as are you, Mr. Darcy?" Her eyes betrayed her joy as she traced the line of his jaw with her index finger.

"It could not be for my good looks or my wealth so it must be for the new pianoforte in my music room. You will be able finally to practice and become an example of an accomplished young lady." Darcy saw her eyes flicker in anticipation of what she would say next.

Elizabeth laughed at his allowing himself some levity. "Speaking of being *accomplished,* who is to tell Miss Bingley of our marriage?"

"Charles claimed that *pleasure.*"

"Having both Jane and I as part of Miss Bingley's *extended* family should vex her greatly."

"I should offer an additional apology to you, Elizabeth. If I hid my fascination with you better, you would not have suffered so many rebukes at Caroline's hand."

"It seems everyone knew of your love except me."

"Why is that exactly, Elizabeth?" Darcy taunted.

"Because I was so busy finding fault with you, my dear Fitz-william, I never saw the core of the man you are. It never occurred to me until I was at Pemberley how many people's welfares depend on you. How could I have been so foolish?"

"Just now I did not wish to criticize you, Elizabeth. We both changed; you were right when you said anything arbitrarily changed in our relationship would not bring us here to each other."

"It must be the rain which brings out my doom and gloom," she sighed and then quickly brightened. "Speaking of *doom,*" she continued, "when shall you write to your aunt to tell her what has become of all her warnings about my arts and allurements? The shades of Pemberley are to be polluted after all."

"It will take courage to face her wrath again, but it ought to be done, so if I may plead for another piece of paper, I will tell her of my joy and ask for her blessings."

"It is too bad, my Love, that I, too, have a letter to write to an aunt or else I would sit close beside you and admire your meticulous handwriting as Miss Bingley used to do. However, Aunt Gardiner's letter explaining your part in Lydia's marriage hinted at what she perceived to be your fondness for me. I did not answer her directly because I could not believe she saw what I wished would happen. Now, I may happily give her the news and promise her a phaeton ride around the grounds of Pemberley."

Darcy's letter to his aunt was short and very formal. He knew she would not welcome anything he said nor would Lady Catherine change her mind. Elizabeth's letter to her Aunt Gardiner, full of mirth and happiness, fondly acknowledged the Gardiners' part in bringing Darcy and Elizabeth together.

Darcy dispatched a third letter to Edward.

9 October

Cousin,

Your interference in my life may come to a close; at last, Miss Elizabeth agreed to be my wife. I am the happiest man alive, but our aunt, I fear, will find herself in more distress. Get you to Rosings and claim Anne for your own. If you are as lucky as I, you and Anne will live in heartfelt delight.

Elizabeth and I will marry on Monday fortnight in a double ceremony with Mr. Bingley and Miss Jane Bennet. We desire your presence for the ceremony. Although it is probably too much for which to hope, we would enjoy seeing Anne with you. Miss Elizabeth sends you love and respect. She thanks you for your part in bringing us together at last.

Fitzwilliam Darcy

Once they finished the letters, Darcy and Elizabeth retreated to the privacy of the alcove. To be with Elizabeth at last gave him more pleasure than he imagined being possible. Most of the conversation between them dealt with their foolish behavior over the past year, but among these moments of mirthful self-reproach hatched *nuggets* of plans for their future. "Do you have preferences for our marriage travels before we return to Pemberley? Would you wish to see the Lake Country? *Fortunately,* the Gardiners postponed their trip there last summer," Darcy asked during one of these moments.

"I traveled so little, each new place has its own wonder; yet, I do not imagine the roads will be in such good shape at this time of year. May we not wait until summer to travel? I would love to see the Lake Country through your eyes, Fitzwilliam, and maybe some day to visit Scotland. Papa says you traveled there recently."

"It was one of the many ways I tried to forget you, Elizabeth. I threw myself into the running of Pemberley, but it was a futile effort," he allowed a moment of reflection. "Scotland offered me no beauty at the time."

"Then we should travel there together some day."

"There is so much of the world I wish to share with you, Elizabeth." He kissed the back of the hand he held.

"Where shall we go first as man and wife? Jane and Mr. Bingley chose to spend their time at Netherfield; they wish to complete the renovations and refurbishing before celebrating Christmas in their new home."

"I thought," Darcy hesitated, not wishing to speak of where they would spend their wedding night for fear of offending Elizabeth, "we could travel from the wedding breakfast to our home in London at Kensington Place. You never saw our London home, and we could control our privacy there. After that, we could decide where we go next."

"Fitzwilliam," Elizabeth blushed, "that is an excellent idea. To think I will have a house in London," she giggled. "Everything is changing so quickly. It is a bit daunting!" Her mood changed quickly, and apprehension crept across her countenance.

"Elizabeth, I watched you for months." He brought both of her hands within his and made sure she faced him directly. "I can tell your moods by the manner in which you attack your needlework or by the shift of your shoulders or the biting of your lower lip. I know the gamut of your many smiles. There is the smile you have for friends when they need your support, the one where you are excessively happy, the one when you are embarrassed or uneasy, the one when you think of something witty to say, and the one when you laugh to be polite. While I got to know those many mannerisms, I also learned about the woman with whom I wished to spend my life. Your transition into my world will be no great conquest. You already possess all the qualities to be Mrs. Darcy."

She accepted his evaluation of her ability to be the mistress of his many holdings, but she still possessed some self–doubts. Yet, she knew he believed in her, and that made her more resilient and willing to try to please him. Finally, she offered, "London and some privacy would be heavenly. I fear as the news of our engagement spreads, we will be beset with *guests* who will demand much of our time. If we could spend several days in London without interference, I would be delighted to do so. We could choose to attend the theatre or take in a concert or simply just be alone together."

"London could offer me no better draw. Our Kensington Place house will finally be a home." Darcy's face reflected his love.

"May we after a few days ask my Aunt and Uncle Gardiner to dine with us—say, later in the week?" she asked tentatively.

"Certainly," Darcy smiled, "we will have the dinner we missed at Pemberley; we will come full circle."

Elizabeth hugged him although Mary sat in the room, and she was sure Mary would offer her a moral reprimand later in private; yet, she did not care; she would be Mrs. Fitzwilliam Darcy soon. "My aunt and uncle will be so pleased! Thank you, Fitzwilliam."

"I would do anything to give you pleasure, Elizabeth. You will have time to look over the house and to decide what changes you may want to make. I would wish to offer you my mother's favorite room for your private quarters. You will find the room quite comfortable, but it is a bit old-fashioned; neither my father nor I could ever think of changing it after her death."

"Fitzwilliam, I am honored. Having part of your mother's belongings for my use is a distinction beyond words. I am sure the room is elegant." Elizabeth's eyes misted with the knowledge of his love for her. How could she ever think him to possess improper pride? Elizabeth often of late blamed herself for once finding Mr. Wickham attractive and amiable; she felt disloyal to Darcy with each of those reflections.

"Then may I, Elizabeth, send word to Mr. Thacker to prepare the house for us? I will insist no one be aware of our arrival in London; no one will call or leave words of congratulations until we are ready to receive them as man and wife."

"Those sentiments are likewise mine, Fitzwilliam," she teased him by tracing lines up his arm with her fingertips, but Darcy stiffened, and she looked startled. "Have I said something wrong? Have I offered some offense?"

"Heavens, no, Elizabeth!" He softened as he beheld her concern.

"Then you still love me, Sir?" she taunted, leaning in toward Darcy's face and tempting his lips with the warmth of her breath.

"Elizabeth," he said, the trembling in his voice evident, "I love you so much it hurts."

Elizabeth's prediction of their being beset with intrusions on their time became all too accurate. She tried to protect him from both her mother's frequent notice and her Aunt Phillips's vulgar questions about the size of Pemberley and his apparent wealth. Sir William Lucas pompously complimented Darcy on carrying away "the brightest jewel of the county." Darcy bore it well and only shrugged his shoulders and rolled his eyes once Sir William left. Mr. and Mrs. Collins escaped to Hertfordshire to avoid Lady Catherine's wrath once she became aware of Darcy's plans to marry. Charlotte Collins rejoiced in Elizabeth's news, and Darcy's letter angered Lady Catherine. Lucas Lodge offered the Collinses some safety. Having her friend at home to share in her happiness thrilled Elizabeth, but she knew Darcy paid the price by having to tolerate Mr. Collins's attentions. Collins, as usual, paraded about as if he were a man of importance rather than a mollifying clergyman whose living came at the whim of a bitter old woman. Darcy bore all of the pomp and silliness with admirable calmness. Putting up with Mrs. Bennet and her sisters and now Mr. Collins and Sir William took its toll on some of the pleasure of the season of their courtship. All the chaos of the Bennet household increased their desire to be away from all this madness; they needed time alone, and they needed the comfort and elegance of Pemberley and their family together at last.

On one such evening, as Darcy departed Longbourn, Elizabeth stood before him in the entryway; she felt his agitation, and she planned to send him back to Netherfield in a better mood. She gripped the lapels of his suit and pulled him near her, and Darcy found her finely formed features disturbingly beautiful in the flickering candlelight. "Fitzwilliam," she whispered his name as his reaction to the planned romantic gesture made her blush, "I too have observed you for some time, Sir, and you have multiple smiles, but the one I love the most is the one when you look at me." She boldly kissed him before parting.

CHAPTER 18

"Happiness in marriage is entirely a matter of chance."

In less than a week, Darcy and Bingley received responses to their letters. Caroline Bingley's letter to her brother proved to be full of insincere wishes and false platitudes. She even wrote directly to Jane Bennet, telling Jane of her delight in receiving Miss Bennet into the Bingley family. Caroline's words no longer deceived Jane, but she still accepted them graciously. "I will write to Caroline and thank her."

"Oh, Jane, you are much kinder than I," Elizabeth responded. "I do not believe I could be as forgiving as you." The sisters were seated in Jane's bedroom at Longbourn; Darcy and Bingley were out shooting with Mr. Bennet. Jane patted Elizabeth's hand in agreement. "Compared to Miss Bingley's short response to her brother, Miss Darcy's response is a novel. Four sides of paper were insufficient to contain all her delight at Fitzwilliam's news we are to be wed. Listen to what she says, 'Fitzwilliam, I have an earnest desire of being loved by my new sister.' Sweet, Georgiana, her regard will soften the deprivation I will feel at being separated from you."

"I feel the same emptiness as you, Elizabeth. We have been more than sisters, you and I, but our intendeds are such good friends, we will often be together."

"Georgiana will arrive the early part of next week. I look forward to your meeting her. Jane, she is so beautiful and so accomplished, and Miss Darcy takes such delight in helping others. I found her to be of a very generous nature. You will adore her; I am sure of it."

"I will be happy to make her acquaintance. Maybe Miss Darcy and Kitty can become friends. Kitty needs another influence in her life besides Lydia or Mary. I hoped, you and I could bring Kitty to stay with us. She is not as impetuous and uncontrollable as Lydia, and being removed from Lydia's influence and with our proper attention and management , Kitty could be less irritable, less ignorant, and less insipid."

"I agree, Jane. Why did I not think as such? In a better situation than she finds here, Kitty's improvement will be great. I will speak to Fitzwilliam this evening about her studies and training."

Mr. Bennet sought Darcy's company on their outing; he would have plenty of time to learn Mr. Bingley's quirks, but his time with Darcy and Elizabeth drew short. Mr. Bennet felt the pain of losing his favorite daughter. Previously, Elizabeth confided in her father how she was once blinded to Darcy's goodness; she showed Darcy no regard, but she could not resist his dark appeal. She had told her father, "His distance irritated me at first, but I cannot deny Mr. Darcy fascinated me." Mr. Bennet knew of Darcy's reputation as a concerned landlord, and he now had an idea of his strength of character, but Mr. Bennet had difficulty admitting any man would be good enough for his Lizzy. Even though they kept it in check, Mr. Bennet also observed the ardor easily visible between Darcy and Elizabeth; this overwhelming affection for Elizabeth softened Darcy's intolerant breeding; he released his passion while maintaining his discerning mind, according to all reports of those who knew him well. He was still a bit of an enigma, but Mr. Bennet would allow Darcy to prove himself if he made Lizzy happy.

"Mr. Darcy, your affection for my daughter places you in my family, but I feel I know so little about you. I know your *reputation,* but I would like to understand the man to whom my Lizzy gave her heart."

Darcy lacked an easy answer for his future father. "To evaluate oneself is difficult, Mr. Bennet. I fell in love with a woman who demands I talk all the time when in the past, I was content to be silent. Most would say I have an independent mind, and, I believe, your sister Mrs. Gardiner once described me as obstinate. I am often cautious with my opinion and guarded with my heart. That is, until I met your daughter Elizabeth," Darcy chuckled. "Elizabeth has a secret inner strength, a willingness to meet any challenge. I love and cherish two women, Mr. Bennet—Elizabeth and my sister Georgiana. That is the man I have become."

The earnestness with which Darcy spoke stunned Mr. Bennet. "It appears, Mr. Darcy, you recognize the worth of my dear Lizzy."

"Elizabeth," Darcy searched for the words to describe the woman with whom he was consumed, "is a woman who sees my innermost self and accepts my deepest reflections without open flattery. I marvel at her unexpected wit and her devotion to her family."

"Mr. Darcy, I regret ever thinking you did not deserve Lizzy. You are exactly what she needs; yet, I will miss her. Please tell me I may come to see her at Pemberley."

"Mr. Bennet, you need no invitation to come to our home to spend time with Elizabeth. You are welcome at any time."

Mr. Bennet offered sheepishly, "Mr. Bingley tells me the library at Pemberley contains many unusual selections."

Darcy laughed out loud. "Mr. Bingley graciously suffers my censure of the Netherfield library. You will find at Pemberley one may spend many hours lost in the written word. You will enjoy it, I am sure, Mr. Bennet."

Mr. Bennet's estimation of his new *son* increased with Darcy's willingness to receive him regularly at Pemberley. "Mr. Darcy, thank you for your devotion to Lizzy; she will make you a good wife."

"She will indeed, Sir." The image of Elizabeth as the mistress of Pemberley brought him contentment.

Within a few more days, Georgiana Darcy and Mrs. Annesley arrived at Netherfield. When the coach rolled to a stop in front of the estate house, Darcy waited at the coach's door. His sister stepped out quickly, delighted in being there at last. She slid into her brother's embrace and hugged Darcy with much admiration. "Dearest One," he stroked her hair gently, "I missed you."

"And I you, Brother," she bubbled over with pleasure. "Is Miss Elizabeth here?"

"She awaits you on the steps," he gestured toward the main doorway. Georgiana turned to look where Darcy pointed, and she beamed with excitement at seeing Elizabeth.

Bingley came forward, "Miss Darcy, welcome to Netherfield Park. I am delighted to have you at my home after so often being a Pemberley guest."

Georgiana curtsied and allowed him to kiss her gloved hand. "Mr. Bingley, thank you for receiving Mrs. Annesley and me. Your generosity is boundless. May I extend my congratulations on your upcoming nuptials to Miss Bennet."

"Thank you, Miss Darcy. My Jane awaits your acquaintance. May we go into the house and take some refreshments?"

"Nothing sounds more delightful." Darcy offered his sister his arm, and Mr. Bingley attended to Mrs. Annesley.

When they reached the main entranceway, Elizabeth and Jane waited for Georgiana. Elizabeth's smile radiated, encompassing her new sister; they gave each other a quick curtsy, and then they were in each other's arms. "Miss Darcy, I am gladdened to see you again."

"It must be *Georgiana,*" the girl insisted.

"*Georgiana,*" Elizabeth shifted her attention, "may I present my eldest sister Jane Bennet."

"Miss Bennet, I am pleased I finally have an opportunity to meet you." Georgiana offered her a greeting of a bow.

"Miss Darcy," Jane began, "Charles speaks so highly of your friendship. It is gratifying to have you at Netherfield to share in our joy. Please come in. Charles, she will need to freshen up." Jane turned to her prospective husband.

"We are not yet married," Bingley teased Jane as she blushed, "and my future wife gives me orders already." Everyone laughed *at* and *with* Jane and Bingley.

Elizabeth and Georgiana each caught one of Darcy's arms. "No orders for me, my Love?" he grinned down at Elizabeth.

"You, *Mr. Darcy,*" she pretended innocence, "are too incorrigible to take orders from me." How easily her brother accepted Elizabeth's mocking tone initially surprised Georgiana; Elizabeth drew out his spirited side.

When Georgiana joined the group in the drawing room, everyone talked over each other at first. There was so much to be said, and emotions were high. Darcy, as he did at Pemberley, placed his sister next to Elizabeth and took a chair close by.

"Elizabeth, my brother's letter brought such happiness to Pemberley. I am sorry, Fitzwilliam," she turned to him, "but I was too excited not to share the news. I told Mrs. Reynolds and asked her to share it with the staff. Mr. Howard also informed the tenants, and Mrs. Annesley and I shared our delight with the new vicar. Prayers for your happiness have been added to the service."

Darcy's eyebrow raised knowing Elizabeth's apprehension about becoming the mistress of such a large estate. "Georgiana, Elizabeth is feeling a bit overwhelmed, I fear." Elizabeth colored with his words.

"Oh, I am sorry, Elizabeth," Georgiana looked concerned, "I should not have spoken out of place."

"Think nothing of it, Georgiana. I am a bit worried about assuming such a role, but your brother will tell you I enjoy a challenge. Was not creating a new Fitzwilliam Darcy a challenge?" Elizabeth laughed nervously at herself.

"Elizabeth, the staff will love you. Fitzwilliam, by marrying you, tells them Pemberley will continue—it will survive. They have waited for him to choose a wife."

"Miss Darcy," Jane cut in, "my sister is exceptional although she gives herself little credit for her own accomplishments."

Mr. Bingley added, "Jane is right. I have known Darcy for over three years. I never knew him to be so content. Look at him—Miss Elizabeth did that."

The two blushed briefly, but as they looked at each other, the fervor of their love promptly replaced their embarrassment. Darcy's intense stare caused her to shift her weight, and she reached out to him. Immediately, he stood beside her. He rested his hand on Elizabeth's shoulder, having to touch her at that instant. She brought her hand up casually to feel his.

"I thank all of you for your confidence and love," Elizabeth stroked Darcy's hand lightly, and he squeezed her shoulder. Realizing she needed to voice her misgivings before she could conquer them, Elizabeth hesitatingly added, "When I visited Pemberley, Mrs. Reynolds spoke of Fitzwilliam some day marrying; Mrs. Reynolds said she did not know who was good enough for him." There! She said the words. Those words of doubt about her worth wrapped up her disquiet.

Darcy came to kneel beside her and looked deeply in Elizabeth's eyes. All others in the room meant nothing. Only those two existed. "Elizabeth, are you not the girl who once told me—I might have the pleasure of despising your taste, but you always delight in overthrowing those kinds of schemes and cheating a person of his premeditated contempt?" Elizabeth mused over the image of standing next to Darcy at the pianoforte and hearing him say he did not dare to despise her. "You are also the person who accused me of trying to frighten you, but you would not be alarmed. You said there was a stubbornness about you, which never could bear to be frightened at the will of others. Your courage always rises with every attempt to intimidate you."

She stroked his cheek. "It is a shame I gave my love to a man with such an excellent memory." Darcy kissed her hand and then returned to his chair. Elizabeth turned to Georgiana and took the girl's hand. "Your brother is right. I am being foolish; you do not see my sister worrying about being the mistress of this estate." Everyone knew the situation was not the same, but no one voiced his opinion. "Georgiana, we will dine here this evening. Tomorrow we will dine with my parents at Longbourn," Elizabeth continued.

"I am looking forward to meeting your and Miss Bennet's parents."

The rest of the afternoon and evening was spent in renewing and forming acquaintances. Elizabeth wanted to speak to Georgiana alone before Darcy's sister came to Longbourn with her brother so when the opportunity opened, she asked, "Georgiana, would you join me for a walk?"

"I would love to see the grounds up close, Elizabeth."

They walked for some time before Elizabeth came to the point of her conversation. "Georgiana, may we have a seat?" Once they were settled, Elizabeth hesitated briefly and then plowed head-on into what she had to say. "Georgiana, before you come to Longbourn, I want to tell you a bit about my family." Georgiana nodded her encouragement. "My father is a *gentle* man, but he finds the foibles of others amusing. My mother is often making plans to marry off one of us. With five daughters, I understand her desire, but she can be too vocal. My sister Mary takes a dim view of frivolity. Catherine, whom we call Kitty, is your age, but has not had the benefit of your education, but she has great potential, and Jane and I hope to expose her to a finer society once we are married."

"Elizabeth, I am aware of some of this. What is your concern? If my brother accepts you, that is all the proof I need of your worth."

"It is not my worth which concerns me, Georgiana. My concern is my sister Lydia." Georgiana understood the implication and fidgeted nervously. "Other than my father and Jane, my family does not know of your brother's assistance to Lydia. They may speak kindly of Mr. Wickham, and I did not want this to upset you. Lydia will attend the ceremony, and she *will* flaunt her marriage. I dread exposing you to such a position."

"Elizabeth, you are kind to think of my welfare with all the other wedding arrangements, but Fitzwilliam and I spoke of this both before he went to help Mrs. Wickham *and* before he returned to Netherfield. I am ashamed of my foolishness, and I would prefer never to encounter Mr. Wickham again; but at Pemberley with

Miss Bingley you held my hand and showed me I have nothing to fear. If you and Fitzwilliam are close, I will be able to handle it."

"Georgiana, you must not feel as if you failed your brother. Mr. Wickham's lies took me in also, and they nearly tore your brother and me apart. You have taken great steps; your youth led you to make a mistake in judgment. Your brother and I misjudged each other repeatedly, and Mr. Wickham at one time or another took us both in. We are none of us above reproach. Do not be so hard on yourself. Mr. Wickham will have his hands full with our Lydia for she is *our mother's daughter.* Lydia will advertise Mr. Wickham's flaws for all to see. In fact, he will pay doubly with Lydia as his wife."

"Thank you, Elizabeth, for being my advocate. I know it was difficult to say, especially about your own sister."

"You are to be my sister, too, in only a few days. I care about you. Your brother loves you; you *never* disappointed him."

When the ladies returned to the house, Darcy isolated Elizabeth from the others in the library. "Did you and my sister have a pleasant walk together?" he asked as they sat in adjoining chairs while enjoying a cup of tea.

"It was delightful to see Georgiana again," she added, pretending not to notice his keen interest in her conversation with his sister.

"Elizabeth, you know me better than anyone. You know I must hear of what you discussed with my sister so please do not tease me."

Elizabeth chuckled at his frustration, but she did not deny him the information he sought. "I wanted to speak to Georgiana privately before we dined at Longbourn tomorrow. I wanted to forewarn her of the possibility of hearing George Wickham's name spoken of in a positive light. I wanted to warn her of Lydia's presence and her lack of discretion."

"How did Georgiana take this news?"

"Her apprehensions with Mr. Wickham lie in what she sees as disappointment, you, my Love, have in her behavior."

"But I love Georgiana with all my being!"

"Your sister knows your love, Fitzwilliam; what she does not allow herself is knowledge of your forgiveness."

"What should I do, Elizabeth? How do I convey as such to her? I know how to manage her wealth and arrange Georgiana's studies, but how do I show her she has no reason to question how I value her worth?"

"Fitzwilliam, just give Georgiana your love—show her, as you showed me—the value of your love. Tell her your thoughts; share your aspirations; show Georgiana you respect and value her opinions. That is what you did with me. It should be easier, my Dear, because Georgiana's heart was never set against you."

Darcy leaned forward in his chair to look closely at Elizabeth. Each day he found something more precious in her. "You and Georgiana already created a bond; this was my hope for her for many years. I will show Georgiana my true feelings. When I was most vulnerable, it was she to whom I turned. She and I are very much alike, Elizabeth. Securing her happiness has been one of my obsessions, I fear. Thank you for caring for my sister as you do."

Elizabeth shrugged her shoulders as if to say it was nothing at all. She also knew Darcy's propensity for self-reproach so she made an effort to tease him out of his bad humor. "I believe," she said looking around the room, "the last time we were together in this room, you showed me very little attention. William the Conqueror was more to your taste."

"That is where you are sadly mistaken. You have no idea what effect you have on me, Elizabeth."

Elizabeth allowed herself a long look at Darcy's lean frame. "Then why did you not talk to me?"

"You, my Dear, berated me the previous evening for judging others. By that time, although I did not acknowledge it to myself, I was ardently in love with you, but you showed me no encouragement. I swore to remove you from my thoughts. I went for a long ride on Cerberus, wrote letters of business and pleasure, and avoided your presence. I was determined to rid myself of the control you had over me." By this time, Darcy was on his knee in front of her, holding her hand. "I came into the library to hide until you and your sister quit the house. Because of you, I had so little sleep the night before and rode Cerberus so hard, I was exhausted and fell asleep in the chair in which you now sit."

The realization of what Darcy confessed played across her face, and Elizabeth's enigmatic smile returned. "If you were asleep, then how call you out my name, Sir?"

"Must I say it, Elizabeth?"

"Say what, Fitzwilliam?" Her smile now spread freely. "I am but a woman; what would I know of anything?"

Darcy dropped his eyes momentarily, understanding she would demand he tell her what she already knew. "Why is it, Elizabeth, you force a man who prefers silence to entertain you with conversation?"

"You avoid the question, Fitzwilliam."

"I dreamed of you, Elizabeth. There! I said what you already knew."

"Oh, Fitzwilliam, please do not be terse with me. I am still in awe of your loving me so dearly. It fascinates me." She cupped his face in her hands and warmly kissed his mouth. His response to such an innocent act of romance she recognized as his passion, but it still took her by surprise each time it happened. Elizabeth moved back from his kiss slowly, knowing they must wait but not wishing to do so. He, too, aware of their eagerness, rose slowly to return to his chair.

"Elizabeth, we should rejoin the others," he warned.

"Must we, Fitzwilliam? There are so many demands on our time; I could stay in here with you forever and never be wanting. Please may we remain for a few more minutes?" They sat quietly in each other's presence, each contented with being with the other.

Quitting the room at last, they held a new resolve to meet the requirements of a recently engaged couple. Darcy's arm slid around her waist as they entered the main hallway. "Did you, Elizabeth, realize how beautiful you looked standing at the top of those stairs the Sunday morning we went to services together? You took my breath away." As he said so, he pulled her toward him.

"That was an uncharacteristic act of impropriety. What made

you agree with Mr. Bingley?" Elizabeth loved to tease him about his earliest attempts at winning her.

"In reality, my emotions were still so disheveled from seeing you in the library the day before, I could think of nothing else but to put *distance* between us."

"So, your way of putting distance between us was to greet me on the staircase and lead me to a private coach? That is an interesting approach, do you not think?"

"In retrospect, the plan was not foolproof." His smile was enormous.

"I do so love you, Fitzwilliam." She looked him straight in the eye. "We have only a week before the wedding; we waited this long to be together; we have a lifetime to love one another. Let us join the others for now." He tapped her chin with his index finger. In more of a question than a statement, she added, "I saw you make the same gesture with Georgiana."

"I did so since she was a babe; it is an endearment between us two."

"I like it; you have my permission to do so as often as you like." She took his hand as they entered the drawing room, promises of love and life exchanged with a simple caress.

The dinner at Longbourn went better than either Darcy or Elizabeth expected. Mrs. Bennet, nearly in as much awe of Georgiana Darcy as she was of her brother, refrained from her usual familiarity although she did ask Miss Darcy several questions on the number of rooms at Pemberley and how many servants there were, but Darcy and Elizabeth deflected the majority of those questions. Georgiana consented to a duet with Mary Bennet, earning Mary's loyalty for the favor of the attention. Miss Darcy also shared the pianoforte with Elizabeth. Georgiana played the harder sections, but Darcy enjoyed the blessing of hearing Elizabeth sing. Mr. Bennet took the time to discuss several books with Georgiana before retiring to his study for the evening. Kitty cornered Miss Darcy to discuss fashion and balls. They seemed to enjoy each other's company although Elizabeth noted how often Georgiana blushed.

"Lizzy," Kitty came to sit with her sister, "Miss Darcy says you want me to come to stay at Pemberley. Is that true?" The girl was bubbling with anticipation.

Elizabeth took her younger sister's hand into hers. "Kitty, it would give me great pleasure for you to come to Pemberley. I would like some time to settle in with my new husband, but I was thinking some time after the first of the year. In fact, I want to ask Fitzwilliam about helping find someone to advance your studies. Jane and I decided you should spend most of your time with us if that would suit you."

"Lizzy, I can think of nothing better. Will there be balls?"

"Kitty, first you will need some lessons before presentations at balls, but I am sure some parties can be arranged."

"Thank you, Lizzy," Kitty hugged her. "I cannot wait to tell Maria Lucas tomorrow."

As expected, Lydia Wickham came to Longbourn for the wedding rather than to send her congratulations. Thankfully, Mr. Wickham's duties, as well as his recent debts in the area, kept him from joining his wife. Lydia flaunted her tales of military balls to Kitty, but Kitty had her own news of being invited to Pemberley, causing Lydia to sulk for a good portion of the evening. Darcy and Elizabeth kept her from giving Georgiana too much notice. Truthfully, Miss Darcy's reserve reminded Lydia too much of her brother to interest Mrs. Wickham's frivolous nature.

As the party drew near its close, Lydia cornered Darcy in the drawing room. "Mr. Darcy, you are a devious man." Used to being the center of attention, she tried to flirt with him.

"I am afraid, Mrs. Wickham, I do not understand your implication." He ignored her advances with his usual haughty manner.

"When you were in London, you should have told me you favored Lizzy. I made such a fool of myself talking about you and her. Lordy, I said she hated you—remember?"

"I recall your words, Mrs. Wickham."

"It is odd—once my dear Wickham was a favorite of Lizzy's—now I am married to Mr. Wickham, and you will marry our Lizzy."

"I will marry Elizabeth," is all the response he gave to her references to George Wickham.

"Oh, by the way, Mr. Darcy, my husband sends you his congratulations." She slipped into his hand a letter addressed to Darcy, written in the distinctive script of George Wickham. He tried not to show the anxiety he felt at seeing it.

"Thank you, Mrs. Wickham." Darcy slipped the message into his pocket to read later. Shortly, he excused himself on the pretense of borrowing a book from Mr. Bennet. Securing the book and stepping into the hallway, Darcy finally read the note in private.

19 October

Darcy,

News of your plans to marry Miss Elizabeth was both a surprise and a revelation. It appears you won the more sensible sister; she was once a favorite, but her lack of fortune decreased her worth for a man such as I. I preferred her conversation to anyone I met of late, but her exuberance will be lost to the solemnity of Pemberley. Oh, well, if that is the life Miss Elizabeth chooses, then she will just have to be happy with your wealth, will not she?

I wish I was aware of your real reason for saving Lydia's reputation. I knew the story you offered did not make sense, but I could not quite make if right; maybe I was too desperate to see things clearly. I imagine now you would gladly pay the ten thousand pounds after all.

You won this battle, but the war is not yet complete. At least, we will once again be brothers.

GW

Darcy's contempt at the audacity of such a note being sent shook his being. He literally shuddered with anger and disdain. Elizabeth, having missed his presence, came to find him. "What is it, Fitzwilliam?" she rushed to his side.

"A letter of *congratulations* from Mr. Wickham." His was a cold laugh.

"Please, Fitzwilliam, do not let this man ruin our time. We all have evil in us, but we all have goodness too. If you let Mr. Wickham cloud these last days of courtship, you allow the evil in, and he wins. I love you so much I would give up my life for you. Let that goodness in instead. Give me the letter; Mr. Wickham's well wishes will make good kindling for my bedroom fire."

He slid the envelope into her hand. "Elizabeth, how I earned your love I do not know, but I am blessed as no man is." He pulled her close to him to escape the darkness he just felt.

She held him there briefly before saying, "Come, Love, Georgiana may need us." She interlaced her arm through his. "Only five more days," she whispered.

If Darcy realized Elizabeth's anger at her sister he may not have left her that evening, but he, Mr. Bingley, and Georgiana returned to Netherfield in due time. Once everyone was to bed, Elizabeth found Jane and Lydia in Lydia's old bedroom. Jane made her "good nights" when Elizabeth entered. "I will see you in the morning, Lizzy," Jane said as she exited the room.

"Good night, Jane," Elizabeth kissed her briefly on the cheek in parting.

Coming to sit across from her youngest sister, Elizabeth first forced Lydia to give her undivided attention, and then Elizabeth spoke in a stern tone, "Lydia, I plan to say this to you only once. You are my sister, and I love you, but Mr. Wickham will *never* be my brother nor will he be Mr. Darcy's brother. Mr. Wickham will *never* be welcomed at Pemberley. If he would be foolish enough to try to come there, it would not be *Mr. Darcy's* wrath he should fear. It would be the wrath of *Mrs. Darcy.* I would have him shot as a trespasser."

"Lizzy, that is foolish; you know nothing about shooting a gun."

"I am sure, Lydia, Mr. Darcy would be happy to teach me how to handle a gun if he knew my purpose was to rid our estate of your husband."

"Lizzy, that is not fair to my husband. How can you think so harshly of my dear Wickham?"

"If you only knew your *dear Wickham*."

"Lizzy, I know you think me to be foolish, but I do know Mr. Wickham's faults, but what can I do, I am his wife."

Elizabeth pitied Lydia, but she would not let that cloud her resolve. "Then *be* his wife and not an instrument for plans of destruction. Lydia, you must grow up—you must as a wife be concerned with something more than balls and officers."

"Lizzy, that is all I have. Jane is beautiful; you are smart; Mary is talented; Kitty is creative. What do I have besides my childish innocence—that is all the charm I have to offer?"

"Do not sell yourself as such, Lydia. You are a Bennet ..."

"I am not valued as are you and Jane. I am sorry, Lizzy, but I have no head for reading or what makes women accomplished."

"Lydia, Mr. Darcy did all he will do for you and Mr. Wickham. He paid Mr. Wickham's debts, purchased for him a commission in Newcastle, and gave an additional two thousand pounds to Mama's dowry for you. You *must* understand; Mr. Darcy will not bail out Mr. Wickham again just because you are my sister. I do not want you to suffer and end up in a place such as in which Mr. Darcy found you in London."

"Lizzy, I cannot manage on what we have to live on!"

"Lydia, Jane and I will help when we can. I may be able to save something from my pin money, but I will *not* ask Mr. Darcy to help Mr. Wickham again."

"I understand, Lizzy." The girl was nearly in tears.

"You need to make your husband understand as well. Tell him what I said."

"I will, Lizzy."

"I do not want to hurt you, Lydia, but I will not have Fitzwilliam abused by Mr. Wickham again. You know me, Lydia. Tell Mr. Wickham this is my final word on the matter!"

"Yes, Lizzy, I will tell him."

"Good night, Lydia." Frustrated with her youngest sister, Elizabeth left the room and stormed to her own room. The fire consumed the congratulatory letter; it burned out quicker than did Elizabeth's anger.

CHAPTER 19

"My mind was more agreeably engaged."

———— ◦◦◦◦ ————

"I say, Bingley, is that not your barouche headed toward Netherfield?" Darcy and his friend took a final tour of Bingley's estate; down to four days before best friends married sisters in Meryton, they both tried to kill the hours before their wedding day by completing the land survey.

"Yes, Jane wanted to make one last walk through of Netherfield and note the renovations for each room before my sisters arrive tomorrow. Caroline and Louisa prefer Jane to choose from their ornate designs." Bingley rose up in his saddle to get a better view of his intended. "Your Elizabeth is coming to spend the afternoon with Georgiana."

Darcy too sat forward in the saddle. It seemed to be a lifetime ago he first saw Elizabeth Bennet walking along the roads surrounding Netherfield; her presence sent a surge through him then, as it did now. "Do you think you have seen enough of Netherfield's lands for the day?" he asked nonchalantly.

"I believe I have," Bingley winked at his friend. "We should return to the house. Maybe we should enter through the servants' entrance, freshen up, and then surprise the Miss Bennets. What say you, Darcy?"

"Bingley," Darcy smiled, "your suggestion is most welcomed." They spun their horses around and headed toward the rear of the house.

By the time Darcy came upon the open doorway of the drawing room, Elizabeth and Georgiana spent a pleasant three quarters hour together. They spoke of family, of music, and of Darcy. An outside observer might think they were sisters forever; a natural respect existed between the two. Their laughter drifted from the room, and Darcy found himself reluctant to enter the space and interfere with their kinship.

"Georgiana, may I ask you something?" Elizabeth looked up sheepishly.

"Anything, Elizabeth."

"Something has bothered me for some time. When I first met your cousin Colonel Fitzwilliam he already knew so much about me. When I asked his source, he said you told him; yet, we never met."

"That is simple, Elizabeth. My brother often spoke of you."

"Really? What could he have said about me? Something devious, I am sure."

"Fitzwilliam never mentioned a woman in his letters before. He related many of your conversations at Netherfield. I could not believe anyone spoke so to him. It peaked my interest. When I thought he was most distracted, I would ask about you."

"My manners were abhorrent. His stories must have portrayed me as less than civilized."

Darcy nearly laughed, but he stifled it wanting to hear more.

"Oh, no, Elizabeth. Fitzwilliam always said wonderful things about you. I wanted to meet you, and I hoped we could be friends." At this Elizabeth reached out and took Georgiana's hand in hers. "I was upset Mr. Bingley quit Netherfield. I wanted to come here and make your acquaintance; Fitzwilliam said he wanted that too." Elizabeth squeezed her hand knowingly.

Then hesitatingly, Elizabeth changed the subject. "Georgiana, now you survived an evening with my family and their references to Mr. Wickham, may we revisit our conversation from the previous day?"

"What do you mean, Elizabeth?"

"With Mr. Wickham, did you believe yourself to feel *regard, affection,* or *love?*" Elizabeth was holding her gaze and looking at Georgiana seriously.

"I am not sure I understand, Elizabeth. I felt all three, of course." The turn of this conversation made Darcy uncomfortable, but he tried to trust Elizabeth's instincts.

"I am not an expert on love, Georgiana, but you are mistaken. If you held Mr. Wickham in regard, you would have felt foolish at your loss, but the romance would have been gone within six months. If you felt affection for him, you would again be foolish, but a year would resolve your loss. If I am correct, you felt one of these emotions rather than love. Am I not correct?"

"Elizabeth, I can see one of these definitions fitting my situation, but then what is *love?*"

"*Real love,* Georgiana, changes your life; your own needs no longer exist. If rejected, you *never* forget the person; as Fitzwilliam did, you might try to run away—you try to find solace some place else, but it cannot be. You might even choose another with whom to spend your life, but there is no love for it died and was replaced with regard or affection. I could not think of loving anyone but your brother; can you say the same thing about Mr. Wickham?"

"I cannot, Elizabeth. I feel nothing for the man. I only feel my own shame at being taken in by him."

"Then may we move on? You are not the person you were then. The Darcys must learn to not be so hard on themselves. Your brother is learning that lesson; can you not also?"

"Elizabeth, you make things so logical and so simple. I am happy to be able to share my life with you. Maybe if you were here before, I would not have made such a fool of myself."

"Georgiana, we all make fools of ourselves. Your brother and I are perfect examples, but what you have now is someone to whom to talk when you have questions. I may not always have the answers, but we will find our way together, and I will always be there to support you."

Darcy could not believe how easily the two of them talked together; at last, Georgiana had a female to whom to turn for advice. He started to step into the room, but held for just a moment when Elizabeth stammered one last question.

"Do you believe Lady Catherine will ever forgive your brother for not choosing Anne? Family is so important to me; I hate being the cause of a family rift."

"My aunt is stubborn, but she forgets Fitzwilliam is the head of the Darcy family now. Those Lady Catherine is able to influence will be easily forgotten."

"But will Edward's marriage to Anne create other problems for your brother?"

"If Fitzwilliam married Anne, our aunt could stay at Rosings because Fitzwilliam is rich enough not to need Anne's fortune. When Edward marries Anne, Rosings becomes theirs, and my aunt will become Dowager de Bourgh and be relegated to a small country manor. She has more problems than your marrying my brother."

"I cannot help but feel I destroyed your family, Georgiana."

"That is nonsense, Elizabeth. My brother loves you."

Darcy could hear no more; he stepped into the room. "My sister is correct, Madame, you have bewitched me body and soul." He stopped only a few steps within the doorway. Both ladies jumped to their feet as if caught misbehaving; Darcy and Elizabeth locked eyes. She blushed deeply.

"You, Sir," she began haltingly, "should not be eavesdropping."

His eyes flashed with humor. "How else may I know when the two women I cherish most are conspiring against me?"

Elizabeth raised her chin as if to challenge him, but her bottom lip quivered telling him her words about women always conspiring against men had nothing to do with what she was really thinking.

"You do not intend on rejecting me again do you, Elizabeth? I am afraid my heart could not take it another time," he taunted her.

Tears filled her eyes as she said, "My loving you can hurt you; I do not want you to ever regret loving me."

The changes in her brother enchanted Georgiana. He openly professed his love for Elizabeth, not caring what others thought or saw. "Elizabeth, I will not give you up again. If necessary, I will carry you off and make you my wife over all your objections. You would not make me do something so uncharacteristic, would you?"

She knew he teased, but she rushed into his arms, burying her tears into his chest. Soothing her head, he said, "Shush, Elizabeth, we will have no more tears over Lady Catherine's disapproval. Do you not think I suffered enough at your hand?" As he said this, he brought her palm to his lips and kissed it gently. "Georgiana," he diverted his eyes to his sister briefly, "why do you not go to your room and retrieve the gift you brought for Elizabeth?" Georgiana curtsied and left quickly.

Elizabeth raised her chin, drinking in Darcy's face with her eyes. "These hands, Sir," she said at last, "will never give you pain again." As she said this, she stroked his chin line and moved in closer.

He dropped his arms down to her waistline, pulling Elizabeth even nearer. Darcy's gaze encompassed her features and settled upon her lips. The familiar lavender wafted over him. "Madame, in a few moments, I may forget I am a gentleman and you are a gentleman's daughter."

Elizabeth's giggle was nearly a purr, silently revealing her undying love. "Ungentlemanly like behavior," she teased, "will have to wait a few more days, but I would not object to a kiss to seal our promise to each other."

His breath was ragged with anticipation; Darcy kissed her long and hard. "You see, my Dear, our love will go down in history," he whispered.

"Will it now?" she whispered back, her lips only inches from his.

"Great loves are always remembered. We will be Fitzwilliam and Elizabeth."

"Ooh, that is way too long. It does not roll easily off the tongue—Darcy and Elizabeth has more lilt to it." She nibbled on his lower lip.

"So, it is agreed; our love will be of what makes great legend." He turned his head burying it in her hair. "We will be as Romeo and Juliet or Othello and Desdemona."

She turned her head back toward his face. "I hope we do not have to die for our love. May we not be more like Petruchio and Katherine or Benedick and Beatrice?"

Darcy laughed softly. Even in the middle of an embrace, she would challenge him. Life with Elizabeth Bennet would be anything but boring. "So, the lady prefers comedy to tragedy, does she not?" He kissed her lightly, brushing his lips over hers.

"Our relationship has been a comedy of errors at times." She returned his kiss, as her fingers caressed the hair along the back of his neck. Her nearness captured Darcy; he bowed his head to hers once more and kissed her warmly.

Georgiana watched this scene from the doorway not wishing to disturb them. *This is the type of love I want. It should be obvious to the world when a woman is in love. It should not be hidden. Thank God my brother kept me from making that mistake. How could I be deceived into thinking what Mr. Wickham offered me was love? What Fitzwilliam has with Elizabeth is real love.* She cleared her voice to announce her presence; the lovers ceased the kiss, but they did not jump apart as one might expect upon being found in such an intimate embrace. They parted naturally, not ashamed of the affection they shared.

"Elizabeth," Georgiana began, "my brother wanted you to have something special for the wedding." She presented Elizabeth with a golden box tied with a ribbon.

"Fitzwilliam," she beamed at him, "you should not have given me anything else; the lace for my wedding attire was enough."

"This was my mother's wish," he said. "She left this in my father's care; when he died, he gave it to me; it was to be a gift for my wife."

"My brother asked me to take it to London; we agreed it needed to be reset for you. I hope you like the design; I chose it myself; I thought it was *simple sophistication*." Georgiana looked on with anticipation. "Open it."

Brother and sister crowded around as Elizabeth, hands shaking, removed the ribbon and cracked open the lid of the box. The emeralds and diamonds necklace sparkled out at her. "Fitzwilliam, I cannot accept something so expensive."

"Have you not heard, my love," he leaned down and gave her a quick kiss on the cheek, "I am worth ten thousand pounds per year?"

She laughed but was beyond words. "Turn around, Elizabeth, and let us try it on." Georgiana giggled, "There—see in the mirror—what do you think?"

"It is not often I am at a loss for words. Georgiana, the design is exquisite! I do not know what else to say." Elizabeth hugged her soon-to-be sister excitedly.

"What about me?" Darcy chuckled.

"You, Sir, I will pay later," Elizabeth teased. "I love you, Fitzwilliam," she hugged his neck tightly.

He turned her back toward the mirror catching her eyes with his in the reflection. Suddenly, it dawned on Elizabeth; Fitzwilliam Darcy made no moves spontaneously. The necklace was a token of his love for her, but it also symbolized to the world: This is my wife! You will respect her as you respect me!

Elizabeth hugged both of them again, whirling both around in her enthusiasm. Georgiana turned to her brother. "Elizabeth and I were going to take a stroll over the grounds. Would you care to join us, Fitzwilliam? We will learn to be a family; how say you, Brother?"

His laughter was contagious. "Georgiana, you have no idea how often I pictured such a future for us; Elizabeth will complement both of us nicely." They turned in unison toward Elizabeth as if on cue. Her joy written across her face told them all they should remember this moment; it was a promise of things to come.

Walking the paths of Netherfield together, Darcy's heart pounded in his ears; he never thought such happiness could exist. Elizabeth and Georgiana bubbled enthusiastically at his side. "Fitzwilliam," Elizabeth began hesitatingly, "Georgiana and I have been talking about our home."

He interrupted her by saying, "Pity is the man who is at the will of two beautiful ladies."

Both females felt the blush of his jovial remark. "Fitzwilliam," Elizabeth paused, "I wish to speak to you of a matter of some importance."

Darcy's amused look faded as he too stopped and faced her head-on. "Then speak your mind, Elizabeth. I am inclined to give you what you request."

"I am sure you will want to share in what I ask, Sir. Once we return from our wedding holiday, I would like for Georgiana to return to Pemberley with us. There is no reason for your sister to stay in London."

"Elizabeth," Georgiana stammered, "I am so inclined, but you and my brother need your privacy."

"Nonsense, Georgiana," Elizabeth took her hands. "Pemberley's vastness can easily afford your brother and I all the privacy we desire. Yet, your presence can give me the confidence I need to become its mistress. I need you there with me; your brother needs you there. We cannot celebrate the Festive Season at Pemberley if you are in London."

"We have not been at Pemberley," Georgiana explained, "during the Festive Season since the passing of our father, Elizabeth."

Darcy watched in stunned disbelief; both women turned toward him with beseeching eyes. "Georgiana," he began slowly, "it seems my marriage to Elizabeth is a new beginning for Pemberley, and we have grieved for its losses long enough. Would you prefer to be at Pemberley?"

"Oh, yes, Brother," she was all smiles. "Pemberley bedecked for the festivities is the most beautiful of houses. May we return to Pemberley as a family—you, Elizabeth, and I?"

"It is settled. The Darcys will celebrate together at Pemberley." The ladies so happily hugged him repeatedly.

Georgiana gasped, "Fitzwilliam, may I tell Mrs. Reynolds this year we reopen Pemberley to its greatness?"

"Certainly, my Dearest," he said as he pulled Elizabeth close to his side. "Your soon-to-be sister and I will be distracted elsewhere. You may let the household and ground staffs know the Darcys will be at home together."

Georgiana hugged first Elizabeth and then her brother one more time. Her excitement showed as she nearly skipped along the path. Elizabeth's eyes misted with tears as she took in Darcy's countenance, and the piercing darkness of his eyes mirrored his sister's elation.

Fitzwilliam Darcy tossed and turned through most of the night; one would expect him to finally rest; after all, his wedding day had arrived; in a few fleeting hours, Elizabeth Bennet would be his forever. Lying diagonally and wrapped haphazardly in the bedclothes, Darcy replayed all the details of the day he began planning over a year ago. How often he doubted this day would ever come; Elizabeth won his heart, but he was a different man then. He knew not himself, nor did he really know Elizabeth; it began as merely physical attraction, but she was more to him now. Elizabeth was his other half; there could be no life without her for Darcy.

Knowing sleep would not be his, Darcy unwrapped himself from the counterpane; slinging his long limbs over the edge of the bed, he reached unconsciously for the bell cord. Although it was still dark, his man appeared within moments of being summoned. A light tap on the chamber door signaled his presence. "Come," Darcy called.

"Mr. Darcy, do you desire something, Sir?" the valet asked.

"Yes, Henry, please tell the stables to saddle Cerberus at first light."

"Do you desire riding clothes, Sir?"

"No, Henry, I do not want the full riding *frock*. I simply wish breeches, boots, and a shirt; Cerberus will rid me of my premarital anxiety. We both need the exercise, I fear."

The valet smiled at his master's disheveled appearance and exited the room. Darcy ran his fingers through his hair and tried to compose his thoughts and calm his heart. He wished to be at Pemberley instead of at Netherfield; being Bingley's guest required Darcy to curb his anxiety on this momentous day; if he was at Pemberley, Darcy would be pacing the halls of the east wing by now.

Henry returned shortly and helped Darcy don the breeches, shirt, boots, and greatcoat, and then Darcy followed Henry down the narrow back stairway leading from the servants' quarters. He used the same steps only a few days before in order to surprise Georgiana and Elizabeth; Darcy paused briefly as the images of that day sparkled brilliantly in the candlelight. Free of the confines of

Netherfield, Darcy strode quickly through the morning mist to the stables. Cerberus awaited him at the mounting block; as he approached, he took the time to pat his favorite mount before swinging up into the saddle. With a "cluck" of his tongue and a light tug on the reins, Darcy turned the cream-colored stallion toward the rolling hills and woods of Netherfield Park. He rode firm but not with speed; he wanted to melt into the haunches of the horse and absorb its strength, and without realizing it, Cerberus carried his master to the rise from which Darcy first saw Elizabeth Bennet.

A deep laugh escaped his throat and was carried upon the morning by the withdrawing mist. As Darcy looked intently upon the place he first saw Elizabeth, Cerberus turned in circles wanting to chase the sound of his voice. He pulled the reins to the right, "Come on, Boy, I know where we can go." A three miles' journey, which Darcy traversed daily since Elizabeth accepted his proposal, led to Longbourn, so why not do so today? Of course, he would not go to see her on their wedding day; Mrs. Bennet's "nerves" would never survive such an intrusion, but he would go close enough to observe the house in which Elizabeth prepared for their life together. It would satisfy Darcy to know Elizabeth would be that close; even without saying so, she would know he waited for her.

Instead of following the road, Darcy snaked Cerberus along the hedged fields with a smattering of sheep grazing tentatively on the remaining shoots of grass. He brought the horse up when they crested the hill leading to Longbourn and dismounted, letting the reins drag the ground. He walked slowly to an overhanging boulder, leaning against its dampness and letting the coolness of the rock calm his heart. Longbourn in the morning sun took on a pictorial solemnity; peacefulness falsely exuded from its walls. Darcy could just imagine Mrs. Bennet scolding servants and daughters left and right—Jane Bennet's knowing smiles and the roll of Elizabeth's eyes. He chuckled thinking about a sweet revenge on Mrs. Bennet; Darcy would take Elizabeth away from all this chaos.

Staring hard at the house in the distance, he could see Elizabeth at the window of his imagination. Finally, he turned to pick up Cerberus's reins and began to mount, but a movement in the morning haze caught his attention. There coming through the rising mist was his Elizabeth clothed in her night shift and a pelisse. For a brief second, he thought it a trick of the mind, but the clutching of his heart by his chest told Darcy she was real.

The lovers' eyes locked on each other, peering into each other's souls, and they moved forward as if in a trance. Without saying a word, they embraced as the sun danced behind them. "Elizabeth," Darcy whispered her name into her hair.

"Fitzwilliam," she laid her hand upon his chest and welcomed his nearness. Their hearts beat wildly as they envisioned the happiness awaiting them.

"Dearest, Elizabeth," he lifted her chin to look into her eyes. "What are you doing here?"

"I could ask you likewise, Sir," was her tempting reply.

"I could find no sleep for images of you. I sought my release by riding here to assure myself this was not a dream, and I find a living, breathing Elizabeth," he stammered.

"Fitzwilliam, you have no fear of finding yourself alone ever again," she stroked the stubble of his beard. "For you, Sir, stole my heart and only you may be rid of it. It is at your whim."

Darcy brushed his lips across hers in an inviting tease. "We should not be found together like this," he said unwillingly.

"'Tis, true. My father might be required to defend my honor on my wedding day," she said, bestowing a full kiss upon his faintly trembling lips. His arms enveloped her as she moved closer for a long, tender moment.

As they separated, Elizabeth's fingers gently traced his lips; he caught her hands and kissed her fingertips. "I will await you at the church," he smirked as she turned to go.

"Do not forget to bring my heart," she taunted him over her shoulder.

"Elizabeth," he called.

Turning slowly and giving him an enticing gaze, she pursed her lips, "Yes?"

"You did not answer my question. Why came you here this morning?"

"Did you not will it, Sir?" She laughed and walked briskly back to the house.

Still feeling her breath upon his cheek, Darcy watched her leaving until he could see her no more, and then he recovered Cerberus's reins, mounted, and rode toward Netherfield.

"Edward, it is so good to see you here; I feared your relationship with Lady Catherine would keep you from coming." Darcy extended his hand in welcome.

"I had to make sure you did not change your mind, Cousin," Edward laughed.

"You always play to the full house, right, Edward?"

"Anne sends you her regards, Fitz. She will send out our announcements tomorrow if you make it through the day." Edward could not give up the playful nature of the conversation.

"Cousin, if I was not the happiest man in the world this day, I might call you out for your references to my cowardice." Darcy was in a good mood. "In reality, Edward, I could not be here today without your good counsel. You were more than a cousin; you were my salvation. I pray you and Anne live long and are happy."

"Thank you, Fitzwilliam. I wish you and Elizabeth the best life has to give. You won an amazing woman."

"Will you escort Georgiana back to Pemberley after the ceremony?"

"Back to Pemberley? Will you not be in London for the Festive Season?"

"Elizabeth and Georgiana want to be at Pemberley. It is time to stop grieving for my parents."

"Fitzwilliam, you will be fine. Elizabeth will help make Pemberley greater than it ever was."

"I hope to have a small gathering at New Year's. Would you and Anne consider being our guests?"

"I will not promise; much needs to be finalized at Rosings, but we will try."

"You and Anne are always welcome in my home; come any time, Edward." Darcy looked around nervously. "I believe it is nearly time to begin." Edward hugged Darcy, slapping him on the back several times. Both men had gigantic grins as they moved into the church.

"Fitzwilliam," Georgiana came forward and lightly kissed his cheek, "I just saw Elizabeth; she is the most beautiful bride ever. The lace delicately frames her face; she looks like an angel."

Darcy could not imagine Elizabeth looking more beautiful than she did this morning walking toward him out of the mist; the passion rushed through him. "Georgiana, you are prejudiced on Elizabeth's behalf."

"'True, Fitzwilliam. I am nearly as anxious as are you."

"I doubt that," he laughed lightly. "Edward will accompany you back to Pemberley."

"The colonel and I will take great pride in singing your praises, Fitzwilliam," she giggled as she hugged him one last time.

Darcy and Bingley took their places at the front of the church. Moments later a hush fell over the congregation, and Darcy turned to see Mr. Bennet with Jane on one arm. Then his gaze fell on Elizabeth on the other side. She looked exquisite! The fine muslin and white satin drape of the dress hung close to her body revealing her curves. The dress scalloped round the bottom was finished with a green ribbon twist. The delicate lace she chose to trim her bonnet also decorated the long sleeves, which were scalloped to correspond with the bottom of the dress and ornamented with more green ribbon. A green silk sash encircled her waist. Green ribbons accented the neckline, and green beaded hairpins peppered her close curls. The diamonds and emeralds glistened as they caressed the soft indentation of her neck, and the green of her eyes pierced his soul; Darcy was not sure, but he thought he let out a moan. Then she was by his side. Mr. Bennet took her hand and placed it in Darcy's, and he accepted the love she gave him this day.

Remembrances of the actual ceremony were not to be had; Darcy was too busy looking down at Elizabeth's face, noting again the thickness of her lashes, the blush of her cheeks, and the ghost of a grin playing about her lips. Flashbacks of the past year—the assembly, her singing at Lucas Lodge, Elizabeth's mud-covered petticoat, the Netherfield Ball, the walks at Rosings, her initial refusal, the lawn at Pemberley, her acceptance—danced through his head. When asked, Darcy's resonant "I will" brought titters from some of the younger town girls and a loud sigh of disgust from Miss Bingley, but other than that, nothing remarkable happened. Both couples retired to Longbourn following the proceedings for the traditional wedding breakfast. Mrs. Bennet was the "perfect" hostess for a "perfect" reception; at least in her opinion, everything was "perfect." She managed to marry off her eldest daughters to two of the area's most eligible bachelors. "Oh, Mr. Bennet, we are so blessed—three daughters married."

Mr. Bennet looked less enthusiastic than did his wife. Although Jane would be close by at Netherfield, his Lizzy would be far away in Derbyshire. Mr. Bennet learned to respect Mr. Darcy over the past few weeks, but that would not lessen his feelings of loss. Kissing his daughter's forehead, Mr. Bennet's eyes welled up. "Lizzy, this house will be so lonely without your laughter; I will miss you child."

"Papa, no one will replace you in my heart. I will always be your Lizzy." She kissed him on the cheek.

"Mr. Darcy," Mr. Bennet cleared his throat as he turned to his new son, "Elizabeth is very special; I expect you to respect her worth and to protect her from any harm."

"I will, Mr. Bennet. Trust me; I will." Darcy spoke softly as the charge from Mr. Bennet was solemn; the man was losing his favorite child, and Darcy understood his sentiment.

Never comfortable in large gatherings, Darcy accepted the congratulations of each guest with as much civility as anyone recalled seeing him do. Being always no more than an arm's length from Elizabeth throughout the gathering helped him persevere. His arm often slipped around her waist to keep her close to him; she rewarded Darcy with smiles, which reflected her happiness. A squeeze of his hand reminded him in a few more minutes they would be alone on the road to London. Each time she did so increased the intensity of Darcy's gaze directed exclusively toward Elizabeth.

They were standing close together whispering endearments when the Bingley sisters approached to offer their respects. "Miss Eliza," Caroline Bingley began, "you look lovely today."

"Thank you, Miss Bingley. Being so deeply in love makes it easy for one to appear *lovely.*" Elizabeth smirked.

"Congratulations go to you, Mr. Darcy." Caroline did not mean what she said, and disappointment laced her voice.

"Thank you, Miss Bingley, for your congratulations; I must agree with you; Mrs. Darcy is beautiful. Of course, I always thought she had *fine eyes.* They pierced my soul." He enjoyed being part of his wife's cut.

"Yes, I recall your saying as such on several occasions." Caroline bit the words.

"Did you really, Fitzwilliam?" Elizabeth turned to her new husband and feigned innocence.

Darcy looked down at her lush lips and nearly drank of their sweetness in front of everyone. Caroline and Louisa stepped back slightly as if they invaded their privacy. "I believe, Mrs. Darcy, I saw no face but yours since the assembly at Meryton." He pulled her closer.

"Miss Eliza," Caroline fought for Darcy's attention even if it meant speaking to his wife, "is your necklace a family heirloom?"

"It is, Miss Bingley," Elizabeth enjoyed baiting the woman, and Darcy knew Caroline did not stand a chance.

Caroline was taken aback. "Really!"

Elizabeth laughed lightly. "Oh, Miss Bingley," Elizabeth's voice was all sugary and sweet, "you thought I meant the Bennet family. The necklace is not a Bennet heirloom; Fitzwilliam gave it to me for I am a Darcy now."

"Actually, it is a gift from my mother for my wife," Darcy added quickly. "The diamonds and emeralds are almost as superb as is Elizabeth. Do you not agree, Miss Bingley?"

Caroline could barely disguise her disgust. With nothing more than a nod of her head and a curtsy, she made her exit.

"Fitzwilliam Darcy," Elizabeth teased, "you are almost as *evil* as is my father. You enjoyed Miss Bingley's humiliation."

"And you did not, Mrs. Darcy?"

"I am afraid I am my father's daughter—I truly enjoyed seeing Caroline in misery. You married a shallow woman, Mr. Darcy. You still have time to ask for an annulment if I offend you." Elizabeth leaned in closer for a quick kiss.

"Do you expect me to consider an annulment when you tease me with your nearness?" Darcy was lost to her alone.

"Then you must suffer forever, Sir. It is my intention of always teasing you with my closeness." Elizabeth brushed his lips with hers.

"May we leave soon, Elizabeth?" Darcy's voice was shaky with anticipation.

"I do believe we should say our farewells, Fitzwilliam." Her voice betrayed her feelings for him. "We have a long drive to London. Come, Love, let us circulate about the room before we leave." Taking his hand, Elizabeth led Darcy from one cluster to another to bid her neighbors and friends adieu.

At last, they came to Jane and Mr. Bingley. The sisters hugged for a long time, and both fought back tears. "I will miss my nightly talks with you, Jane," Elizabeth whispered.

"We may write often, Lizzy—long letters of our lives."

"Our husbands may find our postage expenses extreme," Elizabeth tried to laugh and to lighten the moment.

"Bingley," Darcy interjected, "I would like to have a small party at Pemberley at New Year's. Would you and Mrs. Bingley be our guests?"

"Oh, yes," Elizabeth added quickly. "The Festive Season will be coming to an end, but Pemberley will still be fully decorated. Please, Jane, I want you to see Pemberley."

"It would be nice to be away from the full house we should have at Netherfield," Bingley added cautiously while looking directly at his sisters and Mr. Hurst.

"Your coming to Pemberley will be a good excuse for everyone's departure," Darcy agreed.

"Then we will see each other at New Year's," Elizabeth chimed in. "Thank you, Fitzwilliam. Thank you, Mr. Bingley. You made Jane and I happy brides today." They exchanged pleasantries, and the couples parted to begin their new lives.

Elizabeth made her final goodbye to her family as the trunks were loaded onto Darcy's coach; Darcy moved away to find his sister. "Dearest One," he took her in his arms, "I will miss you."

Georgiana smiled at him. "You should not be thinking about your sister, Fitzwilliam. Think about Elizabeth; love her, and be happy." Her hug expressed her hopes for his future. Elizabeth came over to join them; Georgiana turned her attention to her new sister. "Elizabeth, your being part of our family makes both my brother and I richer in what matters."

Elizabeth hugged the girl she accepted from their first meeting. "We will soon join you at Pemberley."

Colonel Fitzwilliam offered his "best wishes," and then Darcy and Elizabeth boarded his coach to leave for London. Elizabeth watched out the coach's window until none of Longbourn or Meryton could be seen. Darcy took her hand and kissed the palm, no words needed between them.

CHAPTER 20

"We neither of us perform to strangers."

━━━━◦◦◦━━━━

They spent twenty minutes in complete silence; Elizabeth already missed the security of her family; Darcy searched for a way to allay her fears. Eventually, she did the characteristic shift of her shoulders, the one that told Darcy she was ready to meet the challenge of being his wife and the mistress of Pemberley. She turned to him and met his eyes. "Fitzwilliam, how large is Pemberley?"

The question stunned him, not expecting her to evaluate his land. He moved beside her on the coach's bench. "Do you want an estimate or do you require the surveyor's specifics?"

She waved her hand to let him know she had not worded the question well, and he should ignore the wording. "What I would like is to learn to ride a horse well. Could I have my own horse? I want to ride out with you; I do not want to be without you; may I have my own horse, Fitzwilliam?"

More vulnerable than he ever saw her, Darcy knew the horse symbolized her fear of being Pemberley's mistress, but he did not say so. "It would give me pleasure to choose a horse for you. We have many already in the stables at Pemberley, but we may choose another if you find nothing you like. We will buy you appropriate riding clothes while in London. Do you know anything about how to ride?"

"I have ridden Papa's horse, but not well, not like I want to ride. I want to be free to see all of Pemberley."

"We will find you the right horse, Elizabeth." He tapped her chin with his index finger, and she weakly smiled up at him.

"Elizabeth, we will be fine. You are one of the strongest people I know." The tears started to flow, and he knew not what to do. "Elizabeth, please, I cannot bear to see you sad."

After several loud sobs, she said, "I am not sad, Fitzwilliam; I am the happiest I have ever been in my life."

"Then why are you crying?"

She snuggled into his chest. "I do not know why I am crying; you married a foolish woman."

"Elizabeth, foolish or not, I love you with every ounce of my being."

She looked up at the man she chose as her husband, "I love you, Fitzwilliam. I really love you." His mouth smothered hers with a kiss long, hard, and passionate. The kiss threw a shadow over any preconceived ideas of love; they melted into each other; an astonishing amount of everything they ever knew disappeared in the new knowledge of each other.

Reluctantly, he stopped the kiss, but he did not release her from his embrace. "Elizabeth," he could barely breathe, "I do not wish our first time to be in this coach, but I swear if you kiss me as such again, I will not guarantee my ability to resist you."

"You can not resist my arts and allurements," she traced his chin line with her fingers; then she giggled. "Lady Catherine warned you of my ability to trap you, Mr. Darcy, but you would not listen to her advice." Elizabeth nibbled on his lips.

Darcy joined her tease; it was a way to still enjoy her closeness without abandoning social norms. "Although she is quite obstinate, my aunt is a wise woman." Darcy pulled her closer and kissed the side of her neck, rubbing his lips against her skin.

His action had the desired effect. "Maybe we should . . . talk for a while," she said, feeling a bit out of control herself. She sat up and looked lovingly in his eyes.

Darcy breathed deeply and resettled himself in the carriage, but he never let go of her hand. His fingertips massaged the lifeline leading along the palm of her hand.

"There is something I did want to discuss with you, Elizabeth."

She caught a glimmer of seriousness in his tone and turned to receive his address. "I planned to discuss this later, but it will give you time to ask questions. Your father agreed to a jointure, a way Pemberley will remain with you if something should happen to me."

"Fitzwilliam, please do not talk as such!"

"It is a fact, my Love; if nothing else, I am a practical man. I want to teach you all the aspects of the running of Pemberley. Many will not understand my doing so; it is not characteristic for a woman to assume such responsibilities. Besides you and Georgiana, there is nothing I love more than Pemberley. It must survive; if Pemberley lives, so does my family's name. You must promise me you will help me save Pemberley."

"Fitzwilliam, are we in a position where we could lose the estate?"

"No, not financially, but the times change. Men leave the land for the city every day. I need someone who shares my dream for Pemberley. That is one of the reasons I never chose to marry before now. I needed a mate whom I could trust with my family's legacy."

"I will do what you want, Fitzwilliam. People will simply have another reason to offer up censure on our behalf, but that will not change what we do for our family. You teach me, and I will share the knowledge with our children; Pemberley and you are my home now."

He cupped her face in his hands. "I trust you with my heart, my soul, and my name." His kiss this time held flashes of trepidation as well as hope. When she opened her eyes, he still cupped her face, and his forehead rested against hers. She reached up and took both of his hands in hers. "You have my heart," she kissed his fingertips, "my soul," she pulled his hands around her waist and moved in closer, "and I bear your name." Elizabeth returned his last kiss with one full of her strength and her determination. Afterwards, she rested her head on his shoulder while he stroked the side of her face. They rode for nearly an hour in quiet contemplation of what their life together would bring.

The coach pulled up in front of his Kensington Place home. He alighted and then dismissed the footman with a wave of his hand. No one would assist his wife but himself. Elizabeth took his arm and looked up lovingly into his eyes. "Are you ready?" he whispered, and Elizabeth nodded her head in affirmation. They entered the house knowing their lives would never be the same after this evening.

The butler met them at the door. "Good evening, Mr. Darcy; it is good to see you safely at home, Sir."

Handing the man his greatcoat, hat, and walking stick, Darcy turned to his servant. "Thank you, Mr. Thacker. It is good to be back at Kensington Place. Mr. Thacker, may I present my wife Elizabeth."

"Mrs. Darcy, the staff extends its congratulations. Yours and Mr. Darcy's happiness brings joy to us all. We wait on your desires."

"Thank you, Mr. Thacker." Elizabeth blushed with the realization the staff knew this was her wedding night.

"Your rooms are ready, Sir. I will have the trunks brought up."

"Thank you, Mr. Thacker. We will have dinner in about an hour. I wish to show Mrs. Darcy around the house first."

"Yes, Sir." Mr. Thacker bowed and made his exit.

"Let me show you some of the downstairs rooms, Elizabeth, then we will freshen our clothes before dinner."

Going down the hall, Elizabeth noted Darcy spoke to each of his servants, calling him by name. "Fitzwilliam, do you know all their names?" she whispered.

"Of course, most of the staff served my parents or are relatives of the staff members. They served the Darcys for many years; no one here served us less than five years." Elizabeth never thought about how Darcy would treat his staff. She approved of his attitude; she would make an effort to learn the staff's names too.

Darcy showed her several of the rooms; she found them to be more ornate than those she saw at Pemberley, but they each reflected his tastes for fine art, tapestries, and furnishings. In each room, Darcy brought her to the center and then stepped back to watch her reaction. Elizabeth acted like a small child moving away from a parent to try something new and then running back to the security of the parent's arms. She would often lightly touch the statues and figurines or rub her fingertips across the tables; then she would giggle to herself and move quickly back into his embrace.

"Fitzwilliam, it is magnificent; I never imagined . . . I should have after being at Pemberley, but I did not expect such a home." Her eyes sparkled with merriment.

"Then you approve of your London home, Mrs. Darcy?" he teased her innocence.

"Am I your source of entertainment, Mr. Darcy?" She stuck her lip out in a pretend pout.

Darcy lifted her chin and nibbled on the protruding lip. "Mrs. Darcy, you claim to love to laugh."

"At other people's expense, Sir," she pretended offense, "not at my own."

Darcy laughed. "Let us see some of the upstairs and then change for dinner." He coaxed her toward the door.

She took his arm to ascend the staircase. "I have arranged for Margaret to attend you while we are here, but you may choose your own attendant once we return to Pemberley. I took the liberty of ordering additional items to be placed in your dressing room; I hope they meet your approval. We may have fittings for new clothes while in London if you like, Elizabeth."

"Fitzwilliam, you do not need to buy me new things; I did not marry you for your money." Elizabeth put her arms around his waist. "In fact, your money has not been of what I have been thinking today." She tilted her chin up and looked in his eyes.

Darcy's passion rose quickly whenever she was near him. "If not for my money, then why did you marry me, Elizabeth?"

"For your great wit, Mr. Darcy. I would not tolerate children of lesser intelligence." Elizabeth turned from him to enter the dressing room door. "I will see you in a few minutes, Mr. Darcy."

"I love you, Elizabeth," he whispered.

"I love you, Fitzwilliam." Then she was gone.

Darcy entered his own dressing room with images of Elizabeth playing with his senses.

The meal was delicious, but neither of them showed any interest in the food. They both picked at the offerings, and their eyes never strayed from each other. Eventually, without saying anything, he took her hand and led her to her dressing room again. Darcy lifted her chin and kissed her lips tenderly; then they parted.

Using the lavender oil she preferred for years, Elizabeth bathed slowly, tentative about what the next few hours would bring. Margaret helped her slip on her new nightgown and to brush out her hair. Earlier, when she freshened her clothing for dinner, she bubbled in conversation with the maid about the trip from Hertfordshire to London, but now she was silent, lost in thoughts of Darcy.

Like his wife, Darcy was more pensive than usual, but his calmness possessed an intensity he knew not before. Finishing his ablutions quickly, he entered Elizabeth's bedroom to wait for her. He lit several candles and took a seat facing the door to her dressing room; yet, the door opened before he could settle his nerves completely, and Elizabeth was framed in the backlight of her dressing room. He remembered her being framed in the doorway at Netherfield with boots and her petticoat covered in mud. He actually thought her lovely then; now she was beautiful. With the light behind her, Darcy could see her lilt body through the gown. They looked at each other entranced by the moment until she stepped slowly into the room, and the door closed behind her. Darcy could not stand to not be near her; he rose and crossed to where she stood.

His touch of her skin sent a shiver through Elizabeth's body; he cupped her chin as he lifted it to kiss her lips—the kiss warm and tender. She moved in closer encircling her arms around his waist, realizing she never saw him without his jacket, waistcoat, and boots, and then she instinctively slid her hands up under Darcy's shirt and up the muscles of his back. He trembled as he kissed her again while slowly pulling her closer to him and letting his hands rest on her hips. Their breathing became shallow as the kisses became more intense.

Darcy scooped her into his arms and carried her to the bed,

laying her gently back against the pillows. She shifted nervously as his gaze grew in its eagerness. Darcy lowered himself beside her and kissed her repeatedly, his hands searching her body beneath her gown as his lips moved down her neck. Elizabeth reached out and pulled him to her; she was his at last.

Languishing in each other's arms, Elizabeth snuggled into the curve of his shoulder and rested her arm across his chest. Darcy stroked her forearm with his hand and kissed the top of her head. "Elizabeth," he began, but she reached up and placed her fingertips on his lips to stop his words.

"May I not be *Lizzy* again?" she teased.

Darcy laughed and pulled her closer to him. "Your name is Elizabeth Darcy, is it not?" He kissed her forehead as he hugged her tightly to him.

"I am Elizabeth Darcy, but your calling me *Lizzy* was very tantalizing." She kissed him enticingly and stretched her leg across his body. "May I not convince you to call me *Lizzy* again?" Her hand slid across his chest and down his abdomen to his thigh.

"Lizzy," he moaned in response to her touch; then he kissed her more impassioned than before.

This time they slept following their love, satisfied to be in each other's arms. When Elizabeth awoke, she turned to find Darcy propped up on one arm and looking down at her. Realizing her gown had long since been discarded, she blushed and reached for the sheet. Darcy caught her hand and held it in place. "In this bed, you have nothing of which to be ashamed."

"I am surprised to find you in my bed, Sir," Elizabeth teased to cover the uneasy feeling his gaze created in her. "I thought society's refined husbands returned to their own quarters after . . ."

"Some husbands feel the need for privacy." His voice was soft and gentle, and he began to trace circles across her abdomen. "But I never want to leave your side, Elizabeth. Where you sleep, I sleep; this is *our* bed." Her arms circled his neck, and she began to kiss along his chin line. "Shall I call you *Lizzy* again?" he teased.

"I hope to never be *Elizabeth* ever again." She nibbled on his earlobe as he once again encircled her with his arms.

"I love you, Lizzy," were the last words he got out before she covered his mouth with hers.

Daylight streamed through the windows when she woke him by rubbing her palm over the stubble of his beard. "Mr. Darcy, you are more handsome when you are not so properly dressed." Her laughter started as a gurgle in the back of her throat. "Do you have any idea of the time?"

"Do you have a pressing engagement elsewhere?" He pulled her closer to kiss her tenderly.

"I was just considering my need for nourishment. If I am to spend the rest of my life in bed with you, Sir, I will need the occasional meal to maintain my strength."

"So, you never want to leave our bed either?" A look of contentment overspread his face.

"Fitzwilliam, I want to be wherever you are, but this bed has a special appeal," she taunted.

He moved casually from the bed to retrieve her gown. "I will have someone bring us something to eat and have the room freshened. Maybe you would like to find a robe to add to your wardrobe," he handed her the gown. "I will get rid of this stubble." He rubbed his chin across the back of her hand.

Unable to contain her smile, Elizabeth slipped on her gown and disappeared into her dressing room before he put on his trousers and pulled the bell cord for the servants.

Elizabeth, not used to having people wait on her every whim, looked surprised to see Margaret enter her dressing room, but then she realized Darcy summoned her.

"Mrs. Darcy, I am having bathwater brought up; I assume you would like a bath."

Elizabeth knew her appearance must be an open book of her

night with Darcy; she blushed at the thought, but she managed to say, "Thank you, Margaret, that would be nice." She even offered the woman a hint of a smile.

Two younger maids entered with vases of yellow roses and put them on Elizabeth's dressing table. "What are these, Margaret?"

"Mr. Darcy had them brought from Pemberley for you, Mrs. Darcy. He had them cut as buds, wrapped in newsprint, and kept damp until they got here so they would not go bad. They were supposed to be here yesterday, but the driver had trouble on the road. Mr. Darcy wanted them for your bedroom last night, Madam; I hope he is not upset."

"It is fine, Margaret. I am sure Mr. Darcy did not notice."

"You are right, Madam. With a wife as beautiful as you are, a man should not be looking at flowers. I beg your pardon, Mrs. Darcy, sometimes my mouth runs away from my good sense." Elizabeth let the woman know she offered no offense, and then she blushed with a remembrance of Darcy's passion last night.

Margaret moved a screen to block Elizabeth from the view of the servants carrying in the bathwater. Once they left, Elizabeth leisurely lay back in the warm water and let it seep around her body. Images of her husband played in her mind; she could not believe how easily she and Darcy became comfortable with each other; she knew she should not have looked on him or touched him as she did last night, but Darcy accepted her interest in his body—his pleasure as natural; it was liberating. Her mother would have been horrified; Mrs. Bennet, Charlotte, and Lydia painted pictures of what happened between a man and woman in the bedroom. Everything she ever gleaned about her "wifely duty" did not occur in her bedchamber last night. Darcy created a place where her desires often took precedence over his; images of the firmness of his shoulders and back and his arousal danced behind her closed eyes. When she finally got out of the tub, Margaret brought her a fresh gown, this one of white satin. "Another gift from Mr. Darcy, Madam."

Elizabeth sat down at the dressing table; as she did at Pemberley she reached out gently to touch the petals of the roses. Margaret picked up the hairbrush to tend to Elizabeth's hair when Darcy came up behind her. "I will do it, Margaret."

"Yes, Mr. Darcy." She curtsied and left.

Elizabeth held one of the roses in her hand and took in its fragrance. She said nothing to him as he took the brush and gently swept her hair back from her neck. She watched his reflection as he caressed her neck, kissing the nape; she turned to face him, tears forming in her eyes. "Elizabeth, is there something wrong?"

"It grieves me I did not see the man you were before now," she whispered.

"I am a different man because I met you, Elizabeth."

"These flowers are from your mother's plant, are they not?"

"The yellow represents the constancy of my love for you; each day the yellow sun rises in the sky is a day I will love you, Elizabeth." He wiped away the tears streaming down her cheeks. "Are all women so emotional?" he teased. "You cry when you are happy and when you are sad."

She gave him a hint of a smile before her arms encircled his neck tightly. "It is part of my arts and allurements," she whispered in his ear.

"Let us go and eat what we have in *our* room so we can return to *our* bed," he said softly into her hair for she still clung to him tightly. He picked her up and carried her back to the bedroom.

Darcy set her down in one of the chairs; she still clutched the rose in her hand; then he sat down across from her. She was so solemn it perplexed him as to what to do next. He took some of the fresh fruit on a fork and offered it to her. Elizabeth took it in her mouth and chewed it thoughtfully. Once she swallowed, she turned to Darcy and said, "Fitzwilliam, I never want you to be sorry you married me. You gave me so much already; I have nothing to give you in return."

"Elizabeth, give me your respect, help me maintain Pemberley, and love me as you did last night. No man could want for more."

Although she still felt a bit inadequate to deserve such a man as

Fitzwilliam Darcy, Elizabeth nodded her head, but she did not answer. Instead, she picked up the fork, took a piece of fruit on it, and placed it in Darcy's mouth. *It would all be good,* she thought. *I will prove myself worthy of his love.*

Later, when they returned to the bed, Darcy laid back with the pillows propped behind him and Elizabeth's head on his chest. "Poor Jane," Elizabeth sighed.

"You are in our bed and thinking about your sister. I lost my appeal to you, I see."

"On the contrary, Sir. I was just thinking Jane and Mr. Bingley are trying to be husband and wife in a house full of guests and my family three miles down the road. Jane deserves this kind of happiness; she and Mr. Bingley should be somewhere alone as we are." She turned over and moved where she could reach his mouth. "Now, I am in need of a different kind of sustenance; one of your kisses would greatly restore my energies." Darcy took her in his arms, letting the lavender overtake him.

For six days they sought no one else's company but each other's. Although they no longer took their meals in the bedroom, they spent the majority of their time there. Other times, they read together in the library taking turns reading to one another or just sitting close together as they read. "What are you doing, Elizabeth?" Darcy asked as she placed a book back onto the shelf in the library.

"I wanted to save the roses you gave me." She seemed a bit embarrassed. "I put two of them in this book of poetry so they would be here each time we returned to Kensington Place. The others I dried to make a sachet." She crossed the room to where he sat and leaned down to kiss his lips. "Constancy in love must be preserved," she teased as he pulled her onto his lap and kissed her again.

On other days, Elizabeth played the pianoforte, and Darcy turned the music for her; she even rewarded him by singing for him one evening. He thought to try to teach her billiards, but whenever he encircled her body with his arms to show her how to hold the stick correctly, she always turned to kiss him, and the game was lost to their passion. They were never more than a few feet apart. Darcy often came to her dressing room to just be with her while she bathed or to brush her hair. For a love, which took so long to find, they wasted no time in building a bond no one could destroy.

After a week, they decided a walk through the park would do them well as both were of a nature to spend time out of doors no matter what the weather. With Elizabeth on his arm, Darcy felt he saw London for its beauty for the first time. They walked along busy streets, but they saw no one. Reaching Hyde Park, they chose one of the lesser-traveled paths, enjoying the company of no one else. When they emerged from the secluded path to the main one leading through the park, Darcy stopped short hearing someone call his name. "Darcy, is that you my boy?"

"Your Lordship!" Surprise reflected in his voice while Darcy made his bow.

"It is you, Darcy. It is good to see you."

"If I knew you were in London, Sir, I would have left my card."

"Nonsense, do not fret so, my boy. Is this your new bride?" The man looked closely at Elizabeth.

"My apologies, Sir. Lord and Lady Pennington, may I present my wife Elizabeth?" Elizabeth made her curtsy to Darcy's companions. "Elizabeth, Lady Pennington is my mother's cousin."

"I am honored to meet you both," Elizabeth dropped her eyes.

Lady Pennington reached out and touched the side of Elizabeth's face. "Fitzwilliam, she does not appear to be a witch with magical powers," her ladyship smirked.

"I see you heard from Lady Catherine," Darcy added as he pulled Elizabeth closer.

"Do not go on so, Fitzwilliam; no one pays Lady Catherine much attention in such matters. Her strict nature makes her opinions less than appealing," Lady Pennington assured him. "We received news of Anne's and Edward's engagement two days ago. Lady Catherine *was kind enough* to add her note to the announcement."

"I am glad to hear Edward won Anne's heart; I hope they will be happy." Darcy's affection for his cousins genuinely showed.

"Mrs. Darcy," Lady Pennington turned to Elizabeth, "would you two care to join us for some tea?"

Elizabeth looked up to Darcy before she answered, "We would be pleased to join you, Lady Pennington."

They found a confectionery shop, which also served tea, and took a table. The conversation happened naturally although Elizabeth consciously controlled her tendency to be too mirthful. Darcy and Lord Pennington discussed the current political scene while Lady Pennington pumped Elizabeth for details of the wedding. "A double wedding with your elder sister—how delightful! Is Mr. Bingley that amiable young man you brought with you to the earl's birthday celebration, Fitzwilliam?"

"He is, your Ladyship."

"Is that not romantic? Sisters married best friends."

Darcy and Elizabeth smiled at her words of approval. A sudden thought hit Lady Pennington. "Fitzwilliam, please tell me you gave Mrs. Darcy your mother's necklace for her wedding. That was one of the last things she said to me before she passed."

"I did, your Ladyship."

"Good . . . . It was important to her; it was her request for your wife to have it. She always said the green reminded her of Pemberley in the summer and the white, it in winter. Together the jewels were a history of Pemberley worn about her neck. Were they not beautiful, Mrs. Darcy?"

"The necklace was a splendid gift from my husband, but your story made it priceless. Thank you for sharing it with me, Lady Pennington."

"Of course, my dear." She reached out and patted Elizabeth's hand, then she stood to take her leave having finished her tea. "This place was adequate, but I cannot say I enjoyed it as much as Gunter's on the east side of Berkeley Square. You must have Fitzwilliam take you there in the spring, Mrs. Darcy—just drive up in an open carriage, and the waiters will bring out the finest teas, sorbets, and ices. I adore the burnt filbert cream ice." Then she turned to Darcy. "Fitzwilliam, you chose well; your mother would be happy with your choice. It will give me great pleasure to let the rest of the family know your wife is exactly what you need, and Lady Catherine is a bitter old woman. When you are ready to rejoin society, you will come to stay with his lordship and me. You will bring Georgiana too; it has been too long since we saw her."

"We will do so as soon as possible, your Ladyship." Having made his promise, he bowed; taking Elizabeth's hand in his, he repeated his thanks; he knew any censure from his family for marrying Elizabeth was solved. Lady Pennington's opinion in the family easily outweighed anything Lady Catherine could offer.

Although it was the middle of the afternoon, Darcy and Elizabeth lounged lazily across the counterpane on the bed. Exhausted, Darcy lay back with his arm across his eyes; Elizabeth lightly kissed the upper part of his arm not because she wanted him again, but her new husband still fascinated her, and she needed to touch him when he was near.

They spent several hours the last couple of days going over the books of expenses for Pemberley and their other holdings. Once she agreed with Darcy to learn about how to run the estate, she took to the information with a desire to please him. How quickly she grasped the basic information surprised Darcy. There was still much for her to learn, but his plan brought satisfaction. Elizabeth's security and the future for their heirs depended on her understanding about their various holdings. Most gentlemen would never consider sharing such information with their wives; it was not in their domain, but Darcy knew having Elizabeth as his partner, and not his dependent, would offer his family security in these uncertain times. Her strength of character would be an asset for their future success. Lost in his thoughts, he did not expect her to slide her arm across his chest and bring his attention to the present moment rather than future plans. He reached out and encircled her in his arms, turning on his side to enclose her in his embrace. "Fitzwilliam," she giggled lightly, "would you buy me a gun? I would like to learn to shoot."

This was clearly not the conversation he expected in the middle of a tender moment. "Dare I ask what brought on this request? Does my embrace drive you to violence?"

Elizabeth started to laugh, and she began to kiss his chest and move up his neck. "You, Sir, create a strong emotional response in me, but I would not call it violence."

He could barely remember her request by the time her kisses reached and consumed his mouth. "Then why do you need a gun?" He finally got the words out.

Elizabeth continued to kiss his face, but she managed to answer, "I told Lydia I would shoot Mr. Wickham if he ever showed his face at Pemberley. I would like to keep my word."

Darcy took both hands and pulled her head back where he could see her expression to see if she teased him. "You are serious, Elizabeth? What brought this on?"

"You know me, Love. My mind jumps about uncontrolled. Mr. Wickham's expenses were in the ledger today; it reminded me of my confrontation with Lydia."

"What confrontation?"

"It was after Mr. Wickham's congratulatory letter. I warned Lydia I would not tolerate her being a part of any plan Mr. Wickham may have. I told her if he ever tried to come to Pemberley, I would see him shot as a trespasser."

Darcy could not control his laughter. "Elizabeth, you are amazing! I can think of no other woman who would speak as such. Although I would not wish you to experience death, a woman should be able to defend herself," he reasoned. "I know the perfect gun for a woman such as you are. I married a woman who would shock the world if they knew."

She began to kiss his face again. "You are right, Mr. Darcy, you married a shameless woman. I desire your constant attention; I desire a secure future for our children; I will let no one hurt you. I am afraid you chose poorly; I possess too much gall and not enough sugar. Are you sorry for your lack of foresight?"

He kissed her deeply before answering. "Lizzy, I need no one in my life but you. In hindsight, I am blessed to have such an amazing woman in love with me. My only regret is I denied my love for you to myself and others so long."

"You are forgiven, Mr. Darcy." She kissed him lightly. "However, forgiveness has its price."

"What payment shall you demand as penance, Lizzy?"

She ran her hand up his body, sending shivers of pleasure through him. "I have but one true vice, Fitzwilliam—you." Their love was all-consuming; the world could choose to judge; but they were secure in each other, and such judgments were of little consequence.

CHAPTER 21

"Men of sense . . . do not want silly wives."

———❦———

They were in London a fortnight although they went out very little. A few evenings of concerts and the theatre, some shopping, walks in the park, and a satisfying evening with the Gardiners met their need for outside entertainment, but they decided the draw of Pemberley could be denied no longer. "Mr. Thacker, we will spend the Festive Season at Pemberley this year. I will send you word of our return to town."

"Yes, Mr. Darcy."

"Mr. Thacker, I want you to see Mrs. Rowling gets some rest. She has been ill for several days. Call a physician if necessary." Elizabeth walked past her husband as she placed several items in the hands of a waiting servant to load onto the coach.

"I understand, Mrs. Darcy."

"Do not let her tell you otherwise, Mr. Thacker. You tell her those are my orders if necessary."

"She is stubborn, Mrs. Darcy, but I will see to it."

In the few weeks they stayed at Kensington Place, Elizabeth established a rapport with the servants. She knew the majority of them by name already, and Darcy overheard more than one of them praise her for her graciousness. Her husband did not foresee the many facets of Elizabeth Darcy, but both he and his staff welcomed them. Darcy was pleased with himself for winning Elizabeth's love, and he marveled how life sprang into action whenever she walked into a room. He doubted he could ever *command* people's respect as she did.

"Are you ready, Elizabeth?"

"That is what you asked me, Fitzwilliam, when we came here for our first night together."

"Is your response the same as it was then, Mrs. Darcy?"

"It is, Sir." She took his extended arm. "I am most anxious to go home to Pemberley." The smile on his face reflected the pride in his heart at having Elizabeth as his wife.

They stopped for the evening at the same inn where he left the rest of the party the day he discovered Elizabeth at Pemberley. He delighted in the irony of the tale. "Just think," she teased, "if you had not done so, you could be sharing your room tonight, Mr. Darcy, with Caroline Bingley."

"Elizabeth, that is not funny!" However, he laughed because that was what they did: she teased, and Darcy laughed.

When they entered the inn, Mr. Harvey, the innkeeper, rushed to greet them properly. Darcy easily accepted such homage, increasing Elizabeth's amazement at the customary *reverence* as being normal. She was more inclined to wait her turn where Darcy was the type to move to the head of the line. "Mr. Harvey, this is my wife Elizabeth. We will require your best rooms tonight."

"Of course, Mr. Darcy, we are honored you chose our establishment once again. We heard from Miss Darcy on her return to Pemberley you took a wife. We extend our well wishes, Sir. Mrs. Harvey will show you to your rooms, and I will have your trunks brought up, Sir. Will you be joining us in the dining room, Mr. Darcy?"

Darcy looked about the room crowded with common travelers often found on the roads leading to and from London. No one of consequence was noted and inroads of his former disdain for others showed on his face and in the manner in which he said, "No, Mr. Harvey, we will take our meal in the room."

"Yes, Sir, I will have it delivered shortly."

With the requirements for all their needs outlined to the innkeeper, Darcy took Elizabeth's arm in his, and then they ascended the steps to the room. She watched him intently throughout this charade he played whenever they were in public. Two different men possessed his body. Although not as severe as her first impression of him, Darcy still possessed the same haughty reserve he used with her and others in Hertfordshire. Then there was the man who shared her bed, brought her flowers, and searched for her approval. Elizabeth supposed his breeding taught him to expect a certain amount of veneration from others. She found it both amusing and exhilarating how he could command a room simply by stepping through its doorway. She assumed she would never be able to duplicate such power over others. He may teach her the "workings" of Pemberley, but she doubted she could ever *command* people's respect as he did.

During the evening, Darcy became quieter and more resistant than she had seen him, and Elizabeth felt unsure as they neared Pemberley whether he ventured second thoughts about their relationship or whether he tired of her "silliness." He stared at his wife, but it was not the stare that displayed his passion for her. This look showed contempt and disorder. Conversation was minimal, and when they crawled into bed that evening, Elizabeth felt disappointment because for the first time he did not take her into his arms. She could tolerate his not talking to her over dinner, but she did not think she could live without his touching her. Distraught, she began to sob although she fought to hide her feelings.

It was sometime before she felt his hand taking hers. They lay on their backs staring up at the ceiling's darkness. Darcy held her hand, but that was all he offered her. "Elizabeth?" His voice came out distant and shallow.

"Yes, Fitzwilliam." Elizabeth waited for his rejection; she did not think he would deny her in public, but she would just be "Mrs. Darcy" from now on. The tears rolled down her cheeks, but she emitted no sounds; she would not let him know it hurt her.

It was a long time before he spoke again. "I do not . . . I do not want to lose what we had in London." She allowed herself a little gasp. "I was standing downstairs giving orders to Mr. Harvey, and I realized how little I changed after all. It frightened me I could so easily slip back to the way I was before there was Elizabeth Bennet." The tears flowed more freely, but the darkness shielded them from Darcy's view. "Elizabeth, please say something."

She swallowed hard before she answered. "Fitzwilliam, you cannot control your station in life; it is what you do with the position which will define you."

He rolled over to caress her face when he realized she cried. "Elizabeth, have I offended you?"

The tears flowed faster as the tenderness in his voice swept over her. "I thought you held second thoughts of taking me to Pemberley. I thought you sorry for your decision to make me your wife."

"Elizabeth, do you not know by now I could never deny my love for you? I think of nothing else; you control—consume me. Even when I acted as such downstairs, it was my perverted way of protecting you from others."

She began slowly, trying to find the words to bring him peace. "I too was amused at how you slipped in and out of both social modes," she stammered, "but, Fitzwilliam, you were never what you may seem to others; you could not change completely—no one can change all the experiences which define him—the man in whose arms I fall asleep each night is the man you always were; the other is your protection from the world—the same as I face the world with a saucy manner. I am impetuous, and at one time saw only faults in others; ironically, those faults I found within myself as well." During this, his face was buried in her hair, and she stroked the back of his head. "We are very much alike, my Love; we are neither purely one thing nor another; there are no pure breeds here; we are a *mixed breed* as will be our children." Darcy allowed himself a chuckle at this reference. "Fitzwilliam, please, we can be conventional and gracious at the same time. There was a time I renounced your social sense; now I value many of those same practices as part of the man you became. You do not have to decide to be one or the other; you may be the man your parents wanted you to be in all your glory and social standing and also be the man who graciously receives the love and respect of those who know him.

Your parents would want that man to be the master of Pemberley."

Elizabeth knew from the short bursts of his shoulders he too sobbed. Finally, he spoke softly. "It seems we see things in each other no one saw before. We are only perfectly understood by each other."

She laughed lightly. "I always said, there is a great similarity in the turn of our minds." Then she said more seriously, "Fitzwilliam, I wanted nothing but to be with you at Pemberley for months now, but I will not settle for the house. I want the man with whom I spent the last two weeks. I want the passion; I cannot live without your touch. Can you not be both? A person can only be known by the quality of his performance."

His kisses began at the back of her neck, as Darcy's hands moved slowly up her body; he encircled her with his and hearing her breath catch and feeling her body rise to meet his, he was spellbound by his love for her. "Lizzy, I love you more than life itself. I cannot be anything without your love."

"Then let me judge your performance, Mr. Darcy," she giggled.

"Your wish is my command, Mrs. Darcy." They melted into one.

It became evident to both of them on this trip they would occasionally face moments of self-doubt, but not questions of their devotion to each other. The morning brought them a few minutes of quiet reflection before they began to prepare for the final part of their journey. As usual, she lay across his chest. "Fitzwilliam, may we look about the village before we leave? A short walk would be pleasant if it is safe to do so."

"The woman refuses to shop in the finest establishments in London, but she wishes to stop her journey to her new home to see what the local merchants have to offer."

"You knew I was a small town country girl when you proposed, Mr. Darcy," she taunted him once again.

As they walked about the village, Elizabeth glowed with happiness. She conversed with the shopkeepers, eventually choosing a few small trinkets for Georgiana but also for Mrs. Annesley and Mrs. Reynolds. "They will be surprised by the gift," is all Darcy said.

As they prepared to leave, a brown and white pup came scampering across the wooden walkway and hid in the hem of Elizabeth's skirt. She stepped back gingerly and picked up the pup, caressing it while scratching behind its ears and making cooing sounds. She held it up to her husband. "Is it not adorable, Fitzwilliam?"

"It is a dog, Elizabeth. Most dogs are not adorable."

"Well, this one is." She held it in the air and made the cooing noise again. "Look, Love, it has those same sad Darcy-type eyes. I bet it could duplicate *the look.*"

"Elizabeth, you never cease to surprise me. Tell me, if I offer to purchase the dog from Mr. Harvey, I will not find it in our bed at night."

"Oh, Fitzwilliam, I never had a pet before; Mama would never allow it." She was so excited he could not hide his happiness at giving her something she wanted.

He cautioned, "This is a Springer spaniel, Elizabeth. It is an outside dog—a hunting dog—a gun dog; it is not a lap dog one sees in the finer homes in London."

"I understand, Fitzwilliam. Could we not train it to go out with me on my walks or when we ride?"

Darcy pulled her close and then tapped her chin with his index finger, and she gifted him with a quick kiss although they were on the streets of the village. "I will speak to Mr. Harvey before we leave." He rolled his eyes.

In the coach the dog slept at her feet or curled up on her lap the rest of the way to Pemberley. Darcy feigned annoyance, but she knew he enjoyed her enthusiasm. "I cannot wait for someone to ask what wedding gifts I gave you, Elizabeth. They will think I married a soldier when they hear you asked for a horse, a gun, and a hunting dog."

"I keep telling you I am a foolish woman, Sir." She put the pup down on the floor and crawled into his lap. "You do not think me to have no feminine qualities, do you, Fitzwilliam?" She giggled when she saw his face soften and felt his body hardened to her advances. With her arms wound tightly around his neck, she professed her love for him by starting her kisses in the soft indentation of his shoulder and working her way up.

"I admire all your feminine qualities, Mrs. Darcy." He pulled her closer to him and enjoyed the heat of her kiss.

Arriving at Pemberley, Elizabeth alighted from the carriage to be greeted by the staff lined up along the drive and entryway. On his arm as usual, Darcy cupped his free hand over hers and held it tightly in place, fearing her taking flight at seeing the enormity of the change in her life as his wife. He took his time and allowed each of the staff members the courtesy of acknowledging his new mistress. Darcy introduced Elizabeth to key staff members, and she made an effort to learn as many names as possible in such a short period of time. To see her comment on the flowers offered by several of the children and her reaching out to touch the hand of many of those in attendance pleased him. She knew not what impression she gave to those anxious to know something of the woman he chose for his wife, but Darcy missed not one reaction. Elizabeth's approachable manner and genuine smile made her an instant favorite. He knew many staff members feared someone such as the infamous Miss Bingley, a woman whom all found intolerable at best; Mr. Darcy's good sense at marrying a woman who was both handsome and in possession of pleasant airs impressed them.

At the top of the steps stood Georgiana, Mrs. Reynolds, Mr. Howard, and Mrs. Annesley. Georgiana's excitement caused her to fidget in place waiting her turn to greet her brother and Elizabeth. Darcy reached out and took her hand to pull Georgiana to his side while introducing Elizabeth first to Mr. Howard and then to Mrs. Reynolds. Darcy stood in awe of Elizabeth's command of the situation. Although not accustomed to such formal settings, Mr. Howard took the hand Elizabeth extended and made his sincere congratulations. Mrs. Reynolds, who held the Darcys in warm regard, was beside herself with joy with Elizabeth's arrival as Pemberley's new mistress. "I am pleased to welcome you to Pemberley, Mrs. Darcy."

"Thank you, Mrs. Reynolds. I will be depending on your help and guidance. Mr. Darcy's trust in your ability to run Pemberley will be invaluable to me as its new mistress." Such accolades won Mrs. Reynolds early. Then unexpectedly, Elizabeth gave Mrs. Reynolds a quick embrace. Although Darcy realized Elizabeth's motivation came more from the memory of the woman's part in bringing her and Darcy together, the unabashed enthusiasm displayed increased Elizabeth's regard in the opinions of those on staff who saw it, and Darcy found nothing to which to object.

Elizabeth dropped her eyes quickly when she looked up at Darcy; she realized too late her hugging Mrs. Reynolds was a break in decorum before she even entered the house, but Darcy slipped his arm around her waist to pull her closer and to assure her he was not upset with her impetuous act. They both greeted Mrs. Annesley, and the two elderly women reentered the estate together. That just left Georgiana; Darcy and Elizabeth turned together toward the girl who bubbled with excitement. The three embraced each other repeatedly and talked over one another in greeting. Happy as he had ever been, Darcy entered the main hallway with Elizabeth on one arm and Georgiana on the other.

A rather formal act, she took his arm for their first ascent of the staircase, symbolizing their marriage coming together at last. They left Georgiana in the second floor drawing room, and he escorted Elizabeth to their chambers. Beforehand, he gave orders to bring the pup to Mrs. Darcy's dressing area. At the top of the staircase he said, "For many nights last fall at Netherfield, Elizabeth, I fell asleep imagining you standing on this very staircase. Now my dreams are complete; you are no longer here standing and waiting for me; you are now at the top of the staircase and entering our chambers as my wife. Life is good." He bent to kiss her gently on the lips. "It is pleasant to be no longer waiting for you." His smile of contentment encased her.

"It has always been just you, Fitzwilliam. It is just you I love."

When the weather permitted, Darcy and Elizabeth rode out across their land each morning. He chose a horse of a gentle nature but deceptively fast for Elizabeth, and how quickly she learned to ride pleased him. A natural and not easily intimidated, Elizabeth's spirit played out as they raced across valleys and over rises. They could be seen spurring their mounts—laughing and chasing each other at a whim. Those of finer societies would object to their exuberance, but they did not care; they were together. Darcy introduced her to his tenants, making a point of her knowing about each family. His ability to call all his tenants by name and to listen to their concerns impressed her and gave her a great sense of pride. Along with Mr. Howard, they examined the fields and the smaller structures on the estate. Mr. Howard was uncomfortable with the idea at first, but he soon found Mrs. Darcy's ability to adapt to each situation in which she found herself fascinating. Darcy protected his wife, but he also shared all aspects of his life at Pemberley with her. Mr. Howard knew of no relationship like the one he viewed at the great house. Mrs. Darcy was privy to plans for expansion, renewal, repair, and refurbishing of the estate; Darcy was adamant about her need to be a part of every decision affecting his holdings.

Watching Elizabeth spend time each day with Georgiana satisfied him. The two played music and went for walks. They spent time with their needlework and helping the new vicar administer to the poor. In Darcy's view, even though Elizabeth had been at Pemberley only a fortnight, an outside observer would have thought her to be born there.

One afternoon, she and Darcy walked the path upon which they met that eventful day in August. The pup trailed after her when it did not chase the game birds by the stream. They walked hand-in-hand reliving the feelings of their finding each other again. "I was embarrassed you found me here. I thought you would believe me to be trying to curry favor with you once again." Elizabeth paused to look at him.

"Elizabeth, all I thought was God gave me a second chance. I decided if God gave me such an opportunity, I would declare my devotion to you and hope you would receive my intentions!"

"Now, we have been married a month; God moves in mysterious ways, my Love." Elizabeth put her arms around his neck. "Even when hope of our finding love was against us, I still hoped." Going up on her tiptoes, she kissed him, engulfed in his nearness. Darcy nipped at her ear as his arms wrapped around her waist. His gaze settled on her lips, and Elizabeth leaned in where only their breath separated them. "You have married a shameless woman, Mr. Darcy. I choose to kiss you in front of God and anyone who may be watching."

"Mrs. Darcy, I do not seem to be withdrawing from your advances." Frozen with desire, he did not move.

"This is true, Mr. Darcy." The blush of her face told of her need to have him. "Where does that leave us?"

"I believe our walk has come to an end," he said, not letting her go. "Some quiet reflection in our chambers could answer your question, Elizabeth."

"I believe you are correct, Mr. Darcy." She giggled with anticipation. They turned back toward the house. "Come, Hero," she called to the dog.

"Must that dog always go where we go?" he teased. "I knew I might regret giving you what you want."

"That is too bad, Fitzwilliam," she countered, "because what I want right now is you."

Darcy's ardor grew quickly; he turned and kissed her again. "I am a man who dotes on his wife, it seems." He took her hand and led her toward the staircase.

CHAPTER 22

*"A woman especially if she has the misfortune of
knowing anything, should conceal it as well as she can."*

Darcy was at his desk in his study when both Elizabeth and Georgiana entered. "Fitzwilliam," Elizabeth said, so excited she rushed to his side, "Georgiana and I were going through some of your mother's things. We came across a ledger and some notes about an annual celebration she held for the tenants between Christmas and New Year's. Do you remember those?"

"Of course, Elizabeth, but that was years ago; they stopped with her death." Remembering his mother brought him a renewed sadness, one he had not felt since returning to Pemberley with Elizabeth as his wife.

"Georgiana and I would like to bring back the tradition if you have no objections."

Looking at both of them, Darcy's eyes sparkled with a new resolve. Georgiana came forward. "Fitzwilliam, months ago you said you would share your memories of our mother with me. May we start with this tradition?"

He came around the desk to embrace his sister. "My memories are those of a young boy, but you remind me more of her each day—the way you turn your head and that look when you are excited about something for the first time. Georgiana, I do not object, but will you and Elizabeth be able to organize this in such a short duration?"

Elizabeth joined them. "Fitzwilliam, I have nothing to do for our gathering on New Year's nor for decorating the house for

Christmas. Mrs. Reynolds took care of all those details. Georgiana and I both want to be a part of your vision for Pemberley. May we begin with reestablishing your mother's connection to this estate?"

"How may I refuse the three women I have loved?" But Darcy's cautious reserve betrayed his doubts. "Our mother loved this estate; she was devoted to preserving it. Please keep this simple. Read our mother's notes, Georgiana; she knew what was best for our home."

"We will, Fitzwilliam. Come, Elizabeth, we have much to do. Thank you, Brother." She gave him a quick kiss.

"Thank you, Fitzwilliam." Elizabeth's embrace revealed the passion she always felt when close to him. "We will honor your mother's memory. I promise." The women left him with his doubts and his sense of dread. Neither Elizabeth nor Georgiana had experience with such arrangements; he hoped for no regrets, but Darcy feared disaster.

"Elizabeth, my mother's notes tell me little about what she planned," Georgiana's frustration showed.

"I asked Mrs. Reynolds what she remembered. From her recollections, the tenants and some of the villagers came to Pemberley in the afternoon to pay their respects to your parents. Your family greeted them, and everyone was given cider. The children were given candy. This took place in the stable and barn area, I believe. An area was blocked off, cleaned out, and tables were set up for the refreshments. Some traditional music was played, but that is all Mrs. Reynolds could recall. It has been too many years for her to remember all the exact details."

"That is what I see here in my mother's notes, but I envisioned something more. Without wishing to belie my mother's memory, this is a disappointment. I thought it would be more; my parents have a reputation for their generosity." Georgiana felt she betrayed her mother's memory by vocalizing her thoughts.

"Georgiana, your mother lived in a different time. What she did was appropriate for her time, but we may choose to do what is appropriate for our time." Elizabeth's assurance came across stronger than what she felt; she did not know yet how to be a part of Pemberley.

"Will Fitzwilliam agree to our changes, Elizabeth?"

"I promised we would honor your mother's memory, Georgiana. That is what I intend to do; is that not your intention also?"

"Elizabeth, I hope you are correct. I would never wish to upset Fitzwilliam."

Nearly a week passed before Darcy began to have a sense of what all Georgiana and Elizabeth planned. On the day when he stormed into Elizabeth's sitting room, along with Mrs. Annesley, they busied themselves creating pieces of needlework to give to the cottagers. Darcy, of the nature to control everything dealing with his estate, found his lack of knowledge disconcerting. He planned Pemberley's future by teaching Elizabeth its workings. He knew not what upset him; he could not explain why he felt betrayed, but not having control over this celebration caused him consternation, and he overreacted to what he saw. "Elizabeth, what is all this?" The room was full of various items of clothing. "I thought we agreed to keep this celebration simple! This does not look simple!"

"Fitzwilliam, Georgiana and I thought this through. We know what we are doing! Please do not speak to me in that tone; I am not a simpleton!" She jumped to her feet to meet his attack for his censure touched a nerve. If he realized her self-doubts, Darcy would tread softer, but he still placed his family's reputation above his reason.

"Mrs. Reynolds tells me you ordered items removed from the public rooms because you intend to use those for your gathering. What is wrong with the barn area my mother used? Did you not think you should seek my permission before you rearranged *my* house for *your* celebration?" The words cut through her; Darcy saw her stiffen and the fire rise to her eyes. He really did not mean the words he said, but his foolish pride would not allow him to apologize immediately. At all costs, he must save face in front of Mrs. Annesley and his sister.

"Fitzwilliam," her words came out like cold daggers, "I do not know which hurts me more—the knowledge this is *your* house or the knowledge you do not trust me to make decisions which affect our future." The tears came to her eyes as Elizabeth stormed from the room, and he knew instant regret.

Darcy turned to look at his sister. Both she and Mrs. Annesley remained suspended in the moment when one sees a destructive act but one cannot stop the destruction. Neither woman raised her eyes to him for fear of his disapprobation. They did not move; their needles pierced the material but did not complete the loop. Darcy stood there staring at them seeking answers they did not have. Finally, he strode from the room, slamming the door on his way out.

Mrs. Annesley spoke first. "Georgiana, you must go to your brother. You must make him see what he just did to his wife."

Fearing the look in his eyes when he left the room, she said, "I cannot, Mrs. Annesley. He will not listen to me."

"Georgiana, he values you. Your brother is not upset with Mrs. Darcy. He wants things to remain the same as when your parents were alive. People when they remember those who are passed select the memories they will keep of the person. Your brother's memories of your mother are idealistic; she died before he matured enough to realize she was not perfect. Mrs. Darcy cannot live up to such perfection; she will always be found wanting. If he lets this go too long, he will lose Mrs. Darcy's love."

"Do you believe it to be that severe?"

"This was not a simple fight. A crack in their affection opened today; for the first time, they distrusted each other's judgments. If it is not sealed immediately, it will forever plague their time together. Neither of them can help their natures."

Georgiana listened intently; she felt the blame for this misunderstanding; she encouraged and welcomed the plans created by Elizabeth; Georgiana liked the independence the project gave her. Cautiously, she went to find her brother.

Darcy, sequestered in the library, brooded and replayed his words with Elizabeth. He heard Georgiana's light tread, but he turned not to see her, hoping she would leave him to his anger. Instead, she came and sat on the floor at his feet, placing her head on his knee. Instinctively, he reached out to stroke her hair. They sat as such for several minutes before Darcy broke the silence. "I suppose you came to tell me I acted as a foolish ass."

"I would never contradict you, Brother; you must judge your actions."

"A very diplomatic response," he chuckled ironically.

"Instead, I came to speak of our mother. Do you remember anything about our mother which was not pleasing?"

"There are no memories of such for me," he continued to caress her head as she rested on his leg.

"Then our mother was *perfect*?"

Darcy stopped stroking her hair, and she raised her head to look at him. "It is not likely," he said slowly, "our mother made no mistakes." He sat in contemplation realizing his folly. "I think I understand your implications, Georgiana."

"Fitzwilliam, by today's standards our mother did very little for our tenants on Pemberley. I read her notes and was disillusioned. Our parents lived in a different time—you have said so often. If you wanted things the same, you should have chosen someone besides Elizabeth. She will *never* act as our mother acted. Do not force her to be someone she is not. Did you not fall in love with her because she was not what you expected but was what you needed?"

"How do I wipe away the hurt I saw in her eyes?" His self-reproach arrived.

"I do not know what you should say, but if you do not do so immediately you will hurt Elizabeth beyond repair."

Realizing his foolishness, Darcy helped Georgiana to her feet, caressed her cheek, and went to find his wife.

In her dressing room, Elizabeth stared at her reflection, but she saw not her likeness; she saw only the hurt felt within her heart. He entered the room from their bedroom and stood in the doorway for a long time wondering what he could say or do to remove the pain he caused, but she did not move or acknowledge his presence. Eventually, Elizabeth stood and walked toward him. "Excuse me, Mr. Darcy," she said as she started past him, "even though this is *your* house, I assume as *your* wife I am allowed the privacy of my own quarters."

Darcy caught her arm to impede her passage. "Please, Elizabeth, let me explain, I did not mean . . ."

"What did you mean, Fitzwilliam?" Her voice came colder than the disdain he suffered at Hunsford. "I can be your wife and your partner in the privacy of this bedroom, but when the public is involved I am still inferior to your family."

"Elizabeth, I . . ."

She furiously pulled her arm from his grasp and picked up her pelisse. She started for the door's entrance, pausing to look back at him. "Fitzwilliam, my father warned you I would not be caged by your society's regulations; you continue to see me as your inferior; if that be so, I am entitled to the same privileges you provide your staff—my privacy; I can no longer bear to look at you; please do not come to this room again." Saying so, she left him standing arms akimbo, watching her retreat down the hall into the late afternoon shadows.

Several hours lapsed before Georgiana found him sitting in his study staring at nothing at all. "Fitzwilliam, please," her voice held her agitation, "Elizabeth has not returned to the house."

"What? I thought she came back." He sprang to his feet immediately.

"It has been nearly three hours, Fitzwilliam. The temperature has dropped, and snow has started to fall. What is worse is Hero returned to the house without Elizabeth. I am worried."

Instantly, he headed toward the door. "Tell Mr. Shepherd to saddle Cerberus. Where is the dog?"

"Mrs. Reynolds has it under control in the front hall."

"Hurry, Georgiana, find Mr. Shepherd!" Full of fear, he ran the length of the hallway. "When did Hero return, Mrs. Reynolds?"

"Nearly a quarter hour ago, Mr. Darcy. Mrs. Darcy often returns after the dog, but she is never this far behind. Something must be amiss."

"Keep the animal here, Mrs. Reynolds." He ran toward the stables. Within minutes, Darcy reined Cerberus toward the abrupt rise his wife preferred on most of her walks; he hoped she would be a creature of habit today. The light snow gave him some ideas— Hero's paw prints clearly visible; yet, if he did not find Elizabeth quickly the ever increasing snowfall would soon fill in the dog tracks. Darcy prayed she had not met with danger, but his instincts told him otherwise. Elizabeth was too impetuous! But if she was hurt, he was at fault! Trying to spot the dog's tracks, he urged Cerberus across the pathway. Darcy's eyes scanned every tree, every rock, and every rise of the land hoping desperately he would turn his head, and she would be there. Something could not—could not—happen to Elizabeth. He would never forgive himself.

At the bottom of a sharp precipice the dog prints stopped, but Darcy noted the animal clearly ran back and forth on this spot several times. He dismounted the horse and began to frantically call her name. "Elizabeth!" He climbed, nearly crawled, the rock surface, thinking he could see best from the height. "Elizabeth!" The snow came down steadily now, and the smooth surface of the rock made climbing difficult. Reaching the summit, Darcy turned round and round in a circle—heart racing—trying to decide what to do next—fighting the fear which crept steadily through his chest. Then his heart stopped; lying in a clump about thirty feet down on the backside of the climb lay Elizabeth. She did not move even when he called her name. *Please God!* He quickly pulled off his outer jackets and began to snake his way down the slope, holding onto tree limbs and broken rocks, inching his way toward the ball which was Elizabeth.

At last, Darcy reached her. "Elizabeth," his voice calm compared to the tension in his body, "I am here." He turned her over slowly, not wanting to know if she did not live. Her body shivered, and

Darcy gave God a heartfelt thanks. "Elizabeth," he said again.

"Fitzwilliam, you came," her voice barely audible as the coldness racked her body. Mud and snow and scratches covered her face. A bruise showed at her left temple, and dried blood seeped down the side of her cheek.

"I love you, Elizabeth; of course, I came. I will not lose you again." He pulled her close. "I must get you out of here. Put your arms around my neck and hold on no matter what." Darcy scooped her in his arms, holding her tightly to him with one arm and using the other to pull the two of them to safety. He was scared; he was *terrified*—he could not do this, but he must or Elizabeth might die. Perspiration filled his eyes—stinging them, but he would not blink—would not lose focus. He moved slowly up the precarious, weather-beaten side of the cliff, using splintered logs and roots for support. He pulled their weight up—inch-by-inch—often dodging rocks he loosened, covering Elizabeth's head defensively, as debris plunged like bullets at his head. Working as fast as he could, he traversed the muddy, narrow pathway leading to the top. After several intense moments, covered in snow, sweat, and mud, they emerged over the rock's surface. Frantically, Darcy ran his free hand up and down each of her arms and legs to look for protruding bones. Finding none, he held her there, rocking Elizabeth in his arms as he regained his breath.

Finally, with tears stinging his eyes and silent prayers being offered to Heaven, he wrapped Elizabeth in his greatcoat and carried her down the rock's flat surface to where Cerberus waited. She said no more than his name when he picked her up the first time, and now she buried her face into his chest as he carried her to safety; her heart beat as if in his chest; the pain of it clutched his own; he wanted to sob for his loss, but he could not give up hope. He caressed her head and repeated, "I love you."

Elizabeth allowed him to release her long enough to place her on Cerberus's back. He forcibly swung up into the saddle behind her and settled her in his arms once again, the tightness with which she clung to his neck being the only tension in her body; otherwise,

Elizabeth's body drooped and withered in his embrace. He wrapped the coat around her and turned the horse toward Pemberley.

Georgiana was out the main door when she saw him ride into the courtyard. "Oh, my God, Fitzwilliam, is she hurt?" she gasped at her brother's appearance and the bundled body of Elizabeth.

"I do not know, Georgiana." He slid off the horse, still carrying his wife. Irrationally needing to somehow protect her, he lifted her closer to him, afraid if he loosened his grip, Elizabeth might slip away from him forever. He quickened his steps, nearly staggering up the stairs and heading towards his private quarters. He took the steps two at a time. "Send Mr. Shepherd after the physician. Tell him to hurry! She fell over the precipice!"

Exhausted from his efforts, Darcy leaned heavily against the door, his weight swinging it wide. Kicking open the door, Darcy carried her to his bedchamber and laid her gently back on the pillows. He pried her fingers from around his neck to lay her down completely and to examine how fragile she seemed. "Mrs. Reynolds," he screamed. As much as he could, he again checked Elizabeth's arms, back, and legs to look for injuries. Finding nothing evident, he removed his neck cloth, poured some water from the pitcher into the basin, and began to bathe her face and hands with it. His heart raced; she breathed, but Elizabeth did not move nor did she open her eyes. All the time he gently called her name and repeated his love for her; prayers came and went along with anger at how easily he could lose her. He lost everyone he ever loved; he could not lose Elizabeth, too.

The housekeeper entered the room. "What may I do, Master Fitzwilliam?"

"I need clean water and bandages," he snapped.

"Yes, Sir." In a fit of frenzy she ran from the room.

In a little over a half hour, Mr. Spencer, the physician, entered the room followed closely by Georgiana. While Mr. Spencer completed his examination, Georgiana convinced Darcy to go to Elizabeth's dressing room and change his clothes. He did so, reluctantly, not able to abandon the scene—the hurt and the anger—which played out there earlier. If only he did not let her leave, she would not be injured and lying helpless in his bed. How could he be so stupid? His insecurities compounded by those Elizabeth felt as Pemberley's mistress could cost him the woman he loved. He touched her brush on the dresser, and the sadness enveloped him.

Some time later, Georgiana knocked lightly on the door. "Fitzwilliam, Mr. Spencer would like to speak with you." He wiped his eyes quickly on his shirtsleeve and found the doctor.

"Mrs. Darcy has no broken bones, which is the good news. From the multiple scratches and bruises, it appears she slid down the surface rather than falling freely. An impact from that height would have caused more severe injuries. She did hit her head and will probably spend several days sleeping most of the time; these types of injuries can be serious, Mr. Darcy. Your wife may not recover right away, but Mrs. Darcy is young, and I, truthfully, expect her to have no serious complications. Someone should stay with her at all times until she is conscious. When she does come around, she will not be able to stand on her left ankle until the swelling goes down. There are various cuts and bruises, which will need attending. Have her maid bathe her thoroughly and dress the wounds."

"No, I will do it, Mr. Spencer." Darcy's insistence surprised the doctor, but he would not argue with a man of prominence in such a matter. "Did my wife say anything, Mr. Spencer?"

"Just your name, Mr. Darcy." The man hesitated. "I have known you, Mr. Darcy, since your birth; may I make an observation?"

Not taking his eyes from Elizabeth's delicate body lying on his bed, Darcy absentmindedly nodded.

"Although we must watch her carefully, I suspect your wife has no major injuries. A bad headache and a sore ankle is a little price to pay for such a fall as what your sister described. Those will easily heal; why she was outside for so long on such a day as this may take longer to heal." He patted Darcy on the shoulder as he prepared his bag to leave. "I will come to check on Mrs. Darcy in three days unless things change and you need me before then. I will leave you several draughts for pain; once she is awake, she may need them."

"Thank you, Mr. Spencer." Darcy allowed himself to breathe again. He kissed Georgiana's forehead as she caressed his hand. "Without you . . . ." he whispered, but he did not finish his thought. Trancelike, he turned back into his room and closed the door. Georgiana knew, without being told, to order more hot water and bandages to be brought to her brother's room.

Darcy set about the necessary charge of cleaning Elizabeth's wounds. He placed a screen around the bed to protect her from the view of others. So fragile looking, he did not want to move her anymore than was necessary so he went to her room and found her sewing scissors and began to cut the clothes from Elizabeth's body. He talked to her the whole time, describing what he was doing, telling her of his love, of her beauty, and of his sorrow for hurting her. He prayed out loud, thanking God for sparing her life. Then he used the warm water and gentle strokes of the cloth to bathe the dirt caked on her arms and legs. Finally, he dressed the wounds, which were deep enough for infection and needed attention. He doubled the counterpane over her body and then collapsed in the chair next to the bed. He took her limp hand in his and brushed the hair from her face. As he sat back in the chair, tears flowed freely down his cheeks, and the sobs finally smothered his chest. "Stay with me, Lizzy," he whispered.

Exhausted, Darcy drifted in and out of sleep, but the dreams were filled with images of Elizabeth's frail body lying on the rocky ledge and the anger on her face when she stormed from the room. When morning came again, Georgiana appeared to check on Elizabeth's progress as well as that of her brother.

Rousing him by touching his shoulder, she said, "Fitzwilliam, you should get something to eat. I will sit with Elizabeth."

"I cannot leave her, Georgiana. I hurt her—something I swore to God I would never do. I am the most wretched of men. It should be I lying there or worse."

"She would not want that, Brother. Elizabeth loves you."

"With her last words to me in this house she told me she never wanted to see me again. I cannot live without her."

"Elizabeth did not mean what she said. You hurt her so she had to hurt you to be even; you were like children playing some game which neither of you could win. It was your name she called when the doctor was here; it is you she loves even now. You cannot help Elizabeth if you are unwell yourself. Please, Fitzwilliam, go downstairs and eat something. Then you can come back to tend to her."

Darcy hesitatingly agreed, swearing to be gone no longer than ten minutes. Before he left the room, he adjusted the counterpane, knowing Elizabeth would be embarrassed if someone saw her undressed. Georgiana took his seat and Elizabeth's hand; as he left, Darcy heard his sister talking softly to her, professing her affection for Elizabeth and begging her to come back to them.

He gulped down some hot rolls and butter, washing them down with some coffee, knowing anything more would hurt his stomach. Darcy just left the morning room to return to his chambers when he heard Georgiana calling him. "Fitzwilliam, come quick! Please hurry!"

Taking the stairs two and three at a time, he rounded the corner to find Georgiana on her way to find him. "She is awake. Elizabeth calls your name, Brother."

In a fraction of a second, Darcy was kneeling beside the bed holding her hand and brushing the hair from her face. "Lizzy, I am here. I am here, Lizzy."

Her eyes fluttered—opened and closed—but Elizabeth managed to say, "Fitzwilliam." He kissed her hand. "You found me."

"I love you, Lizzy. You are my life. Where you are, I will always —*always* come for you."

The effort of her thoughts made it difficult for her to put the words together she wanted to say. "I love you, Mr. Darcy." She attempted to smile. "I cannot sleep without you. I need to sleep, Fitzwilliam."

"Shush, Lizzy, I am here." He gingerly crawled in the bed beside her, fearing his touch might hurt her more. Elizabeth pulled his arm across her body and closed her eyes. He too closed his and dreamed as he always did—he dreamed of her. Georgiana, watching from the hall, pulled the door shut, knowing *real love* once more lived at Pemberley.

CHAPTER 23

"Till this moment I never knew myself."

It was another four and twenty hours before Darcy emerged from the room again. Elizabeth was alert and wanted something to eat. "I lay awake beside her for hours, Georgiana, just watching the breath slide in and out of Elizabeth's body," he told his sister when she came to his room. "I made a pact with God—give me Elizabeth, and he could have everything else. The money—the house—it all means nothing without her."

"God wants you and Elizabeth together, Brother. He has plans for you." His sister's sage-like words brought him comfort.

Later that day, he gently carried Elizabeth to his tub and bathed her more thoroughly than he had while still wrapped in the counterpane of his bed. She winced as the hot water seeped into the many cuts and scratches on her arms and legs, and he cautiously touched her sensitive skin. Elizabeth so filled his life, Darcy never allowed himself to see her as a woman in need of protection. In fact, he viewed her often as his protector from the grief he experienced in his life. He came so close to losing her. Luck had once been his—he found her when he needed Elizabeth in his life. *What if she turned from him now? What if his pride pushed her away?* He always observed her strength—her resolve. Foolishly, he never saw Elizabeth as someone he needed to not only protect from the world, but also from himself. She gave him her heart completely, and he nearly destroyed her. Miserable, he dutifully washed the curves of her body with the sponge, thinking she was vulnerable—vulnerable

340

only to his censure. His pride would hurt her no more. Finishing, he helped her dress and carried her back to her bed. "If you are not careful, Mr. Darcy," she teased, "you will put Hannah out of a job." Her arms embraced his neck once again, and she rested her head on his shoulder.

"I would gladly spend the rest of my life tending to you, Lizzy." Darcy kissed her cheek as she again buried her face into his chest. When he laid her back on the pillow, she pulled him to her and kissed him tenderly. "Please, Fitzwilliam."

"Elizabeth, I do not want to hurt you."

"You have never hurt me in this bed. I need to know you still love me. I cannot live without you, Fitzwilliam."

"Elizabeth, do what you want. I never meant to question you. I built up a picture of this perfect house—this perfect marriage—a perfect wife." He sobbed as she cradled his head to her abdomen. "I planned everything; except you had ideas I did not plan; I controlled everything for so long, I have difficulty allowing anyone else their due. You did not deserve my wrath. I do not want to destroy your love for me, Elizabeth. Can you love me again as you did before?"

"A few foolish words cannot destroy us, my Love. Do you know what I thought as I lay on that ledge? I thought: *Fitzwilliam loves me. He will come for me.* That is all I kept thinking—despite what I said when I stormed out of this house, I knew you still loved me, and I knew I loved you. Please come to me in our bed, Fitzwilliam."

He began to kiss her stomach and then moved up her body. By the time Darcy got to her lips, Elizabeth's body rose to meet his. "I love you, Lizzy."

Darcy was out of the house when Mr. Spencer called to check on Mrs. Darcy's progress. Propped up on the pillows of her bed, she happily greeted the physician. "Mrs. Darcy, your husband would make an excellent nurse. His care for your well-being was exactly what you needed."

Elizabeth remembered Darcy's passionate kiss before he left and knew what she needed from him, but she had another more pressing question for the doctor. "Mr. Spencer, did the fall hurt my baby?"

"So, you did realize you were with child? These great men are concerned with their heirs; and when Mr. Darcy did not ask about the child when I was here the other day, I knew he did not know, but you could not tell me if you had knowledge of it. I did not tell him for he was too distraught over your health. He would allow no one else to tend to you, Mrs. Darcy."

"When I realized I was falling, I tried to protect the child. I grabbed at every rock and branch to slow down my descent. Please tell me I have not hurt it."

"The three days we waited should be enough time for the injury to show if the fall hurt the child, but I would like to wait at least two more weeks before we can be sure. These types of injuries are sometimes slow to surface."

"I do not want Mr. Darcy to know until we are sure, Mr. Spencer. If there is a chance I will lose this child as a result of my fall, I wish to spare him knowledge of wanting it and then losing it. It would be best he had no time to dream of its life here at Pemberley. His nature is not one to forgive his part in my accident; you must know of his self-reproach." The doctor nodded his head. "My husband plans a New Year's celebration with family and friends. I wish to tell him then. We will be married two months by that time. From my last catamenia, I suspect the child came from our first few nights together. Is that possible, Mr. Spencer?"

"It is quite common, Mrs. Darcy, especially for young, healthy girls as yourself. Would you allow me to examine you now, Mrs. Darcy?"

"Could we pretend you need to check my injuries again in two weeks, Mr. Spencer?" She asked in a conspiratorial tone.

"I delivered both Mr. Darcy and his sister; that was the last of the joy this house saw. After Lady Anne's death, a veil hung over Pemberley; both husband and son loved her too much to let joy back into their lives. There has been too much death and not enough life in this house; I will help you keep your secret, Mrs. Darcy, until the new year if you promise to limit your walks to the flat land for the time being."

"Gladly, Mr. Spencer—gladly." Elizabeth's hand instinctively rested on her stomach. After Mr. Spencer left, Elizabeth wondered at his words. Obviously, what she once thought to be Darcy's contempt for others was, actually, his sorrow at having no one to whom to turn to for love. Georgiana was too young, and Mr. Darcy grieved for his wife. No one helped Fitzwilliam to deal with his own pain. As she lay back across the bed, nursing her wounds, she rued the day she thought him to have improper pride. She would make sure he never felt alone again; Elizabeth would always be there for him.

Since the time Elizabeth swore Mr. Spencer to secrecy a week passed; everything turned snowy and white at Pemberley, and a level of normalcy returned to its halls. She walked carefully, avoiding slippery paths; Darcy guarded every move she made, but she enjoyed the extra attention and allowed him to indulge his concerns. There were still eleven days to the celebration she and Georgiana planned, and many little details needed addressing. She was at the desk in Darcy's study when Mrs. Reynolds entered.

"Excuse me, Mrs. Darcy, a Mr. Chadwick Harrison is asking for Mr. Darcy."

"Show him in, Mrs. Reynolds."

"Mrs. Darcy, thank you for seeing me." He made the obligatory bow. Elizabeth automatically sized him up—proper gentleman in dress—too young to look so serious—pleasant countenance otherwise—a bit unsure of his welcome at Pemberley—old money but new ideas.

"Mr. Harrison, you must excuse my manners. I had a nasty fall last week, and my ankle will not support my weight for more than a few minutes at a time. I just returned from a short walk, and my ankle will not tolerate my rising to my feet again so soon."

"That is quite all right, Mrs. Darcy," he nodded to her.

"Please have a seat, Mr. Harrison. My husband will return shortly. May I be of service to you in the meantime?"

He took the seat she offered. "I heard Mr. Darcy recently married. May I offer my congratulations?"

"Thank you, Mr. Harrison. Do you know my husband well?"

"In reality, I have not seen Mr. Darcy since I was about the age of three and ten; Mr. Darcy, I believe, was off at the university in those days. My late father owns an estate in Dove Dale; I recently returned from the Americas to assume my rightful position as his heir."

"Were you in the Americas for an extended time, Mr. Harrison?"

"For a little over a year, Mrs. Darcy—we had property in sugar-cane, but my family and I objected to the conditions of the workers. I sold the property to small farmers to break up the slave trade."

Speaking his political stance to a perfect stranger shocked Elizabeth, but before she had a chance to respond, Georgiana entered the room. "Elizabeth, the baskets for the meals arrived," she stopped short when she saw the stranger in her brother's study.

Georgiana blushed, and her beauty froze Mr. Harrison in place. Elizabeth took in their first impressions with great interest before she made the proper introductions. "Mr. Harrison, may I present my husband's sister, Miss Georgiana Darcy."

Harrison bowed to her, but his eyes never left Georgiana's face. "Miss Darcy, it is good to see you again."

"I am afraid, Mr. Harrison, you have the advantage. I do not recall our meeting before today."

Harrison chuckled. "I do not doubt it, Miss Darcy, you were a precocious child of seven or eight years, and I came to Pemberley with my parents Mr. and Mrs. James Harrison." Harrison felt a strange sensual awareness as he looked at Georgiana Darcy, and he could not force his eyes from her countenance.

Georgiana blushed and did not answer so Elizabeth added her insights. "As you can easily see, Mr. Harrison, my sister is no longer precocious or a child."

Harrison realized his impropriety. "Forgive me, Miss Darcy, although I am no longer that skinny youth, it did not occur to me you would change so much."

Recovering graciously, Georgiana said, "Have a seat, Mr. Harrison," she came to join them. "You say our parents were acquaintances? How well do you remember my parents?"

"I am afraid I have only childhood memories of coming to Pemberley. It overwhelmed me then as I must admit it does now." His words talked of the house, but Elizabeth suspected his eyes spoke only of Georgiana.

If Georgiana realized the implications of his words, she did not indicate it in her demeanor. Of course, Elizabeth was aware of how easily the Darcys hid their true feelings so she watched this scene play out with interest.

"May I have some tea brought in?" Georgiana offered.

"Of course, Georgiana. Let us have some tea and get to know Mr. Harrison while we wait for Fitzwilliam's return." Elizabeth, like her father, played to such amusements.

How easily Georgiana conversed with Chadwick Harrison entertained Elizabeth. He traveled the world, and Georgiana had questions about the world. In between his anecdotes, Elizabeth ascertained Mr. Harrison sought Darcy's advice on his estate. Darcy assumed control of Pemberley at about the same age, as is Mr. Harrison now. Harrison could seek the advice of some of his closer neighbors, but all those estates had elderly owners, and many were in decline. Darcy had a reputation for innovation, and Pemberley had not been, reportedly, impacted by the draw of the larger cities. Chadwick Harrison wanted Darcy's insights.

When Darcy strode into his study, he did not expect the mirth and laughter borne into the hallway. Elizabeth and Georgiana engaged in an animated conversation with a young gentleman. He stepped to Elizabeth's side and leaned down to kiss her hand, a symbol of his claim on her in case the stranger had other thoughts.

"Fitzwilliam, we are so pleased you finally returned. We entertain Mr. Harrison." Elizabeth gifted her husband with a broad smile.

"I see, Elizabeth." His voice held some hesitation.

"Mr. Darcy," Harrison rose to his feet and made his bow, "I am Chadwick Harrison; my parents are Mr. and Mrs. James Harrison of Hines Park."

"Of course, Mr. Harrison, our parents were acquaintances. I offer my condolences on your father's passing."

"Thank you, Mr. Darcy. I am apologetic for intruding on your time. I came here today to leave my card and request a date when we might talk."

"Mr. Harrison seeks your advice, Fitzwilliam," Elizabeth added, "on the running of Hines Park."

"I would be happy to speak to Mr. Harrison today if you ladies will allow me to reclaim my study." He spoke to them all but looked only at Elizabeth.

"Obviously, I can go nowhere by myself; Mr. Spencer ordered me off my feet. Do you believe I might prevail upon you for assistance?" Their playful teasing returned to their conversation in the past week.

"Come, Mrs. Darcy," he laughed as he swept her in his arms.

"Ask Mr. Harrison to stay for dinner, Fitzwilliam." She looked back at Harrison and Georgiana as Darcy carried her toward the door. "Georgiana and I want to hear more of his stories."

Darcy half turned to his visitor. "I will return in a few minutes, Mr. Harrison, once my new wife has her amusements at my expense." Darcy pulled her to his chest as he carried her from the room, and she rewarded him with a kiss on the neck.

Georgiana stood to make her exit. "We hope you will stay for dinner, Mr. Harrison."

"Thank you, Miss Darcy, I can think of nothing more pleasurable."

Chadwick Harrison quickly became a favorite at Pemberley. He rode the estate with Darcy in the morning, walked the grounds with Georgiana in the afternoon, and dined with all the Darcys in the evening. They asked him to leave his lodgings at the Royal Crown in Lambton and stay with them at Pemberley through New Year's.

"We are expecting my eldest sister and her husband, as well as Kitty, one of my younger sisters. Jane and I shared our wedding day. Her husband Charles Bingley is Fitzwilliam's best friend," Elizabeth added during dinner.

"So, best friends fell in love with sisters. Needless to say, that is unusual."

Darcy laughed, "Charles married the sister with the more pleasant disposition."

Elizabeth countered, "Jane found the more amiable husband." Then she reached out to squeeze Darcy's hand, and he kissed her fingertips tenderly. "As you can readily tell, Mr. Harrison, my dear husband and I at one time had a contentious relationship, but our devotion grows each moment of each day we spend together."

Their banter often amused Harrison; he found Georgiana too enjoyed a spirited relationship with her brother and his wife. In Harrison's opinion, Pemberley offered a refreshing look at English country estates.

"My cousin Colonel Fitzwilliam has also been asked to join us. He is a neighbor of yours; his father owns a large estate in Matlock, but as a second son he chose the military as his career. Along with myself, he serves as one of Georgiana's guardians," Darcy added.

"The good colonel," Georgiana turned to Harrison, "recently became engaged to our other cousin Miss Anne de Bourgh of Rosings Park in Kent. Her mother Lady Catherine is the sister of our mother. We hope Anne's health allows her to join us."

"The last of our guests, Mr. Harrison, will be my aunt and uncle, Mr. and Mrs. Gardiner, from London. They were very instrumental in bringing Fitzwilliam and I together so they are among our favorites."

"That will be our New Year's party group along with the new vicar and Mrs. Annesley," Georgiana was a bit anxious. "We hope you will agree to stay with us until then, Mr. Harrison."

"Having no close relatives in this part of England, being able to share your celebrations will make the time more memorable." Georgiana blushed, but she looked forward to his company. "Plus, I am anticipating the gathering you are having for the Pemberley tenants between Christmas and New Year's. It is an ingenious idea, Mr. Darcy."

"I can take no credit for this celebration; it is the creation of my wife and my sister as a way of remembering our mother, but their plans far exceed anything of which my mother ever dreamed," Darcy deferred the thanks. He no longer worried about the outcome of the celebration. Because he trusted Elizabeth with his heart, he trusted her with Pemberley too.

"Fitzwilliam, what do you think of Mr. Harrison?" They lay across their bed having exhausted themselves in love.

"He is pleasant enough. His political beliefs are more pronounced than are mine, but I admire his plan to save his land. Why do you ask?"

"Because he has that look." Absentmindedly, she drew lines up and down his chest with her fingertips.

"What look?" He turned and propped himself up on his arm.

"He has the look you had when you looked at me at Netherfield. Mr. Harrison looks that way at Georgiana."

"She is but seven and ten, Elizabeth!"

"I am but one and twenty, Fitzwilliam. You are nearly eight years my senior. They are closer in age than are we."

"Do you believe she is interested?"

"Georgiana is comfortable in his company. We need to be observant of the speed of their developing relationship. I would prefer she wait to see the depth of Mr. Harrison's affection. Mr. Wickham was the only experience by which she may measure Mr. Harrison's regard."

"I am not sure I can be reasonable when it comes to Georgiana's heart. You will have to help me, Elizabeth, to see what is best for her. I realize it to be foolish, but I would never wish to have her live anywhere but Pemberley. She trusts you and will tell you things she will not tell me. Although our relationship is stronger than ever, Georgiana sees me as a *parent* as well as her brother."

"You have been an excellent guardian for her, Fitzwilliam. You were no more than a child yourself when you began to be responsible for Georgiana. It must have been difficult to give up your youth to take care of her. You will make an excellent father." Elizabeth rolled over and hid her face in his chest, thinking she said too much and knowing if Darcy looked at her at this instant, he would see her secret in her eyes. "Mr. Spencer will come tomorrow to check my ankle again. I want to be sure I can stand during the celebration for the tenants."

"I will miss carrying you from room to room; I admit having you so close to me gave me great pleasure." Darcy wrapped her in his arms. "Your ankle was a good excuse to embrace you several times a day without being censured for our lack of social grace."

"It seems to me, Mr. Darcy, as this is *our* house, we should be able to set *our* own standards. I give you permission to take me in your arms anytime you so desire."

"Then I would never let you go, Lizzy." Darcy's breath came in short, shallow bursts as he moved in closer to her.

"That would not be intolerable by any means, my Love." She kissed him warmly as she returned to his embrace.

Christmas came to Pemberley; the house shimmered exquisitely, and Elizabeth loved everything about her new home. Mr. Spencer gave her a clean report, and she thought the baby bump became more evident although in her heart she knew it to be too soon. Her hand unconsciously drifted to her stomach several times a day, and she imagined Darcy's joy when he found out.

For such a *rich* household, the gifts were simple—chosen books, a new walking stick, a muffler, a simple bracelet, a fan, sheet music, lace, and ribbons. These were gifts of love not of show; the pleasure came in being together as a family at last. Watching his eyes as he gave out gifts, Elizabeth took time to imagine Darcy with the child next Christmas. She decided he would spoil it with gifts of every kind.

Mr. Harrison allowed Elizabeth, Georgiana, and Darcy time alone before he joined their party, offering each a gift of his appreciation of their friendship. The Darcys dined on a Christmas goose with chestnut stuffing, bread sauce, mince pies, and Christmas pudding eaten with sugar and cream. The Yule Cake, soaked in ale and toasted, supplied the party with tradition. Darcy could not have been happier; Elizabeth hung on his neck most of the day, and they snuck off to various rooms to share intimate moments. During one such interlude, Darcy gave her a necklace of small pearls. "Elizabeth, the pearls caress your neck so beautifully; every time I look at you it is as if I see you for the first time."

"But the first time you saw me, my dear husband, you stated I was tolerable but not handsome enough to tempt you." She kissed his neck and nibbled on his earlobe.

"Mrs. Darcy, you once said I was the last man you could ever be prevailed on to marry." He kissed her mouth with the rush he felt each time he held her in his arms. "Can we not forget the past, Lizzy? There is nothing in my life before you—before you agreed to be my wife."

"Then it is agreed—our life began on the road to Meryton; but may we remember our time here in August?"

"I doubt I can ever forget you in the conservatory," he whispered.

"Then let us save the good memories and leave the bad behind."

The day of the tenant celebration came at last. Elizabeth and Georgiana rushed about taking care of last minute details. Some of the public rooms had been rid of excessive furnishings, leaving only chairs and several small tables in each. Cold meat, bread, pie, and cider were found in each of the rooms, displayed on tables covered by simple cloths, dishware, and centerpieces of pinecones and berry branches gathered from Pemberley's grounds. When the tenants first arrived they stood to the side of the room barely talking to anyone and not knowing what to expect, but Elizabeth and Georgiana moved from room to room talking to each family and pulling them out of their trepidation. Soon, more and more people gathered around, enjoying the food and the social time. Elizabeth took delight in hearing her husband praised for his tenants' concerns and his efforts on their behalf. She learned of his spending two nights with the Lawford family waiting for the passing of their mother and how he rode into Lambton to get medicine for the little Damron girl when the child was sick. Meanwhile, Darcy walked about the rooms genuinely talking to the families and watching Elizabeth's magic as she met each cluster of people. When she took the children onto her lap, Darcy fantasized about her holding their own children. She held a small baby while the mother found something to eat, and he could not resist being by her side any longer. Emotions filling his reason, he came behind her and rested his hands on her shoulders for a few minutes before moving on. As he did so, she smiled brilliantly at him and mouthed the words "I love you" before releasing him with her eyes.

Some of the men brought instruments, and impromptu dancing occurred, but mostly the children played around, rhythmically moving to the music. Georgiana brought out the gifts the three women made for the families—scarves, gloves, lace, ribbons, baby items—all decorated by the ladies for the extended Pemberley family. More than one mother cried at seeing her children so happy with new things.

Darcy and Harrison watched all this from their respective corners of the largest room. Harrison wondered at the scene as it played out, making mental notes of how the celebration shaped the opinions of Darcy's tenants. Darcy, usually miserable in large gatherings, took comfort in watching Elizabeth's and Georgiana's smiles. Eventually, Mr. Howard sought out Darcy. "Mr. Howard, are you enjoying yourself?" Darcy shook his steward's hand.

"It is a pleasant gathering . . . . Mr. Darcy, if I may make an observation," Mr. Howard started, "your wife and sister created more goodwill today than all my ministrations to running this estate. I originally questioned your wisdom in involving Mrs.

Darcy in the running of Pemberley, but it was a brilliant idea, Sir. All I hear is how these people did not want to come here today." The steward stopped suddenly, knowing he said too much.

"Why not, Mr. Howard?" Darcy asked, unexpectedly curious.

"I do not want to say anything, Sir, which may seem inappropriate, Mr. Darcy."

"I will take no offense, Mr. Howard. We have known each other for years; I trust your confidences."

"Your mother's memory is precious to those who have been at Pemberley for a long time, but those years are gone; for all her generosity, Lady Anne kept the social classes; these people expected to be entertained in the barn and then sent home to their drafty houses and hard lives; but your wife opened up your home to them; they are calling her the *mother* of the land." Darcy found this reference amusing, but his eyes instinctively sought Elizabeth; she interacted with the people in the room in the same way he admired her doing in Hertfordshire—one of the reasons he fell in love with her—he knew when he saw her there he needed her in his life. "Lucas and Jefferson changed their minds, Sir, about going to the city to look for work; they plan to stick it out here; they credit Mrs. Darcy for treating them like one of the Pemberley family. They still know their place, Sir, but they also know someone cares about their future. They agreed to try the four-crop rotation after all." Howard continued his observations although Darcy watched only Elizabeth. "These people are not sophisticated, Mr. Darcy; they live their hard lives based on their beliefs and their traditions. Old Mrs. Fleming over there swears the mosaic art at the Tissington well dressing this summer was your wife and sister."

"Mr. Howard, you know I take no notice of such superstitions."

"You may not, Mr. Darcy, but most of the people in this room do. Even good Protestants keep these deep-rooted heathenish superstitions. If you live in Derbyshire, you know one-third of Britain's population died during the Black Plague while most Derbyshire villages escaped such devastation. If you ask the locals, the well dressing celebrations with the blessing of the villages' waters were the reason we were spared—just like the plagues of Egypt, we were passed over. The Tissington mosaic was of two women in a field of wheat and barley; they were dressed in green and brown. Look at what she has on; your wife looks like the emerald green valleys of Pemberley in the early spring and your sister in the brown earth hues; they epitomize the changes coming to Pemberley, Mr. Darcy, but they also show these people who profess loyalty to your family the land will always be there for them. Mr. Darcy, you chose well, Sir—very well, Sir."

Darcy listened intently, never taking his eyes from Elizabeth. "Thank you, Mr. Howard; enjoy your evening." He urgently wanted to be near her; he must tell her how much he appreciated her. Darcy came up behind his wife and caught her around the waist. "Have I told you this afternoon how very beautiful you look, Elizabeth?"

She smiled up at him tenderly, and her eyes sparkled with delight. "Do you not think the green is too bright? I wanted a more leafy forest green, but the dye did not take as well as I wanted."

"Yes, it did, my dear. Mr. Howard says the people relate it to the green valleys of Pemberley in the spring." He whispered in her ear.

Glee overtook her face. "Then it worked. Georgiana's brown velvet is the rich land, and I am the life springing from it. It was a silly ploy—an idea sprung from a tale Hannah related last summer when I stayed at the Royal Crown about maids in the field being good luck—but I hoped it would create a mood."

"And from where may I ask did you learn such devious manipulations, Mrs. Darcy?" His smile portrayed an interest he had never spoken.

"From the master, my Love—from you." She smiled generously, and he tapped her chin with his index finger before moving on. He found Harrison still staring at the proceedings.

"Mr. Darcy, you are blessed with two very progressive thinking women in your household."

"Some would not call progressive thinking in a woman a *blessing,* Mr. Harrison."

"Then, they would be a foolish prats, Mr. Darcy. Look how well they orchestrated this evening. People are happy; they are praising your family as caring landowners: they praise you, Sir, for your attention to the land and your wife and sister to their attention to the people. This is a lesson I wish to replicate at Hines Park, Sir. It is amazing how something so simple may be so ingenious."

"My Elizabeth changed me, Mr. Harrison. She gave Georgiana a *voice,* and now she weaves her magic over my ancestral home. You are right, Sir, I am blessed."

Elizabeth approached, "Come, Fitzwilliam, we need to bid our guests farewell. You know everyone. It will help me learn them too if I hear you call the names. Mr. Harrison, would you consider helping Georgiana with the baskets to be given to each family?"

"Gladly, Mrs. Darcy." He moved past her to find Georgiana in the hallway.

"What is in the basket, Elizabeth?" Darcy asked, curious as to what she thought the people needed.

"The basket is your sister's idea, Fitzwilliam. It has some cold meat, bread, a few potatoes, corn, candy, and some tea. She even added a candle and a branch of consecrated mistletoe to proclaim in each dwelling a happy new year; and I should not forget a slice of our family's Christmas plum cake to be shared on New Year's for luck. Georgiana wanted everyone to have a good meal on New Year's. She has a very generous nature, Fitzwilliam."

As each family left to return to their lodgings, Darcy and Elizabeth spoke to them, wishing them a fulfilling New Year's, and then Georgiana and Mr. Harrison gave them a gift of fresh food so all would have a fulfilling meal to start the new month and year.

"Elizabeth," Darcy whispered in between families, "I was wrong; my mother was not perfection; you are, my Lizzy, you are."

"Then I please you, Sir?" she teased and reached up to caress his cheek.

"Our matrimonial felicity, I may assure you, Mrs. Darcy, is guaranteed. By the way, the green accents your eyes."

"Yellow is my preferred color, Sir, as well you know, but the green is a nice alternative." She squeezed his hand before greeting the next family.

As they prepared to ascend the staircase that evening, they were both very satisfied with the day. "I will be happy to see all our guests tomorrow, Fitzwilliam. I miss Jane's company desperately, but if I have my way, we will not see much of her or Mr. Bingley for the first few days. I know it is devious, but I gave them rooms secluded from the rest of the party. I want Jane and Mr. Bingley to find time for each other."

"Who says they did not do so already, Elizabeth?"

"Fitzwilliam, they truly have more affable natures than do we. They tended Bingley's sisters and Mr. Hurst, as well as my mother and sisters. Could you imagine our distress if we were at Netherfield?" Darcy rolled his eyes; the image of having so many unwelcome people about would easily have him more than a bit irritable. He thought he would probably resort to physically throwing them from his home. "If it is up to me, we will not see them for at least eight and forty hours."

"My sister's romantic nature is influencing you, Mrs. Darcy." He laughed at her feigned innocence.

Elizabeth tried to put on a happy face, but she was wearier than she expected; her energies spent. She sagged against Darcy as they climbed the stairs. "Are you not well, Elizabeth?" The concern he could not hide.

"I am just a bit tired, my Love." She pushed her hair back from her face and fanned herself. Something I ate has not set well, Sir; that is all."

"I will not have you wearing your energies so thin, Elizabeth. You try to do too much." He picked her up to carry her to their room.

Enjoying a renewal of his attentions to her health and wellbeing, she whispered, "I will cut back, Fitzwilliam; I promise. After New Year's, you, my Love, may control my schedule."

"Elizabeth, I plan to hold you to that promise. Your fate will be mine."

"My fate has been yours, Fitzwilliam, for so many months. I cannot remember a time when there was no Fitzwilliam Darcy in my life." She kissed him passionately, and then she sank back against him.

"Tonight, my Love, you sleep in my arms, and I do mean sleep."

"Yes, Fitzwilliam, I need some sleep."

CHAPTER 24

*"I can imagine he would have that sort of feeling—
the mixture of Love, Pride, and Delicacy."*

Two days before the new year, the Gardiners' coach rolled onto Pemberley's grounds in the late morning hours. As visitors, they saw the estate in early August, but now they were to stay as guests, the honor not lost on them. Mr. Gardiner brought gifts for all the members of the household. Darcy's special gift, another picture of Darcy and Elizabeth—this one of them as husband and wife, came from Cassandra Gardiner. Darcy placed it in his study beside the one given to him earlier where he could see it as he deliberated over business dealings. He picked up the child and hugged her; later, after dinner, she sat on his lap and fell asleep in his arms as he gently stroked the girl's head; and the scene brought Elizabeth great joy. Warmer than what was expected for this time of year, Mr. Gardiner took advantage of the weather and showed his sons how to fish although he knew fish were not to be had. All the children played with Hero and helped the dog chase the game birds along the wood line. "Come, Aunt Gardiner, I promised you a ride around the grounds." Elizabeth's joy showed as they headed for a phaeton ride, a promise sealed months earlier. The Gardiners knew the joy of seeing Elizabeth in love and at Pemberley.

Jane and Bingley did not arrive until late in the day. "Jane, we worried for your safety," Elizabeth said as she greeted her sister.

"They decided to sleep in," Kitty whispered as she hugged Elizabeth. Jane blushed when she overheard Kitty's comment, but she also could not help smiling. Elizabeth giggled at the prospect of Jane and Mr. Bingley enjoying the same kind of pleasure she did with Darcy. When she caught Jane's arm going into the house, Elizabeth could not help but murmur, "Jane, if you want to sleep in tomorrow, you have my blessing."

Jane blushed again, but she said, "Maybe I will, Lizzy. Maybe I will." Then they both burst out laughing, enjoying the secret.

Darcy welcomed Bingley in his study; they had not seen each other since their wedding day, and they had much to share. "I am happy to be at Pemberley, Darcy. I must admit I have seen enough of my sisters and my brother Hurst for a while, and after only two months, Netherfield's proximity to Longbourn has lost its appeal even for Jane. We are considering looking for another estate if things do not change."

"I am sorry to hear of your need for privacy. Elizabeth and I spent a glorious fortnight in London."

"Darcy, I feel sorry for Jane. She does not deserve such treatment; my sisters had her running everywhere to try to please them. I promised her a lifetime of happiness, but the drudgery of everyday life already takes its toll on our relationship. It was luxurious this morning to not have obligations to others."

Darcy began to laugh, and Bingley fidgeted with embarrassment. "I am sorry, Bingley; I do not mean to make light at your expense. I laugh because your sister Elizabeth spreads her magic again. She decided days ago, you and Jane should have rooms away from everyone else. Obviously, Elizabeth realized Mrs. Bennet's lack of civilities would not take a holiday once you married. She wishes for you and Jane to be as happy as are we."

"Darcy, remind me to thank your wife properly." Bingley laughed.

"If I know Mrs. Darcy, your making Mrs. Bingley your priority will make Elizabeth happy without any thanks. At Netherfield, Elizabeth delighted in your attention to Jane."

"That reminds me, Darcy; you were quite cunning in getting

me to invite Mrs. Darcy to stay at Netherfield. I thought you did so to allay my agitation over Jane's illness; little did I realize you had other motivations."

"Your concern for Mrs. Bingley was my initial thought, but I willingly admit Elizabeth possessed my heart even then, although I fought my feelings for her. I was a man torn between two worlds—a dutiful son and a man in love with an amazing woman. I never realized I could be both—no choice was necessary."

"How are we so fortunate to marry such intelligent ladies, Darcy?"

"It is for sure we succeeded where many others fail."

Kitty looked forward to spending time with Georgiana Darcy. Since Lydia left for Brighton, Kitty had no one else with whom to share her questions about love and about men; they had shared several "intimate" sidebars when they met at Longbourn before Elizabeth's wedding to Mr. Darcy. Kitty hoped Georgiana would look on her as a close friend and confidante. Kitty Bennet knew Georgiana Darcy to be more refined than anyone else of her acquaintance, and Kitty felt she could learn something from her. Jane and Elizabeth found excellent matches because they presented themselves as "ladies." Lydia's husband at first seemed appealing to Kitty, but she learned Lydia's life was not so easy. They were often in debt and forced to change living quarters, and it was not in a good way. She decided Elizabeth's offer of continuing her studies and of coming to Pemberley was a better way of finding her own "excellent" match.

At Pemberley, she concluded, she would learn what it took to attract a man of consequence—a man with a future. Being able to attend balls and private parties with eligible young bachelors would be to her advantage. Being Mrs. Darcy's sister would also be to her advantage. The prospect of staying at Pemberley and *not* returning to Longbourn with Mary's religious rants and her mother's nervous condition delighted Kitty's youthful imagination so she was pleased, then, to meet Chadwick Harrison even though he obviously had eyes only for Miss Darcy. At least, if she made a good impression on the man, he might introduce her to someone promising.

The house echoed with life, and Darcy's expression reflected the joy he felt at last. Only the absence of Colonel Fitzwilliam and Anne brought him any sense of regret. He hoped for a resolution with the de Bourgh household although he never expected one. Friends and loved ones in the same house changed how he looked at the world. He and Elizabeth found each other; Georgiana grew into a young woman; and Pemberley loomed larger than ever.

He rolled over in the bed to look at a sleeping Elizabeth. Her hair draped down over her shoulders, and her body curled in a ball around a pillow she hugged to her bosom. They married only two months ago, but Darcy had no adult memories of which she was not a part. Wanting to allow her time to rest because she seemed so tired of late, he slid out of the bed and snuck off to his dressing room. He called for hot water and immersed himself in the tub. Relaxing back in the water, he closed his eyes and reflected on his happiness. The warmth combined with his thoughts of his wife lulled him into a dreamlike state. He could see *his Elizabeth,* the woman he loved nearly from the start; she certainly consumed his every thought even back then. Darcy laughed softly to himself as he reached for the sponge. Taking the soap in the hand, he began to slowly rub the lather against his upper thighs.

Finishing, he finally returned to her bedchamber, expecting to find Elizabeth where he left her; but an empty bed surprised him. Searching, coming softly into her dressing room, he waited in the doorway, holding back, watching her as she perched precariously on the edge of her own tub. She toweled her hair dry, the unruly auburn curls playing across her shoulders and down her back. Her silk dressing gown clung to her damp body, and the cinched belt accentuated her tiny waist. The gown opened at her knees, and Darcy drank of her slender leg and ankle with his eyes.

Sensing his presence, Elizabeth looked up slowly, meeting

his intense gaze. Without looking away from him, she said, "That will be all, Hannah."

"Yes, Mrs. Darcy." The maid offered them both a quick curtsy before exiting to the hallway.

An amused smile kissed his lips. "I thought you would still be abed."

"You left me alone, Sir. I cannot sleep when you are not with me." She chastised him although he felt no guilt. He looked up to see her signature enigmatic smile, welcoming him into her world. "Perhaps I should, my Husband, no longer be in charity with you." Her voice held a veiled reprimand.

Darcy pushed away from the doorframe, advancing slowly towards her. "I did not wish to disturb your slumber." He could feel the heated sensation of her presence.

Realizing his intent, Elizabeth stood quickly. "Fitzwilliam," she stammered, while backing away slightly.

Darcy paused, allowing his eyes to trace her form. "Yes, Elizabeth." A wolfish grin turned up the corners of his mouth.

"We cannot." Her eyes grew larger the closer he came. "We have a house full of family and friends."

"Mrs. Reynolds will see to their needs. I hoped you would see to mine." Suddenly, he playfully dipped his hand into the sudsy water and flicked a spray of droplets in her direction.

Elizabeth squealed as she brushed the dampness away from her face with her sleeve. "You are incorrigible, Sir," she taunted.

By now Darcy stood directly in front of her. "And you, my Lizzy, are exquisite." He bent his head to brush his lips against her cheek. Without thinking, he scooped her up into his arms and spun her around, teasingly tossing her up as if he would throw her lithe body away.

Laughing gleefully, Elizabeth kicked and squirmed, clawing desperately at his shoulders and arms. "Fitzwilliam," she gasped, "put me down."

He stopped suddenly, afraid he had hurt her, but the sparkle in her eyes told Darcy she enjoyed his attention. "Put you down? Put you down, my Love?" He pulled her to him. "Where should I put you down, my Lizzy?" As he spoke he turned towards the center of the room and the filled tub. "Should I put you down here?" He extended his arms, balancing her body above the tub.

"Fitzwilliam, you would not!" she warned as she tightened her hold on his neck and tried to pull herself even closer to him. Seeing his intentions more clearly, she tried to reason with him. "You would ruin the new silk dressing gown you bought me."

"I will buy you another," he said matter-of-factly and then pretended to release her.

"No!" she screamed as his laughter filled the room.

Her ire flashed. "Fitzwilliam!" She began to reprimand him for real, but his mouth found hers, and her anger gave way to the passion of the moment. He clutched her to him, and as he seated them on a nearby settee, Elizabeth nestled into his lap.

"I will buy you another," he whispered as he kissed her cheek. "And another." His lips lightly touched the corner of her mouth. "And another." This time the kiss deepened quickly. "Lizzy, you are the most bewitching woman I have ever met."

She snuggled closer to him, resting her head below his chin and turning her body into his chest. After a few elongated moments, she tilted her head back, engaging his eyes in a merry dance of love. "Tomorrow when we awake it will be a new year. I wanted this year—the one in which we found each other—to be memorable. Will you remember this year, Fitzwilliam?" Her voice was laced with the dim recesses of her mind.

"I do not know how to describe what you have brought to my life, Elizabeth. Every sensation is so real. Sometimes you are the most impossible woman God ever placed on this earth, but I only find happiness when I am in your presence—when you are in my arms. I will love none but you."

She kissed him fervently, welcoming the strength of his arms around her. Darcy held her there to him, their arms encircling each other, their legs entangled, their breathing jagged, their hearts pounding into each other's ribcages. It seemed that there was nothing he needed more than to be loved by her. The outside world as they knew it stopped—it was only the two of them left in their world.

New Year's Eve late afternoon brought the carriage carrying Edward and Anne to Pemberley. Darcy met them in the courtyard. "Edward, you are here at last; I feared you would not come."

"We had some *difficulties*, but we are happy to be here, Fitz. May we stay several days at Pemberley? Anne and I need to make some arrangements before we go to Matlock for my parents' anniversary party."

"Of course, Edward; you do not need to ask." Darcy shook his hand. Then he turned to help Anne from the coach. "Anne, it pleases me to see you looking so refreshed. I hope you are well."

"Edward keeps me from dwelling on my illnesses, Fitzwilliam. I feel so much stronger when I am on his arm."

Darcy smiled with the knowledge Lady Catherine's hold on Anne would soon be over. "Let us go into the house, shall we?" He offered Anne his arm, and she actually smiled up at him.

"Darcy, where are Mrs. Darcy and Georgiana?" Edward asked.

"Elizabeth went to find Georgiana when she saw your coach. They will join us shortly. We have several other houseguests; let me introduce you."

Elizabeth discovered Georgiana in the music room listlessly sitting on one of the window seats and staring outside. "Georgiana, Colonel Fitzwilliam and Anne just arrived. Your brother asks you to come greet them."

"What?" Georgiana's distraction caused confusion. "I am sorry, Elizabeth, did you say something?"

Elizabeth came to sit beside her sister. "Georgiana, what is wrong? You have not been yourself the last few days. What bothers you?"

"It is a foolish idea; forgive me, Elizabeth. I am distracted, but I really do not know why."

"Is your distraction related to Mr. Harrison?" Elizabeth recognized the signs.

Georgiana blushed and turned her head to divert her eyes from Elizabeth's knowing glance. Elizabeth turned her chin and forced her sister to look at her. There was a long pause, and then Georgiana blurted out, "Mr. Harrison spends his time with your sister Kitty. He and I have not walked the grounds in two days, Elizabeth. He seems to have found other amusements." Tears filled her eyes.

"Oh, Georgiana," she hugged the girl closely to her. "Mr. Harrison has eyes for no one but you. He knows your every mannerism; Kitty is flirtatious, but Mr. Harrison wants a woman who shares his vision; Kitty is not that woman."

The tears and sobs consumed Georgiana; she could barely speak. "What do I do, Elizabeth?"

"Georgiana, your brother would never agree to a proposal from Mr. Harrison at this time, and I would not support it either. Mr. Harrison will need to wait for you. Your brother would not consider such an alliance until you are at least eight and ten. He feels he just found you himself; Fitzwilliam will not be anxious to have you leave Pemberley. You must learn more about Mr. Harrison before you give your heart to him. Find out does he have the same honor your brother possesses; does he have the humor of Colonel Fitzwilliam. There are many things you need to know about a man before you agree to be his wife; I would not want you to marry unless you found *real love*—real passion. Do not settle on a man who offers only agreeable company. He should accept your opinions and arouse your feelings."

"When did you realize you loved my brother?"

"I cannot tell you the exact time or date. As I look back, I feel he always fascinated me; he would make me so angry I would try to find fault with him; then he would do something so unpredictable. He helped me carry water to my sister's room at Netherfield, out of everyone he could have chosen, he honored me with a dance at the ball, and he shared walks and the field of wildflowers at Rosings. One moment I professed hating him, and then I found I could not take my eyes from his, and I wanted the regard he once offered me. Obviously, he did the honorable thing; your brother saved my family because he loved me. I finally saw him for the man he always was and allowed myself the pleasure of truly loving him. Now, he gives me more than I could imagine. I am not talking about the wealth of Pemberley; of what I speak is a more intangible gift. Your brother allows me to be a woman with her own independent ideas. Although we rarely disagree about issues, I could differ from him, and Fitzwilliam would listen and be accepting. He allows me to love him on my own terms without the demands society might place on us. I find that for a man who once required society's approval for his every move, your brother is able to see what merits real 'worthiness' in a relationship."

"But what if Fitzwilliam wants to present me to society this season? How may I disappoint him and still maintain Mr. Harrison's regard?"

"I will speak to your brother about waiting another season before your presentation, but I will not lie to him about the reasons."

"Thank you, Elizabeth. I could not face Fitzwilliam without you."

"Now, your brother wishes you to come greet the colonel and Anne. Tell him I will be there shortly; I must see Mrs. Reynolds about something for tonight."

As Georgiana turned toward the drawing room, Elizabeth went to find Mr. Harrison; he lounged in the billiard room although he did not play. "Mr. Harrison, I sought your company."

"Mrs. Darcy, may I be of service to you?"

"I want to speak of something serious, and I desire you to speak the truth." She came in close to let him know she wanted his absolute attention.

"Of course, Mrs. Darcy." He escorted her to adjoining chairs.

"Mr. Harrison, I am not a foolish woman; I see how you look at Miss Darcy."

"I am afraid I do not hide my feelings well. I would seek your husband's approval if I thought Miss Darcy returned my feelings."

"Mr. Harrison, Mr. Darcy would not accept such a proposal at this time regarding his sister, and I told Georgiana I would not support her relationship with you."

"Am I such a poor choice for Miss Darcy?"

"This is not what I meant, Mr. Harrison; my early inclination is to believe you to be an excellent choice for my sister; you listen to her and treat her like a woman whom you would respect as well as love."

"Then what is your concern, Mrs. Darcy?"

"For all her fine learning, Georgiana is a delicate young girl who wears her heart on her sleeve, and until I am sure you will not break her heart, I will not *persuade* my husband to give his approval. What I am going to suggest is you return to Hines Park and, literally, get your house in order. Prove to Mr. Darcy your regard for his sister has nothing to do with her fortune. Allow your affection for Miss Darcy to stay in check until both of you feel *real love*. I have no objections to your occasional visit to Pemberley, but until at least the end of the summer and Georgiana's next birthday, I *forbid* your obtaining a promise from Miss Darcy. I want her to be free to choose you without any obligation to do so. Do you understand my wishes, Mr. Harrison? I will not allow you to trifle with Georgiana's heart. If you two are to really love each other, it will stand the test of time."

"Mrs. Darcy, your wisdom is never a question."

"Neither should be my resolve, Mr. Harrison."

"I will abide by your wishes, Mrs. Darcy, but when the time expires, I will make my declaration to Miss Darcy and pray she will accept."

"Come, Mr. Harrison, my husband has guests for you to meet." She took his arm as they returned to the drawing room. "One of them, Colonel Fitzwilliam, a man trained in how to kill another efficiently, is Georgiana's other guardian." Elizabeth smiled deviously.

"I thoroughly understand, Mrs. Darcy." Harrison looked uncomfortable as he mulled over her words.

"Elizabeth, there you are," Darcy called as she entered the room on Mr. Harrison's arm. She quickly left Harrison and slipped into Darcy's outstretched arm.

"I am sorry, Love; I wanted to let the staff know the colonel and Anne have joined us. I did not mean to be so long." She slid her arm around his waist as she turned her attention to their guests. "Edward, you are most welcomed, and Miss de Bourgh, we cannot tell you what joy you brought to this household today. I am excited you are here."

"Thank you, Mrs. Darcy; Edward and I have been anticipating the pleasure."

Turning back and gesturing to Harrison to join them, Elizabeth said, "Colonel Fitzwilliam, Miss de Bourgh, this is one of our houseguests, Mr. Chadwick Harrison of Hines Park."

Edward made his bow. "I know Hines Park; I did not realize you took possession of the estate, Mr. Harrison."

"I have, Colonel Fitzwilliam; my father passed recently."

"We offer you our support, Sir," Anne added softly. Harrison made an acknowledging bow and took his leave.

"Georgiana, why do you not show Anne and Mrs. Jenkinson to their rooms? I am sure she would like some time to freshen up."

Anne turned to Edward. "I will return shortly." He smiled and squeezed her hand.

"Edward, I realize the trip was exhausting, but would you do me the favor of taking a stroll through the garden before going to your room?" Elizabeth smiled knowingly.

"I would love the exercise, Elizabeth," he stammered, not un-derstanding her impetuous request. "A few moments to stretch my legs would do me well."

Darcy looked offended. "May I not join you?"

"Colonel, your cousin always was jealous of our private rambl-ings," she teased. "Should we include him today?"

"I believe he earned that right, Mrs. Darcy."

Elizabeth smiled up at Darcy and took his hand. "Come, Love, we must hear all of Edward's news." Realizing she wanted some privacy, both men followed her outside.

They walked a short distance from the house before Darcy caught her hand to bring her to the point of this extemporaneous walk. "Elizabeth, Edward should return to his room. Would you like to tell us the purpose of this sudden need for the outdoors?" Darcy looked confused.

"I spoke to Mr. Harrison this morning. His interest in Georgiana grows, Fitzwilliam."

Quick to react, Darcy began, "I will not have it, Elizabeth."

She caught his arm to stop his thoughts. "Georgiana believes herself to have feelings for the man," she continued. "I also spoke to her."

"Do you not think, Elizabeth, Georgiana is too young for marriage?" Edward questioned.

"In age, she has reached a common time for marriage, but I agree she is too vulnerable to recognize her own worth. Mr. Harrison, I concede, would treat her well—would value her fine mind; I wish only for Georgiana to find real love, and I told her this." Darcy paced as she talked. "Fitzwilliam, *please*; I told them both, you would not approve of such an alliance at this time, and I would not try to persuade you otherwise." Her words lessened some of his concern.

"What else did you tell Mr. Harrison, Elizabeth?" Edward realized she took charge of the situation.

"I *forbid* Mr. Harrison from requesting a promise of Georgiana until after her next birthday. I *suggested* he secure the future of Hines Park to prove to you, Fitzwilliam, he sought Georgiana's love and not her fortune, and I *suggested* that if someone were to hurt Georgiana, you Edward were skilled in the ways of killing." Because of it seeming initially out of place, both men laughed at this last reference. "Fitzwilliam, Mr. Harrison agreed, but he will present himself to you when Georgiana turns eight and ten. Between now and then we should learn all we can of Mr. Harrison's past and his prospects; and we should expose Georgiana to various social gatherings. If it is meant to be a match, time will tell of its success."

"Mrs. Darcy," Edward began, "you are wise beyond your years. No wonder my cousin wanted to keep us apart at Rosings. He feared I might realize your worth." Then Edward slapped Darcy on the back as he started toward Pemberley. "We will talk more later, Fitz," he called over his shoulder.

Thoughts of losing Georgiana agitated Darcy, but Elizabeth's manipulation of the situation brought him some relief. "Mrs. Darcy, my cousin is correct; although I always appreciate your wit, your astute insights are often unexpected."

Elizabeth hastened to his waiting arms. "You are not upset with my interference into Georgiana's life? I should not intrude in your family's affairs. Did I do anything correctly, Fitzwilliam?"

"First, she is your sister too so what is there to censure? You gained Georgiana's trust while forestalling Mr. Harrison's attention; you earned a promise from Mr. Harrison, giving us time to assure his feelings for Georgina and his ability to provide for her. I am glad you are not a man with whom I must do business regularly. You handled it more amiably than I." He hugged her tightly to him and kissed the top of her head. "Did you really threaten to have the colonel kill Mr. Harrison?" He seemed befuddled by the implications. "First, you threaten Mr. Wickham and now Mr. Harrison. I begin to fear for my safety, Elizabeth," he mugged.

"You have nothing to fear from me, Fitzwilliam; the worst you have to suffer is my loving you to death." She kissed him warmly. Elizabeth looked about nervously. "I am looking forward to this evening, are you not, Love?" she said tentatively.

"Any evening which ends with you and I in our bed is a glorious occasion," he beamed.

"Then we need no company, Sir; we should send them all away." Her teasing always aroused him, and Darcy felt sensual warmth creep into his body.

"Do not tempt me, Elizabeth—do not tempt me." They walked back to the house arms around each other and in contentment.

The last of the party joined everyone for dinner. As the new vicar, Clayton Ashford met the Darcys on several occasions outside of church, and the dinner invitation honored his work in the village. He knew the Darcys to be generous, and how well they maintained the devotion of the community impressed him. He thought himself fortunate to be given a living in such a community. Many of his fellow clergymen had to cower and bow to their benefactors; the Darcys allowed him much latitude in the way he administered to his flock. Miss Darcy embraced the drive to help the poor, and Mr. Ashford hoped he could convince them to support his idea for a village school.

Clayton Ashford was a novelty to many in his parish for he was nothing like the previous clergyman. His appearance pleased the females in his congregation, but he could not be called handsome. He held himself with poise, although some saw his manners as a bit distant. His polite conversations addressed the needs of his parishioners, but he was easily distracted and rarely initiated the discourse. His sermons rocked the congregation with his passion for the church, but he lacked social worldliness. Ashford showed promise of being worthy of Darcy's patronage, but Mr. Darcy still wondered if he made the right decision by giving the man the living; Ashford's aloofness sometimes bothered Darcy because it reminded him of Darcy's own dislike of social gatherings.

Entering the Darcys' drawing room, Mr. Ashford did not anticipate a pleasing evening because he disliked such social exchanges, but he knew the Darcys served as his financial benefactors, and he would put forth a good effort. His host came forward to greet the vicar, and then Mr. Darcy handed him off to his wife for the introductions—the Bingleys, the Gardiners, several cousins, Mr. Harrison—and then Ashford's glance fell on a young girl with sparkling eyes and a fetching smile; he had to concentrate to discover the girl's name—Kitty Bennet, Mrs. Darcy's younger sister. Being single, Ashford schooled himself when being introduced to young ladies. Never did he immediately take an interest in them, no matter how pretty they were. Yet, as soon as he saw her, Ashford's eyes could not leave Kitty's face. He felt riveted to the floor, and if he were the type to curse, he would have done so for he felt foolish just standing and staring at her. Kitty Bennet offered him an encouraging smile so Ashford took advantage of the empty chair beside her. Although he had been in Derbyshire nearly nine months, not once had Clayton Ashford willingly sat next to an attractive young lady and willingly conversed with her.

Kitty Bennet held no idea the impact she had on the man; she simply enjoyed his attentions. She listened intensely to what he said, although she did not always understand his ideas. He spoke of John Wesley, Samuel Johnson, and Sir Joseph Banks. Ashford said these men offered opposing ideas of Christianity, but she knew them not; yet, she was willing to find out if it would please Clayton Ashford. As the evening progressed, she let her sister know her sentiments. Going to refill her tea, Kitty cornered Elizabeth. "Lizzy, thank you for inviting Mr. Ashford; he is a most interesting young man."

"I am pleased you found someone to entertain you, Kitty," Elizabeth held the amused look Kitty associated with their father.

"Would it be possible, Lizzy, to be seated near Mr. Ashford during dinner?" Kitty's anticipation crisscrossed her face.

Elizabeth smirked, "I will try, Kitty."

"Do not tease me, Lizzy. You know my temperament."

"I know, Kitty; I know very well. Do not be too forward; he is a clergyman." Elizabeth warned her warmly.

"I thought all clergymen were like Mr. Collins or old Mr. Aiken. Clayton Ashford is nothing like what I expected." Kitty giggled and moved back to the chair she vacated moments before.

Darcy came up behind Elizabeth and put his arms around her waist. She leaned back into him and felt his warmth. He bent down to whisper in her ear. "Elizabeth, Lady Catherine may be right; your arts and allurements are spreading."

She turned to glance over her shoulder at his profile. "I do not understand, Fitzwilliam."

"Look at the love in this room—families together—husbands and wives—young regard—friends—all caring for one another.

Pemberley lacked this kind of happiness until there was you."

She closed her eyes and leaned back even further to feel his strength enclosing her in his love. Elizabeth reached up and caressed his cheek, and the joy was evident on her face. He kissed the side of her head before he released her to return to his guests. Elizabeth's eyes followed him as he moved away, and he turned back and looked at her—his eyes infinite depths of intelligence and understanding. The intensity of his stare always brought a sudden flush of heat rising to her cheeks. He knew sadness and loss of those he loved, and for a long time he hid his hurt behind a façade of arrogance. Now Darcy allowed himself to love again, risking the pain which only lost love could bring, yet, he did not fear losing Elizabeth's love; their love, he realized, could not be displaced.

Sixteen people sat to New Year's Eve dinner of beef, capons, cole-worts, potatoes, cream soups, fresh fruit, and a bread pudding—a meal served over three courses. The animated conversation reflected the care each person felt for the other. Darcy watched Elizabeth at the other end of the long dining table; she picked at the food except for the potatoes of which she took two helpings. She noticed his concern and offered him a slight shrug of her shoulders, a large smile, and pursed lips as if she expected a kiss. His eyebrow rose as if to question her until the unstated twinkle in her eyes easily ignited his ardor; he closed his eyes to imagine Eliza-beth's closeness. No one at the table could deny their love; anyone who bothered to look at either of them, obviously, recognized the love they held for each other.

After dinner, the Gardiner children played hoodman blind and hot cockles. The adults enjoyed their antics and their joy; Darcy gave a wooden boat to each of the two boys and a rag doll to his favorite Cassandra. The children rewarded him with squeals of happiness and a hug from Cassy. Elizabeth noted how his features softened when the children were near, and she hoped he would take more delight in his own child. Tonight she would tell him of their child; she planned the moment in their bedchamber and what she would say; she anticipated his happiness and how tender his love would be this evening.

The children went to bed, and the men retreated to Darcy's study to smoke their favorite cigars and share glasses of fine port and brandy over conversation. The women entertained themselves in the dining room. Jane and Kitty led the conversation, reliving the escapades of the Bennets and of Bingley's sisters at Netherfield. Elizabeth's only regret lay in Anne hearing of her family's lack of decorum; the stories proved Lady Catherine's concerns, and Elizabeth wished the subject would change to something pleasanter. Tomorrow she would tell all these women her news; she would write her parents. Sharing the news would relieve her of her stress and her exhaustion.

Soon the men returned to the drawing room; Darcy and Edward sought her attention. She stood to the side talking briefly with Anne about their plans for the anniversary party for Edward's parents. Coming into the room as in mass, the odor of the cigar smoke hung on the men's clothing, and the smell permeated every corner. Elizabeth felt her stomach lurch, but she tried to hide her increasing need to regurgitate. Darcy and Edward came to stand beside Elizabeth and Anne. As he always did, Darcy pulled her to him, and she fought to control her gag reflex. "Elizabeth, Anne and Edward plan a late June wedding; I have told them we will attend the ceremony."

Turning her face away, Elizabeth struggled against the surge in her stomach. "Fitzwilliam, you may attend, but I will not." She felt as if she did not find relief soon she would surely embarrass herself.

Not expecting her resistance, Elizabeth's words shocked Darcy and offended Edward and Anne. Darcy tried to allay the umbrage betrayed on his cousins' faces. "Come, Elizabeth, we all understand your resentment at Lady Catherine's attack, but we must put those feelings aside for Edward's and Anne's sakes." He pulled her closer to relay his need for her to say the right thing.

Elizabeth's hand went to her mouth to force herself to swallow hard; the color fled from her face. "I am sorry, Fitzwilliam; I cannot attend." She fled from the room.

"Elizabeth!" Darcy called and started after her, but Mrs. Gardiner stopped him. "I will take care of Lizzy, Mr. Darcy. Stay with your guests."

Mrs. Gardiner found her niece on the exterior entryway; Elizabeth leaned over the stair railing relieving herself of what little she took for dinner. Mrs. Gardiner came up behind Elizabeth and gently rubbed her niece's back. She pushed back Elizabeth's hair from her face. "How far are you with child, Elizabeth?" Her aunt's voice caught her off guard, but it also offered Elizabeth comfort.

She turned toward Mrs. Gardiner. "How did you know?"

Her aunt laughed; she handed Elizabeth a handkerchief, which she dipped in water as she chased her niece down the hallway. Elizabeth wiped her face with the cool cloth and handed it back; a combination of the cloth's dampness and the fresh night air settled her stomach's uneasiness. "My trigger was the smell of pork cooking with Cassandra; for both boys it was any floral scent. What was it for you tonight?"

"The cigar smoke! Other smells have played havoc with my senses, but the smoke could not be ignored. How long does this last?"

"Usually no more than a month or two at most." Her aunt gently wiped Elizabeth's face again. "I assume Mr. Darcy does not know."

"I planned to tell him tonight. I told you about my accident, Aunt Gardiner." The woman continued to wipe Elizabeth's face with the cloth while acknowledging what her niece was saying to her. "Once I fell, I did not want to tell Fitzwilliam until I was sure the baby did not suffer from my foolishness. He was so consumed with my recovery; I did not want to cause him more distress."

"Did you speak to the physician?" Her aunt's concern relayed her tone. "Are there problems for the child?"

"Mr. Spencer examined me on three different occasions. He assures me I have no reason for concern because of the accident."

"Then answer my question, Elizabeth: when will be your lying in?"

"It appears this child is a result of our first nights together as husband and wife. I am nearly two months along. How could I tell Fitzwilliam in front of the whole room I cannot attend Edward's and Anne's wedding because I am to have a child? I want to tell my husband first before I tell everyone else."

"Tell me what, Elizabeth?" She jumped at hearing his voice; Elizabeth turned to see him standing by the open door. Darcy crossed the landing to take her in his arms once again. "What is the reason for your distress?"

Although her stomach was now empty, the urge did not go away. The smell of the cigar smoke remained on his jacket; she jerked her head to the left, grabbed her mouth again, and pulled away from him. Looking back with tears streaming down her face, she paused only briefly before she darted through the doorway to the staircase leading to her chambers.

"Mrs. Gardiner, why is Elizabeth acting this way? Did she say anything to you? This is uncharacteristic of her nature. What have I done for her to keep running away from me? How have I offended her?" Darcy's confusion could not be concealed; he turned to follow his wife.

Mrs. Gardiner caught his arm. "Mr. Darcy, Elizabeth must tell you her reasons; they are not mine to give, but if I may be allowed an opinion, you must ask the right question to get the answer you want."

"I do not understand, Mrs. Gardiner."

"Trust me, Mr. Darcy. A reassurance of Elizabeth's love for you is not what you should question. Give me your jacket, Mr. Darcy." He did not know of what she asked. "Give me your jacket, Mr. Darcy, and then go ask Elizabeth why cigar smoke is bothering her." She reached up and took his jacket from his shoulders. "Go, Mr. Darcy." She caressed his cheek as he looked at her with bewilderment.

Darcy took the steps with his usual speed; his search for Elizabeth ended in their bedroom. She laid eyes closed—face down across the bed, a wet cloth in her hand. He entered tentatively. "Elizabeth?" He feared coming too near—not knowing why she kept retreating from him. "Elizabeth, please," his voice pleaded with her senses. He moved cautiously to the foot of the bed.

Elizabeth sat up and looked at him. Darcy's confusion and concern asked questions his mouth could not. Finally, he said, "Your aunt says I need to ask why cigar smoke bothers you. This makes little sense to me; would you care to explain to me what troubles you?"

Her tears could not be withheld. "Fitzwilliam," she sobbed, "it was not supposed to be this way! I had it all planned!"

He came to the side of the bed and took her hand. "Had what planned? Elizabeth, this should make sense, but it does not; help me to understand."

She nearly knocked him over when she jumped into his arms, hugging him tightly. On her knees on the bed, she was nearly as tall as he, and he did not have to bend to see her face. Her tears rolled down his neck as she buried her face, ashamed of what she had to say to him. "Elizabeth, there is nothing which could make me love you less." He held her tightly to him and stroked the back of her head.

She would not look at him, but she did try to say what she needed to tell him. Still holding him as closely as she could, she spoke to the air, which surrounded them. "Fitzwilliam," her voice was small and difficult to hear at first, "you slept in the same bed with me every night for two months, did you not notice I never suffered from . . . suffered from . . . ." This was harder to say than she expected.

"Suffered from what, Elizabeth?" He would like to look at her during this, but he would take what she was willing to give him so he continued to embrace her.

"Help me say it, Fitzwilliam." She burrowed deeper into his shoulder. "From my female . . . ."

She knew he understood without her saying the words; the realization of what she just said shot through his body. He pulled back her tear-filled face. "Lizzy, please tell me it is true."

"I am with child, Fitzwilliam. We will have a child the latter part of July or early August."

She could not predict the reaction playing across his face. A shout of exhilaration grew from deep inside him as he picked her up and spun her around and around and smothered her face with kisses. "Elizabeth," he said at last, "how long have you known?"

She dropped her eyes, "I suspected as such before the fall."

"Why did you not tell me?"

"I wanted to be sure the fall did not endanger the child; I wanted to be sure all was well before I told you. I could not bear to hurt you."

"Mr. Spencer has seen you?"

"Mr. Spencer knows and believes me to be healthy."

"Then what happened downstairs?"

"The cigar smoke," she looked embarrassed, "made me sick. I am sorry." Her tears started again.

"Do not fret, Elizabeth. I will gladly give up cigars for such news as is yours." Pulling her so close she was a part of him, he kissed her. "May we tell the others?"

"I cannot enter that room again, Fitzwilliam. I have made a fool of myself; plus, the smell of the smoke unsettles my stomach too much."

"I will change my shirt; we will tell the others. I will ask the others to change also; all will be well." Darcy kissed her quickly and started toward his dressing room.

"I cannot ask our guests to do so." She looked at him helplessly.

"I cannot keep this news to myself, Elizabeth; our guests will understand." He rushed back across the room to her, kissed her passionately, and then hurried to his chambers.

In the dressing room he began to change his clothes and wipe any trace of cigar smoke from his being. He moved quickly, using the tepid water to wash his face and arms, finally pouring more water over his head to wash fragments of the cigar smell from his hair. *Elizabeth carried his child—an heir for Pemberley grew within her.* The realization struck him, and Darcy sank into a chair—legs weak from the knowledge. He would be a father—a father; the news brought tears of joy to his eyes, and he buried his face in his hands. *A baby—his baby*—no more horseback rides for Elizabeth, and she must limit her walks. Maybe they should not spend so much time in acts of love—he had so many questions for Mr. Spencer—he would call on the man tomorrow. *A baby—Elizabeth was to have his child.* He had to go back to her; she must be in as much tumult as was he right now.

"Any traces of cigar smoke?" he asked, returning to their bedroom and taking Elizabeth in his arms. "When you said I could control your schedule after New Year's, is this the reason? Is this why you have no energy lately and why you pick at your food?" Darcy caressed her face; it was as if he saw her differently somehow.

"I believe part of my problems of late has been my worry over the child's safety and part of how you would take the news."

"Did you think I would not be happy?"

"It is so much at once—the marriage—Pemberley—and now this. Can we handle all the changes in our life, Fitzwilliam, without it destroying our love?"

"Elizabeth, when I begged God to spare your life, I told him I would give up everything for you to be well again and to love me again. Then Georgiana said God has his plan for us; he gives us no more than what we can handle."

"Then if it is God's will, what more may I say." She sighed but was not so easily convinced.

"May we go tell the others, Elizabeth? I must say the words out loud to verify the knowledge of what you say to be true."

"Then say the words to me, Fitzwilliam. I need to hear the joy in your voice."

Uncharacteristically, Darcy sank to his knees in front of her and placed a gentle kiss on her stomach and lightly stroked her abdomen. "Our child grows within you, Elizabeth." He looked up into her face.

She briefly held his head to her stomach, and then she pulled him to her. "I do so dearly love you, Fitzwilliam."

He took her hand and kissed the palm. "This kiss belongs to our child." He placed her hand on her abdomen and cupped her hand with his. They stood that way for a long time, looking deeply into each other's eyes.

He said at last, "We should go."

"If we must." She was hesitant to leave so he held her tightly once again. Eventually, she took his arm tentatively and raised her chin. "Let us go, my Love."

Going down the steps, he could not take his eyes off her face; Elizabeth was so beautiful, and she loved him. Darcy's heart could hold no more happiness. "Are you ready?" he asked, kissing her cheek tenderly. She nodded her agreement as his eyes searched her face. When they came to the drawing room, he reached out to open the door with his free hand. It reminded him of the first time he walked her back to the Parsonage at Rosings. "I love you, Elizabeth," he whispered. Her eyes sparkled up at him.

When the door opened, all eyes fell on them, and silence filled the room. Darcy heard her sigh deeply, and he pulled her to him. "Elizabeth and I have something to share with all of you." Elizabeth heard Jane gasp and saw her Aunt Gardiner start to cry. "We will be parents in late July." Darcy's voice was shaky as if he could not believe the words himself. There was dead silence for a few infinite seconds, and then all in the room started to rush forward to congratulate them. Darcy instinctively shoved Elizabeth behind him to protect her; then he put his hand out to stop their progress. "Gentlemen, it seems Mrs. Darcy is having trouble stomaching the smell of our cigar smoke so although this is an unusual request, I am asking each of you to go to your rooms and change before you extend your congratulations."

Mr. Gardiner started to laugh as he turned to his wife. "It is just like you and the smell of flowers." He caressed his wife's cheek and then chuckled again as he headed for the stairs. "Come, gentle-men," he said, "in this room I am the only one with experience in this area; trust me, a woman is a delicate creature, but we cannot live without them." The other men looked confused, but they too started to leave.

Mr. Ashford had no change of clothing so he seemed befuddled as to what to do; Bingley took note of the situation. "Come, Mr. Ashford, I am sure I have something you may borrow for the evening."

"Thank you, Mr. Bingley, I should probably take my leave."

"Nonsense, Mr. Ashford, we now have something to celebrate; plus the snow comes down again. You should stay," Jane offered.

"Yes," Darcy added. "I will have Mrs. Reynolds show you to rooms for the evening."

"Thank you, Mr. Darcy," the man looked a bit uncomfortable.

Once the men left the room, Darcy stepped aside to let the women surround Elizabeth. Jane was the first to reach her sister. "Elizabeth, I am overwhelmed with happiness. You and Mr. Darcy are so blessed to have each other; why did you not tell me? Your countenance shows such contentment!"

Kitty and Georgiana followed her closely; both hugged their respective siblings. "I will be an aunt," Kitty squealed.

"We will both be aunts," Georgiana chimed in. Georgiana hugged Elizabeth for a long time. "From the first day I met you at the Royal Crown, I knew you would bring happiness to Pemberley. I love you, Elizabeth."

"I love you too, Georgiana." Then Elizabeth hugged Kitty again. "Kitty, would you stay at Pemberley to help Georgiana and me prepare for this child? I will write Mama tomorrow if you agree."

"Of course, Elizabeth." Kitty hugged her sister warmly.

Anne came forward to offer her congratulations. "I apologize for the offense earlier, Anne. I wanted to tell Fitzwilliam tonight, but your announcement of a June wedding created a problem. I did not know how to respond without exposing the news."

"Fret not, Elizabeth. Fitzwilliam's face tells me how much he loves you. That is all I could ask for my cousin."

Finally, her Aunt Gardiner made her way to the arms of the happy couple. "All is well, Lizzy?"

"It is not as I planned, but Fitzwilliam is happy."

"Life is rarely as we plan, Lizzy. You and Mr. Darcy are meant to be together. I knew that from the moment I met him in August. You will live a life of which others may only dream. You found a great love, Elizabeth."

"I have, have I not? To think I once refused him, and now I cannot breathe without him. Fitzwilliam will have an heir for Pemberley."

Darcy came over to join them, not able to be away from Elizabeth any longer. "Mr. Darcy, thank you for giving our Lizzy the life she deserves. You have a love, which will transcend time." Elizabeth hugged Darcy as her aunt addressed her husband.

When the gentlemen returned, they too offered their congratulations, but naturally Bingley, Edward, and Mr. Gardiner showed their excitement the most. "I remember when you were a mere babe yourself, Lizzy." Her uncle hugged her and offered Darcy his hand.

Edward accepted Elizabeth's apology, offered her a kiss on the cheek, and embraced his cousin with true felt admiration. "Lady Catherine will be most displeased," he whispered to Darcy.

"Tell her the shades of Pemberley are thus polluted." Darcy was too mirthful to care what his aunt thought.

Bingley's smile could not be contained. "Darcy, next to hearing those words from Jane, I cannot be happier than I am now. I must practice my legible handwriting once again. Caroline will be beside herself with envy."

"She and Lady Catherine must console each other, I fear." Darcy laughed out loud.

Jane came back to join Darcy and her husband. "Mr. Darcy, be thankful the roads are poor this time of year; it will keep Mama from coming to Pemberley immediately."

"Without wishing offense, Mrs. Bingley, even your mother could not defer my happiness this evening."

Jane hugged him. "I am pleased you are in Elizabeth's life, Mr. Darcy. You were right; she is your other half. To have Elizabeth so happy gives me more joy than you could know."

"I will devote my life to loving her, Mrs. Bingley."

The party took on a whole new level of enjoyment; no one wished to go to bed. New Year's Eve and a new baby gave everyone too much joy. Mrs. Annesley played, and all the couples enjoyed impromptu dancing, giving Darcy and Elizabeth the pleasure of starting the first dance.

"Mr. Darcy," she taunted as she passed him in the form, "you have the reputation of despising to dance."

"I am very discerning in my choice of partners is all the censure one should give to my reputation." He smiled happily at her. Each time they came together, their conversation continued. "I was disappointed when you refused me at Lucas Lodge."

"Then I cross-examined you at Netherfield."

"Why did you finally honor me with your hand, Elizabeth?"

"So you would always be in a humor to give consequence to a young lady who has been slighted by other men." She reminded him of his first cut to her at Meryton.

"I was a fool, Elizabeth."

"As was I, Fitzwilliam."

The last time they passed, Elizabeth could not help but to touch him, and Darcy caressed her cheek; their eyes, as always, found each other.

Unusual for him, Darcy also danced with Jane, Georgiana, Mrs. Gardiner, and Kitty, but he still watched Elizabeth as he completed each form. She spent time with Bingley, Edward, and Mr. Harrison. Kitty was happy to dance with Bingley, Mr. Harrison, and several times with Mr. Ashford. Not being a formal ball there was no strictures on multiple dances. Mr. Ashford lacked the finesse of a gentleman, but his dancing did not create a spectacle; he found the pleasure of holding Kitty Bennet's hand an inducement for enjoying the music, and he briefly thanked God for bringing these new people into his life. The group simply enjoyed being together.

Georgiana cornered Darcy as the evening progressed. "Are you happy for me, Dearest One?" he asked when she came near.

"Fitzwilliam, to see you so well-situated is the most joyful of times. Elizabeth is so beautiful; see how she beams with love."

"Georgiana, I may have given up my pursuit of Elizabeth if you did not intervene, and if you did not realize she was in danger, I may have lost her forever. What might I say to you to tell you how much you are loved?"

"Words are not necessary, Fitzwilliam. I am thankful you finally have love in your life. You gave up your youth for me and for Pemberley; it was never fair for you to take on so much at such a young age."

"I never regretted what I did for you, Dearest One."

"Now we are creating our own Pemberley, Fitzwilliam. I believe we are repaid ten times over for our good deeds. God gives us blessings because of what we do for others."

"You are more devout than I, but I have come to a new understanding of the infinite power of God since Elizabeth came into my life. I never knew such love of life."

"Love life and Elizabeth, Fitzwilliam." She kissed his cheek; as she turned to leave him and rejoin the others, Georgiana pivoted toward him with one last remark. "Did you know, Brother, the Greeks did not extol a man's accomplishments upon his death? They simply asked one question of his family and friends: did he live his life with undying passion?" She gave him her own version of an enigmatic smile and left.

As the evening wound down, Darcy offered a toast to Elizabeth. "To my wife, Elizabeth Bennet Darcy, a woman of unexpected wit, a devotion to her family, silent courage, and strength combined with innocence and sweetness—I learned from you how to be a brother, a man, and a husband. Soon I will learn to be a father. You are the love of my life." Her eyes welled up; there was a time when

Elizabeth looked for love—a fiery cannonball of emotions; now she knew true love, deep compassionate love—a consistent flame, which never burns out.

When the others retired for the evening, Darcy and Elizabeth sat together in the drawing room; he reclined against the back of a settee with one leg stretched out and the other dangling to the floor; Elizabeth lay back against him, lounging lazily between his legs where she could easily touch his face and feel his warmth. He held her head to his chest and kissed the top of it as he rubbed the side of the arm, which she laid across his chest. She stroked his chin line and periodically lightly kissed his neck. The fire was burning down, but neither of them wished to move, fearing the spell would be broken.

"Are you truly happy to be a father so soon, Fitzwilliam?"

"Of course, Elizabeth, dare you ask?"

"We have been together for such a short period of time; I feared you would think it too fast."

Fascinated by the fact she was with child, he reached out to place his hand lightly upon her stomach. Looking deeply in her eyes, he said, "Georgiana said earlier I gave up everything for her and for Pemberley. The truth is I gave up some of my youth to know true happiness. My blessings are just coming closer together than I expected." He offered a soft chuckle to lighten the moment.

"What if our child is not a son? Would a daughter disappoint you?"

"There was a time I felt anything but a son would be settling for less, but I will admit to seeking the approval of Cassandra Gardiner more so than her brothers. I would walk across England for one of her hugs. Holding her in my arms yesterday evening as she fell asleep offered me such ease. Having three females in my household would be a blessing. I remember how little Georgiana looked as a baby; I was afraid to even touch her at first, but my mother taught me to hold her and to look upon her. She would wrap her hand around my finger and hold on so tightly I knew she asked me to protect her from harm."

"You will be a phenomenal father, Fitzwilliam."

"You taught me to love spherically, Elizabeth—in several directions at once. I learned so much about love from you."

The open professions of Darcy's love moved her, and she rose up to where she could press her forehead against his and caress his cheek. How quickly his passion rose the first time they lay together surprised her, but her equally passionate response she found more astounding; British women in fine houses were not supposed to feel about their husbands the way she felt about Darcy. Marriage was to be a convenience, not a time of seeking pleasure from one's true love. He gave her a liberating freedom, something she did not expect from a man who once seemed so haughty and reserved; Elizabeth could not think of anything but the *real love* she held for this man. Darcy treated her as no man she knew treated his wife. He gave her the right to be herself and to demand his love when she needed him.

"Elizabeth," she felt the familiar shift of his body telling her he wanted her. She snickered with the knowledge of his desire.

"Fitzwilliam, I told you the bed at Kensington Place had special appeal." She began to tease him with kisses across his chin while rubbing her lips across his mouth.

"May we conceive other children there?" Darcy's voice betrayed his thoughts. She silenced his lips with a fervent kiss, drawing near to him and responding to his passionate touch, which searched her hips.

"Elizabeth," a moan started in the back of his throat, "you have no idea what you do to me."

"You, Sir, have no idea what I want to do to you." Elizabeth giggled, as the moan became a distinct groan; the passion she now recognized as being the man she loved. Her mouth found Darcy's as she slid up his body, and his arms encircled her.

"Lizzy . . ." he began.

"Good . . . I love it when you call me *Lizzy*."

RESOURCES

Austen, Jane. *Pride and Prejudice*. Clayton, Delaware: Prestwick House Literary Touchstone Press, 2005.

Beckinsale, Kate, John Corbett, John Cusack and Jeremy Piven. *Serendipity*. Directed by Peter Chelsom. Simon Fields Productions, 2001

Cressbrook Multimedia. "Well Dressing." *Peak District Multimedia Guide*. 1997. http://www.cressbrook.co.us/features.wellhist.htm.

Decker, Cathy. "Images of Real Regency Clothing." University of California at Riverside. April 20, 2004. http://hal.ucr.edu/~cathy/rd/rd.html.

Eardley, Dennis. "Discover Derbyshire and the Peak District." December 2003. http://www.derbyshire-peakdistrict.co.uk.

Graves, Beverly: Commentary. "People to Meet from the Obit Page." *Suburban News Publication*. February 9–16, 2005.

"Gunter's Tea Shop." *Georgian Index*. August 2006. http://www.georgian index.net/Gunters/gunters.html.

Myretta, Barbara, et.al. "Pride and Prejudice." The Republic of Pemberley. 2004–2005. http://www.pemberley.com/janeinfo/pridprej.html#Toc.

Overton, Mark. "Agricultural Revolution in England 1500–1850." September 19, 2002. *BBC*. http://www.bbc.co.uk/history/british/empire_seapower/agricultural_revolution_06.shtml

Ross, David. "English History: Georgian England." *Britain Express*. Little Rissington, Gloucestershire, England. http://www.britain express.com/History/Georgian_index.htm.

Shakespeare, William. *Much Ado About Nothing*, act 5, scene 2, lines 57–68. Edited by David Bevington and David Scott Kastan. New York: Bantam Classics, 2005.